THE TRAITOR PRINCE

Also by C. J. Redwine

Defiance

Deception

Deliverance

Outcast: A Defiance Novella

The Shadow Queen

The Wish Granter

The Blood Spell

THE TRAITOR PRINCE

A Ravenspire Novel

C. J. REDWINE

Balzer + Bray
An *Imprint of* HarperCollins*Publishers*

Balzer + Bray is an imprint of HarperCollins Publishers.

The Traitor Prince
Copyright © 2018 by C. J. Redwine
All rights reserved. Printed in the United States of America.
No part of this book may be used or reproduced in any manner whatsoever without
written permission except in the case of brief quotations embodied in critical articles
and reviews. For information address HarperCollins Children's Books, a division of
HarperCollins Publishers, 195 Broadway, New York, NY 10007.
www.epicreads.com

Library of Congress Control Number: 2017943274
ISBN 978-0-06-265299-7

Typography by Sarah Nichole Kaufman
18 19 20 21 22   PC/LSCH   10 9 8 7 6 5 4 3 2 1
❖
First paperback edition, 2019

For Clint, who was once the Javan to my Sajda.
Thank you for being the kind of man who doesn't leave.

URRVENSKEYR MOUNTAIN

LAKE SKYLLIVRENG

ELDR

ISLAND OF ICHIL

SEA OF ICE

SILBER RIVER

VALLÉ DE LUMÉ

THE CHRYSÓS SEA

SÚNDRAILLE

LLORENYAE

ONCE UPON A TIME . . .

A BRISK WIND scoured the packed dirt streets of the peasant quarter in Makan Almalik, tossing grit into the night air and clawing at the robes of the young man who walked briskly down a side road, his cowl pulled over his head to guard his face against the onslaught.

The streets were deserted at this time of night. The lanterns hanging in their metal cages every quarter block illuminated rickety wooden shops with their shutters closed and goat hair tents with their flaps tied shut. Only a fool would venture out at midnight to face the tumultuous moods of Eb' Rezr. The god of wind and rain was a capricious master—one the aristocrats of Akram had stopped serving over a century ago, after Yl' Haliq, the all-powerful, had vanquished the lesser gods—but the peasants didn't have the luxury of betting their survival on a single god.

Rahim buried his face in the coarse wool of his cowl as another gust of desert wind tore at him. The moods of Eb' Rezr were useful to the FaSaa'il, the rebellious faction of aristocrats who sought to use Rahim as their puppet. The wind kept people inside—their prying eyes far from the faction and its activities—as they mumbled prayers and set aside tiny offerings from their already meager supplies to gods who couldn't or wouldn't help them.

Pathetic.

Rahim didn't pinch mouthfuls of food from his meals to toss to the ground for Mal' Enish, the goddess of animals, or cut strips of cloth from his robes for the priests' collection barrels in honor of Sa' Loham, the god of the poor. He needed no god, and neither did the superstitious peasants who clung to the belief that their offerings would somehow bring them rescue.

The fact that he'd been forced to spend seventeen years in a tent just like them, surrounded by poverty and desperation, was a bitterness that poisoned him with every breath. He should have been raised in the palace in Makan Almalik, claimed by his father, his every whim catered to. Instead, he'd been raised in his mother's tent in a small desert town far from the palace. He'd toiled in heat and misery—by day learning the trade of a tailor and by night dreaming of the destiny that should have been his.

A destiny that could still be his if the FaSaa'il's plan was successful.

Grim determination lent strength to his body and sharpened his thoughts as he passed a tiny mercantile shop, its walls shaking beneath Eb' Rezr's onslaught, and entered an alley that stank of camel dung and trash.

Two shadows detached from the wall as he approached, cowls pulled over their heads so that all he could see of the figures were their eyes—sharp and hungry.

Rahim's eyes were sharp and hungry too, but there the likeness ended. His skin was a darker shade of bronze, his cheekbones set slightly higher, his chin a bit more pointed—all gifts from the royal blood that ran through his veins. He was the spitting image of a Kadar, and the resemblance was going to change his future.

"Yl' Haliq meet you and keep you safe," the taller man said.

Rahim's heart thudded angrily, and it took all of his restraint to keep the sneer from his face. Instead, he answered, "Yl' Haliq be praised."

The man drew back, and his companion opened a narrow door in the side of the shop. Rahim moved past them and into the well-ordered stockroom as the door closed behind him. Before him stood five figures, shrouded in cloaks, though the material of their garments was far finer than anything he'd ever owned. The closest figure, a man with broad shoulders and an even broader gut, strode to Rahim's side and wrapped a hand around his shoulder.

"Here he is, friends. The answer to our problems. Yl' Haliq be praised that I happened to catch him trying to steal from me at the racetrack a few months ago!" The man's fingers dug into Rahim's shoulders, but the boy didn't flinch.

Yl' Haliq had nothing to do with any of it. Rahim had left his mother's tent in the dead of night, traveled the distance between her town and Akram's capital on foot, and then spent nearly five months on the streets of the city, his eyes downcast, begging for scraps from the priests, while he listened and learned.

It hadn't taken long to pick up on the whispers of discontent among some of Akram's aristocrats—families whose businesses had been heavily penalized by the king or who had lost royal favor for one transgression or another. It had been a simple thing to strike up a friendship with a servant from each house until he had the information he needed. Simpler still to target Lord Borak, the man he'd judged as the leader of the FaSaa'il, and get caught stealing.

One look from Borak at Rahim's features had been enough to spare him a trip to Maqbara prison.

"This will never work." A woman who stood on the opposite side of the room crossed her arms over her chest. "You can't just have him trade places with the prince. Someone will notice."

"Our friend in the palace will help confirm his identity. Besides, look at him." Lord Borak reached up and yanked Rahim's cowl back to reveal his face. An older woman gasped and took a step toward him. "Remarkable. You can't even tell he's half peasant."

Anger flashed through Rahim, heating his cheeks and curling his fists. It took effort to smooth his expression into something bland and nonthreatening. More effort to uncurl his fists and pretend his heart wasn't slamming against his chest as these pathetic aristocrats sized him up like a horse on an auction block.

"See?" Lord Borak sounded triumphant. "He's the spitting image of his father, Prince Fariq."

"Who walks and dresses like a peasant," the woman at the far end said. "I'm willing to bet he sounds like one too. He'll be discovered, and he'll give up our names, and then we'll be killed, our families will be exiled, and our holdings will be turned over to the crown."

Rahim shook off the man's hand and stepped forward. Giving his voice the crisp polish Lord Borak had drilled into him over the past four months of instruction, he said, "Forgive me, madam, for my uncouth clothing, but I'm afraid until the trade is made, I must continue to blend in with the peasants. I assure you, I am entirely capable of passing as royalty when necessary."

"But even if he looks like an aristocrat, the king will surely know his own son." The man closest to Lord Borak frowned as he swept his gaze over Rahim.

"The king hasn't seen his son in the ten years that the prince has been at Milisatria Academy in Loch Talam," Lord Borak said.

"A father knows his son, no matter how long it's been," the man argued.

"Not when the father is taking daily doses of poison and can barely remember his own name," Lord Borak shot back.

"You can't be sure of that," the man said.

"I have sources placed all throughout the palace. I am sure of everything," Lord Borak said. "Now—"

"But what about the prince? The real one? Surely he'll return to fight for the crown," the man said and then took a step back as Rahim's cold gaze landed on him.

"I am the real prince now. Anyone claiming otherwise must be put to death."

The man flinched. "I didn't join this group to kill a boy."

"Quit being disingenuous, Lord Halim," the woman at the back said. "You were the one who provided the poison our ally is giving to the king in place of the daily tonic he takes to treat his weakening heart."

"But a boy—"

"'Sometimes blood must be shed for the good of the king-dom,'" Rahim said.

Lord Borak shot him a look, and Rahim forced himself to

incline his head respectfully. Better to let them believe they controlled him. That the puppet they thought they'd fashioned from a street rat would never turn on them the second he had the chance.

"We are doing what must be done," Lord Borak said grimly. "The king has neglected the old ways, and has acquiesced to demands from both Ravenspire and Balavata at our expense. We've all lost land along the shifting lines of the kingdom's borders. We've had sanctions placed on our horse races, our goods taxed, and our property invaded on accusations that we're violating the new laws against selling child slaves or that we've thrown debtors into prison on false charges just to take over their businesses." His voice rose as the others nodded in agreement. "We're out of favor and losing power, and the only way to regain the upper hand is to put our own prince on the throne and take back what is ours."

There was a beat of silence after Lord Borak finished speaking, and then Lord Halim said, "Let it be done. But this boy had better fool the king. I'm not going to die for treason."

Rahim met Lord Halim's eyes and then slowly moved his gaze around the room as each of the five aristocrats pledged their support to the plan. Kidnap the true prince after his graduation from the academy in the northern kingdom of Loch Talam. Kill him and send Rahim back to Akram in his place. Push for a quick coronation due to the king's failing health, and once Rahim was installed on the throne, rule through him.

He bared his teeth in a smile as the pact was made.

He was no puppet.

By his father's blood and his own tenacity, he was a prince. A ruler. A god among men.

And once he was through carving his destiny out of the blood and bone of those who stood in his way, everyone in Akram would bow before him, his name the prayer they raised as they begged for his mercy.

FOUR WEEKS LATER

ONE

WAITING WAS AGONY.

Javan Samad Najafai of the house of Kadar, prince of Akram, paced the stone corridor outside the headmaster's office because staying still felt impossible.

He'd spent the past ten years at the prestigious Milisatria Academy for the Comportment and Education of the Nobility in the northern kingdom of Loch Talam, far from his family. He hadn't seen his father since the moment the king had escorted him into the school at the age of seven and solemnly reminded him of his duty to his mother's *muqaddas tus'el* before returning to Akram.

He'd done his best to fulfill his mother's sacred dying wish that her son would earn the most honors of any prince educated at Milisatria. He'd studied hard for every exam. Taken extra classes and turned down invitations to visit the taverns and theaters in town so he could do schoolwork instead. He'd worked tirelessly to prepare himself mentally and physically for the challenge of earning the academy's top honors, and now everything came down to the thin sheet of parchment the headmaster would soon be nailing to his door.

"Stop pacing. You're making me nervous," Kellan said. The crown prince of Balavata was slouched lazily against the wall opposite the headmaster's door, eating a sandwich as if learning which ten students had qualified to compete in the upcoming final exam for the position of top honors was of little consequence.

Javan glanced at his roommate, his heart jumping in his chest. "Nothing makes you nervous."

Kellan spoke around a mouthful of thick oat bread and ham. "I am pretty unflappable."

Javan rolled his eyes, forced himself to breathe past the surge of nerves that wanted to close his throat, and continued pacing while two dozen of his friends and fellow students joined him in the corridor, their eyes lit with anticipation, their conversations echoing throughout the stone hallway.

Kellan shoved himself away from the wall and offered half his sandwich to Javan. "Here."

"I'm not hungry." And Yl' Haliq knew if Javan tried to swallow anything right now, he'd choke.

"You're always hungry." Kellan raised an eyebrow at Javan, and the prince shook his head.

"I can't eat right now. My stomach is in knots."

Kellan grimaced and took a small step back. "Last time you said that, you vomited on my boots two seconds later."

Javan punched Kellan's shoulder. "That was in fifth year. And you said you'd never bring it up again."

"Just making sure that's the only thing that's coming up."

Kellan winked at Javan, and the prince laughed, though it felt like his lungs were constricting.

He'd make the cut. Of course he would. He'd studied longer and worked harder than anyone else at the academy.

But what if?

What if the tricky question on his applied mathematics exam had knocked his grade down a point? There were three other students who were naturally better at math than he was.

What if he'd used the wrong codex to interpret the obscure quote on his philosophy exam? He could name five others who would never make that mistake.

What if the margin of victory he'd tried so hard to achieve was a fragile thing easily lost by a single mistake?

Yl' Haliq be merciful, Javan couldn't return to Akram without fulfilling his mother's *muqaddas tus'el*. He'd never be able to look his father in the face again.

"Stop it." Kellan smacked Javan's back, his dark eyes glaring at the Akramian prince.

"Stop what?" Javan frowned at his friend, refusing on principle to rub the spot where Kellan's handprint felt singed into his skin.

"Stop obsessing. You'll make the list. You make *every* list. You always get everything you set your mind to. If I hadn't spent the last ten years with an up close and personal view of your many flaws, I might be jealous."

Javan snorted. "Since when are you jealous of anyone?"

Kellan grinned, but any reply he might have made was lost as the headmaster's office door swung open. Silence descended on the corridor as every student watched the tall man with close-cropped gray hair and a neatly clipped beard step out of his office, a sheet of parchment in his hands.

"Greetings, students," he said, his low voice filling the corridor.

"Greetings, Headmaster," the students answered as one.

"Exams for individual subjects have all been graded, and your marks over the course of your tenure at the academy have been tallied." The headmaster's gaze slowly roamed over the small crowd of tenth-year students gathered around him. "I'm proud of all you've accomplished, and you should be too. As you know, only the ten students with the highest overall scores will be allowed to compete in the upcoming final exam to win the crimson sash and the title of Most Honored at the commencement ceremony."

The headmaster's eyes caught Javan's and held for a brief second before he turned his back on the students and raised a hammer to nail the parchment to his door. Javan's heart was thunder shaking his chest as he surged forward with the others once the headmaster stepped out of the way. His eyes skimmed the list rapidly, and then the world snapped into sharp focus as he caught the fourth name on the list.

Javan Samad Najafai.

The pressure in his chest eased.

He'd made it. Now all that was left between him and the sash was the final exam—a multifaceted assessment designed to rigorously test students mentally and physically through a series of challenges. There were others on the list—Kellan included—who were better at individual events in the exam, but Javan could hold his own. And he knew that victory wouldn't go to the student who was most naturally skilled at each of the five tasks. Victory would belong to the student who approached the exam with the best strategy. Figuring out how to win was like solving a puzzle, and there wasn't another student at the academy who was better at strategizing than Javan.

"I suppose it's bad form to say I told you so," Kellan said from Javan's left.

"Terrible form." Javan laughed and turned to offer Kellan his hand. "Congratulations on making the cut."

Kellan shook Javan's hand and then shouted, "This calls for a celebration! To the tavern!"

"To the tavern!" Many of the surrounding students echoed back, though a few whose names weren't on the list were slinking away.

"Are you coming?" Kellan asked, even though never once in all of their years of friendship had Javan ever gone to town to celebrate anything. There was always another exam to study for, another weapon's technique to practice, another goal to hit.

This time was no different.

Javan started to shake his head, and Kellan rolled his eyes. "The exam isn't for another three days. Are you going to start overpreparing already?"

"You know me." Javan shrugged as if missing out on a night at the tavern with his friends didn't feel like another moment in a long chain of lost opportunities that he'd never get back.

He'd have a chance to socialize once he returned to Akram, having brought honor to his family name and peace to his mother's spirit. He could invite Kellan to visit from Balavata and show him the racetracks, the roasting pits full of pistachios and marinated goat meat, and the dimly lit salons with their citrus-flavored liquor and their harp players whose nimble fingers flew across the strings until you couldn't help but dance.

A pang of homesickness hit. Ten years was a long time to go without seeing his father. The other students returned home for the winter and summer holidays, but not Javan. He'd stayed to study. To practice. To sit with the headmaster or a tutor and do his best to live up to the expectations that rested on his shoulders.

Soon it would all be worth it. He just had to enter the exam with the best strategy, stay focused, and win.

"If you change your mind, we'll be at the Red Dwarf. You can come embarrass yourself with your poor drinking and conversational skills," Kellan said.

"I think you'll be embarrassing enough for the both of us," Javan said with a quick smile for Kellan as the other boy crooked his arm through the elbow of the closest girl, flashed her a charming smile, and walked out of the building with a pack of students on his heels.

"You don't want to celebrate with your friends?" the headmaster asked, pinning Javan with his gray eyes. "Not even for an hour?"

"I can't. The exam—"

"Isn't for three days."

"Only three days to study the tasks and come up with a plan—"

"Only four days before commencement and your friends scattering to their own kingdoms." The headmaster smiled at Javan, though there was a sadness in his eyes. "You've pushed yourself hard for your entire tenure at the academy. No student of mine has ever given more to his studies. But being the best at everything isn't all that matters."

"It is to my father." The words were out before Javan could

stop them. Heat flushed his cheeks at the expression of pity on the headmaster's face. "I didn't mean that the way it sounded."

"We should never apologize for speaking the truth, no matter how uncomfortable it might be to hear."

"It's just . . . I'm the only heir. My uncle Fariq doesn't have any children, and even if he did, he's my father's cousin, though he's been treated like a brother. Only a direct descendant can inherit the throne. I'm the last of the Kadars, and we've ruled Akram for nearly two hundred years. I have to bring honor to my kingdom."

The headmaster moved to Javan's side and rested a heavy hand on the prince's shoulder. "No student has brought more honor to his kingdom than you. Taking an hour away from studying won't tarnish that. If anything, it will improve your ability to be an excellent ruler." At Javan's raised brow, the headmaster squeezed his shoulder. "People matter more than competitions and grades. *You* matter. I hope you realize that you are more to your father than the honors you bring home from school. And I hope you know that you are more to me than any of your accomplishments."

The warmth in Javan's cheeks poured into his chest, and he stood a little straighter. Earning his father's respect and fulfilling his mother's dying wish were the fuel that pushed him to the limits of his endurance every day. But earning the headmaster's affection—seeing love and pride in the eyes of the man who'd been like a second father to Javan for the past ten years—was a light that burned steadily in the prince's heart.

"And before I forget, another letter arrived for you." The headmaster reached into his robes and produced an envelope with creased corners and a gritty coat of the burned red sand of the Samaal Desert that separated Akram from Loch Talam.

Javan took the envelope, and the light inside him burned a little brighter.

Maybe he hadn't seen his father since he'd arrived at Milisatria, but the letters his father sent—as infrequent as they'd become in the last five years—kept Javan tethered to the family he'd soon be returning to.

"Thank you, Headmaster. I need to go now," Javan said.

"I hope you mean go to the tavern with your friends," the headmaster called to Javan's retreating back.

The prince clutched the letter to him as he exited the building and turned toward the dormitory. Moments later, he was inside his room and sliding a slim dagger across the envelope's edge, leaving the royal purple wax seal with its Kadar family crest intact as he always did.

There was a single piece of parchment inside, and Javan tried to quell the sting of disappointment at how few lines were written on it. The first letter his father had sent him, three months after he'd arrived at Milisatria, had been two full pages detailing the comings and goings of Uncle Fariq, who loved to travel, the antics of Javan's pet leopard Malik, and the growth of the jasmine he'd planted on the queen's grave. Until five summers ago, his letters had contained a wealth of details that kept Akram alive in Javan's mind and strengthened the connection he felt with his father.

But then the letters had begun to change. Less description. Less interest in Javan's life. When the letters began arriving every six to eight months instead of every three months, and Javan found entire paragraphs that didn't quite make sense, the prince had finally sent a letter of his own to his uncle asking after his father. His uncle had assured him that King Samaal was simply busy—distracted by the heavy burden of ruling Akram.

Javan had absorbed both the hurt and the comfort in his uncle's reply and had redoubled his efforts to prove to his father that he too was worthy of the burden of ruling Akram. Turning to the latest letter from his father, Javan's eyes devoured the two short paragraphs greedily, lingering on the last sentence.

I am sure you will do your duty.

Slowly, he placed the letter in the box that contained the rest of the correspondence from his father. A band of pressure wrapped around Javan's chest as he slid the box back under his bed.

Javan's duty wasn't to Kellan or the rest of his friends, no matter how much he might wish to spend an afternoon with them at the tavern.

His duty was to fulfill his mother's wish, earn his father's respect, and return to Akram ready to rule his people with strength and honor when the time came for him to take his father's place. Nothing less would do.

And to do that, he had to earn first place in the final exam.

Without hesitation, he sat at his desk, pulled out a sheaf of parchment and a quill, and began to plan.

TWO

THE DAY OF the final exam dawned cold and damp, and Javan woke with a prayer on his lips and a coiled tension in his chest. A heavy mist clung to the rocky hilltops and belly crawled over the fields as the ten students who'd earned the honor of taking the test filed out of the dormitory and headed toward the stables for the first of the five tasks.

The headmaster met them at the mouth of the stables, while behind him grooms saddled horses and assembled armor and lances.

"Good morning," he said.

"Good morning, Headmaster," the students answered.

"A brief reminder of the rules," he said. "Each task is a test of your strength, your skills, and your strategy. You must remain at that task until you have earned enough points to move on. Jousting requires ten points. You receive one point per touch, two points for hitting the center of someone's chest, and three points for unseating your opponent. Once you've reached ten points, you may leave for the next task. I will wait for you on the final field where you will try to gain the sash by using your combat training to defeat any challengers who arrive at the field with you. A touch from the weapons will count as an injury." His eyes narrowed. "Any actual injury caused to a fellow student will result in your immediate disqualification. Good luck."

Javan's stomach felt as though he'd swallowed rocks, and his mouth was dry as he wished Kellan and the other students luck and then quickly moved into the stable and chose a mount.

He was decent at jousting. Maybe not as skilled as Cora or as fast as Eljin, but he could keep his seat and put points on the board in quick order, and that was all that mattered. He simply had to hold his own in the first three tasks and not fall behind. The fourth task was where he planned to take the lead. Pulling a hauberk over his head, he reached for a helmet and mounted the horse.

It was time to fulfill his mother's dying wish and make his father proud.

Two hours later, Javan was in serious danger of the one thing all of his planning hadn't accounted for: being eaten by a dragon.

The beast crouched at the edge of the precipice above Javan, its talons digging into the rugged stone cliff, its wings casting a shadow as wide as seven men lying end to end, and its dark eyes locked on the prince. The morning sunlight glanced off the dragon's dull gray scales and disappeared in the shadow of the beast's black underbelly. A long, jagged scar ran the length of the dragon's chest, from the base of its neck to its stomach. Javan swallowed as the creature's lips peeled back from a row of knife-sharp teeth, smoke pouring from its nostrils.

Fear was lightning spiking through Javan's veins, threatening to send his carefully crafted plan into chaos as images of being snapped up in the dragon's immense jaws filled his head.

He was trapped. A dragon in front of him. A treacherous climb through slippery, shale-covered hills behind him. And no one he could call for help.

He'd been certain of his strategy. He'd walked the academy's vast grounds long after he should have been asleep, memorizing the craggy landscape—the green hollows that dipped into pools of shadow, the gray-blue rivers that reflected the stars, and the rocky peaks that pierced the sky like a smithy's nails, looking for an advantage over his fellow students.

He'd found the trail that sliced through a cluster of steep, rocky hills two nights ago. By his calculations, using this trail to get to the final task instead of staying on the main path that neatly dissected the academy's enormous estate into tidy quadrants would save him valuable time.

The rest of his strategy had worked beautifully. He'd held his own in jousting, trapped his opponent in a game of kingdoms at war within twelve moves, and completed the obstacle course with only two students ahead of him. He'd banked his success on the fourth task. Archery had always been one of his best sports. Arriving at the grounds for the fourth task in a tie with three other students, including Kellan, he'd grabbed a bow, nocked an arrow, and then sent it flying dead center into the target. Two more quickly followed, and then he'd tossed the weapon to the grass and left the archery grounds at a dead run while the others were still reaching for their second arrows. Veering left at the tumble of rotting tree trunks that marked the intersection between the north quadrant and the east, he'd ducked behind a rocky outcrop and hurried toward the shortcut.

Everything had gone according to plan until the headmaster decided to block the shortcut with a *dragon*.

The beast exhaled, a long, rasping growl of breath that shivered through the air and sent smoke curling toward the thick gray clouds that scudded across the sky.

Javan forced himself to breathe as well. Fear out. Courage in.

This was just another test. Another way to make sure that only the truly deserving wore the crimson sash at tomorrow's commencement ceremony.

Doubtless there was another equally daunting obstacle blocking the others on the main path. Javan shoved all thoughts of his friends and fellow competitors from his mind and focused on the problem of getting past the beast.

The dragon beat its wings, slowly at first, and then shale began sliding down the hill as the beast picked up speed. Every flap of its wings was a leathery slap of sound that sent a chill over Javan's skin.

He had no weapons. They were forbidden between tasks.

He had no allies. He'd left them behind on the main road.

He had nothing but his instincts and his brain.

That didn't seem like enough to best a dragon the size of a small house, but the headmaster wouldn't have allowed it to be here if he didn't believe his students already had the skills to beat it.

Fear out.

Courage in.

Javan looked away from the dragon to quickly scan the area, forcing himself to catalog his options as the dragon's talons scraped the rocky precipice, sending chunks of rock tumbling past the prince.

He needed a weapon. He needed shelter.

He needed a way through the hills to the fifth task before one of his classmates got to the sash first.

His list of options was pitifully short. There were plenty of small pieces of shale. There were rocks ranging from fist-size to ones as large as a carriage. There was the hill in front of him, but no tunnels that could offer safety while keeping the dragon at bay. And there was Javan himself with his tunic, his boots, his pants, and his belt.

His belt.

The dragon rose, blocking the pale sun, its immense shadow swallowing Javan whole.

The prince was out of time. Whipping off his tunic, he leaned down and scraped a hand through the shale until he found a piece sharp enough to cut his skin. He scooped it up along with a few rocks the size of pomegranates. The dragon's roar shattered the air above him, and Javan's heart thudded as he dumped the rocks onto the center of his tunic, tied the sleeves into a makeshift knapsack, and then scrambled for the incline that led to the hill's precipice.

Doubtless the dragon would try to block Javan. He'd just have to find a way to distract it or fend it off long enough to get through the pass.

The dragon dove for him, the air whistling past its body as fire poured from its mouth.

Yl' Haliq be merciful, the dragon wasn't just trying to block his progress. It was trying to *burn* him.

Javan leaped to the side, crashing onto the shale as the fire seared his left arm. The dragon slammed into the ground beside him, sending a wave of rocks skidding down the rest of the hill.

Terror lanced Javan, bold and bright. Fragments of prayer tumbled from his lips as he reached for his tunic full of rocks with shaking fingers. The beast wasn't trying to stop Javan. It was trying to kill him.

Javan lunged forward, grabbing sharp outcroppings to haul himself over the slippery ground, his breath sobbing in his lungs as he whispered a prayer for deliverance.

The outcroppings sliced into his hands, and soon his palms were slick with blood. The dragon's wings swept the air, and Javan had to brace himself to keep from being flattened by the gusts of wind that hit him.

As the dragon rose into the air once more, Javan forced himself to reach. To climb.

To hurry.

The precipice was three body lengths away.

The dragon was circling overhead, smoke pouring from its nostrils.

"Yl' Haliq, save your faithful servant," Javan breathed as he dug deep for more speed. More strength. As he tried to push the blinding terror into the corner of his mind so he could *think*.

The dragon's roar thundered as Javan's bloody hands closed over the spiny ridge of the hill. The prince pulled his legs under his chest, planted his boots against the shifting shale beneath him, and leaped.

Fire exploded against the side of the hill as Javan cleared the ridge and landed on the narrow flat strip of the hill's precipice. Throwing his makeshift knapsack to the ground, the prince tore the knot loose and grabbed the sharp piece of shale. Four quick slices and he ripped a patch of fabric the size of his hand from the bottom of his tunic.

The dragon dove toward him. Javan threw himself forward, skidding on his hands and knees as the beast's talons dug into the ground, leaving long gashes where the prince had been crouched.

Javan's hands shook as he flattened the square of fabric and gouged a slim tear into two opposite sides of the patch. Above him, the dragon flew into the air and began circling. The prince grabbed the braided cord of his belt, unwound it from his waist, and shoved one end through the tear in the right side of the patch. The dragon's roar shook the ground.

Fear wrapped around Javan's chest and squeezed. Hastily pushing the end of his belt through the other tear, he centered the patch in the middle of the corded rope while the dragon dove.

This time, Javan didn't move fast enough. The beast's great leathery wing collided with the prince and sent him spinning toward the edge of the precipice. Javan dug into the ground with his elbows and feet, his hands still clutching the slingshot he'd fashioned.

The beast flew into the air and circled back.

Javan jumped to his feet and dove toward the cache of rocks sitting in the middle of his ruined tunic.

Smoke gushed from the dragon's mouth and hurtled toward the prince with every flap of the creature's wings.

Javan's hand closed around a rock, and he centered it in the piece of tunic even as he spun to face the dragon's next assault.

There would be no time to dive out of the way if he missed.

The dragon roared.

Javan pulled the rock back with one hand until the cord of his rope belt was taut.

With an enormous whoosh of smoky air, the beast locked eyes on the prince and came straight toward him.

He was going to die.

The words chased one another inside his head as his stomach dropped and his knees shook. He was going to die, and he'd never been to a tavern or kissed a girl or seen pride in his father's eyes.

Terror threatened to turn Javan's limbs to stone as the dragon closed in, and he forced himself to breathe.

Fear out.

Courage in.

Flames gathered in the back of the dragon's throat.

Javan leaned his weight onto his back leg, stared at the space between the dragon's eyes, and let the rock fly as fire began pouring from the beast's mouth.

The flames rushed for Javan as the rock sailed through them and struck the dragon's left eye.

With a guttural cry, the dragon wheeled away, clawing at its face with its front talons.

Javan lunged forward, ducking beneath the wave of fire and wincing as the heat seared the bare skin of his back. Grabbing another rock, he readied it in the slingshot even as he hurtled over the far edge of the precipice and began sprinting down the incline and toward the path that wound through the next cluster of craggy hills.

For a moment, he thought the dragon wouldn't follow. It hung in the sky, wings pushing at the air while it clawed at its injured eye. Javan focused on the slim space between the third and fourth hills in front of him and reached deep for another burst of speed. His boots crunched on the shale beneath him as he closed in on his way out.

Behind him, the dragon roared. Javan risked a glance over his shoulder and his mouth went dry at the light of blind rage that glowed in the dragon's uninjured eye. The beast snarled and dove for him.

"Yl' Haliq be merciful," Javan breathed as he raced toward the slice of light that glowed between the hills.

He couldn't stop. Couldn't turn around and aim the rock at the dragon. One misstep, one lost instant of forward momentum, and he wouldn't be able to outrun the fiery death that was closing in on him.

Heat swept his back as the dragon sent a fireball toward him. Javan cried out in pain, but didn't stop. Reaching the space between the hills, he abandoned the slingshot, grabbed both sides of the rocky outcrop, and swung his body through. Without pausing, he skidded down the steep incline, sending showers of rocks onto the small meadow at the base of the hill.

Carved wooden stakes marked the four corners of the meadow, and at its center was a raised stone platform the size of a table that could seat twenty. The academy's coat of arms was carved into the front of the platform. A small selection of weapons was arranged on the left of the dais, and on the right stood the headmaster, the crimson sash in his hands. His back was to Javan, his focus on the main road where in the distance the three students Javan had left behind on the archery grounds were running toward the meadow.

"Weapon!" Javan yelled as his boots hit the grass.

The headmaster pivoted, his mouth an O of surprise as

behind Javan, the dragon crashed into the space between the hills and exploded through it in a hail of dust and debris. The sash fluttered to the ground as the older man lunged for the other side of the platform and grabbed a bow and quiver.

Javan stumbled as he crossed the meadow, the painful burns along his arm and back searing into his nerves, and the headmaster yelled, "Catch!"

The bow and the quiver flew toward the prince. He scrambled to his feet and caught them as the headmaster hefted a long sword and began running toward Javan.

Whirling to face the dragon, Javan planted his feet, nocked an arrow, and took a breath as he aimed the weapon at the incoming beast. Its scales were impenetrable. He'd have to hit it in an eye again.

The headmaster reached his side as Javan drew back the bow, prayed he'd calculated wind speed and velocity correctly, and let the arrow fly.

The arrow arced through the air. The dragon's lips peeled back, fire blooming in its throat. The headmaster raised his sword.

And then the arrow buried itself in the dragon's injured eye.

The beast screamed, a half-human half-dragon sound that sent a chill shuddering through Javan.

This wasn't a wild dragon from the north. This was a Draconi, a dragon shape-shifter from the eastern kingdom of Eldr. Why would a dragon shape-shifter be ordered to kill anyone who tried to get through the hills?

As the other competitors rushed into the meadow, the dragon clawed at its injured eye while the other eye glared balefully at the humans in the meadow. When it saw the prince's friends grabbing weapons and joining him, it gave one last roar and then turned, its massive wings beating the air as it flew south.

Javan remained poised, another arrow nocked, though his chest heaved with every breath and his back was lit with white-hot pain. His friends surrounded him, their gazes on the sky until the dragon was no more than a tiny speck in the distance. Finally satisfied that the beast wasn't going to return, Javan turned toward the headmaster and said, "That thing tried to *kill* me."

The headmaster was staring at the southern horizon, his face ashen. "I know."

Javan clenched his jaw and forced himself to speak respectfully to his elder. "Please help me understand why you would instruct a Draconi to guard the hill pass and kill anyone who came through it."

"I didn't." The headmaster's voice was soft, but there was anger in it.

"Then who did?" Javan asked, unease coiling in his stomach.

The headmaster's eyes narrowed. "I'd very much like to find out."

THREE

JAVAN STOOD AT the window of the room he shared with Kellan as the crowds for commencement day began pulling their carriages onto the academy's long half-circle drive. His gaze flicked between the people below and the sky above, his pulse racing every time he caught sight of a dark, distant cloud and wondered if it was the dragon returning to finish what it started.

"What are you looking at?" Kellan asked.

Tearing his gaze from the sky, Javan glanced at the academy grounds again. "The extra security the headmaster ordered for the commencement ceremony just arrived." He winced as he carefully pulled a clean tunic over his shoulders. The poultice the academy's physician had spread over the burned skin on his back had taken away much of the sting, but it was still tender to the touch. "If that Draconi comes back, it's in for trouble."

Yl' Haliq be praised, this time Javan wouldn't be in the fight by himself.

Javan's stomach knotted as he watched the security reinforcements move past the slow line of carriages carrying the noble parents of Milisatria's graduating class from across the three western kingdoms. Somewhere in that line there would be a sleek carriage made of polished teak and ebony with the Kadar family crest painted on its doors. Somewhere in that line was Javan's father, whose deep grief over the death of his wife hadn't caused him to miss a single day of ruling both Akram and his son with an implacable resolve.

A true ruler was fit—body, mind, and soul—and Javan had spent every ounce of his considerable willpower becoming a worthy heir to Akram's crown. The look of pride he'd finally see on his father's face would be his reward.

The thought was both exhilarating and somehow terrifying.

"Move over. Let me have a look." Kellan shouldered his way to the window frame and gave an appreciative whistle. "The headmaster went above and beyond with security this time. I guess he's still worried about that Draconi returning. Look at this! Royal knights, trained wolves, and an entire contingent of elven archers wearing black patches with a constellation insignia on their left shoulders." Kellan's eyes were lit with excitement. "Those are dark elves, Javan. Do you know how long I've wanted to meet one? Let's go introduce ourselves."

Javan shuddered. "So they can poison our minds with their magic and use us as slaves? No thanks. The only good elf is a dead elf."

"I'm sure these must be safe elves. Why else would the headmaster allow them on the grounds?"

"*Safe* elves." Javan snorted and looked over Kellan's shoulder as the security forces began spreading out to cover the academy's grounds. "There's no such thing as a safe elf. Maybe if your people had been captured and enslaved by those monsters like mine were, you'd understand. The only reason they're here is because the headmaster needs something that can kill a Draconi in case the dragon comes back, and the city's baron is hosting a contingent of dark elves from the northern land of Ystaria. The elves are visiting Loch Talam to convince the king and queen that the peace treaty they recently signed is solid. What better way to assure them of the elves' good intentions than to voluntarily protect the academy the king's children attend?"

"How do you always know everything?" Kellan demanded as he turned from the window to grab his commencement robe. "It's annoying. Useful, yes. But annoying."

"Because while you were out constantly looking for new and creative ways to kill yourself on some ridiculous adventure, I spent my time listening, observing, and learning." And if that sounded just a little bit boring, it didn't matter. Javan hadn't been sent to the academy to have fun.

"I've done plenty of listening, observing, and learning. Which is how I know that the girls from hall six will be celebrating at the Red Dwarf tonight." Kellan wiggled his brows, and Javan laughed, though his eyes were once again drawn toward the sky.

"Hey!" Kellan snapped his fingers in front of Javan's face. "You. Me. The girls from hall six and some of the best whiskey in Loch Talam. You're coming, right? It's your last night."

Javan hesitated. What would it feel like to laugh and linger and not worry about his studies? This one night was all he'd get. Once he returned to Akram, he'd assume a new set of duties. A new routine that would bind him to a set purpose the way his father's instructions had bound him to his tasks at Milisatria.

At the thought of his father, Javan's smile slowly disappeared, and he drew in a deep breath.

"I know that look." Kellan folded his arms over his chest.

"I'm sorry. My father will finally be at Milisatria tonight. It's been ten years since I've seen him. I can't go anywhere."

"My mother will be here too. That's why we're sneaking out after they settle into the guest rooms for the night."

Javan scanned the horizon while he searched for a way to explain his refusal. His gaze lingered on the craggy rock hills in the distance. He couldn't find any sign of the dragon who'd attacked him, but still a queasy sense of dread pooled in the pit of his stomach.

"Javan, are you coming with us or—"

Regret filled him, a painful weight that bowed his shoulders. "I can't. If we were caught, my father would think . . . It would cast doubt on everything I've accomplished. I've worked so hard to make him proud. I'm not going to risk losing that."

Kellan said nothing.

Turning away from the window, Javan shrugged into his sky-blue commencement robe and lifted the crimson sash. Once the dragon had disappeared in the distance at the previous day's competition, the headmaster had awarded the sash to Javan for arriving at the meadow first. The prince had offered to defend the sash from the other competitors, as was proper, but his friends had unanimously declined. Something about not wanting an arrow in their eyes.

"Look at you, wearing that red sash." Kellan's tone was easy, as if Javan hadn't just turned down the last invitation he would ever issue, but his gaze was thoughtful. "You'll be drowning in fair maidens by the end of the ceremony. I will, of course, graciously offer to dance with a few of them just to give you some breathing space." Kellan winked at Javan as he flung his own golden sash— the standard color for all graduates—around his shoulders.

Javan rolled his eyes. Approaching the room's looking glass, he smoothed the crimson fabric that was draped over his neck, its beaded ends hanging even with his waist. "I've never once been drowning in fair maidens."

"That's because you've always ignored them in favor of studying. Now that you no longer have to constantly bury your face in a book, you'll finally have a chance to impress a girl."

Javan stared at his reflection for a moment, searching for pieces of his parents, of his heritage, in his face. He found his father in the arch of his cheekbones and the tilt of his chin. Saw his mother in the line of his jaw and the slight curl to his hair. Felt the deep ties of duty and faith they'd instilled into the very fabric of his being. He was every inch their son, inside and out, and tonight his father would see that for himself.

Javan tied his shoulder-length black hair back with the ceremonial *zar'ei* his father had given him, his fingers lingering over the strip of leather with its narrow band of inlaid garnets—his mother's birthstone. She'd grown hazy in his memory, the passage of time breaking her into bits and pieces. Her laugh when they'd walked through the citrus grove, plucking lemons from the trees. The way the sun had gleamed against the roses in her cheeks. The smell of honey and jasmine that didn't have an image attached to it but felt like home all the same.

If earning his father's pride meant the world to Javan, then sending his mother to her peaceful rest by fulfilling her wish was the sun, the moon, and the stars.

Kellan looped an arm around Javan's shoulders and grinned at him. "Ready?"

Javan met his friend's gaze. "Ready."

Ordering his knotted stomach to relax, he moved toward the door, Kellan close behind.

He'd done everything that was expected of him and more. He was going to stand on the commencement stage wearing the crimson sash, proof that he was capable of ruling in his father's stead when the time came, and he was going to see pride on his father's face. Something soft and bright glowed in his chest at the thought of it, and Javan smiled as he stepped out of the room and made his way toward the academy's performance hall.

The hall was crowded. Rows of chairs in neat, horizontal lines faced the stage that occupied the north wall. Parents, siblings, and extended family filled the aisles, hunting for seats and scanning the graduating students—who sat quietly on the stage behind the headmaster—looking for their own child.

Javan stood to the right of the headmaster, slightly in front of the first row of students. His place of honor for being the top of his class. He kept his body still, his chin lifted, but his heart thudded painfully against his rib cage as his gaze skipped from one family to the next, searching for his father.

Would the king's shoulders stoop now? Would his long black hair have silver running through it? Twice, Javan was sure he'd seen him, but both times he'd been wrong. By the time the crowd was seated and quiet, the knots were back in Javan's stomach, and he'd given up pretending that he wasn't actively looking for his father.

The headmaster's voice rumbled beside Javan, filling the room. Candelabras moved gently in the breeze from the bank of open windows to the west, their shadows dancing along the floor. Javan strained to see every corner of the room, his eyes racing from one row to the next until he forced himself to slow down and methodically look at every person seated before him.

His father wasn't there.

The headmaster spoke Javan's name, and applause filled the room, but Javan couldn't find the will to force a smile. His chest ached like he'd run the entire perimeter of the academy, and the knots in his stomach had turned to stone.

He hadn't come.

Ten *years*. Ten long, arduous years of sacrifice, duty, and honor. And his father hadn't bothered to show up.

As the ceremony ended, and the crowd surged toward their children on the stage, Javan turned on his heel and walked away. Through the clusters of parents and grandparents, their smiles and tears salt on a wound Javan had never expected to be dealt. Past the pair of dark elves that stood sentry at the ballroom's west entrance without sparing them a glance. Over the lush green lawn of the academy proper and onto the cobblestoned road that led away from the academy.

There he stopped as the sun sank into the western sky, a ball of fire disintegrating into darkness.

"Javan!" Kellan's shout came from behind him, but Javan didn't turn.

He'd spent a decade with the single-minded purpose of honoring his mother and earning his father's regard. What was he supposed to do now?

Kellan came to a stop beside him, and they stood in silence for a moment. Finally, Javan said, "He didn't come."

The words were ashes in his mouth.

"I'm sorry."

Javan didn't want to be sorry. He wanted to feel like what he'd done mattered. He wanted to smile and laugh and feel better than the boy who'd been left behind and then forgotten.

And he knew exactly how he was going to do that.

The ache in his chest became a flame of anger as he turned toward Kellan and said, "Is the invitation still open?"

Kellan blinked. "If you're referring to girls, whiskey, and dancing, then, yes. Of course it is."

Javan glanced once more down the road his father's carriage should've traveled and then turned his back and met Kellan's gaze. "I'm in."

FOUR

THE RED DWARF was a low-slung gray brick building on the southern edge of town in the middle of a warren of crowded, twisted streets and narrow alleys. It had taken Javan, Kellan, and five of the girls from hall six nearly an hour to walk there. The slender fingernail of a moon did little to illuminate the roads, but the street lanterns were still lit, and there were plenty of people moving through the town in carriages, on horseback, or on foot.

Kellan and Javan had flanked the girls as they walked, their hands resting on the hilts of the daggers they'd strapped to their waists. Three of the girls had daggers too. None of them mentioned the dragon who'd attacked Javan, but they'd spent much of the hour-long walk craning their necks to examine rooftops and skylines, just in case.

The fact that they'd made it to the tavern without incident was slightly reassuring. If the Draconi had been acting alone, the injury it had sustained had kept it from returning. If someone had sent the dragon, the security on the academy's grounds had kept any further threats at bay. Javan wasn't sure how that would also keep the students safe when they left the academy's property, but perhaps the headmaster had employed extra security throughout the town of Abhahan as well.

Javan shoved thoughts of the dragon to the back of his mind as he approached the tavern. Tonight was his chance to see what he'd been missing all those years of turning down invitations so he could study. His chance to have fun without worrying that he would somehow disappoint his father.

His jaw clenched tight, and he reached for the tavern's door handle.

It was hard to disappoint someone who didn't care enough to show up for the most important moment of your life. The fact that the headmaster had received a message that the royal coach would arrive to collect Javan in the morning was somehow worse than being forgotten completely. Maybe Uncle Fariq was wrong. Maybe the king's letters had grown impersonal and infrequent because Javan had become nothing more than another duty in a long list of responsibilities weighing on the king's shoulders.

Pushing thoughts of his father into the same corner of his mind where the dragon crouched, Javan opened the thick wooden door to the tavern and was hit with a wall of noise. Fiddles played a lively jig. Wood crackled in an enormous fireplace that took up most of the far wall, and a din of voices was raised in merriment. A quick peek confirmed his suspicions—most of the graduating class was inside. Holding the door open for the girls, Javan raised a brow at Kellan.

"I thought it was just going to be the two of us and the girls from hall six."

Kellan grinned. "I guess word got around."

Javan rolled his eyes. "Somehow with you, it always does."

Kellan's grin widened. "If you play your cards right, it will still be just us with the girls from hall six."

The tavern's door closed behind him with a soft thud, and Javan's gaze swept the room. Square wooden tables filled half the floor, surrounded by chairs painted red, green, or black; and the other half of the floor already had a few couples dancing. Exposed wooden beams divided the ceiling into smaller sections, each lit with its own simple iron chandelier. To his left, a long counter separated the dining area from kegs of ale, racks of mugs, and bottles of whiskey. A swinging half door at the far end of the bar counter led to the kitchen.

Javan's stomach rumbled as he followed Kellan to two empty tables near the fireplace. The tavern smelled of roasting pig, fried blackberry tarts, and the sharpness of fermented grain, reminding Javan that he hadn't eaten since that morning. As Kellan pushed the two tables together, Javan held out a chair for each of the girls and then shrugged out of his cloak and settled into the one closest to the fireplace, his back to the wall, his eyes on the rest of the room.

Maybe he was just being paranoid about the Draconi, but there was no point in taking chances.

Javan smiled at Bria, a short girl with bright red hair and an adorably freckled nose, and prepared himself to be charming and fun. Unlike Kellan, Javan had been too busy with his studies to learn how to flirt. Still, if Kellan could do it, so could he. Javan had never once failed at anything he set his mind to, and this would be no different.

A waitress laid platters of roasted pig, stewed apples, wilted greens, and fried blackberry tarts in front of them. Once they'd eaten their fill, Javan met Bria's eyes and said a line he'd heard Kellan say a hundred times.

"You look lovely. I don't know what material your dress is made of, but I'd love to find out." He winced visibly the second the words left his mouth, and Bria's eyes widened. His voice rose. "I mean . . . no! Not like that, I just . . . I meant dancing. Dance with me! That's what I meant."

Yl' Haliq be merciful, this was a disaster. How did Kellan get away with saying such awkwardly awful things?

"You want to dance with me so you can touch my dress?"

"Yes. No! I'm not . . . I'd just be touching you." That sounded so much *worse*. His face felt as hot as the fire at his back. He had to fix this. Fast. "Unless you don't want me to touch you. I don't have to touch anything! I can just . . . We can dance. That's all. Is it hot in here?"

He tugged on the collar of his shirt and prayed that Yl' Haliq would open up the floor and swallow him.

"Um . . ." Bria cast a quick glance at her friends. "We can dance, but I think you'll have to at least touch my back since they're playing a *pallestaya*."

"Of course. That's perfect." Javan stood abruptly, and reached for Bria's chair, but she was already pushing it back, her cheeks pink.

He cast a quick look at Kellan, but his friend already had a girl on each arm and was whirling them both into the sweeping movements of the *pallestaya*. Javan offered his arm to Bria and led her to the dance floor without once looking at her face. Thank Yl' Haliq he knew how to dance. It was a required course at the academy, so Javan had dedicated himself to excelling at it. Now he just had to get through the next few moments without saying anything stupid, and he would have redeemed himself.

Javan spent the entire dance excruciatingly aware of the space between himself and Bria. He couldn't think of a single thing to say. He was too busy making sure he didn't sway too close or allow more than his fingertips to rest against her dress. How did one enjoy dancing while constantly monitoring oneself to make sure not a single dishonorable message was sent, even by accident?

By the end of the dance, Javan's shoulders were knotted with tension, and all he wanted was his chair in the back corner of the tavern again. Instead, one of Kellan's partners cheerfully offered to swap with Bria, and Javan found himself once again painfully aware of how difficult it was to keep a proper distance while dancing. Kellan didn't seem to mind. He whirled around the floor, his hands firmly on his partners' backs, his face leaning toward theirs while they all laughed.

A third dance started, and Javan found himself facing Kellan. His friend leaned close and said, "You look like you're being forced to dance with old Mrs. Denham from the dining hall. Relax. You're supposed to be having fun."

"I'm trying!" Javan rolled his shoulders to release some of the tension and glared at Kellan.

Kellan made an exasperated noise in the back of his throat as he grabbed Javan and led them both into the movements of the dance. "Having fun isn't a skill you have to learn. This isn't a test. It's just dancing and conversation."

"That's what I've been doing," Javan said through clenched teeth.

"No, you've been perfectly executing your dance steps while trying not to touch your partner." Kellan swept Javan into a flawless dip, and Javan glared.

"I'm trying not to send any dishonorable messages. And stop spinning me. Why are we even dancing together?"

Kellan spun Javan out three steps and back in. "Because I wanted to prove to you that you can dance and talk and touch another person without looking like you swallowed rancid milk. Plus, it's fun. See?"

"It would be a lot more fun if I didn't have to look at your ugly face while doing this." Javan took the lead and flung Kellan into a dizzying spin. "Also, how do you get away with saying such terrible lines to girls? I tried one, and it was a disaster."

Kellan laughed. "It's all about the delivery. You have to say them with confidence and a sense of humor."

"Even though they're the worst things to ever come out of your mouth?"

"Those are hardly the worst things to have come out of my mouth."

Javan laughed. "Point taken. Now stop dancing with me. I'd much rather pick a different partner."

"You wound me." Kellan winked as he smoothly handed Javan off to Cherise, a softly rounded girl with blond hair and stunning blue eyes.

Javan lost track of time as he danced, laughed, and danced some more. Friends slapped him on the shoulder and congratulated him for achieving top honors. Others offered to buy him an ale and toast the fact that he'd sent a dragon running. And, miracle of miracles, he had no lack of dance partners, despite the fact that he refused to say another one of Kellan's stupid lines.

By the time the tavern began emptying, Javan's feet were sore, his bladder was full, and his spirit felt lighter than it had in weeks. He was going to have to make it a point to have fun more often. A difficult task for the heir to Akram's throne, but Javan was no stranger to accomplishing difficult tasks.

The thought of returning to Akram, and to his father, was a dash of cold water on his spirit. He was ready to fulfill the destiny Yl' Haliq had set for him.

He wasn't ready to face his father.

The thought sent a dull pain through Javan's chest. Before the hurt could show on his face, he bowed to his last dance partner and caught Kellan's eye as he reached for his cloak.

"I'm heading out back to the privy. Do you mind escorting the remaining girls back to the academy without me?" He prayed Kellan would say yes and give Javan some time to wrestle with his thoughts.

Kellan glanced at the two girls from hall six who still remained. "Happy to do the honors if you'd rather walk back alone."

"Thanks." Javan let the tavern's door shut behind him and headed toward the privy in the back. The slim crescent of a moon was hidden behind clouds now, and knee-high ribbons of fog clung to the deserted city streets. He used the privy quickly, checked that his dagger was securely strapped to his waist, and then stepped out of the little outbuilding.

A whisper of sound came from his left, and Javan whirled as someone's fist crashed into his face.

The blow rocked him back on his heels. He reached for his dagger, and someone slammed into him from the side. He lashed out, sweeping a leg that connected with someone's knee. A man swore viciously, and something inside Javan went cold.

That was an Akramian peasant's curse.

There was no reason a band of Akramian peasants would cross the desert and lie in wait outside an ordinary tavern in Loch Talam to rob just anyone.

They were here for him.

Had the dragon been waiting specifically for him as well?

Pain exploded across the back of Javan's head as something hard connected with his skull, and he crumpled to the ground as darkness closed in and the world went silent.

FIVE

It was finished.

The FaSaa'il's hired team of assassins had killed Javan, and no one was the wiser. In the chaos of moving day at Milisatria, no one had looked closely at Rahim as he stayed inside the Akramian carriage and waited for the coachman to pack Javan's belongings in his dorm room and haul them outside. One boy had tried to hail him, but his guards, ordered to protect the prince's wish for solitary prayer, had immediately blocked the way. Soon, Rahim would leave the misty, craggy land of Loch Talam—and most of the people who knew what the real Prince Javan looked like—far behind him. The Akramian aristocrats whose children had attended Milisatria with Javan would be dealt with in Akram.

Rahim allowed himself a small, satisfied smile as the last of Javan's belongings—the last of *his* belongings—were loaded atop the sturdy carriage and tied into place. Soon the coachman and the quartet of royal guards the king had sent to collect the prince from Milisatria would finish securing the load, and it would be time to leave for the long stretch of desert road that would eventually bring Rahim back to Makan Almalik.

He'd left the city as the bastard son of a poor seamstress. He was returning as the heir to Akram's crown of fire. And there was no one left who could stop him. Not even the FaSaa'il who thought Akram's new prince was their puppet.

"We're ready, Your Highness." The coachman stood outside the carriage door, awaiting instructions.

"Then let's be off," Rahim said, careful to put an aristocratic polish on his words. "I'd like to cross the Sakhra bridge and be on the desert road by nightfall."

He took a deep breath and forced himself to relax against the seat again as the coachman hoisted himself into the driver's box. Soon, he'd be in the desert staying at inns where no one would dare question the occupant of Akram's royal coach. He'd eat as much as he wanted. Wear Javan's fine robes and plan what he'd say when he finally saw the king face-to-face for the first time. And what he'd do once the king either died or abdicated the crown, and every citizen of Akram was at Rahim's mercy.

He'd had seventeen long years of living in a seamstress's tent to dream about how it would feel to be a god among men, but nothing he'd imagined came close to the blazing heat of triumph that warmed his blood now.

"Wait!" A man's commanding voice cut through the air, and the coachman pulled the horses to a stop.

Rahim rapped sharply on the carriage's ceiling. "Continue!"

"Prince Javan, I'd like a word before you leave." The man sounded close to the carriage door. Rahim stiffened, but then relaxed as two of his guards stepped down from their perches on the side of the vehicle and blocked the way. "I'm the headmaster here, and this is a matter of urgent security for the prince."

Unease curled in Rahim's stomach. Did the headmaster know something was wrong? What other security issue could he be talking about? If he didn't suspect anything, he would surely anticipate Javan gladly opening the door and receiving him. If he *did* suspect, refusing to talk to him would simply confirm his suspicions. Rahim had seen the dark elves stationed at the academy's entrance. If the headmaster raised the alarm, Rahim wouldn't make it off the school's grounds before those monsters destroyed him with their magic.

There was only one solution.

The unease settled into cold determination as Rahim made the only choice he could.

Plenty of rulers began their reign with blood on their hands. His would be no different.

"Allow him to enter," he said quietly, lest his voice give him away to the headmaster before he'd had a chance to put his hastily constructed plan into action.

The guards stepped aside. The carriage door opened. Rahim turned his face into his shoulder as the headmaster, a sturdily built man with gray hair and creased skin, climbed into the vehicle. Reaching past him, Rahim grabbed the carriage door and pulled it closed.

"Kellan told me you were already in your carriage by the time he returned to the room early this morning, and that your guards wouldn't allow him close enough to say good-bye. I understand your eagerness to return home after so long, but do you really think ignoring your friend is the best way to leave?"

Rahim remained silent, and the headmaster sighed.

"I'm uneasy about that Draconi attack during the final exam," the man said. "While I have no proof that the creature was after you specifically, I'd like to send a small contingent of extra guards—"

He broke off abruptly as Rahim lifted his face to look him in the eyes.

"Who are you? Where is Javan?" The man glanced around the carriage's lush red interior as if Javan might be hiding in a corner.

Rahim crossed his arms over his chest and slid his hands into the pockets he'd sewn into his tunic beneath his armpits. The metal throwing stars concealed in their depths were a solid weight in his hands. "I am Prince Javan."

The man's eyes narrowed. "You most certainly are not."

Rahim smiled coldly. "I am Prince Javan Samad Najafai of the house of Kadar. Anyone who says otherwise must die."

Something flashed in the man's face, and he reached for the short sword that was strapped to his waist.

Rahim whipped the throwing stars out of their pockets and let them fly, thankful now for the hours spent practicing with the weapons while he was a boy stuck in a desert town with little else to do besides sew garments with his mother and dream of the life that should've been his. The weapons' razor-sharp tips buried themselves in the old man's chest. He gasped—a strangled, wet sound—and reached for them as if to pull them out.

It was too late. Blood was gushing over his chest, pooling in his lap, and dripping onto the floor.

It was fortunate the carriage's interior was already red. That stain was never coming out.

Rahim didn't understand what the headmaster meant by a

Draconi attack—a pity he hadn't been able to keep up the deception long enough to get more details—but if there was a threat from the Eldrians against Loch Talam, that was all the more reason to leave this damp, craggy kingdom far behind.

Rahim's hands shook as he reached past the headmaster and rapped on the front wall of the carriage. "The headmaster has decided to accompany us to our stop tonight as he has business there. Let's go."

The coachmen called out to the horses, and the carriage lurched into motion again.

Clenching his hands into fists to stop the shaking, Rahim lifted the purple sash he wore across his shoulders and wrapped it around the lower half of his face.

He hadn't known blood would smell like sweetly decaying metal. Hadn't imagined the awful way a body sagged when the spirit that once inhabited it was gone.

And he would never have guessed that killing someone would be so unsettling.

The future king of Akram couldn't afford to be unsettled by the taking of a life.

Slowly lowering the sash from his face, Rahim forced himself to breathe in the scent of blood. Forced himself to stare at the awkwardly slumped body with its glassy stare until it was no longer unsettling. No longer upsetting.

Until it was nothing at all.

The path to a king's throne was often paved with the bodies of his enemies.

Rahim had only just begun.

SIX

JAVAN JOLTED FROM unconsciousness when his body hit water. His eyes flew open, and he dragged in a quick, startled breath as he broke the surface of whatever body of water he'd been thrown into. The sun was a pale light in the sky, and Javan's heart raced. He'd lost the chunk of time between leaving the tavern and dawn. Was anyone out looking for him yet?

For a second, he could see the faces of his attackers—three Akramian men with rough woolen cowls pulled over their heads—and then they disappeared from sight as murky water rushed over Javan's face and pushed against his lips like it wanted permission to flood his lungs.

Javan tried to lift his arms, but his hands were tied behind his back. Tried to kick, but his legs were tied together at the ankles. He was trussed up like a pig on a spit, and the sunlight that grazed the surface of the water was quickly disappearing.

He was sinking.

Jerking his body, he kicked his legs as one, trying to swim

without using his arms, but he kept steadily drifting toward the bottom of the lake.

Panic hit, slicing though his thoughts like a hot knife.

He was going to drown. Suck the murky water into his lungs and never be seen again. Jerking against the ropes that tied him, he thrashed and struggled while his lungs began straining.

Why was he sinking?

Forcing himself to stop struggling, he tried to think.

Weights in his cloak pockets. It had to be. There was no other explanation for his rapid descent. His lungs begged for air as his pulse pounded inside his head.

He had to get his cloak off. It was his only chance.

His chest ached with the need to take a breath as his feet grazed the bottom of the lake, his boots catching on the rocky surface. Yl' Haliq be praised that the lake was shallow enough to allow a faint sheen of sunlight to help Javan see his surroundings.

Prayers tumbled through his mind as he frantically looked around the lake floor, searching for something he could use. He was surrounded by algae-coated rocks. Ignoring the fierce pressure in his chest, Javan crouched in front of a rock the size of his torso and thrust his bound hands toward its sharp edges.

A quick bite of pain snaked up his arm, and blood bloomed in the water around him as the rock sliced into his palm. Desperately rubbing the rope against the rock, Javan pressed his lips closed while a faint ringing sounded in his ears and spots danced at the edges of his vision.

Yl' Haliq be merciful, he didn't want to die.

His thoughts began to fray, and panic screamed through him. Gritting his teeth, Javan called on his remaining strength and scraped the rope against the rock as hard as he could.

It gave. Heedless of the cuts that sliced into his skin, Javan scraped harder, tugging and pulling at the rope as it began to unravel. Seconds later, as the ache in his lungs became a burning pain, the rope loosened enough for Javan to pull one hand free. Quickly freeing the other, he shoved the cloak off, kicked his feet against the ground, and shot toward the surface.

At the last moment, he realized the men could still be on the shore watching for him. His lungs spasmed, and he nearly coughed. The ringing in his ears was deafening. When at last he couldn't avoid breathing for another moment, he turned onto his back and let just his face clear the water.

Air rushed into his lungs, and the pressure eased. He stayed like that for nearly an hour, floating on his back just beneath the surface, letting his mouth leave the water long enough to take a breath before he submerged again, before he finally dared poke his head out of the lake to search the shoreline for his attackers.

They were gone.

Quickly, Javan swam to the bank, hauled himself onto the shore, and assessed the position of the sun.

The sun was halfway toward midday. That meant the royal coach was at Milisatria and everyone would be wondering where he'd gone.

He needed to get back to the academy to enlist the help of the royal guards and the headmaster to flush out the three men who'd tried to kill him and get some answers. It was unlikely Akramian peasants could afford to hire a Draconi assassin, which meant they were probably working for the same person. Javan had no idea why someone would want him dead, but the why mattered less right now than getting to safety before those who wanted to kill him realized he was still alive. Turning in a slow circle, he got his bearings and then started moving south toward Milisatria.

It was nearly noon by the time he reached the academy. There were still a few carriages scattered about the academy's semicircular drive, but a quick glance showed that none of them were the teak and ebony vehicles preferred by Akram's aristocracy.

Was the royal coach late? Or had the same person who'd sent men after Javan attacked his coachman and his guards too?

Javan hurried toward his dorm. Maybe Kellan was still here. Maybe one of his remaining classmates had seen something that would give Javan a clue about why anyone would want to kill him.

Did a rival family want to declare him dead and make a move to put themselves in line for the throne instead?

Was this a ploy to break his father's will or punish him for something?

He brushed past a pair of third years who were hauling a chest between them and edged around a woman with a wide skirt and an even wider hat who stood, arms akimbo, in the center of the hall calling instructions to a trio of servants as they scrambled to empty her child's room of its belongings.

Taking the stairs two at a time, he reached the top floor quickly, but then had to lean against the wall as dizziness swamped him. His head still ached from the blow that had knocked him unconscious, and his near drowning had only served to make the pain worse. When the spell passed, he entered his hallway and moved to his room.

The door stood open, and the room was empty of all but the beds, dressers, and desks the academy provided for students' use.

Javan blinked and moved a few steps into the room.

Where were his belongings? His blankets. His framed painting of Makan Almalik at sunset. His copy of the sacred texts.

He pulled open the drawers of his dresser while confusion warred with dread within him.

Everything was gone.

It was as if he'd never been here.

So now he was supposed to be dead and also moved out of Milisatria? How did that benefit the person behind this?

Javan's thoughts raced, but he couldn't make sense of it. Why take his belongings if he was dead? And where were his belongings now? A hint of red caught his eye, and he leaned down to find the crimson sash he'd worked so hard to earn crumpled up beneath his bed. Whoever had packed his belongings must have missed this. Pulling the sash out, Javan folded it with shaking hands and slid it inside his tunic.

Turning his back on the empty room, Javan retraced his steps through the dorm, past the commons, and back to the academy's drive. Four carriages remained, and the academy's staff were already busy sweeping the walks, washing the windows, and entering the buildings with buckets and mops.

Javan glanced around, expecting to see the headmaster bidding farewell to students and their families as was his custom, but he was nowhere to be seen. Scanning the staff members closest to the drive, he found one he knew fairly well.

"Aaler!" he called as he approached the liveryman.

The shorter man gave the load strapped onto the carriage beside him a thorough appraisal before nodding his approval to the family's coachman and then turning to face Javan. His eyes widened in surprise, and he glanced at the drive again as if looking for the prince's carriage.

"Did the headmaster decide he'd rather stay at the academy, sir?" Aaler asked.

Javan frowned. "The headmaster?"

"Where is your carriage?" Aaler craned his neck to see farther down the cobblestoned road where it wrapped around a bend in the hill and disappeared from view.

"I don't have one. Where is the—"

"Of course you have one. I approved the load at least an hour ago. Maybe more." Aaler met Javan's gaze, the confusion on his face a perfect match for the prince's own.

"You sent my carriage on its way without me?" Javan kept his voice even, though he wanted to shout in frustration. All his belongings, and apparently the carriage his father had sent, gone.

But why would the coachman drive away without the prince?

"No, sir. You know you were inside. You and the headmaster." Aaler took a step back as Javan quickly closed the space between them.

"I wasn't in that carriage. Why are you lying to me?"

"I'm not lying!" Anger sparked on the man's face. "You were inside the carriage while your coachman packed up your room and then had your guards help load the trunks."

"Did you actually see me?"

"Yes!" Aaler paused. "Well, from a distance. I saw you look out the window once. And then the headmaster entered your carriage to talk to you, and he decided to ride with you to your first stop."

Javan lifted his head to stare at the distant southern hills that edged the border of Loch Talam before giving way to the enormous Sakhra bridge and then the road that cut through the Samaal Desert. Someone had been inside the carriage posing as Javan. Someone who looked enough like him to fool others at a distance.

He had no idea why the headmaster would enter the carriage and travel with the occupant, but he was certain of one thing: he had to reach the carriage before it entered the city of Makan Almalik.

No one besides Uncle Fariq and the parents of a few of his Akramian peers had seen him in ten years. Including his father. If someone was making a bid for the throne by posing as Javan himself, there was a very short list of people who would even recognize the deception. A short list Javan felt certain the person who'd set a Draconi and then a team of assassins against him would have no compunctions about killing.

"If you weren't in the carriage, my lord, then who was?" Aaler's voice rose. "And what have they done with the headmaster?"

"I don't know. But I intend to find out." Javan met Aaler's gaze. "I'm going to need a strong horse and provisions for the trip. You can put it on my father's account."

Moments later, Javan sat astride a sturdy black gelding. He'd traded the clothes he'd worn to the tavern for the flowing white linen pants and tunic that were acceptable for traveling across the desert. A hooded woolen cloak hung from his shoulders. It wasn't the royal purple and silver of Akramian royalty since his had been taken by the impostor in the carriage, but it would do. A satchel containing spare clothing, a bedroll, a feed bag for his horse, and several skins of water was bound to the saddle behind him. Aaler hadn't been able to give him any coin since only the headmaster had the keys to the trunk that held the academy's spare funds, but Javan, after strapping on a short sword and two daggers, had taken several extra daggers from the armory and packed them into a soft leather bag that hung by his side. He'd be able to trade a weapon for provisions and shelter along the road if necessary.

He hoped it wasn't necessary.

He hoped to catch up with the carriage before dawn, expose the impostor's charade, and put a stop to the entire thing before any damage was done.

Bidding Aaler farewell, Javan turned his horse south and nudged him into a brisk trot. The cobblestoned road banked around the base of the hills, and then cut south through a pair of silvery lakes. The imposing stone facade of Milisatria grew small behind him as the cobblestones gave way to the packed dirt of the main road that wound past the final craggy hills and meadows of Loch Talam before reaching the imposing length of the Sakhra.

Javan urged his horse into a canter and anchored the bag of weapons to his side with one arm so that it wouldn't bang against the horse's flank. Traffic on the road was light. Most people had no interest in crossing the Sakhra and entering the desert at night when temperatures plummeted and bandits roamed.

As the giant pillars of the Sakhra came into view, Javan pulled the gelding into a walk, both to give the horse a chance to catch its breath and to assess what he was seeing.

Built of glistening dark stone that curved gently upward before arching in the middle and then descending to the far distant edge of the desert that pressed against the banks of the enormous Abhainn Liath river, the Sakhra was wide enough for four carriages to travel abreast. Intricately woven black rope formed a safety netting on either side of the bridge. A small crowd of late-afternoon travelers were clustered at the edge of the bridge staring down at the body of a man that lay crumpled on the shore beside the bridge's entrance as if he had been tossed from a moving carriage.

Javan's heart pounded and his hands grew clammy on the reins as he drew closer.

The body was unnaturally still, and no one made a move to offer medical aid. The man's official Milisatria uniform was stained dark with blood, and the dying light of the sun painted his gray hair gold.

Javan slid from his horse, tied the reins to the closest bridge post, and stumbled to the edge of the shore.

"Careful there, son. Don't want to end up going in." A man reached for him, but Javan couldn't feel the hands that held him back.

Something wild and awful awoke in his chest and grew until it was a monster howling beneath his skin. He fell to his knees and dug his fingers into the rocky sand as he stared at the body of the man who'd been as much of a father to him for the past ten years as the one who'd given him life.

"Son?"

"Did you know him?"

"Might be his first dead body. Can be a shock."

"Night's falling. We can't stay."

The words swirled around Javan, passing over him without a ripple as the monster in his chest swelled into his throat until it was difficult to breathe.

The impostor in the royal coach.

He'd done this.

Killed the headmaster for trying to have one last word with Javan.

Killed him because the headmaster had seen the impostor. Because he had known something was wrong.

And because to fake your way onto a throne, you had to remove anyone who could dispute your claim.

If Javan hadn't accepted the invitation to go to the tavern. If he hadn't decided to use the privy and walk back by himself. If he'd fought harder. Escaped sooner. Run faster.

The headmaster would still be alive.

The monster tore into him with feral teeth, drawing blood from the scars of grief that covered the wound of his mother's death. Javan threw his head back and howled at the darkening sky.

His mother was gone. His father hadn't shown up. And now he'd lost the headmaster, a man he'd loved like family.

The hands that were holding him back let go. The voices that were talking over him gradually ceased. The prince bowed his head, grief sinking into him until the blood in his veins felt turned to stone.

It took two hours to dig the grave in the thick dirt above the shoreline. Another hour to carry the headmaster, arrange him with dignity and honor, and gently cover him with soil to keep him safe from carrion eaters until word could be sent back to Milisatria so that they could collect him and give him a proper burial.

Darkness was a vast, cavernous presence across the land, dusted by the distant glitter of cold white stars, as Javan laid a heavy stone across the top of the headmaster's grave and scratched the man's name into the rock with the tip of a dagger.

Resting his hands on the stone, Javan murmured a lament for the dying. It was supposed to be prayed before the loved one passed over into the next realm, but Javan knew Yl' Haliq would understand.

Just as he would understand the deep dishonor that had been done this day, and what Javan had to do to make it right.

The sharp edges of his grief hardened into determination as he mounted his horse, lifted his hood over his head, and set his course for the desert.

SEVEN

RAHIM WAS SO close to being recognized by Akram as its prince, he could almost taste it.

He'd been traveling the Samaal Desert for over three weeks now, passing inns and long stretches of road with nothing to see but the ruins of altars to the lesser gods and the iron-caged effigies of dark elves ready to be lit on fire during the week of *Tu' Omwahl* as Akramians remembered the war six generations before that had finally freed them from servitude to the monstrous creatures from the far north.

By the week of *Tu' Omwahl*, the FaSaa'il would have either finished poisoning the king or Rahim would have convinced him to abdicate. Either way, Rahim would be ensconced on Akram's throne, the crown of fire on his brow, and the bodies of all who'd opposed him strewn in his wake.

It would be interesting to kill again. He'd acted so quickly with the academy's headmaster that he hadn't had time to really savor his victory.

He sniffed as he glanced across the carriage at the ruined upholstery. He'd been right about the bloodstain. It was never coming out. The velvet was crusty and matted, and the man's bright red blood had dried an unsightly brown. As the unforgiving desert sun beat down on the carriage, the smell that lingered in the stifling confines coated the back of Rahim's tongue with sharp bitterness and almost made him wish to ride atop the vehicle with his guards.

Almost.

But Rahim had spent too many years in the burned red sand of the desert, sewing garments to help his mother eke out a living and nursing his rage, to ever travel as anything less than the royal he was.

Besides, it was good to sit with the smell. To realize that he was strong enough to kill those who caused him problems and live with it afterward. Ordinary people couldn't stomach it, but Rahim was hardly ordinary.

A sharp knock sounded on the door, and then a guard poked her head into the carriage, her eyes scraping over the bloodstained seat as if it didn't exist.

None of the guards and coachmen had questioned Rahim when he'd demanded they stop the carriage at the entrance to the Sakhra bridge. Not even when they discovered his reason for stopping was to dump the body of Milisatria's headmaster onto the shore.

If the power of being Akram's prince was this intoxicating, Rahim couldn't wait to experience what it was like to be king.

"Forgive my intrusion, Your Highness." The guard's voice was brisk. "We'll be entering Makan Almalik soon. The journey is almost over."

He nodded his thanks and leaned forward to sweep the curtain from the carriage's window as the guard closed the door and resumed her post.

Makan Almalik spread across a bowl-shaped valley deep in the heart of Akram. Gentle hills dipped and curved, and the copper pipes, which funneled rainfall during monsoon season into enormous holding tanks, gleamed at the edges of the city.

Rahim drank in the sight like a starving man staring at a feast. A few months ago, he'd arrived in the city as a peasant. Now he was entering as its prince. Pride swept through him, fierce and possessive.

There were the gleaming white clay homes with their colorfully painted rooftops lining the hills in stately elegance. The cinnamon trees with their rust-brown bark and lemon groves with their rich green leaves and thorny stems. There were the packed-dirt streets and the brilliant sashes tied to balconies to flutter in the wind and give early warning of incoming sandstorms. The wooden stables painted in bold hues of peacock blue, apple red, or sunlit gold and the racetracks with their betting halls and trampled sweet grass seats for the peasants who paid five wahda to watch the aristocrats race their steeds.

And there, rising above the warren of streets, orchards, and buildings was the palace—the shining jewel in the crown of Akram. White pillars capped with domes tiled in crimson and gold glowed in the early morning light like torches. Carved marble tigers, the animal on the Kadar family crest, stood sentry along the glistening white walls that hemmed in the enormous palace estate. Royal purple banners hung from the upper balconies.

Rahim smiled as the carriage entered the city and began

winding its way toward the palace.

He'd done it.

Influenced the right people, said the right things, made bold decisions, and won the right to enter the palace as the true prince.

Soon, he would be crowned king, a worthy successor to the current ruler whose failing health would surely inspire him to quickly put his newly returned son on the throne.

And once he was king, he would test the loyalty of those who'd helped give him the crown. They'd better be prepared to pass his test. Their lives depended on it.

His smile stretched wide and feral as he pulled away from the window and looked at the bloodstained seat across from him while the carriage pulled to a stop and waited for the palace gates to open.

Hoofbeats thundered toward the carriage from the road behind him, and Rahim's heart kicked up a notch. A shout echoed from the top of the vehicle, and Rahim spun toward the door in time to see a boy yank it open, kick a guard onto the ground, and then launch himself straight for Rahim.

EIGHT

JAVAN LUNGED FOR the carriage's interior as shouts and the rasp of a sword leaving its sheath echoed behind him. Pulling the door shut, he threw the bolt and ignored the sound of a weapon slamming repeatedly against the latch.

Ice slid down his spine as he turned to stare at a face that looked remarkably like his own. High cheekbones. Sharp jawline. Narrow chin.

No wonder Aaler had been fooled.

The boy sat on the carriage seat, his lips pressed tight as he glared at the prince. Javan moved closer, studying the boy intently. Javan's skin was a darker shade of bronze, his brow was wider, his ears set closer to his head. But if someone hadn't set eyes on the true prince for a decade, if someone was simply expecting to see a young man who resembled a Kadar, the boy would pass inspection.

Javan would worry about what that meant later. Right now, he had a promise to keep.

The boy rose into a crouch, arms up to fight.

Good. A fight was exactly what Javan was looking for.

"You're supposed to be dead," the boy said. He looked furious.

"You're about to be."

The boy smiled, sharp and vicious, and Javan drew his short sword.

"This is for killing my headmaster. May Yl' Haliq deal justly with your soul." Javan feinted left and then dove straight for the boy as he jerked to the right.

The sword sliced into the boy's upraised arm as Javan crashed into him, sending them both sprawling. Blood flowed, and the boy kicked and fought, making it impossible to raise the sword again in the confined space of the carriage.

Fine with Javan. Abandoning the sword, he drove his fist into the boy's stomach, and then rocked back as the boy's head slammed into his own. Lunging forward, Javan punched, elbowed, and kicked, absorbing the answering blows and ignoring the pain, until he had the boy beneath him again. Until his hands were around the impostor's neck.

"You dishonored my friend, my family, and my kingdom," Javan said, his breath heaving. "As the prince of Akram, I sentence you to death."

The guards outside the carriage finally smashed the lock with their swords. The door flew open behind Javan and hands grabbed him roughly, hauling him off the impostor and out of the vehicle.

"Wait!" Javan cried as a trio of guards grappled with him, driving him to his knees in the dirt beside the carriage. "He's an impostor. A threat. I'm the real Prince Javan. I can prove it."

The cold scrape of swords leaving their sheaths filled the air. Javan twisted in the grasp of the guard who held him. "Get the king. Please. Or Prince Fariq. They know me."

Desperation closed in as the guards ignored him. A second guard sheathed his sword to help the first hold Javan, while the third aimed his sword at the prince's heart.

"I'm the prince! Please, just get the king. He'll recognize—"

"What is the meaning of this?" Prince Fariq's voice cut through the air as he strode out of the palace gate.

Relief rushed through Javan, turning his knees to water. "Yl' Haliq be praised. Uncle, there's an impostor in the carriage. A boy claiming to be me." Javan met Fariq's gaze. "He killed the headmaster of Milisatria and tried to kill me." Javan jerked against the guards who held him, but they refused to let go.

"A boy claiming to be you?" Fariq laughed, an unpleasant sound that sent a whisper of warning over Javan's skin as the boy climbed from the carriage, a bruise blossoming along his cheekbone, his arm still dripping blood. "Why would my beloved nephew claim to be anything other than the prince he is?"

Javan's mouth dropped open, and the words died on his tongue as his uncle moved to the impostor's side and wrapped an arm around the boy's shoulders. Dread bloomed in his stomach like sickness as he studied the two of them together. The same jaw, ears, and hands. The Kadar eyes set just a bit wider apart than Javan's. The resemblance between the two was strong enough that the impostor could be Fariq's son.

"Yl' Haliq be praised for your safe arrival," Fariq said to the boy.

The desert air felt trapped in Javan's lungs as he stared at Fariq. Hands whisked over Javan's body, removing the two daggers he wore, and someone pulled Javan's arms behind his back and wrapped a short length of iron chain around his wrists. He could barely find the strength to struggle against them.

"Uncle!" Javan's voice shook. This was his father's cousin, raised in the palace as if he was his brother. The man who'd come to Milisatria six times over the past ten years at the king's behest to check on Javan's progress and to bring him new clothing, honey cakes, and news from the palace.

This was the family Javan had been trying to protect from the impostor.

This was a traitor.

Fariq swept Javan with a disdainful glance, though he didn't meet the prince's eyes. "Do not speak to me as if you know me."

Anger swelled, hot and thick, and Javan yanked at the chain that bound him. "Do not speak to me as if you don't. I demand an audience with my father." He craned his neck to look at the guards. "I want to see the king."

The boy laughed and then spit blood on the dust beside Javan's knees. "Traitors don't get audiences with the king."

"I'm no traitor!" Javan struggled to get to his feet, but the guards pushed him down. "I am Javan Samad Najafai of the house of Kadar, esteemed prince of the Kingdom of the Sun and heir to Akram's crown of fire. Test me." He looked at the guards. "Ask me anything. Ask me something only I would know."

Most of the guards wouldn't meet his gaze, but one—a thin man with graying hair and a black armband indicating a position of command, stared directly at him, a frown on his face. A flash of recognition hit Javan. He remembered this man. Abbas. The guard assigned to Javan's mother. Javan opened his mouth to say something, but the man turned away from him and bowed deferentially toward Fariq and the impostor.

"Enough of this." The impostor stepped away from Fariq's side and stood in front of Javan. With quiet malice, he said, "You have dishonored your kingdom. As the prince of Akram, I sentence you to death."

Panic hit, a shock of fear that shook Javan's knees and set his heart pounding as the guards hauled him to his feet and dragged him away from the palace.

"Wait! Please! I swear I'm Prince Javan. Let me talk to my father. Keep me in chains if you must, but let him see me. He'll know me." Javan's words tumbled out, fast and desperate, but it was no use. The guards had orders from Fariq, and nothing Javan could say would change their minds.

He was going to die.

"Please listen." Javan's breath came in quick gasps and his pulse roared in his ears. The iron chain binding his wrists behind his back cut into his skin as he walked the streets of Makan Almalik, led by Abbas, the guard who used to be assigned to Javan's mother.

"My name is Javan Samad Najafai of the house of Kadar. I just graduated with top honors from Milisatria Academy in Loch Talam and am returning home for the first time in ten years. The boy who told you to kill me is an impostor." Javan's voice was hoarse from pleading his case as the guard escorted him to the magistrate's courtyard in the heart of the city where he would be beheaded for the crime of attacking the prince of Akram.

The irony was not lost on him.

"I can prove it," Javan said, for what felt like the hundredth time. "One minute in the king's presence, and he will recognize me. One minute. That's all I ask."

"Those who attack the royal family of Akram don't get to ask for favors." Abbas spoke with unflappable calm.

Javan's voice rose as they reached the base of the hill, the palace perched high above them, and turned toward the center of Makan Almalik. "That boy isn't Prince Javan of Akram. I am. He plotted to replace me because he looks enough like me to fool those who haven't visited the academy in Loch Talam."

"Prince Fariq visited Javan in Milisatria," the guard said quietly. "Are you saying he failed to recognize his own nephew?"

No, Uncle Fariq hadn't failed to recognize Javan. How could he? He'd seen his nephew just last year on a two-day stop as he traveled to visit the king and queen of Loch Talam. Javan's heart ached, and grief pressed sharply against the back of his throat. Fariq had lied. Thrown his support behind the impostor who looked like he could be Fariq's own son, though Fariq himself had once told Javan the best way to deal with a bastard was to kill it before it grew old enough to want what it could never legally have. It didn't really matter who the impostor was. Fariq had turned his back on his family. His honor.

The understanding that his uncle wanted him dead—that he was even now welcoming the impostor into the heart of the palace knowing that Javan was about to be executed—was a live coal sinking into the pit of Javan's stomach.

If Fariq could kill his nephew to put another on the throne, how long would it be until he killed his cousin, the king? Surely Fariq didn't believe he could deceive Javan's father for long. The impostor would make a mistake. Forget one tiny detail. And the king would know.

Maybe his father hadn't neglected to show up to Javan's

graduation on purpose. Maybe Fariq had somehow kept him from it so that the king wouldn't know about the ruse until it was too late.

They were going to kill his father and take his kingdom, and Javan was the only one who knew. The only one who could save his father and his people.

But first he had to save himself.

And he was quickly running out of time.

"You look familiar," he said as they passed a bakery with honey cakes and almond-crusted cinnamon knots on display. The air smelled of hot chicory and sugar, and Javan's stomach rumbled. "I'm certain I remember you."

"Move faster," the man answered as they wove their way past clusters of people standing outside a racetrack wearing white linen with sashes the color of their favorite stables, waiting for the betting hall to open. Several craned their necks to watch the guard escorting the boy whose hands were bound in iron chains.

Frantically, Javan cast about until he unearthed a memory—faded and blurry, but it was the best he could do. The picture of happier times, easier times, was a bittersweet pain that bloomed in the hollow space carved out by Fariq's betrayal.

"You carried me once," Javan said softly. The racetrack disappeared behind them as they turned onto a street lined with stately white buildings whose tiny courtyards each had a single fountain flanked by a pair of orange trees. The road ended in front of a wide building with a brown domed roof and a courtyard fountain, only this fountain wasn't flanked by orange trees. It was flanked by a pair of *muqsila*, their large blades affixed to their iron frames and hanging suspended over the stocks below, ready to decapitate anyone whose crime deserved death.

Javan's stomach pitched, and the thick, sun-soaked air felt impossible to breathe.

He spoke faster, trying hard to keep his voice from shaking. "I think you were assigned to guard my mother. Your name is Abbas, right?"

The guard ignored him. They were halfway up the street, and Javan couldn't take his eyes off the *muqsila* blades glittering like silver glass in the sun.

He'd get to plead his case before the magistrate and ask for evidence and witnesses to be produced, though it was unlikely he'd get much of a stay of execution when everyone believed the crown prince was the one who had ordered Javan's death. Especially with Prince Fariq ready to lend credence to the impostor's every word.

Would it hurt? Or would it happen too fast to feel anything at all? One moment, he'd be kneeling in the magistrate's courtyard, his arms locked in the stocks, his neck resting on a slab of wood with the blade poised above him. The next, he'd be in the verdant fields and golden cities of Yl' Haliq, earning his reward for his faithful service.

Except that he hadn't completed his service.

He hadn't protected his father or his people. He hadn't done anything at all except honor his mother's *muqaddas tus'el*.

And he was out of time.

"Yl' Haliq, be merciful upon your servant's soul. Grant me absolution from my sins and forgiveness for my enemies." He choked on the second line of the dying man's prayer, but the sacred texts were implacable in their requirements of him. He couldn't die with a pure heart if he harbored hatred for another.

He'd always thought forgiving others before death would be

easy. What did it benefit you to hold an old grudge when you were moving into the next realm?

But now the pain of the injustice done to him lodged in his heart like a splinter of fire.

Abbas roughly hauled Javan into the magistrate's courtyard. Javan glanced at the guard's uniform, at the black armband that denoted him as the head of the palace unit. It was too late for the prince. It didn't have to be too late for his father.

"Please double the guard on the king," he said quietly as they approached the closest *muqsila*. "Even if you don't believe that I'm telling the truth, you must know that he's in danger. Whoever is trying to take the throne can't do that while the king is still alive. Not unless he abdicates, which he won't do once he realizes the boy in the palace isn't his son."

The guard said nothing, and Javan's feet slowed as they reached the bloodstained stocks of the *muqsila*. His lips formed the rest of the dying man's prayer, his words a faint breath of sound as his throat closed and his eyes stung.

Soon the magistrate would step out, flanked by his clerks, and the futile process of pleading for his life against the testimony of a royal would begin. It didn't matter that Fariq and the impostor hadn't accompanied Javan to the magistrate's office. The word of the head of the palace guard would be enough to condemn Javan. He was going to fail to complete the destiny Yl' Haliq had given him. He was going to fail to protect his father.

But he was finally going to see his mother again after eleven long years. The knowledge was an anchor of peace in the center of the raging tumult of fear and grief that stormed within him.

He opened his mouth to ask for the magistrate to take evidence, when Abbas said, "Why do you care what happens to the king? You just tried to kill his son."

"*I'm* his son." Javan raised his head to look at the guard.

They stared at each other for a long moment, their silence broken by the tinkling splash of the fountain and the cooing of doves roosting in the building's dome.

"It's a strange thing for a traitor to want to protect the king," Abbas said.

"I'm not a—"

"Traitor? Of course you'd say that. You'd say anything to avoid being executed." The man's eyes narrowed. "Maybe you'd even pretend to worry about the king to deflect suspicion."

Javan shook his head, desperation lacing his words. "Do what you will with me, but please double the king's guard. Swear it before Yl' Haliq. I'm begging you."

Abbas frowned, and stared at Javan for a full minute before finally saying, "I'll double his guard."

"Thank you." Javan drew in a breath, but before he could say anything more, the guard said, "You definitely look like a Kadar. I'm not sure I remember you. It's been ten years. You could be the traitor, or it could be the boy in the carriage. Either way, Fariq runs the kingdom far more than the king these days, and he gave me an order. I can't disobey without losing my own life."

The man's jaw tightened. His gaze slid from Javan's to the *muqsila* behind the prince. Then he abruptly grabbed Javan's arm and pulled him away from the blades of death and toward the magistrate's office instead.

"What are you doing?" Javan asked as they passed the fountain and began mounting the steps that led toward the front entrance.

"I'm not going to chance having a royal's blood on my hands.

Not when I swore an oath to protect them. Say nothing about who you claim to be. If anyone finds out that you're still alive, I'll be dead, and shortly after so will you." He reached for the door handle.

"What are you going to do with me?" Javan asked as the door swung open and the scent of parchment, ink, and peppermint sticks spilled out.

"I'm doing the one thing that will keep us both alive and, if you're smart about it, could eventually give you what you need to prove your claims."

"All I need for proof is a few moments with my father."

The guard escorted Javan into an entrance lined with framed quotes from the sacred texts and said, "I'm throwing you into Maqbara. Gaining an audience with the king will be entirely up to you."

NINE

THE ENTRANCE TO Maqbara was in the back of the magistrate's building behind a narrow wooden door with a thick iron bolt across its middle. Abbas had left three hours ago after turning Javan over to the magistrate, a small man with ink-stained fingers and a meticulously groomed mustache, on the charge of attempted murder.

No mention had been made of Javan trying to kill the "prince."

The magistrate had accepted the guard's account of catching Javan in the act of trying to run another boy through with a sword. Seconds after the guard had signed his testimony, the magistrate sentenced Javan to thirty years in Maqbara and locked him in a holding cell until he could be escorted into the bowels of the prison. No witnesses called. No evidence recorded.

It was unsettling how easy it was to be convicted of a crime he didn't commit.

Did a palace guard's testimony carry enough weight to excuse the fact that the magistrate hadn't conducted an investigation or allowed Javan to speak in his defense? Whatever the reason, Javan had more important things to think about. He was about to enter Maqbara, Akram's most infamous prison. No one ever got out before their sentence was served, but Javan was going to have to change that.

As the magistrate unbolted the door and swung it open, Javan sent a swift prayer to Yl' Haliq for deliverance. Then, heart crashing wildly against his chest, he started the long walk down the tunnel that led into Maqbara.

The magistrate and two of his guards walked behind him. One of the guards held a lit torch. The air smelled of dust and burning pitch. Javan sucked in one slow breath after another, trying desperately to calm the terrible thunder of his pulse so he could *think* instead of panic.

The guard had said gaining an audience with the king was entirely up to Javan. What did that mean?

The chains that bound Javan's wrists behind his back clinked with every step, a noise that began to feel like the tolling of a funeral bell.

Why would the king grant an audience to a prisoner? It didn't make sense.

Javan's mouth went dry as the truth hit him. Abbas must have lied. He hadn't wanted to kill Javan himself and risk having innocent blood on his hands, and so he'd thrown him in Maqbara to be forgotten.

What would happen to his father while Javan and the truth of his birthright spent the next thirty years in a cell? The tunnel curved gently to the left, and a light glowed faintly at the bottom of the long incline in front of the prince. It took everything he had to keep walking when all he wanted to do was run, even if it meant the magistrate's guards would kill him before he ever made it out of the building.

His head spun, and he forced himself to stop thinking about the prison. About spending thirty years here while his father unwittingly welcomed a traitor into the palace.

Maqbara was a puzzle he had to solve. A task that required him to be at his best physically, mentally, and spiritually.

The riotous thunder of his heartbeat steadied. He'd spent ten years focusing on completing every task set before him. On being the best. The stakes were impossibly high this time, but at the heart of it, Maqbara was a test.

Javan excelled at tests.

He would study the prison and the people in it. He would figure out its weaknesses and exploit them. Every decision, every move he made would be to bring himself one step closer to getting out in time to save his father and his kingdom from whatever Fariq and the impostor had planned.

He wasn't going to be too late.

He *wasn't*.

"Hurry up," the magistrate said, his voice bored. As though he made this trip often. As though locking up a seventeen-year-old boy for the next thirty years of his life on the word of one palace guard was business as usual.

Javan drew in another shaky breath and tasted metal on the back of his tongue. The closer he got to the bottom of the tunnel, the more the air smelled of iron and dirt.

There was a metal gate at the bottom of the tunnel, its open scrollwork letting in the dark gold of the sunset that was unfurling above the skylights set in the prison's ceiling. The thick glass skylights were embedded in the gutters of the streets above, and shadows cut through the sunlight as carriages swept past. The magistrate fished a key from his pocket and jiggled it inside the lock.

For a moment, Javan imagined ramming the smaller man's body into the gate and leaving him behind as he ran for his freedom into the city above.

But of course, that wouldn't free him from the chains that bound him. And even if he miraculously avoided the magistrate's guards, they would unleash every guard in the city with orders to hunt him down and kill him on sight. A boy with his hands chained behind his back would be easy to find.

Maybe he could plead his case. Tell the magistrate who he was and ask for a chance to prove it.

But why would the man believe him when the head of the palace guard himself had delivered Javan to be thrown into Maqbara? Besides, Abbas had been firm in his instructions to remain quiet about who he really was. Despite Javan's despair over being lied to, the guard was right. All Javan had going for him right now was the fact that the impostor thought he was dead.

He couldn't attempt an escape now without losing everything.

Javan let the fantasy dissolve as the door swung open and the magistrate pushed the prince through it. They were at the mouth of an enormous rectangular arena whose wooden floor was scarred and stained, as if battles had been waged within it. On three sides of the arena, stairs led to four levels of seats. Above the seats, another eleven levels were carved into the dark stone. A cacophony of raucous voices drifted down to echo around the hollow space of the arena.

Javan scanned the area around him quickly, trying to memorize everything in case he needed the information later. Two entrances into the arena—the one he'd used and one that led to a row of what looked like iron barn stalls. Nothing that could be used as a weapon. Nowhere to hide unless the stalls were empty.

He looked up. The first level contained fancy platforms with plush chairs and woven rugs. Flags in the colors of the most esteemed aristocratic houses hung on poles in the corner of each platform. The flag directly across from where Javan stood caught his eye, and he took three quick steps forward.

"Not so fast. We're going this way. You'll get your turn in the arena soon enough." The magistrate tugged on the chain around Javan's wrists.

Javan barely heard him. The platform across the arena had a royal purple flag in the corner. He could just make out the edge of the Kadar family crest hidden within the limp folds. But more important, the chair in the center of the platform was a small teakwood throne.

"Is that for the king?" he asked, his voice shaking.

The magistrate huffed. "Of course it is. The royal family likes sport as much as the next person, and Prince Fariq likes it more than most. Now come on. I have a dinner to get to."

Hope flared to life within Javan, a tender, fragile thing that hurt to touch as he followed the magistrate around the southern edges of the arena toward the rows of iron stalls tucked beneath the first level of seats.

The guard hadn't lied. The king attended whatever sport happened in the prison's arena. Javan simply had to figure out how to get close to the ring when a competition was happening. All he needed was to lock eyes with his father. Surely Javan's resemblance to both his mother and the king himself would be enough to at least gain Javan an audience. Especially if he called him Father.

From there, Javan would discuss the one thing he was sure Uncle Fariq hadn't been able to tell the impostor. The one thing Javan and his father shared: his mother's sacred dying words and the sash that Javan still had, folded carefully beneath his tunic in honor of her *muqaddas tus'el*.

"Sajda, new prisoner!" the magistrate called as they came abreast of the stalls.

Javan winced at the sharp odor of fur and fetid water that hung heavy in the air. What kind of animals were they keeping in the prison? Whatever they were, they could do with a bath and some fresh water in their troughs.

"Sajda!" The magistrate turned to survey the rest of the prison. "Where is that girl? Should be close to evening feeding time. I expected her to be here. Never mind—just go find the warden, and be quick about it." He waved one of the guards toward a corridor carved into the stone wall beside the stalls.

The guard started for the hall but then stopped as a tall girl with long black hair and alabaster skin stepped out of a stairwell and moved toward them. She wore solid black from her shirt and pants to her boots. Her wrists were adorned with wide iron bracelets, and her hands were curled into fists.

The animals in the stalls began a chorus of howls, hisses, and snarls that sounded nothing like any animal Javan had ever encountered. It would've been enough to send a chill down his spine except the girl was already doing that.

She moved like a predator—all lithe muscle and efficient grace—and her dark blue eyes were fixed on him as though she meant to tear him to pieces. The skin on the back of his neck prickled, and he fought the urge to slide back a step. She looked to be his age, and Javan would've spent useless time wondering why she was working in such an awful place, but he was too busy hoping she didn't decide to feed him to whatever nasty-smelling animal was currently howling for its dinner.

"New prisoner. Thirty-year term. Looks like he'll be a good competitor." The magistrate whisked another key out of his pocket and Javan's chains fell away.

The girl's eyes narrowed, and she slowly scanned Javan like he was a prize pig she was thinking of butchering. "Maybe," she said finally, her voice cold and quiet. "Looks a little soft, though."

Javan's chin rose, and he glared at her. He'd taken honors in every physical competition hosted at Milisatria with the exception of the disastrous fencing tournament in fifth year. He'd just buried the body of his mentor, ridden hard across the desert, tried to stop an impostor from taking the throne, and been thrown into Maqbara, where he was determined to either gain an audience with the king or escape, whichever came first.

He was anything but soft.

Her brow rose as if his thoughts had been written on his face. "You think I'm wrong?"

"Yes." The word came out before he could think better of it.

For a second he imagined something like regret flashed across her face, and then she said in her eerily quiet voice, "I'm never wrong. You'll either toughen up fast, or you'll be meat."

"What does that mean?"

She shrugged as if she couldn't be bothered to explain herself, and stood silently next to him as the magistrate and his guards hurried across the arena and out of the prison, slamming the door shut behind them.

When the echo of the door's closing died, she said, "Here's the schedule. Breakfast is at first bell. Chores are at second, third, and fourth depending on which level your cell is on. Fifth bell is lunch. Arena practice is divided up between bells six through nine, again depending on your level. Dinner is at tenth bell, rec time is at eleventh, and lockdown is at twelfth. Prisoners will be locked in their cells between meals and tasks. There are six guards per level and all of them will beat you within an inch of your life if you disobey a single order. Tenth bell just rang. Kitchen is on the ninth level. Eat what you can grab. If someone steals it from you, you either take it back, or you don't eat. If you steal food from someone else—"

"I'm not a thief."

"Better not take it from someone stronger and faster than you." She met his gaze, and he forced himself to stand his ground beneath the ferocity in her eyes. "I run the prison when the warden is busy. If you attack me—"

"I would *never*—"

"If you try, I will hurt you until you've forgotten what it's like to feel anything but pain. If you attack other prisoners, you'd better be certain they aren't allied with those who are more vicious than you."

"Miss . . . I'm sorry. I don't remember what the magistrate called you."

"Sajda." She said it like it was a challenge she'd thrown in his face.

"I'm Javan."

"I don't care."

"I can see that. I just . . . I wanted to tell you that I'm not dangerous. I'm not a criminal. I shouldn't be here." He put as much sincerity into his voice as he could, but her expression remained cold.

"Everyone says they shouldn't be here. Only some of us are telling the truth." She turned from him and motioned toward the stairs. "There's an open cell on the fifteenth level. Don't miss lockdown. Any prisoner who fails to answer roll call in his or her cell after lockdown will be hunted down and killed."

"I suppose you do the hunting," he muttered as he followed Sajda toward the stairs.

Her back stiffened. "The warden does the hunting. And if I were you, I'd do everything I possibly could to stay far, far away from her."

He thought he might like to stay far, far away from Sajda as well, but that wasn't an option yet. Not until he understood the way the prison worked and the people who lived in it.

As he climbed the narrow stone steps that led to the next level, he pressed his hand to his heart, feeling the soft brush of the red sash against his skin, and whispered a prayer that he would find a way out of Maqbara before it was too late for his father and for himself.

TEN

RAHIM'S BLOOD CHURNED as he entered the inner courtyard of the palace. So many years spent dreaming of this place—of the famed mosaic fountains and the lush beauty of the hanging gardens. Of the cool tiled halls, the gilt-edged domes, and the massive teakwood throne.

Most of all the throne.

It was unfortunate that Javan had survived his assassins in Loch Talam, but Fariq's quick thinking had bolstered Rahim's claim and silenced any doubt in the guards' minds.

It was a story, though. A whisper that might linger in the air, drifting through the city until it found ears that would welcome it.

Aristocrats who could recognize the real Javan from their visits to Milisatria.

Loyalists who were already suspicious about the king's extended absences and failing health.

Opportunists who would wonder if this was their moment

to seize the throne instead.

As Rahim skirted the largest fountain and brushed past a hanging jasmine vine, he considered his options.

He could call in the aristocrats and have them thrown into Maqbara or killed, but that would be hard to explain to the king. There was no point in taking the risk yet. The families from Milisatria would have to die before Rahim made public appearances, of course, but for now, that could wait.

He could convince the FaSaa'il to get their allies to spy on the loyalists and report any rumors. That seemed the easiest and most productive course of action. Once he knew the rumors, he could figure out how to put a stop to them.

A path of white stone connected the courtyard to a wide veranda with thick, round pillars, scalloped ironwork, and an ornate door dipped in bronze. A small wooden altar for Mal' Enish and an equally small stone altar for Eb' Rezr held places of honor on the westward edge of the veranda but looked as though they were rarely used. Rahim supposed the king preferred Yl' Haliq, who the stories said had first united the smaller nations across the land into one nation under the rule of the Kadar family, joining their diverse customs, teachings, and ideologies into one cohesive kingdom.

A servant dressed in the pale yellow of the palace house staff held the door open, her head bowed in deference.

Fariq stepped aside to allow Rahim to enter first. Rahim brushed past the man who'd fathered him without bothering to claim him as his own until it suited his ambition to do so and entered the palace. Colorful, hand-painted tiles edged in gold formed an enormous rosette on the floor in the circular entrance hall. Bouquets of waxy blooms from the palace garden were arranged in ruby urns and set in front of the six pillars that formed the edges of the hall. Diamonds dripped from a chandelier nearly the size of the royal carriage, and more jewels were inlaid around an altar for Yl' Haliq that was set into the northern wall. There were no altars to the lesser gods in here.

He had to work to keep from staring at the opulence. Javan wouldn't gawk at a diamond chandelier like it was his first time seeing a precious gem.

Of course, Javan's father hadn't condemned him to either be killed by the palace guard or to live in poverty far from his birthright.

The bitterness Rahim had nursed for years snaked through his blood like poison, igniting the rage that always simmered just beneath the surface of his skin. He'd lived in tents, scrounging through trash heaps for food, while Fariq and his useless cousin, the king, lived without a single care in the world.

Pain shot through Rahim's jaw, and he forced himself to unclench his teeth and shake off the tension in his shoulders. He'd never pass for an aristocrat if he allowed his fury to show.

"Javan?" A man's voice, shaky and weak, came from behind Rahim.

The rage coiled and writhed within him, but Rahim carefully blanked his expression as he turned away from the grand entrance to find the king standing in a corridor to the left, a tremulous smile on his face.

Rahim froze, his blood racing. The king would instantly recognize him for a fraud and demand to see his real son. He'd call the guard, and Rahim would follow Javan to the *muqsila*. Fear clawed at him as the king hesitated, and Rahim reached for the throwing stars hidden in his tunic. He might not be able to escape with his life, but many would die while he tried.

The king frowned, but then Fariq swept past him and said in a booming, jovial voice, "Look who's returned from Milisatria at long last, Cousin!"

Rahim hesitated another beat and then let go of the throwing stars to rush forward, following Fariq's lead. "Father!" he cried, forcing himself to sound as if the sight of the stooped, frail man before him was cause for joy.

The king opened his arms, and Rahim stepped into them.

He would only have to play the king's dutiful son until the king died or decided to abdicate the throne because of his poor health. Then the FaSaa'il would fall in line or be eliminated, and all Akram would belong to Rahim.

Enduring the king's cloying embrace took enormous effort. When the king stepped back, he patted Rahim's shoulder with one hand as he stared hungrily at the boy's face.

"You've changed some. I always thought you had your mother's eyes."

"I believe he takes after you," Fariq said smoothly.

The king leaned toward Rahim, raising his trembling hand from the boy's shoulder to his cheek. "I've missed you."

"And I you." Rahim tried to sound sincere.

"Cousin, it has been a long and arduous journey for Javan. Perhaps we should let him rest." Fariq gripped Rahim's elbow and pulled him away from the king, but both of them froze when a low, menacing snarl rose from behind them.

Rahim spun and found himself staring into the amber eyes of a white leopard with black spots and a golden collar around its neck. The beast's whiskers twitched, and its lips curled away from its fangs as it growled again.

"Malik! Don't you remember our Javan?" the king asked, stepping past Rahim to shake a finger at the enormous cat.

The leopard sat back on its haunches and stopped growling, though it flicked its tail and kept its eyes locked on Rahim.

"Does it . . . he . . . Malik often get upset when people enter the palace?" Rahim asked.

The king frowned. "Sometimes, but you know we keep him in the residential wing. I let him out because you were coming home. I thought he might like to sleep on your rug again."

Rahim thought the cat might like to disembowel him in his sleep, but he pasted on a smile and said, "It's been ten years. I'm sure he'll be used to me again in no time. But perhaps for tonight, it would be best if he slept elsewhere."

"Perhaps." The king's gaze wandered away from the leopard, roamed the entry hall, and then landed on Rahim with startling ferocity. There was a keenness to the king's eyes that hadn't been there a moment ago, and though his body still trembled, the confusion was clearing from his face.

He knew.

The cat had given the ruse away.

If the king knew that Rahim wasn't his son, he'd have to be eliminated immediately, but Rahim didn't dare kill him while the leopard watched him with such unblinking malice.

Fariq stepped to the king's side and said soothingly, "Malik is simply upset that Javan abandoned him for so many years. They'll be friends again before we know it. Meanwhile, it's time for your tonic, dear cousin."

"Is it?" The king glanced outside in bewilderment. "I thought I was to take it only once a day."

"The physician has increased it to twice a day. Don't you

88

remember? He told you this last week."

Rahim drew in a slow, calming breath as the king agreed to be handed over to a page who would take him to his sitting room. Once he was out of earshot, Rahim turned to Fariq and whispered, "Lord Borak didn't tell me the leopard might hate me."

"I've been wearing a piece of your clothing each day for weeks. He should've been comfortable with your smell by now." Fariq eyed the leopard, who sat still as stone watching them. "Hopefully he won't try to kill you before we can get the crown on your head. I'd hate to have gone to all this trouble only to lose my shot at the throne."

"*Your* shot?" Rahim's voice rose. "You forget that I'll be Akram's king."

Fariq's laugh was cruel. "You? You're the little bastard who was raised in a filthy hovel in some no-name desert town. Your only value is the fact that you are the same age as Javan. As it stands, I can't inherit the crown because I'm not a direct descendant of the royal line. Once you are crowned, you will sign a law allowing any surviving member of the Kadar family to rule."

Rahim shook with fury. "And then what? You try to kill me and take the throne?"

"Not if you do exactly as you're told. You get to wear the crown in public. The FaSaa'il gets their property and favor restored. And I make the decisions from behind the scenes." He smiled, slow and vicious. "I've spent a lifetime watching my cousin get all the power while never trusting me with a single bit of it. Cutting off my royal allowance when he thought I bet too often at the tracks. Revoking my diplomatic authority in Balavata and Ravenspire when their rulers complained that I was sanctioning slave trade. Ruining my reputation so that even though I'm making most of the decisions for him now, many of the aristocrats are watching me like a hawk, waiting for a chance to drive me out. That's over now. I will take what I've been denied, and I will do with it as I see fit. Behave yourself, and once I die, the throne is yours free and clear. Understood?"

Rahim matched Fariq's smile with one of his own and said quietly, "Understood."

ELEVEN

MAGIC HISSED THROUGH Sajda Ali's blood, stinging her skin as she swept her long black hair into a ponytail, careful to leave the sides low enough to cover most of her ears. She ignored the bite of the magic she'd inherited from the father she'd never met and tucked her black shirt into her black pants as the underground prison of Maqbara slowly came to life around her.

She'd overslept, a rare mistake that would have cost her dearly if the warden had been in residence, but the woman hadn't returned yet from her trip to negotiate for a shipment of monstrous creatures from the remote desert villages that dotted the Samaal. Frustration hummed through Sajda. She might not be in trouble for oversleeping, but she'd missed most of her opportunity to work on the only thing that truly mattered to her: a way to escape.

After splashing water on her face, she rubbed some on the tiny raised scars that crisscrossed the skin beneath the cuffs she wore—a reminder of the times when the magic in her blood had fought the rune-inscribed iron that was meant to keep it at bay. Every year, the warden locked new cuffs on Sajda's wrists, the freshly carved runes keeping the iron free from rust and trapping the magic in her slave's blood. And every year Sajda dreamed of finding a single instant, a tiny sliver of time between one cuff falling to the floor and the other one snapping into place when she could use her magic to overpower the warden and gain her freedom. But the warden was too smart to unlock an old cuff before the new one was in place, and Sajda didn't have the luxury of dreams that would never come true. She hurried from her room. There was still time to make progress on her plan if she moved quickly.

Besides, she didn't want to be caught alone in the fifth floor corridor when the iron bars opened to let the prisoners out of their cells. The last time that happened had been disastrous. She was still nervous about the precarious lie she'd spun to keep the prisoners from suspecting what she really was. It was hard to explain how a sixteen-year-old girl had nearly broken a tall, muscular man in half for attacking her.

She could handle two or three prisoners attacking at a time. She couldn't survive an onslaught from the entire prison, and she had no doubt that's what she'd be facing if the inmates of Maqbara ever learned the truth.

Shutting her door firmly behind her, she locked it and then moved swiftly down the corridor. The prison was lit with the subtle glow of dawn breaking through the dusty skylights set far above the cells that were carved like a honeycomb out of the bedrock beneath Akram's capital city. The faint thud of hoofbeats clipped along the packed dirt streets aboveground, sending puffs of dust spinning into the faint beams of sunlight like bits of gold, and eerie cries of hunger drifted out of the stalls that housed the prison's current population of monstrous beasts.

Sajda held her head high as she followed the narrow passage that wound around the fifth level, in full view of the prisoners who were now awake and waiting for the iron bars at the mouth of their cells to rise. To one side, a railing separated the corridor from the vast empty space of the arena far below. The first four levels of the prison were nothing but platforms of seats encircling the combat ring. The cells began on the fifth level. Each of Maqbara's fifteen levels hugged the outside wall and was joined to the rest of the prison by narrow sets of stairs cut into the stone every thirty cells.

The light streaming in through the skylights at the top of the prison changed from faint yellow to rosy gold. The sun was up in Akram, and the aristocracy would be getting ready for an afternoon of bloody entertainment at the arena, though to their credit most of them attended simply because Prince Fariq had made it clear that those who didn't would fall out of royal favor and be sanctioned accordingly.

Sajda moved faster as the prisoners began beating their bars with their fists, their voices raised as she passed.

"There she is. Pretty girl. Maybe you should join me in my cell tonight."

"It's the warden's slave. Think you're better than me? Lift these bars and find out."

"Better stop ignoring me, *ehira*, or you'll be sorry."

Fear was a jagged blade slicing through her, sending her magic churning. The skin beneath her rune-carved cuffs burned as the iron crippled her magic, leaving her with enough power to defend herself against a few humans but without the ability to do the one thing she'd longed for since the warden bought her from an auction block when she was just five years old: escape.

The prisoners' voices rose, and Sajda moved rapidly toward the staircase. "They're just words," she whispered to herself. To her magic. They were words she'd become so accustomed to, she no longer heard them. Just the voices. The tones. The thin line between bravado and intent that would tell her if she needed to watch herself around one of the prisoners.

The fifth level was where the most dangerous prisoners were kept. These were the men and women who'd beaten their way up the rankings of the last few tournaments. Who'd survived every bloodbath with a body count in their wake. These were the top contenders for this year's prize, though there were plenty of newer prisoners who were hungry to take their place.

None of it was Sajda's problem. She simply had to keep the prison stocked with vicious beasts, run the tournaments that lined the warden's and Prince Fariq's pockets with coin, and stay alive.

Most of all, she had to stay alive.

Rounding the corner to the stairwell, she plunged down the steps until she reached the arena's floor. Hurrying around its outskirts, she entered the double row of iron stalls that hugged the wall closest to the hall that led to the warden's office.

Drawing in a slow, unsteady breath, Sajda ducked into the stalls, her body now blocked from view by the iron wall that kept the prisoners from seeing the predators they'd be facing in the ring. Howls and hisses filled the air as she moved quickly toward the last stall on the right.

"Hush," she whispered. "You'll get fed in a few minutes."

Her words went unheeded, and she rolled her eyes. It was a

testament to the amount of time she spent around monstrous things that she'd started talking to them as if they could somehow understand her.

The last stall on the right was currently empty, though that would change with the next delivery. Shoving a drift of hay aside with her boot, she grabbed the small ax she'd hidden there years ago.

Pausing for a moment, she held perfectly still and listened.

No footsteps. No clamor from the beasts as someone other than Sajda walked through the stalls.

She was alone.

A hay trough, roughly the length of Sajda's legs and the height of her waist, rested against the far wall. Sajda pushed it aside. Dust fell from the opening behind it. Ducking, she crawled through a tunnel that was only slightly wider than she was. After several paces, the tunnel opened up enough to allow her to crouch. She'd hollowed out a space nearly as big as her room with the idea that if the prisoners ever turned on her, she'd have a place to hide, though hiding wasn't her goal. Escaping was.

Moving through the hollowed space, she reached the back where another tunnel was burrowing through the stone. It wasn't much—she couldn't even fit her entire body in it yet—but it was a start. One day, it would lead all the way out of Maqbara, up through the bedrock, and into the open air of the city itself.

Pressing her lips together to keep the dust from getting in her mouth, Sajda began swinging the ax. Bits of rock chipped away, falling into a heap as she painstakingly scraped another thin layer off the back of the tunnel.

Sweat dotted her brow as she finished what she could for

the day. Hurriedly scraping the rock shavings into her hand, she stuffed them into her pants' pocket and left the tunnel. She pushed the trough back in place, hid the ax, and left the stall. She was swinging the door closed when a voice from her right said, "Busy morning, eh, little one?"

Sajda spun, her fists clenched, magic itching in her blood. A short, stocky man with salt-and-pepper hair, a bushy beard, and kind eyes stood two stalls away, his left hand rubbing the arthritic knuckles on his right.

"Tarek, you startled me." Sajda's voice was low and calm, though magic still sparked along her skin, painful little nips that burned like ice. She stalked past him and placed an open palm against the stone wall beside the entrance to the stalls to steady herself. Drawing in the solid, immovable strength of the rock—a trick she'd learned by accident her first week in the prison when, overwhelmed with fear and loneliness, she'd pressed herself against the wall and wished for its strength to become her own. She'd been shocked when the stone had obeyed.

Now, her pulse slowed, and the painful prickle of magic mixed with the essence of the rock and became a cold, unyielding calm encasing her like armor. Pain seared the skin beneath her cuffs and then subsided. Keeping her voice soft, she said, "I've warned you not to sneak up on me."

His smile revealed a missing front tooth—courtesy of the one and only stint he'd done in the arena eight years ago. "Sorry, little one. Thought you would've seen me. Must have been lost in your own thoughts again."

"I could've hurt you."

Tarek's smile gentled as he handed her an orange from the prison's kitchen. "You'd never hurt me."

"Not on purpose." Sajda stood beside the older man. "Where's your breakfast?"

"Cook wasn't finished with the porridge yet. I'll go back up in a bit and get some."

Sajda frowned. "Make it quick. I have to feed the beasts, and I don't like you going to the kitchen when the other prisoners are there unless I can go with you."

He patted her on the shoulder. "Nobody cares to bother an old man like me."

"Not if they know what's good for them. Is Batula here yet?" Sajda asked.

"On her way."

"Good." Sajda tore into her orange and devoured the slices quickly. Within moments, Batula stood outside the stalls, her hands sheathed in leather gloves. Sajda had long since given up trying to guess how old she was. Maybe forty. Maybe eighty. Her golden skin was leathery and sagged along the edges, but her eyes were clear and she was strong enough to help Sajda wrestle the creatures into the arena. She'd lived in the prison since before Sajda's arrival, and Sajda had never figured out if, like Tarek, Batula was a prisoner the warden was using for her own purposes, or if she owned Batula like she owned Sajda.

"Hurry along, now." Batula gestured toward the sacks of food that lined the wall beside the stalls. "These beasties won't feed themselves." Batula reached for the crank on the wall that operated the pulley system for the cell doors. "Guards in place?"

Tarek craned his neck and scanned the fifteen levels above him, searching for the black-clad guards who entered the prison at dawn and left at dusk once the cell doors were back in place. "Guards are at their stations," he said as one of the guards set the first bell tolling, its mournful tone rolling through the air, fat and thick.

"Another day in paradise." Batula cackled as she turned the crank. The harsh clicking of metallic gears catching on chains filled the air, followed by the scrape of iron bars lifting into the stone ceilings. Prisoners poured out of their cells. Most headed toward the kitchen on the ninth level, but some came straight for the arena to get a look at the beasts they might be unlucky enough to face in the afternoon.

Sajda donned a pair of leather gloves and grabbed a sack of sheep innards delivered that morning by one of the local butchers. Breathing through her mouth to avoid the worst of the sickly sweet scent, she opened the sack and moved to the first stall. A man-size white worm was coiled inside a cistern of water. Sajda tossed a handful of sheep guts into the cistern and shuddered as the worm's head whipped up, its jaw stretching wide to reveal a glistening row of sharp fangs.

"I hate the water beasts the most," she muttered to Tarek as he threw guts to a gaunt wolflike creature with red eyes and foam dripping from its muzzle. "Though I think we're having something worse in round three—"

"What have I told you about sharing details of the upcoming combat rounds?" A thick, gravelly voice spoke from behind Sajda.

Sajda's stoic shield of calm cracked, a tiny fissure of pressure that snaked along its surface, finding her weaknesses and burrowing in as she whirled to find the warden standing at the entrance to the stalls.

"You're back!" Sajda reached for the indifferent composure she'd borrowed from the stone, but it disintegrated beneath the menace on the warden's face.

The woman's iron-gray hair was pulled back in its customary bun, and one dark eye watched her slave. The other was hidden beneath a bandage that covered nearly half her face. When she caught Sajda staring at it, she said, "It pays to watch yourself. One moment of carelessness, and the tables turn on you. Do you want me to turn on you, slave?"

Sajda froze, her magic scraping at her skin like tiny knives, her breath clogging her throat as she fought to keep her fear out of her expression. "I didn't share the tournament details with any of the competitors. It's just Tarek—"

"Tarek is a prisoner. A criminal. I don't trust criminals." The warden stepped closer to Sajda, her tone venomous, and grabbed one of the iron cuffs around Sajda's wrist. Heat rippled along the warden's skin, sinking into the iron and burning Sajda's scars until she had to grit her teeth to keep from crying out. "I don't trust you, either. But I know how to control monsters. Isn't that right?"

Sajda nodded, magic snapping impotently at the runes that glowed with heat along her cuff.

"Did you tell anyone else what to expect in the combat rounds?" the warden asked softly while the skin beneath Sajda's cuff burned.

"No. I—"

"She didn't even tell me anything," Tarek said, his voice shaking with fury. "You don't have to punish her."

The warden whipped her gaze toward him, and Sajda instantly moved between them, her arm still trapped in the warden's grip, her magic still throwing itself relentlessly at her palms as if testing the strength of the runes.

"It's all right, Tarek." Sajda tried to sound calm. "I shouldn't have said anything at all. You should just go get your breakfast with the other prisoners."

"That's right, Sajda. You shouldn't have said anything." The warden's smile died before it reached her eyes. "If you want to continue living under my hospitality, you will perform your duties to perfection. That includes keeping secrets." The warden yanked Sajda close, and the girl's magic seared her skin. Lowering her voice, the warden said, "Unless you've decided that we're going to start sharing each other's secrets now."

Sajda shook her head, her stomach tightening.

The warden cocked her head. "Is that a no?"

"No," Sajda breathed.

Leaning close, the warden whispered, "Don't get careless, slave. The only good elf is a dead elf, remember? We wouldn't want the prisoners to know that the monster they fear the most walks among them."

TWELVE

JAVAN HAD AWAKENED to the sound of wind and sand scraping over the skylights in the ceiling outside his cell. The room was a narrow space cut deep into the bedrock with nothing but a small shelf, a privy bucket, and a sagging bed pushed up against the far wall. Javan hadn't seen much of his new home since he'd arrived at his cell after sunset, but even the moonlight shining in through the corridor's skylights had illuminated the layer of grit that clung to the floor and the spiderwebs that draped across each corner.

The prison was still dark as Javan slipped from his bed and got to his knees.

His morning prayers felt harder to speak, his whispered words swallowed up by the immense darkness of Maqbara. He'd waited for the peace that usually filled him to come, but instead his heart had ached, a steady throb of loneliness that was impossible to ignore.

The flame of anger that had stirred in the wake of his grief as he crossed the desert burned steadily, a sharp counterpoint to the ache in his heart.

He shouldn't be here. His father shouldn't be in danger. And the headmaster shouldn't be dead.

And yet Yl' Haliq had allowed it. How could Javan reconcile his divine destiny with his present circumstances? He was abandoned. Tossed into a hole and forgotten. Surrounded by criminals who behaved with dishonor.

He'd finished his prayers, lingering on the last word, his eyes tightly closed as he waited for . . . *something*. A sign. A reassurance that Yl' Haliq still had his eyes on the prince.

Instead, he'd felt nothing but the steady burn of anger at the injustice of it all and the aching pressure in his chest whenever he thought about how alone he really was. Slowly he'd climbed to his feet.

The sacred texts taught that Yl' Haliq was beyond human understanding. His ways were inscrutable, his wisdom unknowable, and his mercy boundless. Though Javan couldn't see how, surely Yl' Haliq was already at work on the prince's behalf.

As first bell rang, Javan resolved to do his part to solve the puzzle of either gaining an audience with his father or escaping the prison. Whispering one more quick plea that Yl' Haliq would bless his efforts, Javan had stretched and reached for a tunic in the murky light of dawn that managed to filter in.

His clothes, stained with the impostor's blood, had been taken from him the previous night, though Sajda had let him keep the red sash with the quiet warning that if any of the more dangerous prisoners saw it and wanted it, they'd tear him limb from limb to get it. He'd been given two spare tunics in a dingy gray cotton, one spare pair of pants in the same hue, three pairs of socks, and several undergarments that were nearly worn thin. Everything was clean, though, and he had much bigger things to worry about than his clothing.

The only prison employee he'd met so far was Sajda. His stomach tightened as he thought of the unrelenting fierceness in her dark blue eyes and the way her body moved like a leopard's—sleek and lethal. He'd hoped to gain an employee as an ally, but it clearly wouldn't be her. He'd have to scout the prison for others today. According to Sajda's coolly delivered list of facts and instructions as she'd escorted him to his cell on the fifteenth level, there were six guards on each level during the day. It was possible Javan could turn one of them into an ally, but it was risky. Better if he could get close to the cook or whoever ran the menagerie downstairs.

In the rush of grabbing a crust of bread for dinner, he'd forgotten to ask about the strange-sounding beasts. He had Sajda to thank for his meal since he hadn't arrived in time to get any food. It didn't surprise Javan one bit that when she calmly demanded food from a prisoner with a full plate, the woman had handed over the bread without dissent.

The prisoner had probably witnessed what happened when someone disobeyed Sajda.

A small, treacherous part of Javan's mind was curious to see that too. Would Sajda be the kind of fighter she seemed to be? If she turned against him, would he be able to stop her?

He was getting out of Maqbara, even if he had to go through Sajda. She might be formidable, but thanks to his training at Milisatria, so was he. And he had far more at stake than the simple wish to get out of prison.

As the iron bars that covered the mouth of his cell slowly

rose into the ceiling, he shoved his feet into the boots he'd been allowed to keep, folded the sash and tucked it next to his heart again, and then hurried toward level nine before all of the breakfast food was taken.

Prisoners were already crowding the stairs on their way to the kitchen as Javan joined those who were housed on the top level with him. Conversation surrounded him, and he moved quietly down each step, listening intently.

"I swear by all that's holy, if it's nothing but toast and lentil spread again, I'm going to kill the cook."

"Haven't seen the warden in days. Best sleep I've had in weeks."

"They don't have enough land beasts. I caught a peek at the stalls when I was scrubbing the royal box yesterday. I'm telling you the next round is going to be water monsters."

He reached the landing for the ninth level and turned right, letting himself get caught in the flow of people making their way into the long galley kitchen with its double hearths, its wooden table the length of five full-grown men lying end to end, and this morning, its cooking staff.

Three people wearing aprons moved between huge cauldrons simmering on the hearths and the table that was already laden with bowls of a soupy-looking porridge, slices of flatbread, and dishes of crushed lentil paste. The fourth—a woman with a bun sliding halfway down her head and a scowl that seemed permanently etched onto her face—stood arms akimbo barking orders to the prisoners to take a bowl, a slice of bread, and a spoonful of paste and then get away from her hearths.

Javan caught her gaze and gave her a polite smile. Her scowl deepened.

Maybe he wouldn't be allies with the cook after all.

The prince got into line behind a short older man with a limp. The man shot him a quick glance, and when Javan smiled, miracle of miracles, the man smiled back.

Making allies with a criminal wasn't on Javan's list of ways to get out of Maqbara, but it couldn't hurt. Besides, seeing something other than anger or cold disdain on another person's face loosened a bit of the ache in Javan's chest.

"I'm Javan," he said quietly.

"Tarek," the man replied. "Don't usually wait so long to get my breakfast, but this morning got away from me." He picked up a bowl of porridge, handed it to Javan, and then grabbed one for himself.

"Thank you." Javan braced himself as a group of prisoners rushed through the door and lunged for the food that remained on the table. "We should get out of the way."

"I'm not staying. Work to do. Take care of yourself, Javan." Tarek smiled once more and turned to go, but there was a large, muscled man with scarred flesh and flat, unfriendly eyes standing in his way.

"What are you doing here without your protector, old man?"

Someone jostled Javan as they went for a slice of bread, and the prince stepped closer to Tarek.

"Running behind, Hashim. Step aside, please." Tarek's voice was firm, but his bowl of porridge shook in his hands.

"Should've eaten already, old man." Hashim moved closer, flanked by several other prisoners.

"Take it, Dabir," Hashim said.

A tall man with small eyes and a beaked nose snatched the porridge out of Tarek's hands and handed the bowl to Hashim.

"You really shouldn't wander the prison without your guard dog. Anything could happen," Hashim said.

Javan's pulse kicked up, and his grip on his own porridge bowl tightened.

A woman on Hashim's right lunged forward and shoved Tarek back into the table. Javan grabbed the older man's arm and steadied him. The flame of anger within Javan fanned into a blaze as he glared at Hashim and his friends.

"Who are you?" Hashim demanded, his gaze flicking over Javan as if assessing an opponent before finally coming to rest on the prince's face.

"Someone who isn't going to allow you to shove this man around." Javan kept his hand on Tarek's arm, though all his focus was now on the threat in front of him.

Hashim laughed, a harsh, unpleasant sound that sent Javan's anger crashing through him, a lightning bolt of furious purpose.

He couldn't afford to make enemies inside Maqbara, especially when he'd yet to figure out how the prison worked.

But he couldn't afford to behave dishonorably either. Not if he intended to rule Akram with a pure heart.

"Don't do this." Tarek breathed the words beside Javan's ear. "It's just food."

It wasn't just food. It was someone with the upper hand using it to hurt a man who couldn't defend himself.

It was a dragon lying in wait to kill a schoolboy. Assassins ready to finish the job. It was Uncle Fariq using Javan's absence against him to take the throne. The impostor killing the headmaster because what he wanted mattered more to him than another person's life.

It was *wrong*, and Javan was sick of people doing wrong.

"You're new here, so I'm going to give you a second chance," Hashim said, his eyes boring into Javan's. "Tarek here gets special treatment from the warden because he's the watchdog's little pet. Makes him think he's better than us, though he wouldn't survive a single round with me in the arena. We can't touch him when his guard dog is near, but she isn't here now, is she?"

Javan frowned. "Guard dog?"

"I'm sure you met her when you got here. Tall, pale skin, black hair, looks like she'd like to kill you? You probably thought she was beautiful, and that you'd like a piece of that little *ehira*."

"You'll watch your mouth about Sajda." Tarek pushed away from the table to move past Javan, who whipped his arm out to stop the shorter man from barreling straight into Hashim's raised fists. "Do what you please to me, but you will not disrespect that girl in my presence."

Hashim laughed cruelly. "How are you going to stop me? Kick my shins?"

Keeping his voice even, Javan said, "Give Tarek back his breakfast, apologize for saying such a filthy thing about Sajda, and we'll all walk away and forget this happened."

Hashim's smile blinked out, and he turned the full weight of his gaze onto Javan. "You need to think really hard about your next words. I can make your stay in Maqbara pleasant, or I can make every day a living hell."

Javan held the man's eyes and said with painstaking precision, "Give Tarek his breakfast, apologize, and walk away."

Hashim's lips twisted. "I'm going to enjoy teaching you your place."

The man's fist shot toward Javan, but the prince was already moving. Lunging to the side, he shoved the bowl in Hashim's hands against his scarred chest, sending a wave of piping-hot porridge sloshing out. Hashim shouted in pain, and the four prisoners who flanked him charged for Javan and Tarek.

Throwing his own bowl of porridge into the face of the man closest to him, Javan pushed Tarek behind him, planted his feet, and started swinging.

Pain exploded across his face as someone's fist connected with his cheekbone, and he hissed as a boot slammed into his stomach, sending him crashing into Tarek and the table behind them. Javan snapped out a kick, sending a female prisoner spinning back into Hashim, but two men were instantly there to take her place.

Javan was surrounded. Back against a now empty table. No weapons except Tarek, who'd put up his fists and was daring anyone who thought they could call Sajda names to get what was coming to them.

"Let me through!" Hashim roared, and tossed aside his friends as he came at Javan.

"Enough!" A cold voice cut through the noise, and Hashim froze, his fists still raised.

Javan kept his fists up too, as did Tarek, but a ripple of silence spread throughout the kitchen until the only sound was the faint pop of the porridge still bubbling on the hearth and the ragged sound of prisoners trying to catch their breaths.

Javan glanced at Sajda as she stalked to Tarek's side, her expression promising pain to everyone in her path. Maybe it was the light from the lanterns hanging from the walls inside the kitchen, but her alabaster skin seemed to glow like she had a sheath of light trapped within.

"Are you hurt?" she asked Tarek. Javan blinked at the gentle edge to her cold voice and then locked his gaze back on Hashim as the man shifted, turning his feral eyes toward her.

"I'm fine," Tarek said. "Thanks to Javan."

Sajda's eyes met Javan's for a moment, though he couldn't read her thoughts. Then she turned to Hashim and said quietly, "I would think someone focused on winning the competition would have more important things to do than bother an old man over his breakfast."

Hashim smiled slowly, and Javan's muscles tensed at the expression on his face. "You're right, *ehira*. I need to practice defeating monsters." His voice dropped as he leaned toward her. "You wouldn't want to practice with me, would you?"

Sajda's eyes narrowed, and she tugged at the iron bracelet on her left wrist. "Leave Tarek alone, Hashim."

"Or what?" he asked.

Sajda matched his smile with one of her own, and Javan's skin prickled. "Or I'll show you why the warden puts me in charge when she's gone."

Looping her arm through Tarek's, Sajda began pulling the old man toward the door. Javan frowned as he tried to reconcile the cold, distant person he'd met the night before with a girl who would protect an old man. She'd gone three steps when Tarek whispered something that brought her to a stop. She stood silent for a moment before sighing and tossing a glance over her shoulder at Javan.

"Are you coming?"

"I . . ." Javan glanced around the kitchen, at the way no one would meet his eyes except Hashim and his friends, who each looked like they wanted to kill him. The guards stationed at the door hadn't even bothered to come inside the kitchen when the fight started, and they showed no inclination to change their positions once Sajda left.

"Suit yourself." She shrugged and turned back toward the door.

"No, I'm coming." Javan let his fists drop and brushed past Hashim.

As Javan followed Sajda and Tarek into the corridor, Hashim yelled, "You're meat. First chance I get in the arena. Better watch your back."

Javan had no intention of facing Hashim in the arena—whatever that meant. He'd blown his chance to quietly and carefully integrate into the prison, judiciously choosing his friends. He'd made a vicious enemy; his allies consisted of a kind old man and a girl who unnerved him completely; and somewhere above the prison, his father was in danger of losing both the throne and his life.

Javan wasn't sure things could get much worse.

THIRTEEN

WHAT WAS SHE supposed to do with the new boy?

The prisoners who joined the ranks in Maqbara were either petty thieves, vicious criminals, or poverty-stricken debtors who couldn't afford to pay what they owed to a member of the aristocracy and who spent their lives in the prison while their families tried desperately to scrape together enough wahda to pay off the debt.

This boy held himself like he owned every space he entered. He met everyone's gaze like an equal. And he spoke with a crisp polish to his words that sounded jarringly out of place amid the softened syllables of the peasants who filled Maqbara's cells.

Plus, he was almost pretty, a fact that shouldn't have offended Sajda but somehow did. His smooth bronze skin, shoulder-length black hair, and brown eyes were a distraction in a place where distraction could get her killed.

"Why didn't the guards on level nine stop Hashim? Shouldn't they protect us from attacks?" the boy asked, righteous indignation filling his words.

"They aren't here to protect you," Sajda said. "They're here to protect the warden and keep the prisoners from breaking her rules. And her rules say nothing about prisoners keeping their hands to themselves."

"It's dishonorable."

"It's a *prison*." Sajda shot Javan a glare as she escorted Tarek toward the stairs with the boy right behind them. He met her gaze without flinching, a hint of challenge in his eyes.

Not the kind of chills-down-her-spine challenge she saw in the eyes of Hashim and several of the other prisoners. Not the threatening kind.

More like he was determined not to show fear in the face of her icy dislike of him.

Which would be admirable, except that Sajda's safety depended on the prisoners fearing her. If they didn't—if they pushed her beyond the speed and strength she possessed—she had nothing left but her trapped magic. Magic she had precious little idea how to use as a weapon.

Plus, using magic against a prisoner would ignite a firestorm of rumors. It wouldn't be long before someone put her magic together with the fact that Sajda's hair always covered her ears and came up with the answer.

Dark elf.

Cursed.

Monster.

If she'd heard it said once, she'd heard it a thousand times: the only good elf was a dead elf.

Sajda had no intention of being a dead elf, which meant the new boy needed to learn to fear her. She knew exactly how to accomplish that. One quick sparring match with her, and he'd see her speed. Her strength. He'd know he was outmatched.

She waited until they'd reached the stalls before turning to Javan and saying, "The magistrate already put your name into the betting pool for tomorrow's tournament, but of course since you're an untried competitor, the aristocracy isn't biting. If you survive tomorrow, maybe you'll move up the ranks a bit, but now that you've made an enemy of Hashim, surviving isn't likely."

"You are quite the optimist," Javan said in his elegant voice, crossing his arms over his chest. "I have no idea what competition you're talking about, but I've had plenty of training, and I'm no stranger to winning contests of sport."

Her brow rose. "*Contests of sport?* Who talks like that?"

He frowned. "Who doesn't?"

"Everyone but you."

"Aristocrats talk like that," Tarek said quietly, his eyes on Javan.

The boy tensed, his gaze darting quickly to Tarek's face before returning to Sajda. "I must have overheard it, then."

Her eyes narrowed. His hands were clenched into white-knuckled fists. The vein at the side of his neck showed that his pulse was beating rapidly.

He was lying. But why?

"I'm sure that's it." Tarek gave Sajda a pointed look and said, "We should check on the beasts. Javan can help. His level isn't assigned chore time until third bell. We'll just tell the guards on level fifteen not to come looking when he doesn't return to his cell at second bell—"

Sajda ignored Tarek. "Why are you lying?" she asked Javan.

His body stilled—prey who'd just sensed a predator closing

in. "Lying about what?"

"Sajda." Tarek's voice was stern, something he never tried with her. "Let's check the beasts."

She shot a glare at Tarek. "I'm not turning my back on him. I don't trust him."

"He defended me." Tarek put his hands on his hips.

"He's lying."

"We all have secrets. The boy proved himself—"

"The boy hasn't even begun to prove himself."

"The *boy* is standing right here and would really appreciate it if you stopped talking about him like he's part of the scenery." Javan uncrossed his arms and stepped forward.

Sajda whipped her arms up and crouched, her body braced for his attack.

Javan froze as he took in Sajda's defensive stance. Raising his hands as if to show he meant no harm, he said softly, "I'm not going to hurt you. I already told you I would never do something so dishonorable."

Why did he talk like an aristocrat? Was he spying on the warden? Surely a woman that vicious had enemies outside the prison.

Sajda's magic bit into her skin as she considered another possibility. Could he be spying on *her*? Had she let something slip—been too strong, too fast, too frustrated by her restrained magic as the runes in her cuffs glowed—in front of someone? The warden had always warned her that if her true identity was discovered, she'd be killed. Maybe there were rumors about a dark elf in Maqbara and this boy had come to the prison to find the truth.

"Why are you here?" Sajda demanded.

"I was sentenced to prison by the magistrate—"

"Yes, but *why*?" She stared him down, magic itching painfully beneath her skin, begging for release. "You aren't afraid of me. You defended Tarek against a pack of bullies. Both of those facts mean you must have combat training, which is rare to find in a prisoner. It also means you must think gaining Tarek's trust, and by extension mine, will benefit you somehow. And you talk like an aristocrat. Aristocrats rarely get thrown into Maqbara. But here you are. I want to know why you're here and what you want. If I'm not satisfied with the answer, you'd better pray your training is enough to save you from me."

The skin beneath her cuffs ached as her magic hissed through her blood, a feral creature anxious to hurt the liar in front of her.

Javan stared at her, the silence between them punctuated by the sand scraping the skylights above and the faint slosh of a water beast in its cistern.

Finally, he said, "I won't dishonor Yl' Haliq by lying, but I can't tell you the whole truth."

"Wrong answer." She rose from her crouch, magic burning, arms extended toward him, this aristocrat masquerading as a prisoner and trying to gain her trust.

Did he know what she was? Had the warden slipped up after all these years and told the wrong person just what kind of slave she was keeping in the bowels of Maqbara?

"Wait!" He kept his hands in the air, palms facing her even as she lunged for him.

"Sajda!" Tarek yelled as she crashed into the boy and wrapped her hands around his throat.

Magic hummed through her blood, stinging her palms as it reached for Javan, hunting for his strength, his truth.

The boy's brown eyes widened as if he could feel the pull of her magic on his blood, and then he brought his arms up beneath hers in a sharp movement that loosened her hold on him and knocked her back a step.

He didn't wait for her to find her footing.

Pivoting, he swept her leg with his, sending her hurtling toward the floor. She spun into the momentum of the fall, landed briefly in a handstand, and then flipped onto her feet again.

"Let me explain—"

She rushed toward him, letting her elven speed carry her fast enough that he never had a chance to brace before she crashed into him, wrapped her arms around him, and threw him to the ground.

He rolled as he landed and was back on his feet in a flash.

Definitely trained. She was going to have to be more elf than human if she wanted to gain his fear and his truth.

Pouring on the speed, she took two running steps forward and plowed her fist into his chest.

He flew backward, but as he fell, he grabbed the front of her shirt and took her with him.

"Let go!" She seized his wrists, magic raking at her skin, hunting for a way into Javan's body. His mind. His weaknesses.

A tiny thrill of pain seared her wrists beneath her cuffs as his pulse beat rapidly against her palms.

She wanted to draw his strength and his composure from him and leave him shaking and weak. Leave him begging her for mercy. She wanted to hear the truth spilling from his lips so she would know if she was in danger or if the warden was the one in trouble.

Her magic prickled and hummed, and she imagined turning

it loose on the boy with the challenge in his eyes and the aristocracy in his voice.

He dug his heels into the ground and flipped them. She hissed as her back hit the floor, her hands still wrapped around his wrists, his pulse fluttering against the heat of her magic.

"Let. Me. Explain." He bit the words out as he eased back onto his knees, his legs straddling her waist as he opened his hands to show her his palms.

A gesture of surrender she couldn't accept while she was at a disadvantage. He'd surrender to her, but it would be because he understood that she could hurt him if he didn't.

Feeling a faint whiff of regret for his pretty face, she concentrated on her strength, on the magic coiling in her blood, and then she sent her right fist straight into his jaw.

His head snapped back, and he hit the ground. Sliding away from him, she lunged to her feet, hands up and ready. He dabbed at the blood welling from a cut that had opened beside his mouth and then slowly stood to face her.

She frowned. His lips quirked.

"Are you *smiling* at me?"

"Yl' Haliq forbid," he said gravely, the ghost of a smile disappearing, though the challenge in his eyes had been replaced by something warmer.

"I just knocked you to the ground—"

"I knocked you down first."

Tarek waved his hands in the air. "Maybe you two could stop fighting, and we could hear the boy out."

"I didn't actually fall. I turned it into a flip." Sajda raised her chin to glare at Javan.

"And I flipped us both." He tilted his head to the side to

study her. "You're fast. And strong. That's a mean right hook you've got."

She smirked, caught herself, and resumed glaring. "I was holding back."

He gave her a slight nod. "I believe you. Whoever trained you truly understood how to help you harness your power."

Her skin went cold, magic piercing it like shards of ice. "What do you know of my power?"

He frowned. "Lower center of gravity since you're female, but still the power behind any combat move comes from the abdomen." He glanced at hers, and then quickly looked away, a faint pink highlighting his cheekbones.

She drew in a slow breath, willing the painful itch of her magic to settle. Either he was the world's best liar, or he knew nothing about her true power. And she'd already established that he was a terrible liar.

"Will you listen to me without trying to kill me now?" he asked. There was a note of deep sincerity in his voice that made her want to walk away.

She didn't want his story. Didn't want to understand why, even when she'd thrown him to the floor and punched him hard enough to split his skin, he hadn't tried to do anything but hold his own.

He hadn't tried to hurt her.

Either he was after the warden, or he needed her trust for something else entirely.

"I'll listen," she said. "But if I don't like what I hear, I'm going to stop holding back."

"Understood." He glanced around them as second bell rang, but they were alone by the stalls. Still, the boy lowered his voice as he said, "I was accused of attempted murder."

Her brow rose. Murder was the last thing she'd expected him to say. If someone wanted to plant an aristocrat in the prison, a murder accusation against a boy whose every move screamed "give me honor or give me death" was a pretty flimsy disguise.

"Did you do it?" she asked, and waited smugly for him to spin a tale about wrongful accusations and misunderstandings and could he please see the warden to sort it all out?

"Yes." He held her gaze, a muscle clenched along his jawline.

Misery and defiance warred for dominance on his expression, and she blinked.

He was telling the truth.

"Who did you try to kill?" she asked.

Defiance won. "The false—a boy who stole my life. Took my belongings, killed my friend, and tricked my father."

"I thought you weren't going to tell me whole truth," she said as her magic settled, a smooth heat coursing through her veins.

His dark eyes settled on her, and something in her stomach twisted in a warm, unfamiliar way. "I haven't. But only because if I do, it could cost someone his life. Someone I owe a debt to for putting me here instead of executing me."

"You're an aristocrat, aren't you?" She gave him a look that dared him to deny it.

"I was."

He wasn't a threat. Not to her. If he'd wanted to prove she was a dark elf, he'd have gone for her ears. Tried to push her into using her magic.

Maybe he'd rescued Tarek out of the sense of honor he wore like a second skin. Maybe he'd been trying to gain allies and had heard that Tarek was special to her.

It didn't matter. She was satisfied that he wasn't after her, and that was good enough for now. He'd made powerful enemies of Hashim and his crew, which meant that once tomorrow's arena competition started, the problem of whether or not to completely trust Javan was going to be moot.

No way would he survive what was coming at him.

She turned away from Javan to check on the beasts, ignoring Tarek's and Javan's discussion of the upcoming tournament's rules and then Tarek's hurried explanation to the guards who'd entered the arena intent on punishing Javan for not returning to his cell by second bell.

It was easy to let their conversation wash over her and float away without leaving anything behind.

It was far harder to silence the whisper of regret that tightened her throat when she thought of the pretty aristocrat lying dead on the arena floor.

FOURTEEN

RAHIM FOLLOWED A page through a long corridor in the east wing of the palace, his woven sandals tapping a sharp rhythm against the mosaic tiles beneath his feet. Sunlight streamed in through windows set deep into the walls, washing the jeweled colors of the tiles with gold.

It had been three days since he'd arrived at the palace, and he'd spent his time doing what he did best: listening. Gathering information.

Planning.

The king was doing poorly. The poison he unknowingly swallowed twice a day dulled his senses and sent tremors through his body. It wouldn't take much to finish what the poison had started, but the FaSaa'il didn't want to make a move until the coronation ceremony, something the king seemed reluctant to schedule. They reasoned that if the king willingly abdicated to Rahim, anyone left who'd known the real prince would have no recourse but to accept Rahim as their ruler. If the king suddenly died, leaving Rahim the crown, and someone raised questions about the new ruler's parentage, the aristocrats loyal to the current king could claim he was murdered and cause problems for the FaSaa'il's bid for power.

Fariq ran the palace, and by extension Akram, while the king was indisposed, but even then, the king tried to keep his cousin's authority on a short leash by refusing to just hand over the royal signet ring and allow Fariq to deal with all correspondence to ambassadors, magistrates, and aristocrats in the king's place. Not that Fariq hadn't found ways to get things done without the royal seal, but it made any true grab for power difficult.

The palace staff seemed evenly divided between those who showed genuine love and concern for the king and those who spied on him and were quick to do Fariq's bidding when the king's back was turned.

Which meant those same servants would be spying on Rahim, reporting his every move to Fariq and the FaSaa'il. No doubt the other half of the servants would also be watching him closely to make sure he truly was as dutiful to the king as a son ought to be.

Neither of them would find fault with him. He would walk the line between faction puppet and honorable prince until he was ready to strike.

"In here, Your Highness," the page said as she stopped before a thick door of carved teakwood.

Rahim nodded his thanks and swept into a room filled floor to ceiling with bookshelves. Dust motes danced in the sunlight as he strode forward to take his seat at the long oval table that rested in the center of the library. Fariq sat at the head of the table. The five FaSaa'il members Rahim had met a month ago at Lord Borak's behest were seated on either side of him, along with a man who hadn't been at the original meeting. Rahim took a seat at the end opposite Fariq.

As soon as he was settled, Lord Borak leaned forward and caught his eye. "You're looking every inch the prince, my boy."

My boy. As if Rahim was nothing more than a trained dog who reflected well on his master. As if they weren't all here because Rahim had been smart enough to see his opportunity and take it.

Schooling his expression into one of bland respect and obedience, Rahim inclined his head and said, "I am the prince, my lord."

Lord Borak laughed and clapped his hands. "Excellent. Didn't I tell you he could pull it off?" He looked around the table, but Fariq rapped his knuckles against the wood, and Lord Borak fell silent.

"The king suspects nothing," Fariq said, "and his health continues to fail. I'm certain our prince can convince him to set a coronation date shortly so that we don't need to worry about rumors or rebellion once Rahim is on the throne. My cousin has always been prone to put the needs of Akram above his own, so that's the approach you use." Fariq looked at Rahim. "Tell him you're concerned about his health and want to ensure a peaceful transfer of power just in case."

"I've tried," Rahim said. "He isn't yet willing to move forward."

"I didn't instruct you to do that." Fariq's eyes narrowed as he glared suspiciously at his son.

A heavy silence fell across the table as the aristocrats shifted uneasily in their seats.

Rahim pressed his palms together and touched his fingertips to his forehead in a show of obeisance. "You told me it was important that the coronation was scheduled quickly. I thought that meant I should take steps to make that happen. My apologies if I misunderstood."

Fariq paused for a moment, and then said, "You didn't misunderstand what needs to happen, but from this point forward, you don't make a move that I haven't authorized. Is that clear?"

"Of course." Rahim smiled through gritted teeth.

The FaSaa'il drew a collective breath and the mood in the room lightened.

"Now let's discuss the rumors about the king's health and how to combat the loyalists who are certain I must be behind it," Fariq said. "We can't have anyone taking issue with the upcoming transfer of power. I'd also like a list of all families with children who attended Milisatria. Those who can't be turned to our side must be eliminated before our prince can make a public appearance. That might raise some questions, so I'll also want a list of other influential families who can be bribed into being loyal to us."

Rahim opened his mouth to suggest that they deal with the Milisatria families in a way that wouldn't raise anyone's suspicions at all, but Fariq whipped a hand into the air.

"You just sit and listen. When we're ready for you to speak, we'll tell you what to say."

Fools, all of them. So sure the puppet they were using to take Akram's throne didn't have teeth of his own.

Rage was a fire churning through Rahim's blood as he folded his hands in front of him, assumed an expression of boredom, and fantasized about driving a sword through the heart of every person seated at the table.

FIFTEEN

THE NEXT MORNING, Tarek was waiting beside Javan's cell door as the bars rose slowly into the ceiling. The old man had two pieces of toast smothered in lentil paste and an orange in his hands.

Javan climbed to his feet, his knees aching from the hour he'd just spent in prayer. Still no peace. No direction. Just anger at the injustice of his position and a sense of wild anticipation that buzzed through him at the thought that today was a round of the competition the aristocracy came to see.

Today could be the day he finally saw his father face-to-face.

Pressing his hand against the sash folded over his heart and whispering one last prayer for deliverance, Javan met Tarek's eyes and moved toward him. Tarek smiled.

"Figured you'd rather not go to the kitchen for your breakfast this morning." He offered Javan both pieces of toast. "Sajda won't be there to keep Hashim and his group in check like she was yesterday for lunch and dinner."

Javan accepted the food and inclined his head in a sign of respect for the older man. "Thank you."

It was a blow to his pride that he'd needed Sajda's help to get his meals, but he couldn't deny that she was the only one Hashim seemed to fear. It was clear Javan's interference with Hashim's treatment of Tarek had bought him nothing but ill will from the man—there'd been eight prisoners flanking Hashim in front of the kitchen's long table at each meal, blocking Javan from the food. Until Sajda, with her predatory grace and her cold-as-stone demeanor, had turned her unnerving gaze on them and quietly asked if they wanted to be fed to the beasts one piece at a time.

Even then, Hashim moved slowly. He'd obeyed her, barely, his expression mutinous as Sajda walked past him like he mattered less than the dust on the floor beneath her feet.

"How did you get out of your cell before the bars were raised?" Javan asked. If there was a way to roam freely, he needed to know it in case his father didn't attend the event. Or in case he couldn't get close enough to be recognized.

He refused to consider that his father might not recognize him at all. That the king might believe the impostor was his true son.

"Been here so long the warden lets me stay in a room with a wooden door instead of bars in exchange for helping Sajda."

"So Sajda isn't a prisoner like you?" Javan asked.

Tarek's expression darkened. "She's the warden's slave."

The toast tasted like sawdust as Javan absorbed Tarek's words. He couldn't reconcile Sajda—with her confidence, her pride, and her incredible combat skills—with the word *slave*. There was nothing submissive about her. "How long has the warden owned . . . How long has Sajda been here?"

"Since she was five."

How had she endured living trapped in the underbelly of the prison for so long? She had to be around his own age, which meant she'd been here for about a dozen years.

Twelve years of holding her own with hundreds of prisoners. Of navigating the treachery and violence that came with throwing the worst of the worst into a hole together. Twelve years of doing what it took to survive.

Suddenly her icy demeanor and relentless distrust of him made a lot of sense.

"The orange is for Sajda. Let's go find her before the competitors crowd the area by the stalls. The prison's normal routine is suspended today. Everyone who is competing will be down at the arena once they're done with breakfast. Everyone else will be back in their cells until the round is over and the audience members are long gone." Tarek clapped an arthritic hand on Javan's shoulder as they moved down the corridor of level fifteen toward the closest stairwell. Already a swell of voices echoed from the arena far below. "Let's talk about getting you out of the arena alive and mostly intact."

Javan shot Tarek a look as they made their way down the stairs. "I'd prefer to remain completely intact."

"Wouldn't we all, but the beasts don't care about pretty faces, and neither do your fellow prisoners. Now remember, each creature is worth a set amount of points. Point values will be written on the wall opposite the king's box. Every creature you kill will add points to your score. Do yourself a favor and make sure the judges standing around the arena's edges see you hold up your kill. Or if the beast is too heavy, make sure you get their attention. Wouldn't want someone claiming a kill that's yours. If you kill another competitor, you will receive a five-hundred-point deduction, but you'll also gain that person's tournament points. There's been a round of competition already, but no one has reached five hundred points, so killing someone isn't a strong strategy yet. Everyone who survives moves on to the next round."

"This is barbaric," Javan said, his stomach churning at the thought of murdering another prisoner just to gain the person's points. The thought of killing wild beasts who'd done nothing to deserve it wasn't much better. Did none of the other prisoners care about the blood on their hands when they finally stood before Yl' Haliq for judgment?

"This is survival, and it happens twice a year. We have a summer tournament and a winter tournament." Tarek's voice was firm. "Collecting bets on the competition is what lines the warden's pocket with wahda. I'm pretty sure Prince Fariq benefits too because he has the palace steward at each match recording which families attend, how much they bet, and how enthusiastically they cheer for their favorites. The better competitor you are, the more you become a crowd favorite. Crowd favorites bring in heavy betting and are granted more leeway by the warden as a result, and everybody wants to win."

"Any crowd favorites yet?"

"Hashim and several others on level five."

"Fantastic." Dread settled into him. "I was young when I left Akram for school, but I don't remember my family ever attending a tournament in Maqbara. When did these competitions start?" And why was his father allowing the dishonor of a tournament that forced people to compete for their lives?

Tarek frowned in thought for a moment. "About five years ago. It was Prince Fariq's idea, I believe. He borrowed it from something they do in the kingdom of Llorenyae."

Five years ago. The same time the king's letters began to change in tone and frequency. Javan couldn't reconcile the father he remembered—the man who put honor and obeying the sacred texts above all else—with the king who would sanction a bloodthirsty tournament for sport. Had his father really changed that much, or was this more evidence of Uncle Fariq's betrayal of everything the Kadar family stood for?

Moments later they were at the double rows of iron stalls where Sajda was finishing tossing sheep guts to whatever monstrous creatures were housed there. An older woman with shrewd eyes and wrinkled skin was walking the arena floor, a piece of parchment in her hands. Using the door to the magistrate's office as north, she counted paces according to the schematic on her parchment, stooping to place a black cloth where each weapon would be hidden. A trio of guards stood beside the arena entrance closest to the stalls, their glares landing as one on Javan.

"No prisoners allowed in the stalls, Tarek." The shortest guard, a man with wide shoulders and an impatient air about him, stepped toward them, one hand resting on the hilt of his sword.

"We have a much larger group of beasts than usual for today's round," Tarek said. "More beasts means more work, and if we're going to have everything ready in time for the warden, we need extra help. If you don't want me to pull beast workers from the prisoners, perhaps you could help us instead? You know how the warden gets if the tournament falls behind schedule."

The man's eyes narrowed, but he took a step back. "Just the one prisoner, then. You know how she gets if the competitors see the beasts before the competition."

Tarek nodded, wrapped a hand around Javan's arm, and pulled him quickly past the guards and toward the stalls.

"Want me to help Batula with weapon placement?" Tarek asked as Sajda washed her hands in a basin beside the last stall.

Sajda nodded as she took the orange from Tarek. "Make sure everything is weighted so we don't have floating weapons to contend with."

"Floating weapons?" Javan asked as Tarek joined Batula on the scarred arena floor to begin sorting through the weapons that had been dragged into a pile at its center.

Sajda pierced the skin of the orange with her fingernail and peeled the skin away in large chunks. The sweet bite of citrus filled the air, and a creature in the stall beside her began snuffling along the doorframe. "The rules of the tournament state that all weapons must be hidden in the arena at the start of the round. It gives the warden another way to collect bets. Which weapon will be found first. Which competitor will get his or her favored item. And it increases the risk because a crowd favorite might die if she doesn't get the weapon she knows how to use. Since today is water combat, we have to weight the coverings over the weapons to make sure nothing moves from its original spot."

"All of that is disturbing, but what do you mean by water combat?" Javan asked as he moved to the stall and stared in horrified fascination at the scrawny creature inside. It looked like a mangy, stunted goat with claw-tipped hooves, razor-sharp spikes running down its back, and fangs that hung past its chin. "And what is *this*?"

"That's a devil goat. From Llorenyae." She sounded impatient.

"You don't have to worry about that one today."

Javan backed away from the stall as the devil goat looked up and gnashed its teeth in his direction. "That's a relief."

"Hardly. That one is relatively easy to kill, though of course it isn't worth many points. You'll have far more dangerous monsters in the water with you today. You'll be wishing for a simple devil goat before long." She popped an orange slice into her mouth and rubbed absently at the skin beneath her iron bracelets.

"There's that glowing optimism again," he said as he moved to the next stall. "Yl' Haliq, what is this abomination?"

An enormous white worm coiled and uncoiled itself in a cistern of water. The worm was easily the size of a full-grown man, and its wide, gaping mouth revealed rows of sharp teeth. A chill chased its way across Javan's skin at the sinking realization that the things he would face in the prison's arena were nothing like the well-ordered contests he'd engaged in at Milisatria.

"A man-eating worm. Also from Llorenyae, as most of our beasts are. It can distend its jaw and swallow a man whole, so you should stay away from its mouth." Sajda finished her orange and turned toward the arena. "There's also a pair of small water dragons, nearly sixty flesh-eating fish, a dozen venomous snakes, a river sprite with a nasty temper, and an enormous blob of a thing called a lake crawler that can disguise itself as its surroundings and swallow you whole if you step on it. I think it looks a little darker than its surroundings, so try not to step on any shadows."

"Thanks for the advice," Javan muttered as the worm twisted and thrashed. His stomach felt like it was twisting and thrashing too. How was he supposed to survive in an arena full of water with all those creatures?

"Want some more advice?" she asked without looking at him. Other prisoners were finished with breakfast and were heading toward the stalls now.

"Only if it's full of your usual sunshine and cheer."

She laughed, and then shot him a glare as if making her laugh was on her list of things prisoners weren't allowed to do. "Don't compete."

"Don't compete? That's your advice?"

She nodded, her gaze back on Batula and Tarek, who were spreading the weapons across the arena, securing some to the floor with heavy stones, while others they hung on hooks around the walls.

"Tarek said every prisoner under the age of forty is required to enter the arena," Javan said. Glancing back at the man-size worm, he found himself hoping she knew a way out. A way to skip throwing his body into the water with the other prisoners, hoping to kill the monsters before they killed him. He could still get his father's attention without being in the arena itself.

"Yes, you have to enter the arena. If you don't, the warden will kill you in front of the aristocracy as an appetizer to the main event. But you don't need to fight." She turned the full weight of her gaze on him, and this time when his skin prickled, it wasn't entirely unpleasant. Maybe because at the moment, she wasn't looking at him as though she wanted to tear him to pieces. Or maybe because he was just getting used to feeling like lightning was skimming over his body whenever he was around her.

She lowered her voice as Hashim and several other prisoners exited the nearest stairwell and came as close to the stalls as the guards stationed by the arena's entrance would allow. "This is the second round of combat for the tournament. There are only three rounds left after today. If you keep your back to a wall, kill any creature that attacks you, and try not to take credit for any kills, you won't be perceived as a threat, and the other prisoners probably won't try to murder you."

"I don't have any points worth stealing," he said. "I doubt anyone would risk taking a penalty to kill me."

"There are plenty of awful things that can happen to someone while they're still alive. And if a group of competitors work together to kill you, they split the point deduction between them." Her voice was cold and calm, but there was an edge to it that he hadn't heard from her before. A thread of darkness that hinted at storms just below her surface.

"When does the king arrive?" he asked, trying hard to keep his voice level even though it felt like a ball of nervous energy was tumbling through his chest. He could get his father's attention without truly participating in this barbaric tournament. He'd meet his gaze, wave the red sash over his head, and this nightmare would be over.

She shrugged. "I don't keep track of royalty. Just stay against a wall and try not to die."

"I'll keep that in mind. Thanks."

"Don't thank me. You helped Tarek. I just paid that debt. Once you get out into the arena, you're on your own." She walked away as Tarek and Batula secured the gates at both ends of the arena. Leaping onto the short wall that ran around the edge of the ring, Sajda walked nimbly toward the center point on the eastern wall, bent at the waist, and cranked a lever attached to a silver pipe cover. The cover lifted, and water gushed into the arena.

Javan left the stall area, avoiding Hashim and his friends, and joined a small group of prisoners who stood at the closest gate watching the water level slowly rise. A guard called out prisoner names and handed each competitor an armband with a number on it to help the judges keep track of their kills and to give the crowd a chance to identify and choose their favorites. Javan tied his armband into place and faced the arena.

Sajda was right. He would secure a weapon, find a space at the edge of the ring, and survive until the last monster was killed. No flashy competition. No trying for the top score. No additional risk that could rip away his chance to save his father and his kingdom. For the first time in his life, Javan was going into a competition without intending to win.

"I can't swim," the man closest to Javan said softly.

"The water will only be waist deep," a woman answered, her hands moving swiftly as she secured her long black hair into a braid. "Get a weapon, plant your feet, and kill anything that comes close to you."

The man shuddered, and Javan said, "If you go under, don't panic. All you have to do is find the floor with either your feet or your hands. Then you can orient yourself and stand up. You'll be all right."

The man shot Javan a quick look and said, "This isn't worth it. We're risking our lives to entertain the aristocracy, and for what?"

The woman laughed, though there was no amusement in her voice. "Well, it sure isn't so we can ask for a boon from the king when he finally shows up during the final round. Hashim and the others from level five have too many points already for any of us to win the prize."

"The king doesn't attend until the final round?" Javan asked, hope fizzling into despair that sank into his bones like stone.

According to Tarek, the final round was at least a month away. Would the king survive the impostor and Fariq that long? Would Javan?

"No, he doesn't. And even then, he barely pays attention. Unless you win the audience with him, he won't even know you exist," the woman said.

"We're risking our lives because if we don't, the warden turns us into meat," another man said, but Javan wasn't listening.

"What do you mean?" He moved closer to the woman, who gave him an irritated look. His heart kicked hard against his chest. "Are you saying we can gain a personal audience with the king?"

"And you get to ask for a boon that he will grant as long as it doesn't break any laws in the kingdom. But only if you win the entire tournament," she said. "And you aren't winning. None of us are. Most of the prisoners from level five already have at least two hundred points each. It's too late to catch up with them, and even if you did, they'd kill you as soon as you had five hundred points."

Something bright and painful burned in Javan's chest as he looked at the board nailed to the wall across from the king's box. Every creature entering the ring that day was listed.

VENOMOUS SNAKE—5 POINTS

FLESH-EATING FISH—10 POINTS

RIVER SPRITE—25 POINTS

WATER DRAGON—40 POINTS

LAKE CRAWLER—50 POINTS

MAN-EATING WORM—100 POINTS

Forget standing with his back to the wall. Forget just trying to survive. The key to getting out of Maqbara was staring him in the face.

If the level five competitors had around two hundred points each, then Javan needed at least that much to even have a shot at qualifying for the final round.

After memorizing the point values of every creature that would be swimming in the water with him, Javan turned his attention to the covered weapons that lined the walls and the floor.

Hashim and his ilk weren't going to gain an audience with the king because Javan was going to compete with a vengeance.

And he was going to win.

SIXTEEN

Javan stood beside the arena with the other competitors. There were about forty-five prisoners preparing to enter the ring. His heart thudded in his ears while the aristocracy filed in. Guards flanked both the prisoners and the doors, swords out in case someone decided to make a run for it while the door was open. More guards stood watch on the upper levels, making sure any prisoners who were too old or too injured from the last round of competition stayed in their cells. The bars stayed up, as they did throughout the day, but the guards pacing the halls with their swords out discouraged anyone from breaking the warden's rules.

Javan's blood was on fire with nervous energy. Every physical contest he'd participated in at Milisatria had been a well-ordered test with clear boundaries and the expectation that every student would obey the ironclad rules against harming one another. This, on the other hand, was utter chaos. Water monsters. Competitors who may or may not have any weapons' training. No rules against attacking other people. And a crowd ready to bet on the outcome. There were so many ways it could all go wrong.

Panic clawed at him, a jagged pulse of fear that tore through his veins. Javan clenched and unclenched his hands, shook out his arms, and paced in the small space between each guard, to the annoyance of those closest to him.

"Will you stop? You're making my nerves worse," the man who couldn't swim said. Sweat beaded his brow and collected beneath the arms of his gray tunic.

Javan shrugged as if to say he was sorry, but didn't stop. The jagged pulse of fear twisted within him. If he stood still, it would paralyze him. He needed to be loose and limber. Fighting a horde of bloodthirsty creatures was going to test the skills he'd learned at Milisatria to their limits. Fighting them with water up to his waist while trying to avoid the other prisoners?

Nearly impossible.

As soon as the thought hit, he banished it before the panic could consume him. Nothing was impossible. Nothing. Not even the daunting task of winning a tournament when he was already hundreds of points behind and when everything in the arena with him wanted him dead. He just had to work for it harder than anyone else. And he'd spent the last ten years doing exactly that.

Pacing, he scanned the crowds as they made their way to their seats, their sashes a bright slash of beauty in the drab stone interior of the prison. So far, he didn't see anyone, student or parent, he'd met at Milisatria, but that didn't mean they weren't there. And if he made enough of an impression—if he drew enough attention to himself—he'd have accomplished two huge steps forward in his plan to get out of Maqbara.

He'd have gained enough points to give himself a chance at qualifying for the final round. And if he was recognized by any families who knew him from the academy, he'd have alerted them to his predicament. They could call upon the king and tell him the truth. Hope churned through him, twining with the fear until he wasn't sure which was worse.

As the judges for the match climbed onto the narrow wall that surrounded the arena and strapped themselves to support poles to keep from falling into the combat zone, someone bumped into Javan. Hard.

He turned to find Hashim glaring at him, his lip curled in derision.

"You're meat. I'm going to see to it personally." The midday sunlight glaring in from the skylights above traced the white scar tissue that crisscrossed Hashim's face.

Javan shrugged. "You're the crowd favorite, I hear. And currently in first place. If you want to give that up by taking a five-hundred-point deduction on my behalf, who am I to argue your strategy?"

Hashim spit on Javan's boots as a sturdily built woman dressed in black walked out onto a platform on level one. The crowd fell quiet as she raised her hands. Her iron-gray hair was pulled back into a bun, and one dark eye glared down on the arena. The other side of her face was hidden beneath a bandage.

Moving away from Hashim, Javan stood next to the non-swimmer again and asked quietly, "Who is that?"

"The warden, you fool."

Javan's eyes narrowed as he stared up at the woman who ran Maqbara and forced her prisoners to fight, sometimes to their deaths, for her own profit. What kind of person dealt in death and violence to line her own coffers?

The same kind of person who bought a child of five and put her to work in the middle of Akram's most violent criminals.

He found himself hoping she'd accidentally fall into the arena.

"Welcome to the second round of this year's tournament!" Her voice was low and gravelly. "We have forty-six competitors still in the running for the prize."

She swept the prisoners with a glance and frowned when her eye landed on Javan. For a long moment, she glared at him, her nostrils flaring as if finding a new competitor in the group was infuriating.

Finally, she said, "It seems we have forty-*seven* competitors. A new prisoner has joined our ranks. If you want to take a gamble on an untried young man, we will be accepting bets for another five minutes before combat starts. Odds on the favorites are listed at the betting table." She gestured to her left, and Javan followed her movement to see a small table set up on the platform with a short, bespectacled woman sitting behind it, her quill flying over parchment as she recorded bets and collected coin.

Turning away, Javan paced again, his knees shaky, his palms clammy. Nausea burned the back of his throat as the realization hit that he was about to get into the water with the vicious, man-size worm he'd seen in the stalls, plus a bevy of other dangerous creatures.

This wasn't sport. It was madness. It was also the only way he could win an audience with his father and save both himself and the king.

Over by the stalls, Sajda, Tarek, Batula, and several unhappy-looking guards were standing beside cisterns and barrels of water. A long wooden chute was mounted to a pole beside them. They could pour the contents of the barrels into the end closest to them. The other end dumped the creatures straight into the water inside the arena.

Sajda met his gaze once, but her expression looked carved out of stone, and he couldn't find a hint of worry or compassion in her eyes.

Not that he needed it from someone who'd made it clear she disliked him and had only given him advice today out of respect for her relationship with Tarek. Besides, it was time to focus. He had a combat round to win.

The warden stepped to the front of the platform again and yelled, "Betting is closed. Competitors, take your stations."

Hashim instantly elbowed his way to the front of the crowd, nine other competitors right behind him. Grabbing the side of the arena, he hauled himself up and over. He landed with a splash and immediately went for his weapon of choice—a short pole with a wickedly spiked ball at the end of its long chain.

Javan stepped away from the throng of prisoners who were being herded by the guards toward the same spot Hashim had used, each trying to scramble into the arena in time to find the weapon he or she wanted.

Gambling that the guards wouldn't see him in time to stop him, Javan sized up his path, and then ran straight for the section of the wall directly between the competitors and the barrels full of beasts.

Someone shouted, but it was too late as Javan grabbed the edge of the short wall and leaped. Twisting in midair, he cleared the wall and landed with a splash. He dove forward, and water rushed over his head as he kicked his feet against the wall, propelling himself directly into the center of the arena where a pair of short swords were anchored to the floor with a stone. Several strong kicks later, and he was there. Shoving the stone aside, he grabbed the sword hilts, found his footing, and stood, his hands shaking as energy flooded his body.

The applause was deafening as he shook his hair out of his eyes and looked up.

All eyes in the arena were trained on him, though he caught several people glancing quickly at the palace steward, who stood alone in the royal box recording participation on his sheaf of parchment. A flurry of conversations erupted as the aristocracy realized the competitor who'd made the grand entrance into the ring was the new prisoner. He swept the crowd with his gaze, meeting their eyes and willing someone to recognize him.

Yl' Haliq be merciful, please let someone recognize him.

As the rest of the competitors landed in the arena and rushed for weapons, Javan felt a chill on the back of his neck. He glanced at Sajda, fully expecting her to be treating him to her I'm-about-to-remove-your-vital-organs glare, but her expression was nothing but icy indifference. Craning his neck, he found himself locking gazes with the warden, who stood on the platform directly behind him.

He imagined there was something familiar in the way she was looking at him, and then shook it off. Of course there was something familiar. Sajda had given him the same treatment. Maybe this was where she'd learned how to intimidate others without saying a word.

Turning away from the warden, Javan swallowed a sudden lump in his throat and braced himself as two guards hefted a barrel and slowly tipped it into the wooden chute. The chute rattled and shook as a dozen venomous snakes slithered down its length and into the water. Javan's knees shook as the jagged pulse of fear exploded into brilliant strands of terror. He forced himself to keep his feet planted when everything in him wanted to swim for the relative safety of a wall.

He couldn't win if he played it safe.

The crowd roared with excitement as a prisoner close to the chute suddenly went underwater. Seconds later a steady stream of flesh-eating fish slid off the chute and into the water, and crimson bloomed where the prisoner had gone under.

Javan looked away as the two water dragons dove into the arena. He couldn't watch the beasts entering the combat zone. He needed all his focus for the water.

Carefully scanning the area around him, he breathed deeply.

Fear out.

Courage in.

There. A pair of darting shadows whisked by his boots and began circling. Another big splash sounded from the chute as Javan held his breath and ducked under the water in a crouch.

The fish were plump silvery things with blue-tipped tails and yellow eyes. He watched carefully, timing their movements, and then drove his swords down as they came for his legs.

His swords each skewered a fish; but before he could stand, something large slammed into him and sent him sprawling.

He twisted, his back to the floor, and raked his sword tips across the belly of a water dragon. A few damaged scales spun into the water, but the moss-green lizard with the spiny ridges and thick fangs seemed unaffected.

As its thick, muscular body passed above him, Javan lunged to his feet. Something tore at his arm, and he stabbed a sword through another fish before flinging himself onto the fleeing dragon's back.

The creature growled, a hoarse, guttural sound, and writhed beneath Javan's grip. Its spiny tail whipped through the air, slicing into Javan's back and sending an arc of water flying.

The water was turning murky with blood—from Javan and from other prisoners around him. The air was filled with cries of pain and rage and the thunderous clamor of the crowd above them.

Terror was a fire burning through Javan, screaming at him to get out of the water. To run because surely no punishment the warden could deliver was worse than the monsters that circled him now.

Ignoring the urge to run, Javan concentrated on the water dragon. The beast was nearly impossible to hold on to. It twisted, its dense body several handspans longer than Javan's, and snapped its elongated snout toward Javan's face. He flung his head back, wincing as the wet end of the creature's nose scraped across his neck.

Panic flared, sending his heartbeat crashing against his ears. How did you kill a water dragon? The scales were impossible to penetrate with a sword.

The creature twisted again, and now Javan was holding the underbelly, which was just as well armored as the rest. Something brushed past his leg, and he prayed it wasn't the lake crawler ready to swallow him whole or the worm with its distended jaw aiming for his exposed body.

Screams rose from a prisoner to his right, but Javan didn't look. He had his hands full. The dragon was rolling like a barrel, its jaw coming perilously close to Javan's arms. He loosened his grip and then grabbed on again as the lizard shot forward. The creature reared back and snapped at Javan's head, and the prince found himself staring past a row of thick fangs to the soft flesh of the beast's throat.

Yl' Haliq preserve him, there was only one way to do this, and it was going to *hurt*.

As the dragon twisted and came at him again, Javan let go of its body with his left arm, aimed his sword, and shoved his arm into the beast's mouth.

The blade bit deep, and the dragon's jaw closed.

Agony blazed through Javan, raw and blistering, as the fangs sank into his arm. Raising the hilt of his other sword, he smashed it repeatedly against the lizard's snout. The creature thrashed wildly, and Javan saw stars at the edge of his vision. But then the dragon's jaw relaxed, and it gave one more feeble twist before going limp.

Trembling from the pain and the residual panic, Javan turned and caught the eye of the closest judge, a girl wearing a red tunic with a white sash, and heaved the body of the dragon toward her. She checked his armband and nodded once as he slid the two fish who'd stayed on his right sword into the water. He'd lost the other sword to the dragon's throat. She wrote his score on the parchment she held while he turned to see what else he could kill.

The entire ring was in chaos.

Prisoners thrashed and fought—with beasts and with one another. The water was clouded with blood, guts, and scales.

Javan calculated quickly. He'd earned sixty points. That wasn't nearly enough. He needed the lake crawler and the worm, if they were still alive.

Something bumped his boot, and he bent swiftly to stab whatever creature it was, only to nearly drive his sword through the man who'd told him he couldn't swim. The man's eyes bulged with panic, and bubbles escaped his lips as he frantically grabbed for the snake that was wrapped around his throat like a scarf, its fangs sunk into the first two fingers of the man's right hand.

A small crowd of flesh-eating fish followed close behind, tearing at the man's arms with their tiny teeth.

Javan struck, slicing his sword through the snake and severing its head. Then he snatched the front of the man's tunic and hauled him to his feet. Tossing the snake's lifeless body toward the judge on his left, Javan grabbed the man's hand and dug the tip of his sword into the puncture wounds, cutting them wide open.

A shadow scuttled across the floor, and Javan dragged the man backward with him as the lake crawler drifted by, the gaping maw in its center nothing but a shadow slightly darker than the rest of its body.

Javan shuddered. This was madness, but there was only one way out of the horror that surrounded him. Only one way out of Maqbara and back to the destiny that was his.

He needed to kill the crawler and find the worm or he was going to lose his chance to gain an audience with his father. But the man he'd saved was shaking now, his teeth chattering as blood flowed from the holes in his arms and the cuts on his fingers.

Javan turned and waded toward the closest wall, dragging the man with him. "How long did the snake have its fangs in you?"

When the man didn't answer, Javan swung around and snapped, *"How long?"*

"I don't know." The man's voice shook. "Not long. I was holding its head, but then it got away from me and bit just before I bumped into you."

Javan reached the wall and pushed the man against it just as the worm skimmed past them, someone's legs dangling from its mouth. Horror crawled up the back of Javan's throat.

"Sa' Loham preserve us," the man cried as he stared in horror.

Javan yanked the man's injured hand toward him and looked at the veins on his arm. They looked normal, but he had no idea if venom left streaks of red moving toward the heart or not. And neither one of them had time for a lengthy discussion about the man's options.

"We have to cut off anything that might have venom in it," Javan said.

The man pulled his hand toward his chest.

"Lose your fingers or lose your life. Which is it?" Javan asked, his patience fraying. Even now the worm could be dead. The lake crawler too. And Javan couldn't catch the tournament leaders if he was busy killing the last of the fish. "Choose!"

"Fingers," the man said.

Javan pinned the man's hand to the wall and removed his first two fingers with one quick slash of his sword. Blood gushed, and the man screamed.

Whipping his tunic over his head, Javan wrapped it tightly around the man's hand. "Raise your arm above your head and stay close to the wall. It's the best I can do for you now."

Javan whirled back toward the competition in time to see Hashim and four other competitors charging straight for him.

SEVENTEEN

"GET HIM!" HASHIM shouted.

Javan dove to the side, but Hashim and his allies were on top of him in a flash. Pain sang up his injured arm as they wrestled his limbs until they had him pinned between them, each holding an arm or a leg. Javan held tight to his weapon and lifted his bare back out of the water as they crossed the arena floor with him.

Prayers tumbled through his mind, fragmented and desperate. Was this the end? He'd survived the Draconi, the assassins, a death sentence, and a stay inside Maqbara only to be killed by criminals in a tournament that went against everything his father and his kingdom stood for?

It was impossible to breathe the fear out and let courage in. Panic was an iron fist squeezing his chest. Frantically he scrambled for leverage, reason, *anything* that could stop what was about to happen.

Hashim and his friends might hate Javan, but they wanted

the same thing he did. They wanted to win. To gain an audience with the king and ask for a boon. Killing Javan would hurt their goal. He had to make them see it.

"You can't afford a five-hundred-point loss," he said, his voice sharp with desperation. "You could lose your place as the tournament leader. You could lose your chance to talk to the king."

A shudder worked its way down his spine as someone else screamed and the crowd applauded.

How did his father condone this bloodbath? How did the audience? Surely sending people to their deaths for sport violated everything the sacred texts taught. It hardly mattered that the people in question were criminals. If their crimes had deserved death, they'd have been sentenced to the *muqsila* instead of Maqbara.

"I told you I would make you regret interfering. I can afford a point deduction. There are still three rounds left," Hashim said, but his eyes darted toward the warden as he spoke.

"Here!" A female competitor with broad shoulders and the outline of a galloping stallion inked into her neck called.

Javan bucked and twisted as he caught sight of the faint shadow spreading out along the floor beneath him.

They were going to drop him on the lake crawler.

The iron fist of panic squeezed, and his throat constricted.

The crowd roared. Someone cried out. But Javan could barely hear past the deafening beat of his heart.

He couldn't die like this. He was the *prince*. His destiny had been foretold by Yl' Haliq. He wasn't supposed to be in this bloodbath trying to survive monsters that should never have been brought to Akram in the first place.

His lungs burned for air as he struggled to breathe past the noose of fear closing around his neck.

He'd have an instant to react once they dropped him. An instant to twist, as he fell through the water, then to drive his sword into the thing that lurked beneath him.

And he had no idea where to aim for the kill shot.

"Now!" Hashim yelled.

The people holding Javan let go.

His back hit the water and he began to sink.

A flash of white shimmered out of the corner of his eye, and he twisted toward it as he fell.

The worm's jaw was already distended—a cave of teeth and tongue.

Javan kicked out, his foot finding someone's chest, but hands were reaching into the water, shoving him down. Panic burned through him. There was no way out of this. Either he dove beneath the worm and landed in the gaping maw of the lake crawler, or he would be swallowed by the monstrous thing surging toward him.

Spinning, he raised his weapon and collided with the worm.

His head slammed into the roof of the worm's mouth, and he drove his sword up, through the soft palate and deep into the creature's tiny brain.

The thing shuddered, and its fangs scraped over Javan's bare skin. And then the worm was sinking, taking Javan with it.

He'd killed the worm only to be eaten by the lake monster.

His lungs burned for air, and his pulse was thunder in his ears as they hit the floor of the arena. Yanking the worm's jaw open, Javan struggled to get his arm out of its mouth, unhooking fangs from his skin and tugging his sword free so that he could face the lake monster.

The shadow was gone.

Hands reached for him, and Javan slashed at them with his sword.

He wasn't getting caught by Hashim's group again. He'd killed the worm. One hundred points to add to the sixty he already had. Sixty-five if the judge had seen him kill the snake. No one was taking that from him now.

Ignoring the pressure that was building in his head as his lungs strained for air, he plunged his sword through the worm's tongue and deep into its jaw. Then, using that as a hook, he dragged the creature over a floor now littered with the corpses of the water beasts and a few human corpses as well. When he could hold his breath no longer, he rose from the water, dragging the huge white worm with him.

The crowd cheered as he stood there, surrounded by blood and bodies, the monster in his hands. He caught the eye of the same judge who'd scored his earlier kills and heaved the worm into the water in front of her.

Fifty paces away, Hashim stood holding the mangled body of the lake crawler and glaring at Javan. The prince glanced around the arena, noting the other competitors who still remained upright. None of them would meet his eyes.

Not even the man who was still wearing Javan's tunic as a bandage.

A bell tolled, deep and sonorous. "This round is over." The warden's rough voice echoed across the arena. "Scores will be tallied shortly and winnings may be collected at that time. Prisoners, you are dismissed. If you need the infirmary, the guards will escort you. Otherwise, return to your cells."

Slowly, every inch of his body feeling battered, bloodied, and bruised, Javan made his way to the side of the arena closest to Sajda and Tarek and climbed over the wall.

His knees gave out as his feet touched the ground, and he went down hard. The stone was rough and cold against his skin, and he lay his cheek against it as he struggled to breathe. To ride out the waves of pain that racked his body now that the distraction of battle was over.

He'd survived. More than survived, he'd put a worthy number of points onto the board.

But he'd only made his situation with his fellow prisoners worse, and he had no illusions. Hashim wouldn't accept the humiliation of failing to defeat Javan. He'd be coming for Javan—in the near future or in the next round of competition. And none of the other prisoners wanted to be in the middle of it.

Javan was on his own.

Tarek rushed toward him as a guard barked an order to get on his feet and go to the infirmary or be beaten for noncompliance. Quickly, the older man slid his arthritic hands beneath Javan's arms and helped the prince struggle to his feet.

"Thank you," Javan said, his chest heaving as he fought to catch his breath. Pain sent a wave of sickness crashing through him as he took a tentative step forward. Gritting his teeth, he moved cautiously, holding his injured arm close.

Sajda stood apart from them, her arms crossed over her chest, her expression cold as he limped past her to follow the other injured prisoners to the infirmary. "What happened to staying near the wall? To not competing?"

Javan met her gaze. "I changed my mind once I learned about the prize for winning." His voice trembled, and he glanced once more at the audience above him, hoping to see a familiar face.

Hoping someone would be staring at him with recognition and horror that the crown prince of Akram had nearly died as a prisoner inside Maqbara.

No one was paying him any attention.

No one but the guard tasked with bringing him to the infirmary.

"I said move," the guard snapped, pulling a thick iron bar from its place on his belt. Javan barely had the energy to flinch as the bar swung toward him and slammed into his back. Staggering forward, he caught himself on the wall beside Sajda.

Her eyes were chips of ice boring into him. "You're a fool. And now you've put an even bigger target on your back. The infirmary is wasted on you. You're as good as dead."

She turned away, calling Tarek to her side. Javan stumbled down a side corridor that led to the infirmary, her words echoing in his head, a prophecy he didn't know how to avoid.

EIGHTEEN

JAVAN COULDN'T STAY in the infirmary overnight. Not if he wanted to survive to see the dawn.

It wasn't because the physician was nothing more than an old prisoner who'd once sold medicinal herbs to feed herself and her children on the streets of Makan Almalik. It wasn't because the cries of pain and anguish from a few of the other eighteen patients scraped against the fragile hold Javan had over himself until he thought he'd scream just to give the helpless despair that had taken root in him somewhere to go.

No, he couldn't survive in the infirmary because four of Hashim's friends were also patients, though they didn't look to be in bad shape, and judging from the hushed whispers that had drifted Javan's way, he had until the guards locked the infirmary door at twelfth bell before all four came for him.

The old woman had smeared a salve over his wounds and bandaged his arm, though it did little to quell the pain. Every move felt as though there were shards of broken glass beneath his skin.

As the heavy, mournful tone of eleventh bell filled the air, Javan slowly pushed his way off the flimsy cot he'd been resting on since the tournament round ended and got to his feet. He swayed for a moment, darkness swarming his vision, and there was a rustle of sound behind him.

Turning, he saw Hashim's friends rising from their cots too, their eyes locked on him.

Forcing himself to go as quickly as the pain would allow, Javan stepped away from his cot and moved down the aisle that bisected the row of beds. Shadows stretched long fingers down the stone walls from the half dozen torches lit inside iron cages, and Javan nearly stumbled over a prisoner's boots left haphazardly at the end of her cot.

"I'm going back to my cell," he announced to the guards stationed at the door.

One of them glanced between Javan and the swiftly approaching prisoners behind him and said, "Better make sure you're inside your cell by twelfth bell, or you'll be hunted down."

He was already being hunted down. Hashim's friends were closing in as Javan moved back down the corridor toward the arena. Sparks danced at the edge of his vision. He couldn't outrun them up fourteen flights of stairs to his cell, and even if he did, they could just follow him inside. He had no protection until the bars dropped. And he was in no shape to survive a fight with one person, much less four.

There was only one place he could think of where he might find any kind of help, and even that was a long shot. Still, a long shot was better than nothing. At the end of the corridor,

Javan turned away from the stairs that led to level fifteen and headed toward the stalls instead.

They were deserted.

Sending a swift, urgent prayer to Yl' Haliq, Javan scanned the area. Sajda had to be here. Her combat skills and the eerie control she exerted over the other prisoners were the only chance he had. She'd said her debt to him for helping Tarek was paid, but he didn't think she was unfeeling enough to let him die at the hands of the same people who'd tried to hurt the older man.

The wooden chute still hung from the side of the iron wall that separated the stalls from the arena. Blood, fish guts, and scales littered the floor, and a snuffling sound came from one of the few stalls that still housed a creature. But Sajda and Tarek were gone.

The faint whiff of hope that had held Javan together unraveled, and his shoulders sagged.

There was no one to help him. No one who cared. Even Yl' Haliq seemed as distant as the stars. Javan had thought he could stop the impostor. Save his father and his kingdom from Fariq's treachery.

Save himself.

He'd believed Yl' Haliq would deliver him. That the destiny he'd been training for since birth was written in stone.

Instead, he was going to die at the hands of vicious criminals, friendless in the bowels of Maqbara, and no one who mattered to him would know to mourn his passing.

"Go get Hashim," the woman with the neck tattoo said as she and the others flanked Javan. "He'll want to do this himself."

"Do what himself?" A cold, quiet voice drifted from the corridor Javan had just left.

Javan's knees shook as he turned to find Sajda standing at the mouth of the hallway, her dark blue eyes a storm of ice and fury as she stared down the prisoners who surrounded Javan.

Maybe Yl' Haliq had heard his prayer after all.

"This doesn't concern you," the tattooed woman said, though the bravado in her voice trembled. "Unless you've decided to take the pretty boy on as a new pet."

"A pet?" Sajda cocked her head, one eyebrow climbing toward her hairline.

"We know you collect prisoners the rest of us want nothing to do with. Tarek. This boy. That woman Maeli who died in the arena two years ago," the man on Javan's right said. Javan recognized him as Dabir, a prisoner who seemed to worship the ground Hashim walked on.

Something dark flashed across Sajda's expression and was gone before Javan could decide if it was grief or anger.

"Twelfth bell is coming," Sajda said, her voice giving nothing away as she faced the man. She looked unconcerned that he was a handspan taller than Javan and nearly twice as broad, or that his small round eyes bored aggressively into hers. "Dabir, you're still recovering from the last punishment you got for not obeying the guards. Better run along to your cells now, or a beating is the least of your worries."

"Hashim already despises you," Dabir said from Javan's right. "You don't want to make an enemy of him."

Sajda smiled, slow and vicious. "Hashim doesn't want to make an enemy of *me*."

The tattooed woman took a small step back, but then glanced at her friends and held her ground. "There are four of us and only one of you. You might be good in a fight, but you can't take all of us."

Sajda's smile became a baring of teeth. "Fine. If you four can knock me off my feet, you can have the boy."

Javan's stomach clenched. She was strong and fast, and her reflexes were incredible, but the odds of her keeping her feet in a fight against four others weren't good. Certainly not good enough that he wanted to bet his life on it.

Hissing in a sharp breath as a shaft of pain blazed a trail from his fingers to his jaw, he raised his fists.

Dabir laughed. "Looks like Sajda's little pet wants to come to her rescue now." Dabir twisted, and even though Javan saw the blow coming, he couldn't block it. Couldn't get his injured arm to hold steady. The man's fist plowed into Javan's chest, and the prince went down.

He had to get up. Get his hands into position and his feet moving. He had to, but his body moved sluggishly and his limbs were weak.

The man aimed a boot at Javan's face, and then he was gone. Flying through the air and slamming into the iron wall of the stalls several paces away.

Javan looked up to see Sajda, her body a blur of motion as she blocked, feinted, kicked, and spun with swordlike precision. The carvings on her iron bracelets seemed to glow faintly in the fiery light of the sunset from the skylights above.

In moments, it was over. All four of Hashim's friends were crumpled on the floor or limping away, and Sajda was still standing.

Javan shivered as the full weight of her gaze landed on him.

Her eyes were cold and predatory, her body a tightly coiled spring held perfectly still as she hunted for more prey.

He had the uneasy feeling that if he said the wrong thing, he would be the next body she sent into the wall. She blinked, and the predator was gone, replaced once again by icy indifference. Bending forward, she offered him her hand. He took it, and tried not to wince as she pulled him roughly to his feet.

"The warden is in a foul mood tonight," she said, encompassing the other four prisoners with her gaze. "Get to your cells now, or you'll be dead by morning."

Javan looked at the stairs, dread pooling in his stomach. He could barely keep his feet. Climbing fourteen flights of stairs before twelfth bell was going to be nearly impossible.

The other prisoners dragged themselves quickly toward the stairs, and beside him, Sajda sighed.

"Lean on me." She sounded irritated.

"If you're sure—"

"Do you want to die tonight?"

"No."

"Less talking, more walking. Let's go." She wrapped an arm around his waist and took some of his weight as she guided him toward the stairs.

"Thank you," he said quietly as they navigated the steps. "For saving me from them and for helping me now."

She sniffed. "You're just lucky I was still cleaning and storing weapons. Usually I'm already in my room for the night."

"What made you want to help me?"

"I've seen enough death for one day."

They cleared the fifth level and hurried toward the sixth, brushing past other prisoners who were returning to their cells from rec hour. Some of them cast curious looks at the pale girl who was hauling the injured boy up the stairs, but most of the prisoners refused to look at them at all.

The despair that had briefly lifted at Sajda's assistance settled heavily on Javan's shoulders once more.

He had no allies beyond a sweet old man and a girl who barely tolerated his presence and who had duties that didn't include constantly watching over Javan. He'd made powerful enemies, both inside and outside the prison. He'd put up enough tournament points to get a foot in the door, but he was nowhere close to being in a strong position to earn a place in the final round. His back was against the wall, and his survival depended on coming up with a better strategy than just fighting hard enough to win the combat rounds.

He needed help, and there was only one person he could ask.

As Sajda assisted him up the last flight of stairs, twelfth bell began tolling, thick and mournful. The iron bars shuddered and began their slow journey toward the floor.

"Move," Sajda snapped as they reached the corridor.

He made himself walk faster, and ducked beneath the bars of his cell as they reached the halfway point between the ceiling and the floor. The dying rays of the sun lingered over Sajda's skin, a rosy glow at odds with the glare she was aiming his way.

"There. Now you'll at least live to see the morning." She turned to walk away as a guard cleared the stairwell and began to take roll, moving from one cell to another, checking to see that each prisoner was inside, his job made easier by the fact that so many cells on the fifteenth level were currently empty.

"Wait!" Javan called, his stomach in knots as she paused and gave him a raised eyebrow. He didn't know how to convince her.

He had no leverage, no wealth, and no power. Nothing to offer.

He also had nothing to lose.

She'd bought him some time. If he didn't find a different strategy, this night could be his last.

Meeting her eyes, he said quietly, "I need your help."

NINETEEN

THE GUARD ASSIGNED to Javan's side of the fifteenth level approached Javan's cell and gave Sajda a quizzical glance. "You're out a bit late, aren't you?"

"Just making sure all the prisoners who decided to leave the infirmary made it safely to their cells," she said, her voice devoid of all emotion. "The warden is in one of her moods."

The guard's jaw tightened, and he quickly ticked Javan's name off the list he held in his hands. "Better get yourself to your own room, then."

Sajda nodded. "I will."

The guard hurried on, making short work of his checklist, and Javan wrapped his hands around the iron bars of his cell before Sajda could leave.

"Please," he said softly. "I really need your help."

"I just helped you. And since you ignored my advice earlier and made a true enemy of Hashim, I don't see why I even felt compelled to stay late working on the weapons so I could keep an eye on the infirmary."

He studied the irritation on her face and took a gamble. "It's because Tarek asked you to, isn't it?"

"He's sentimental. You protected him, and now he feels loyal to you, even though you've proven to be completely foolish."

"And you feel loyal to him, so here you are." He offered her a smile, but her expression only sharpened. "I think maybe we got off to a bad start. I'd like to be friends."

"I don't have friends." Her voice was flat.

"You have Tarek."

"That happened by accident."

He gave her his best attempt at the kind of charming smile that came so easily to Kellan. "We can pretend this happened by accident too."

"No." Her tone was dismissive as she started to turn away. "And stop smiling like that. It's annoying."

"Wait! Please." He softened his voice as she gave him an icy glare. "It's terribly rude of me to push after you've already said no. I realize that, and if you say no again, I promise this is the last you'll hear of it." Though Yl' Haliq knew he couldn't think of a way to survive Maqbara without her.

She opened her mouth, and he raised his hands in the air, palms out in a gesture of surrender. Of desperation.

"Please. Hear me out. That's all I ask."

She stared him down in silence as the rosy glow of the dying sun dimmed into the purple gray of twilight. Finally, she jerked her chin up a notch. He took that as permission to keep talking.

"I want to trust you with the whole truth," he said.

She rolled her eyes. "The whole truth about what?"

"About me. I have to get out of Maqbara." He fought to sound calm. To keep his voice quiet so that none of the other prisoners could overhear. "My father's life depends on it. Akram itself depends on it."

"Well, you lasted longer than most, I'll give you that." She sounded dismissive. "Most start begging for a way out within hours. And I've yet to hear such dramatic stakes. The fate of Akram itself depends on your release. You have to know how ridiculous that sounds."

He adjusted his position and winced as pain shot across his back. "If you think that sounds ridiculous, then you're really going to have trouble with the next part."

She crossed her arms over her chest and waited.

His voice was a faint breath of sound as he said, "I'm Prince Javan of the house of Kadar, heir to the crown of fire."

The words hung in the air between them, and he couldn't read her expression. He tapped his fingers against the iron bars and willed the anxious energy churning through him to subside. He'd told her the truth. If she didn't believe him, or if she used it against him, he was out of options.

When the silence became more than he could bear, he said, "An impostor who resembles me tried to have me killed. There was a dragon and then assassins and all my belongings were stolen, and the impostor returned to Makan Almalik before I could get here, and my uncle betrayed me and said I wasn't Javan, but I am." He drew in a shaky breath and met her skeptical gaze. "I am. My father hasn't seen me in ten years, so he doesn't realize the boy in the palace isn't me. Or maybe he does, and they're going to kill him. Get him out of the way so the false prince can rule Akram with dishonor, violence, and greed. I have to get out of here so I can stop it."

One slim brow climbed toward her hairline. "Right. Because you're the real prince."

"Yes. You don't have to believe me. I know it sounds impossible. But—"

"Escape is impossible. You belong to the warden now."

"I belong to Yl' Haliq. I belong to Akram. And I can't stay here." He leaned closer to the bars, took one look at her expression, and quickly straightened his spine. "It doesn't matter to you what my reasons are. All that matters is that I need a way out, and you know this prison better than anyone else I've met. Plus no one else is interested in talking to me in case they anger Hashim."

Her lip curled in scorn. "Is this the part where you try to bribe me?"

"This is the part where I offer to pay for your services."

She laughed, but there was no mirth in it. Sweeping her gaze over his prison clothing, she said, "With what? You're no better than any of the other debtors who get tossed in Maqbara and forgotten about."

"I'm the *prince*. Once I'm free—"

"If you got free, you'd shake the dust from this place off your feet and never look back."

He straightened his shoulders, ignoring the bolt of pain the movement caused. "I swear upon my mother's life that I would pay your fee. I am a man of my word. Simply name your price."

She shook her head. "What good is wahda to me?" She swept her arms out wide, the first diamond-bright sheen of starlight catching on the marks carved into her bracelets. "What would it buy me? An extra blanket from the weavers when they come to visit next spring so I can warm myself on terribly cold nights? A nice cut of meat from the butcher so I can enjoy its flavor while I eat an animal that knew more of the outside world than I do? Or maybe I can bribe the more violent prisoners to stay away from me for one more miserable day. Tell me, O prince of Akram, which of those fine items should I buy with your coin?"

He'd miscalculated. Badly. And if he didn't find a way to salvage the situation quickly, his best hope to stop the impostor and rescue his father—his kingdom—would be lost.

He would be lost.

"You're right," he said quietly, before she could turn away and leave him alone, teetering on the brink of despair. "I'm sorry. I'm desperate."

"Everyone in here is desperate." Her voice trembled a little, though the stoniness of her gaze was unwavering.

Everyone here was desperate. Everyone.

Including her.

"What do you need?" he asked.

She drew back, eyes narrowed. "What do you mean?"

"You don't need coin. You care nothing for the promises of a prince. But you're right—everyone in here is desperate." He caught himself leaning toward the bars again and stopped. "I have to stop the impostor who wants to take the throne of Akram by killing anyone who stands in his way. That means I need a way out of here. And that means I need you. But it has to be worth it to you to help me."

"And it isn't."

"It could be." Yl' Haliq be merciful, it had to be worth it to her. Javan was out of other ideas. His voice shook as he said, "A fair trade. You show me how to escape—"

"There is no escape." She ran her fingers over the bracelet on her left arm. "Do you think I'd still be here if there was?"

"There has to be *something*." His voice rose, and he clenched his fists against the futile spark of anger in his chest. It wasn't her fault he was trapped in Maqbara, surrounded by enemies. Wasn't her fault the kingdom Javan had dedicated his life to was in terrible danger. He took a deep breath and sent a silent prayer to Yl' Haliq for help.

She cocked her head to study him, and something in her expression told him he'd been found wanting. "There are only two ways to get out of Maqbara before your sentence is up. Overpower the warden—"

"We could do that if—"

"Which is impossible. Or—"

"Nothing is impossible." He hoped.

"Says the boy who thought he was supposed to rule a kingdom, but whose god allowed him to be thrown into prison instead."

He absorbed her words and tried to ignore the ache of doubt that fed on them. Pushing against the heavy sense of despair that wanted to shroud him in stone, he said, "And the second way out?"

That eyebrow climbed toward her hairline again. "Win the tournament and for your boon, ask for immediate release."

He closed his eyes, and swallowed past the sudden lump in his throat. It all came down to that cursed tournament. To surviving the days between combat, though he had enemies throughout the prison and guards who wouldn't lift a finger to help. To gaining enough points in the combat rounds to win while watching his back every second so that no one drove a sword through it.

That strategy had already failed him, and she was telling him there was no other way. Slowly, he opened his eyes to find her watching him, a tiny frown etched into the space between her eyes as if he was a puzzle she was trying to solve.

A puzzle.

He scrubbed a hand over his face. All puzzles had a correct solution, but often there were multiple paths to the same outcome. He'd tried one path, and it hadn't worked. Maybe she could help him forge another.

"If there's no other way out of Maqbara, then I have to win the tournament, but that's going to be hard after today."

She sniffed.

"I have to survive between combat rounds. And I can't fight the beasts and also watch for Hashim and his friends. I need allies. I need leverage. And I need a plan."

She looked annoyed. "I gave you a plan, and what did you do? You ignored it and nearly got yourself killed in the arena for your trouble."

"I ignored it because I learned that if I win the tournament, I get an audience with my father. And I didn't get myself killed."

"Nearly."

"Nearly isn't the same as dead. I can do this. I just need a better plan."

She remained quiet.

"Sajda, I have to win. And clearly, I need help understanding the power structure inside the prison and which prisoners might turn into allies." He met her gaze. "I need you. Please tell me what I can do for you to earn your help."

She stared at him in silence, but the stoniness of her gaze softened into something faraway and troubled.

"What do you need?" he asked softly.

There was a long silence, and then in a whisper he had to strain to catch she said, "Freedom."

"I know you won't believe me, but I can promise that after I'm released, I'll come back and free you." Please let her believe him. He had nothing else to offer.

Her gaze snapped back into the present, and her full lips twisted as though she'd sucked on something bitter. "And then what? I go out into the world and pretend I know how to live there? No thanks."

There was something dark beneath her words. Something that struck a chord in the grief that lived within him. He sifted through her words, hunting for the thing she wasn't saying.

She wanted freedom. That was clear, though he thought she already regretted admitting it. But she was afraid. Afraid of the world outside the prison, because she'd known nothing else since she was five.

Sold as a child. Raised in a prison that ran on violence and bloodshed. It was all she knew. No wonder she was afraid of the one thing she desperately wanted. She knew how to survive in the darkness, but was terrified she'd be lost in the light.

"I can teach you," he said, fragile tendrils of hope threading though his despair.

She folded her arms over her chest. "Teach me what?"

"Anything. Everything. The history of the kingdoms. Tactical military strategy. Applied mathematics. Court customs and manners. Alchemy. The path of the stars."

Her eyes lit up. "You understand the stars?"

"I do." His breath caught in his chest at the way her face glowed when she was unguarded.

They watched each other in silence while far below the sound of the door that led to the magistrate's office slammed shut behind the last guard.

Finally, she said quietly, "We have a deal. But you have to listen to my advice this time. And you have to give me my first lesson within the next three weeks."

"Yes. Anything. That's . . . Thank you. Truly." He paused. "Wait . . . what happens in three weeks?"

"The next tournament round. It's going to take us a while to procure the next group of beasts and get the arena set up. I want to learn about the stars first. In case nearly dead turns into actually dead."

"I do love your optimism," he said, his voice shaky at the edges as relief swept through him. "Thank you."

"Tarek will bring you meals so you can avoid Hashim in the kitchen. He and his friends are on level five and are separated from you during chore and practice hours, so don't stray from where you're supposed to be unless I personally come to get you. We'll see if we can figure out at least four other competitors who can be bribed into liking you enough to be your allies during rec hour and in the arena."

He opened his mouth to thank her again, but she was already walking away.

Holding on to fragile strands of hope that felt as tenuous as a rope made of water, he crawled into bed and prayed until sleep claimed him.

TWENTY

THE PRISON HAD long since fallen silent when Sajda crept from her room, closing the door quietly behind her.

Her body trembled with fatigue, but she couldn't bear to sleep yet. The remains of the creatures from the day's combat had been skinned, chopped, and turned into meals for either the remaining beasts or the prisoners. New monsters had been commissioned from the bounty hunters on Llorenyae. She'd scrubbed some of the arena floor and dragged the bodies of those who'd died to the center of the arena for the warden to deal with in the morning. And of course she'd lost her mind and defended Javan and then agreed to help him gain allies.

She wasn't sure she'd made a good decision. She'd spent the last two years ignoring Hashim's speculative gaze and disgusting suggestions. Shrugging off his questions about why the warden made her wear cuffs. Keeping him in line through an occasional show of power and the composure she borrowed from the prison's stone. She didn't need him to decide she was his enemy.

His eyes already lingered on the runes carved into her iron cuffs. Some days he stared so hard at her while the magic was stinging her blood that she feared the power trapped within her was branded on her skin. She'd met prisoners like him before, and it always ended the same. A confrontation far away from the guards and the warden. A show of dominance and aggression that required her to call on her elven speed and strength just to survive.

She'd endured it all. Years and years of whispers and stares. Of offers and threats. Of violence spilling over, outside the arena.

She'd survived.

And she'd keep on surviving until she could learn how to survive in the outside world too. How to get the cuffs off.

How to escape, not just Maqbara but any hint of the slave she'd been.

Her boots didn't make a sound against the stone floor of level five as she crept past the cells, circling the arena below until she came to the staircase that was nearly opposite her little room. Moonlight drifted in through the skylights above and gleamed against the iron bars of the cells. Sliding into the narrow staircase, Sajda listened carefully.

The quiet snores of prisoners. The faint whisper of the desert wind scouring the ground far above her. But no footsteps. No warden hunting for a prisoner who'd failed to return to his or her cell at twelfth bell.

Satisfied that she was alone, Sajda climbed the steps, pausing at the landing on each level to listen for footsteps. When she reached level fifteen, she turned left and moved silently down the line of cells, many of which stood empty, waiting for new prisoners to be swallowed by the dark depths of the prison. She paused briefly beside Javan's cell, though he was nothing but a dim outline beneath the blanket on his bed, before moving on. The aristocrat who claimed to be the true prince might be able to help her learn how to survive outside Maqbara, but his belief that she could somehow help him survive the next three rounds of competition was optimistic bordering on foolish. Maqbara crushed the innocent and the good. He'd be no different.

Still, she hadn't turned him down. Even though it meant declaring war with Hashim. Tarek was the closest thing to family she had, and he rarely asked her for anything. She hadn't had the heart to tell him the pretty aristocrat with the earnest sense of honor and duty was beyond saving.

At the opposite end of the landing, she came to a small supply closet whose door stood permanently ajar, one broken hinge hanging askew. A few empty buckets, a mop, and several dusty chests filled with old bedding lined one wall. The ceiling had a deep crack running across it, a fissure just a few handspans wider than Sajda's waist. The walls were stained with water that had leaked into the prison during the last monsoon season, and small eddies of dirt covered the floor.

Sajda entered the room and dragged the door as close to shut as it would go. Then she pulled one of the chests into the center of the floor, careful to move slowly to avoid the scrape of wood sliding over stone. Another long minute of listening to be sure no one was coming to discover her, and then she climbed onto the top of the chest, crouched, and leaped for the crack in the ceiling.

Grabbing the edges of the crack, she swung her body up and through, keeping her head low to avoid banging it on the enormous support beam that helped keep the city above from crashing into the prison below. The first time she'd tried crawling into the ceiling, she'd been nine, and even with her magic giving her strength, she'd had to stack two chests on top of each other to make the leap possible. She'd been so sure she could find a way out of Maqbara and into the world above if she followed the support beams long enough. If she explored hard enough.

She hadn't found a way out.

But she'd found something almost as good, and it had sustained her through hundreds of lonely nights.

Crawling out from under the support beam, Sajda half stood half crouched to avoid hitting her head and began moving swiftly toward the far corner of the prison. Dipping her hand into her pocket, she took out the rock fragments from the morning's tunnel excavation and let them fall to the floor where they'd never be noticed. The darkness here in the upper recesses of the prison was impossible for a human to navigate without a torch.

But Sajda wasn't a full-blooded human, and her eyes found gradients within the darkness. Shadows that were a faint shade darker than the air around them showed her where the vertical support beams stood. The beams across the ceiling were solid black stripes against a lighter canvas of the same black. She moved quickly, avoiding pillars and ducking low when necessary, until she reached the corner farthest from the supply closet.

Here, the darkness was bathed in the silvery sheen of the stars that shone through a skylight—the only one outside those that were placed above the corridors and the arena. Sajda wondered if the original plan for the prison had included a larger building. Or maybe skylights over the staircases. Whatever had happened, she was grateful for this abandoned window to the heavens.

The light illuminated the corner, spreading out to nearly the size of Sajda's room. She'd brought blankets and pillows years ago to create a tiny oasis of comfort for herself. Crawling onto the neatly layered blankets, she eased her head back against a pillow and stared at the blue-black sky above her.

The stars were scattered across its surface like handfuls of silver-white jewels. Sajda searched the velvet sky, finding the patterns of the stars that were visiting her at this hour of the night. There was the trio of brilliantly glowing jewels lined up in a row like a drawn sword.

She traced her eyes over the dusting of stars that spread out from the trio and imagined it was shards of broken glass. The remnants of a cage the sword had destroyed. Farther to the right, seven medium-size stars could be a person fleeing if she connected the dots.

She liked to think it was the warden, and that if she could just concentrate hard enough, the trio would become the weapon she needed to destroy the cuffs and leave Maqbara forever.

The group of stars seemed to grow brighter, their silvery glow rushing down from the heavens to linger on her skin. Her magic stirred, an impossible hunger that scraped at her skin until she thought she'd go mad from the want of it.

Lifting her hands, she reached for the starlight, tangling her fingers in the glow and letting her magic absorb the power—cold and unbearably distant. It sank into her, a beauty that tore something inside until tears slipped down her face and her breathing came in ragged bursts.

It was homesickness, though the stars weren't her home.

It was a sense of deep connection, though the stars were unknowable.

It was the closest thing to freedom she could find.

Turning from the trio, she searched until she found her favorite. A tiny prick of light at the far edge of the sky she could see. The star was more blue than silver, and it didn't rotate through the sky the same way the others did. Sajda thought maybe it was another land full of people. What would it be like, living so far from this kingdom of blood and broken promises? If she could get to the tiny blue star, would Akram glow in the distance? Or would it disappear and take all her heartache with it?

Would the faint memory of her mother's face as she told Sajda to be good and show off her ears so someone would offer a generous sum fall into the endless darkness of the night sky, never to haunt her again? Would the taste of fear, chalky and bitter, leave her mouth forever?

Maybe on the tiny blue star, mothers didn't sell their little girls. Maybe dark elves weren't feared by good people and used by bad. Maybe there, she would be loved.

Slowly lowering her hands, she stared at her fingers. At the silvery sheen that seemed to glow from within her. Her wrists ached beneath her cuffs, but she didn't care. She was home when her magic consumed the starlight, and that was worth any pain she had to endure.

She lay on the blanket for an hour, watching the silver-white jewels slowly spin past her skylight. Letting the glow tangle with her magic and wound her with its cold perfection. Feeling the icy, untouchable essence of the stars fill her and lend her the strength to eventually make her way back to the supply closet. Back to the staircase. And back to her little room on the fifth level.

One day, she'd break the cuffs and get out of Maqbara. And when she did, she would find someplace far from people who could hurt her. Someplace under a vast, unknowable sky. And she would be home.

TWENTY-ONE

THE DAY AFTER the combat round in the arena, Javan skipped kneeling for morning prayers. He figured Yl' Haliq, the all-knowing, understood how stiff he was. How every move ignited a bone-deep ache that throbbed throughout his entire body.

Instead, he lay on his bed staring at the stone ceiling above him, waiting for first bell and praying his doubt into words as the sacred texts instructed.

"Yl' Haliq, be merciful on your servant," he whispered. "For I am . . . I feel so alone. Don't you see that? I'm trapped in prison, my uncle has betrayed me, and my only hope is a girl who barely tolerates me." His throat closed, and he blinked rapidly as tears burned his eyes. "Have you abandoned me?"

He closed his eyes and tried to quell the seething doubts. The fire of his anger. Tried to make room for the soft, still voice of Yl' Haliq. "Please. I'm supposed to rule Akram. I'm supposed to protect my kingdom. I can't do that here."

There was no reply, but Javan's heart started beating faster.

An awareness spread through him, tingling down his spine and gathering in his chest like joy and heartbreak and hope all twined together.

"Are you there?" he whispered. "Will you please send your faithful servant a sign? Let me know that I'm not alone. That this is part of your plan for my life."

He fell silent, and in the quiet heard the soft rub of a boot against the stone corridor outside his room. His eyes flew open, and Sajda stood just outside his cell, a chunk of buttered bread and an apple in her hand. The iron bars creaked and groaned as it slowly rose into the ceiling while first bell began tolling.

"Who were you talking to?" She peered around his cell as if he might have someone hidden beneath his bed or behind his privy bucket.

"I was praying." He pulled a tunic over his head, wincing as he pushed his injured arm through the sleeve. The pain was a dull throb today—much better than the sharp knife of agony he'd felt the day before. He decided the more he moved it, the better. He couldn't afford to be too stiff to fight if any of the prisoners decided to come for him. "How much did you hear?"

There was a flash of compassion on her face, gone so fast he almost missed it. "Not much. Here's your breakfast."

"Tarek sent you, did he?"

"He was running behind this morning, so I came on my own." She sounded grumpy.

He got to his feet, brushed his hair away from his face, and accepted the apple. "Thank you. Does this make us friends?"

"Maybe." She frowned at him.

"Your overwhelming enthusiasm is making me uncomfortable," he said dryly.

She grinned, a quick flash of white teeth and sparkling eyes, and it was as if someone had sucked all the air out of the room.

She was beautiful. He'd known that, of course. He'd have to be an idiot to miss it. But it was usually an icy, dangerous kind of beauty that felt more like a warning than a welcome.

He wasn't sure he was ready to see more welcome from her. Not when he was still staring at her face as if he'd never seen it before. Not when the casual words he'd been ready to say had turned to dust in his mouth.

This was ridiculous. He'd been living in close quarters with girls since he was seven. There had been a few who made his heart beat a little faster when they looked his way. He was used to appreciating a girl's smile.

But this.

This was sunshine pouring through a crack in a sheet of ice.

This was starlight dazzling against a snowy hillside.

This was trouble.

And he didn't need trouble. He needed her help. He needed her friendship. And then he needed to leave Maqbara, and everyone in it, behind.

Her smile disappeared, and she cocked her head to study him. "You look a little unsteady."

She had no idea.

"I'm still recovering from the arena."

She nodded. "Best way to recover is to move your muscles. You can get some practice in with the weapons while the others eat breakfast, and we'll talk about which of the remaining competitors might make good allies. You can start figuring out the best approach to them during rec time tonight."

"I can start on it sooner than that."

She shook her head. "You have one hour of chore time and one hour of sparring practice. Besides meals, those are the only times you'll be allowed out of your cell unless you've bribed the guards on your level. And you have nothing to bribe them with. Come on."

He bit into his apple and followed her from his cell.

The arena was a mess. Seven human corpses were laid out in a neat row on the stone floor in the center of the ring. The ring itself was still damp, though the water had been drained after the aristocracy left. The ground was littered with scales, blood, and bones. The smell—a sharp briny scent with the cloying sweetness of decay beneath it—nearly caused Javan to lose his breakfast.

"That's quite a stench," he said as they joined Tarek at the stalls. He'd already fed half the remaining land beasts.

"Enough to make your eyes water," Tarek agreed. "But it'll be gone soon enough once the warden does her thing."

Javan frowned. "Her thing?"

"Meat," the warden's voice said from behind them. Javan whirled to find her standing beside the human bodies.

She hadn't been there a moment ago. Was her office that close? Or did she just move really fast? He scanned the arena but then movement caught his eye. Turning back to the warden, Javan's stomach pitched as he watched her skin ripple. Her bones began expanding, her skin hardening. She disrobed quickly, even as her shoulders doubled in size and talons sprouted from her fingertips.

"What am I seeing?" Javan demanded, his voice shaking. "What is this?"

The warden's skin darkened, small patterns becoming visible

as she hunched over, smoke pouring from her nose. Javan's pulse raced, and a slick sense of foreboding filled him.

"Shape-shifter," Tarek answered, but Javan could already see it. Black leathery wings sprouted from her shoulder blades, and her skin became dull black scales with gray accents. The decay-scented air clogged in Javan's throat as foreboding became truth.

She was a Draconi.

A gray dragon with an injured eye.

She was the creature who still haunted his nightmares.

Horror filled him, followed instantly by rage as she slowly tripled in size, her bones expanding, her muscles filling out until he was looking at the dragon who'd tried to kill him in Loch Talam.

He reached for his sword before remembering that he no longer had one. "Give me a weapon."

Tarek sounded panicked. "Son, you don't—"

"A weapon!" Javan turned to Tarek, his body flushed with the heat of his fury. This was the creature who'd started his nightmare. He'd taken her eye defending himself against her attack.

Now he wanted her life.

When Tarek didn't move, Javan rushed past him to scour the stalls, hunting for anything he could use. The only thing he found was the metal pole that had been used to stabilize the chute from the previous day's competition.

It would have to do.

He turned, and Sajda was there, blocking his way.

"Step aside."

"What do you think you're doing?" she asked, her usually calm voice fraying.

"Killing a monster."

"With a pole?"

"It's all I could find. Step aside, Sajda. She deserves this."

She slapped a hand on his chest, and something that felt like a thrill of prickling heat licked over his skin. "She deserves to be actually killed. Not irritated by a boy with a metal pole."

"I already took her eye. I bet I can take something else she values before she turns on me." Rage was a fever in his blood. A voice screaming that somehow she was the root of all of his problems. She'd been the first thing to go wrong. If he fixed that—if he took from her the life she'd tried to take from him—somehow it would turn everything around.

"What do you mean you took her eye?"

"She attacked me in her dragon form while I was at the academy in Loch Talam. I injured her eye while defending myself, and she flew south. I never thought I'd see her again, but here she is, and this time I'm taking more than her eye."

Sajda wrapped her other hand around the pole and held it still even as he tried to pull it toward him. "You aren't thinking clearly. She saw you compete yesterday. If she wanted you dead, she'd have killed you already. If you attack her, she'll burn you alive, and then who will save Akram from the impostor?"

That got his attention. Looking away from the dragon, he met Sajda's eyes and said, "I thought you didn't believe me."

"It doesn't matter what I believe. It's what you believe." Her voice was low and urgent and very un-Sajda-like. "Do you have a responsibility to the people of Akram?"

"Yes." He ground the word out between clenched teeth.

"Then maybe you should stay alive long enough to fulfill it."

He met her eyes for a long moment, his pulse beating rapidly, his muscles clenched and ready for battle before finally saying,

"It's annoying when you're right."

"You'll get used to it." She took the pole from his hands and slowly removed her hand from his chest. The strange, prickling heat left him as soon as she stopped touching him.

What was wrong with him? First he was knocked off his feet by a single genuine smile from her. Then he was feeling flushed just because she touched him. He needed to stop letting the girl who barely tolerated his presence distract him.

The dragon roared, and Javan stared in horror as she swept the line of bodies with fire. The smell of cooking flesh filled the air, and Javan gagged.

"You never get used to it," Tarek said quietly from a few paces away.

"Why is she doing that?" Javan asked, his fists still clenched like he thought he could beat the dragon into submission.

"They're meat," Sajda said. "If I were you, I'd stick to eating bread and fruit for the next week."

He gagged, caught himself, and then gagged again. When he could trust himself to speak, he glared at Sajda and said, "Is that what you meant when you said I was meat?"

"In my defense, I really did think you'd die in your first round."

He walked away. Away from Sajda's casual acceptance of the violence that surrounded them. Away from the warden as she moved down the line incinerating one body after another.

This was a brutish, barbaric place. Did his father know what went on down here? How could he allow debtors to be tossed into the combat ring with violent criminals? Where was the honor in that? Or was Fariq behind all of it, and the king was somehow kept ignorant?

Leaving the arena behind, he entered the corridor that ran beneath the eastern edge of level one. The unspent fury he'd felt for the warden still tumbled through him, a nervous, jagged kind of energy that made him want to ball up his fist and send it into the wall.

"You're upset." Sajda spoke beside him, and he nearly punched her as he jerked around in surprise.

"Don't sneak up on me like that."

"If you hit me, I'd hit you back, and we both know how well that turned out for you last time." She sounded smug.

"I was trying not to hurt you."

"Oh really? Does that mean you think if you were trying to hurt me, you'd actually beat me in a sparring match?" There was a challenge in her voice.

He matched it with one of his own. "Did you see me in the arena yesterday?"

She snorted. "Rescuing a stranger."

"Killing the top predator."

"Getting jumped by Hashim and his friends."

"Gaining enough points in a single round to put myself above quite a few of the competitors."

"You got lucky," she said, and he rounded on her.

"Or maybe you got lucky when you landed that punch. Care to take another shot?"

Her fist plowed into his stomach before even saw her throw the punch. He doubled over wheezing, pain spiking as his injuries protested. "What the . . . you don't just start a sparring match out of nowhere. You're supposed to shake hands and—"

"There aren't rules for sparring matches, Prince."

"There most certainly are. I think you broke my ribs." He

stayed hunched over and waited.

She paused and then leaned down. "I should've held back. I'm sorry."

"I'm not." He grabbed her left arm and spun her to face the wall. When she brought her foot up to kick him, he hooked his leg beneath hers and tried to knock her off-balance.

She recovered much faster than was strictly fair.

Who had trained her? Had there been a prisoner with extensive combat experience who'd taken an interest in a little girl?

She lunged for the wall, pressed her hands against it, and snapped a double-legged kick in his direction.

He was already ducking and moving, though it hurt to do so. She spun to face him, and landed a glancing blow, but he was figuring her out now. She moved so fast, she relied on her speed to get her in and out of range before he could react. If he kept moving, kept breaking pattern, it threw her off. And when she was off-balance he had a second to react. To tap her shoulder. Nudge her kneecap. Nothing to hurt her, but enough to let her know that the point was his.

When that worked three times in a row, she stopped and glared at him.

"What? Do you need me to stand still so you can punch me?" He was wearing a ridiculous grin on his face. He could feel it stretching his lips too wide, but he couldn't seem to stop.

"Says the boy who still hasn't hit me."

"I'm not interested in hitting you. And according to the rules of engagement, I've now scored three points in a row."

"Points?" She looked at him like he'd gone mad. "Who tallies points when they fight?"

"It's . . . like a game."

"A game?"

"Yes. A game where the person who gets the touch gets the point. The first person to the predetermined amount of points wins."

"I don't usually like games, but I'll make an exception for this one." She gave him a sly smile. "Are you still mad?"

He went still. The anger was still there, but it was banked. A pile of embers steadily glowing instead of a fire raging out of control. The vicious, violent energy that had careened through him had steadied. And the loneliness that had filled him when he'd awakened that morning had lost some of its sting.

He was thinking clearly again.

And she'd given him that on purpose.

"You picked a fight with me to get me to calm down?" He frowned.

"It worked, didn't it?" The challenge was back in her voice.

"Yes." He almost didn't want to ask, but the question was already leaving his lips. "Why did you do it?"

"Because you needed it," she said. "And if I have to be friends with you, then I should get to punch you now and then. Did you give me a point for that? Because I deserved about five."

"You don't get five points for one touch."

"You do when that one touch nearly breaks someone's ribs. Now get back to the arena for your level's chore hour before the guards decide to beat you into submission."

TWENTY-TWO

RAHIM KNOCKED ON the door of the king's chambers and waited. In his hands he held a stack of parchment—orders for the king to sign, correspondence to reply to, and various details that needed his attention. Some of them had been given to Rahim by Fariq with strict instructions to make sure the king signed everything without looking too closely at the contents. One of the pieces of parchment Rahim himself had written in the solitary confines of the small office that was attached to his receiving room, far from the prying eyes of Fariq or any of the palace staff.

He was going to make very sure the king took notice of that sheet.

The door swung open, and Abbas, the head of the palace guard, slowly backed away to allow Rahim entrance. Rahim wasn't sure why the head of the entire guard felt it necessary to personally stay so close to the king, but he was tired of the man watching his every move. He was the prince. Once he took the crown, Abbas would either treat him as a member of the royal family he'd taken an oath to guard, or he would be removed from his post.

He found the king ensconced in pillows on a couch that faced the same lemon grove Rahim could see from his receiving room. A thick woven blanket covered the older man's legs. Several guards were stationed throughout the room—far more than attended either Rahim or Fariq. The king waved his guards out of the room when he saw Rahim approach.

"Javan!" The king smiled and reached a trembling hand toward Rahim. "I do enjoy our daily visits."

Rahim smiled. "As do I, Father. I'm afraid today I'm being used as a messenger by the palace steward, the magistrate's office, and Uncle Fariq." He waved the sheaf of parchment in the air as proof. "Apparently your signature is required on a number of things that you already discussed with them in previous meetings this week."

The king eyed the parchment and then struggled to sit up. "I recall the meeting with the steward and the magistrate, but I haven't spoken to Fariq about anything of importance in quite some time."

Rahim's heart raced. "Really? Well, perhaps I misinterpreted his words."

"Perhaps." The king frowned as he pushed the blanket to the floor and stood on shaking legs. Rahim quickly wrapped an arm around the king's frail waist and helped him walk to the massive ebony desk that rested against the far wall. Carvings of falcons and vines decorated the edges, and its surface gleamed with polish.

The king noticed Rahim admiring the desk and said, "It was a gift from Queen Lorelai of Ravenspire two years ago after she assumed the crown. I moved my old desk into your mother's library. I remember how much you loved to sit at it and pretend to use your little ring to seal letters to her."

Rahim gave the king the warm, slightly sad smile he'd adopted for any conversation that brought up the late queen and then gently steered the king into the chair. "I'll have to go see it again for myself one day soon."

"You'll need to see her grave as well." The king's voice sharpened. "I'm surprised that you didn't do so immediately."

Rahim closed his eyes to hide his annoyance and tried to look stricken. "I'm sorry, Father. It's just that I've been gone so long. And now I see her around every corner, and it's like losing her all over again. I'm not ready to . . . I just need more time."

The king's shaking hand patted Rahim's cheek. "Of course, Son. I should have realized that it would all feel very fresh to you. You haven't had time to make new memories here. Perhaps you could take Malik for a walk around the grounds as you used to. He never gets enough exercise anymore."

Rahim would rather drive a sword through his own foot than go anywhere near that vicious leopard, but he simply nodded and then turned to the parchment. Swiftly separating them into three stacks, he pulled the king's quill and ink pot forward and lit a candle beneath the wax warmer.

"What is this? Magistrate's?" the king asked as his trembling fingers sent one pile of parchment spilling across the desk.

Rahim gathered up the sheets, careful to keep the four that Fariq had slipped into the pile hidden in the middle. "Yes, these are the orders you discussed with the magistrate two days ago. All they need is a signature and a seal. Would you like me to do the seals for you?"

"That would be helpful," the king said as he glanced over the parchment before scrawling his shaky signature across the bottom and handing it to Rahim.

"I'll need your ring, Father."

The king laughed a little as he slid the royal signet ring off his finger and dropped it in Rahim's waiting palm. "Soon enough you'll be the one wearing this."

Something flashed across the king's face as he watched Rahim, waiting for a reply, but Rahim was a fast learner. His first suggestion that they schedule a quick coronation had upset the king. He was ready to try a different approach.

"I'll wear the ring and assume the heavy burden of ruling only when you deem me ready, Father."

The king beamed with pride. "That's my boy."

The older man worked quickly through the magistrate's stack, but Rahim's stomach dropped as the king took the time to glance over each page before signing. If he read the orders Fariq had included, he'd launch an investigation into where the sheets had come from and who was out to destroy the most loyal families in the kingdom.

Rahim couldn't have that.

His mind raced as he glanced around the room, hoping to be struck with inspiration. What he needed was a distraction. Something that could hold the king's full attention. His gaze landed on the window and the glossy green leaves of the lemon grove that spread across the hill beyond it.

As the king slid another page to Rahim to be sealed with wax, revealing the first of the four orders from Fariq, Rahim said, "Have you been out to the lemon grove lately?"

The king looked at the window. "Not for years. Not since . . .

well, you know it was your mother's favorite place."

Yes, Fariq had mentioned that to Rahim in his detailed descriptions of palace life while Javan was a boy. Resting his hand on the king's shoulder, Rahim said, "I haven't been there either. Would you like to go with me?"

Hope flared in the king's eyes, and his smile was warm. "I'm not much for walking long distances now, but perhaps just to sit. I'd love to hear about your time at the academy." He paused, a frown digging into his forehead. "Have we talked about it yet? I sometimes forget things now."

"The academy?" Rahim asked, holding the king's gaze. "Just a bit."

"Did you do it? Did you honor her *muqaddas tus'el?*"

Rahim froze, working hard to keep his expression neutral. Fariq hadn't told him a thing about the queen charging Javan with a sacred dying wish. He was going to have to bluff and hope the king bought it. "Yes, Father. You know I did."

The king's frown deepened. "I do?"

"We discussed this when I first came home." Rahim gave the king a gentle smile, tinged with just enough pity to have the older man straightening his back and nodding sharply.

"Of course we did. That would've been the first thing you wanted to show me. We can take the sash out to her grave when you're ready."

Rahim squeezed the king's shoulder gently while he frantically inventoried the items taken from Javan's room at Milisatria. He couldn't remember a sash, but maybe Fariq would know what the king meant.

"That sounds fine, but let's take that walk in the lemon grove first. Shall we hurry through these so that we can enjoy the light before it's time for afternoon meetings?"

The king's eyes were teary as he turned back to the parchment and quickly signed the rest of the pile. The orders waiting from the castle steward were handled just as promptly, but when the king reached for the last sheet, the one Rahim had filled out himself not an hour ago, the boy said quietly, "That was the one Uncle gave me. I forgot that he wanted it placed in the middle of the pile, but I'm sure it doesn't matter."

It was about as unsubtle as Rahim could be, but it worked. The king was already frowning. Already pulling the parchment close to carefully read every word. His lips pressed together in a tight line, and there was cold anger in his eyes when he finished.

"When did Fariq give this to you?" The king's voice was deadly calm.

"This morning. You seem upset. Have I done something wrong?"

"Did you read this?"

Rahim let a bite of indignation enter his voice. "No. Those weren't mine to read."

"No, of course, my son. Forgive me. I keep hoping to see the best in my cousin, but time and again, he shows me only his worst."

Rahim frowned, though inside his heart was racing. This was it. He'd hedged his bets, banking on the king's distrust of Fariq to put Rahim one step closer to becoming Akram's ruler. If Fariq learned of his deception, he would try to kill Rahim. If the king learned Rahim's identity, he'd order his death as well.

But if both trusted Rahim implicitly and sought only to destroy each other, no matter the outcome, Rahim would be the winner.

"What has he done?" Rahim asked, keeping his hand on the king's shoulder.

"This is an edict proclaiming Fariq to be the regent, to rule in my place due to my failing health." The king's voice shook with anger. "Not only is he trying to supplant me, but in doing this, he is also trying to supplant you."

"But why?" Rahim did his best to sound distressed.

"Because he is greedy for power and angry that Yl' Haliq has seen fit to deny it to him." The king turned to Rahim. "Listen to me now. Fariq has friends within the palace and without. We cannot know who is with him in this plan. You must not tell anyone about this. We have to proceed with speed and caution. I wasn't willing to take this step yet, because it seemed like Fariq was pushing me toward it, but now I wonder if he was pushing me because he knew that would make me resist doing the one thing that can put the crown out of his reach."

"What are we going to do?" Rahim asked as triumph, bold and bright, spread through him.

"We will hold your coronation."

TWENTY-THREE

IT HAD BEEN almost two weeks since the last combat round, and Sajda still didn't know what to do about Javan.

He was surviving, a fact that shouldn't have made her feel anything one way or the other, but which somehow made her glad. He'd kept to the rules she'd outlined for him—eating in his cell with her or Tarek, staying close to the other prisoners on the fifteenth level during chore and arena practice hours since Hashim and the rest of level five had a different schedule, and staying in plain view of the doorway during rec hour so she could keep an eye on him from the hallway in case Hashim decided to pick a fight while all the prisoners were in a room together. Occasionally she was able to get him out of his cell between his sparring hour and the bell that heralded the prisoners' recreation time, but she'd had to invent excuses that wouldn't raise anyone's suspicions and get back to the warden. She'd told the guards that Javan had been given extra cleaning duties, and to make her story sound legitimate, she'd included several others from the fifteenth level as well. They'd scrubbed the arena until it glowed, polished the seats, and wiped the walls; and when they were finished, she had them start over again. Anything to keep an eye on Javan during the hours when Hashim might be able to bribe a guard to let him leave his cell.

He'd had to mingle with the other prisoners during recreation time—it would be hard to make allies otherwise, and he desperately needed those for his next stint in the arena—but Sajda had remained vigilant just outside the recreation room with the guards, her expression daring Hashim to give her a reason to punish him. Hashim had glared right back, and Sajda's magic stung her veins at the memory.

He wouldn't take her interference much longer. Either he'd confront her directly, or he'd do his best to kill Javan in the next combat round.

Worry chased her thoughts during the day and kept her up at night. Her bargain with Javan was a sword held over their heads by a fraying thread. One wrong move, and he could die. One mistake, and the warden could get suspicious and decide to expose Sajda. She couldn't even coach him on the beasts he would face in the next round, because for the first time in the tournament's history, she had no idea which creatures would go into the arena. It was supposed to be a combat round against beasts of the air, but the warden had canceled her shipment from Llorenyae and simply told Sajda she should order plenty of sand.

Instead, Sajda had coached Javan on which prisoners might make potential allies and had tried to hold up her end of the bargain by sparring with him during his arena practice. She thought it strange that he insisted on making it into a game where a simple touch counted as a point, and no one was supposed to use their full strength, but there was no accounting for the ways of aristocrats.

She'd done what she could, but she had the terrible feeling that disaster was careening toward them. She ought to walk away. Protect herself. Focus on surviving.

But he was kind, even when she wasn't. He made her laugh. He listened to her as though her words mattered. He treated her as if she was something far better than a slave, and every time he smiled at her, something warm swirled through her veins like a new kind of magic.

It was strangely exhilarating until this morning when she woke before dawn and realized that the odd, fluttery feeling in the pit of her stomach wasn't hunger.

At least not hunger for food.

Somehow, he'd become someone she wanted to be with each day, and it was terrifying. She wanted to back away. Cut him off at the knees before he had the chance to do the same to her. Before the thread holding the sword over their heads snapped.

But even as she considered what she would say to leave him friendless in Maqbara once again, something dark and aching opened up within her, and the words refused to pass her lips.

What was she going to do when he found out what she really was? When he turned on her and saw the monster instead of the girl?

The only good elf was a dead elf.

Maybe it was better to just show him the truth herself. At least then, he'd be walking away because she'd given him a push.

"Where are you?" Javan asked beside her, and she jumped.

"I'm standing right here in the middle of the arena with a

scrub brush and bucket, just like you," she snapped. "The warden won't be happy if you and the other prisoners don't get your work done before the next bell."

"We'll get it done. I meant where are you up here." He tapped lightly on the side of her head.

"Do that again, and I'll give myself ten points for every touch I get this afternoon during sparring practice."

He gave her an exasperated look. "You can't arbitrarily change the rules just because you're in a bad mood."

"I can do as I please. I did what I pleased for eleven years before you showed up, and I'll keep doing as I please long after you're gone." She'd forgotten to borrow the cold composure of the stone wall outside her bedroom this morning, and everything inside her felt like a rope fraying under the strain of something far too heavy to lift.

He went still, which meant she'd just revealed too much of herself to him. She was looking back through her words to find the problem when he said quietly, "Have I done something wrong?"

"You made me be friends with you." She glared at him as she set her bucket of soapy water by her feet.

"I didn't make you do anything." He set his bucket down too. "Nobody ever makes you do anything."

She ran her fingers lightly over the runes in her cuffs and looked away.

Seconds later his hand brushed lightly across her wrist, lingering on the cuff, one finger resting on the web of scars that peeked out from beneath the iron. "Why do you wear these if they bother you?"

She moved her hand away. "Who says they bother me?"

"Sajda." His voice was gentle.

She met his eyes defiantly. "What?"

"Are we truly friends?"

"I don't know how this happened. I blame you."

"I can live with that," he said. "And you don't have to tell me anything you don't want to tell me. But one day, I hope you trust me enough to tell me why you wear those bracelets if you don't like—"

"Cuffs."

The word slipped out before she thought to stop it, and one look at the slowly gathering thundercloud on his face had her wishing she could take it back.

"Cuffs." His voice was deadly quiet.

"It's nothing. We should scrub the floor."

"It's everything." He waited until she looked into his eyes, so dark and right now so full of fury. "Isn't it?"

She clenched her jaw and willed herself to be a star—distant and untouchable. The thundercloud on his face became a storm.

"The warden did this to you, didn't she? Put iron cuffs on you so that every time you lift your hands you remember that she sees you as her slave." His voice had a lethal edge to it now.

"She doesn't just see me as a slave. I *am* a slave. Bought and paid for." She was a star. A galaxy. A vast, unknowable space so very far from here.

"She may have paid coin for you, but she doesn't own you. You've seen to that. I've never met someone with more confidence and courage than you." He held her gaze with his, but he didn't really know her. He hadn't seen the truth.

The warden hadn't just bought a slave. She'd bought a

monster. And monsters didn't get to keep mothers or homes or friends.

"I'm going to check on the weapons. The warden ordered me to see what needs to be sharpened before the next combat round. You can scrub the floor. And when you're done with that, go offer a sneak peek at the weapons' placement schematic to the four competitors you wanted to build an alliance with. Hashim and his friends will be stuck cleaning the ovens in the kitchen for at least another hour, so you'll be safe." She was already backing away, her fingers itching to touch her cuffs as her magic spun through her like chaos, wild and wounded.

"Sajda—"

She left him in the middle of the arena, surrounded by buckets, guards, and the other prisoners from level fifteen.

He wasn't supposed to hear the things she wasn't saying. No one was. With him, she couldn't hide behind the ice she borrowed from the stars. The spaces between her words left her secrets bare to him.

Friendship was terrifying.

She was a fool for falling into its trap.

Magic churned through her, nipping at her skin. It streaked through her veins with a familiar pain, hunting for a target, but there wasn't one.

She'd allowed this. Dropped her defenses because he'd protected Tarek. Because he'd saved the life of a stranger in the arena at the expense of his own victory. Because he'd said he was a prince, but he treated her like his equal.

Because when he smiled with that hint of challenge in his eyes, something wild and bright woke within her.

The cuffs burned against her skin as her magic thrummed with every heartbeat.

And still she didn't know what she was supposed to do about Javan.

"Well, look at that. I've been hoping to catch you alone."

Sajda whipped around to find Dabir standing behind her, blocking her return from the corridor that led beneath the seating platforms to the small weapons closet.

"That's a very foolish wish." Her voice shook as the magic within her hurled itself against her skin, begging for its freedom. "You're supposed to be cleaning the ovens."

"Hashim thought one of us should go see what you do with your pet all day."

"You'll be beaten once the guards find you."

He shrugged. "I've been beaten plenty since I came here. Once more doesn't matter. Especially now that I can tell Hashim you're using the new boy as a maid during the mornings and a punching bag in the afternoon." His smile made her skin crawl. "And I can tell him he was right about you."

"So you skipped roll call yesterday afternoon to watch level fifteen's arena practice, and you think that means you know something about me?"

"I'd heard the rumors—how you're too fast and too strong to be just a slave girl who feeds the beasts—but until I saw you sparring yesterday, I thought the rumors were just Hashim making an excuse for not subduing you yet the way he'd like to."

Her breathing came hard and fast as she stared him down.

He stepped closer, and she held her ground, even though everything about him made her want to back away. "Now I think he's still making excuses, but I can see why he'd want to overpower all of that speed and strength. Hashim thinks we're just going to leave you for him, but . . ." He shrugged as if to say oh well, I got here first.

Fury and fear twined within her until she could no longer tell the two apart. Her magic buzzed beneath her skin, a hornets' nest ready for blood.

His blood.

He thought he'd seen the limits of her power while she was sparring with Javan, but he hadn't seen anything yet. Raising her fists, she said, "I'll give you one chance to walk away."

He laughed. "You're a good fighter, I saw that for myself, but I've got you by several handspans. It's been a long time since I had to subdue a girl to get a taste of her and there's nowhere for you to run."

Her smile was vicious. "No, Dabir. There's nowhere for *you* to run."

He frowned, but she was already moving. She took three running steps forward and slammed her fists into his face. He flew backward and crashed against the rough stone wall of the corridor. Blood poured from his nose, and her magic whispered and begged and screamed until she fell to her knees beside him, cupped her hands beneath his chin, and let his blood pool in her hand.

She'd never held another person's blood in her hands before. Distantly, she knew she should be frightened or disgusted or worried about the way her magic was scraping at her palms like a rabid animal. But instead, she was fascinated. It was like his blood was the key to a side of her magic she hadn't known existed.

He groaned and tried to slide away from her, but she wasn't

watching him. She was staring at the tiny crimson lake in the center of her palm. Her magic surged, a painful itch that spread along her arm and exploded into her palm with agonizing brilliance.

The blood spun in lazy circles, and images floated into Sajda's mind.

His past.

His intentions.

His fears.

She bared her teeth as she slowly raised her head to lock eyes with him, his darkest nightmares playing across her mind, one after the other.

Dark, small spaces.

A woman with short hair and a loud voice.

Falling into a lake and sucking water into his lungs.

Snakes.

Magic was an implacable force that owned her, rushing through her veins until all she could hear was its intoxicating thrum of power.

He'd wanted to overpower her.

He'd overpowered other girls before her. Left them broken and bleeding when he was finished. She could see their terrified faces in his mind.

"What are you doing?" His words were slurred, blood leaking from the back of his head where he'd hit the wall.

She held his gaze as she leaned down to the little lake of blood in her palm and began whispering. The nightmare took shape in her thoughts, fused with her magic, and became words that fell from her lips with the power of a lightning strike.

The runes on her cuffs blazed red, but she ignored the pain

and let the words rush out, conjuring the images in his mind with every breath.

He saw snakes rising from the stone floor, black and glistening. They coiled and writhed and slithered toward him, while the stone gave birth to more. He shoved himself as close to the wall as he could, and still they came. Golden eyes unblinking. Fangs extended. They rushed across the floor, crawled over his boots, and slid over his skin.

He screamed as her words took a different shape and the walls closed in, skylights turning to hard slabs of black stone. The snakes were churning now, a writhing mass of scaly black, as the room shrank to nothing more than a box.

He wailed, a long, broken sound that startled Sajda out of the story she was weaving. She closed her mouth, letting the rest of the words, the images, dissipate into nothing.

Dabir clawed at his body, searching for snakes that weren't there, and screamed for someone to turn on the lights.

Horror swept over Sajda.

What had she done?

The magic that had borrowed a shield of calm from the stone wall each day to protect her suddenly felt like a weapon that had used her. Controlled her.

Turned her into a monster.

She scrambled to her feet and turned to find Hashim standing at the end of the corridor watching her with curiosity burning in his eyes. Without looking at him again, she swept past and took the stairs to her room two at a time.

But no matter how fast she ran, she imagined she could still hear the echo of Dabir's screams as he fought with the nightmare she'd given him.

TWENTY-FOUR

WITH LESS THAN a week before the next tournament round, Javan and the other prisoners from his level worked an extra hour during chore time at the behest of the guards to once again scrub the arena, the warden's platform, and the spectators' seats. Sajda hadn't returned. Tarek had brought Javan a lunch of stale cheese and bruised apples and said he hadn't seen Sajda either, though the older man thought Javan was safe in his cell until level fifteen's sparring session, as Hashim and crew were distracted by the inexplicable mental collapse of their friend Dabir.

Javan stayed in his narrow, filthy cell, alternately praying and thinking through what he knew of the other prisoners on his level while he waited for seventh bell and the start of his sparring session. With Sajda's help, he'd spent the last two weeks assessing their skills during practice, observing their personalities, their strengths and weaknesses, and how they responded to Hashim's bullying tactics during rec hour. There were four who stood out to him. Four Sajda had agreed could be bribed to become his allies. Tonight during rec hour, he'd make his move and pray for Yl' Haliq's blessing.

Tension knotted his shoulders as seventh bell tolled. If these four turned him down, his options were limited, and the next combat round was less than a week away. He left his cell, shaking out his arms, satisfied that the injuries he'd sustained during his first round were little more than distant aches, easily ignored. It was time to spar with Sajda and mend whatever he'd done wrong.

She never showed.

Worry twisted through him, slick and heavy, as he returned to level fifteen after practice, checked in with the pair of guards assigned to his section, and then obediently stayed within the confines of his cell while levels ten through twelve practiced in the arena far below.

There had been something off about Sajda that morning, though he couldn't put his finger on exactly what it was. Maybe it was that she'd been irritable instead of calm. Jumpy instead of still. She could simply be having a bad day—Yl' Haliq knew being constantly trapped in the dim cavern of Maqbara was enough to set anyone on edge—but Sajda didn't show her nerves. She held her body still, kept her expression cold, and maintained eye contact until sometimes he wished she wouldn't.

But today, she'd been fidgety. Unable or unwilling to meet his gaze for more than a quick glance, her expression haunted. And her fingers had worried the iron cuffs she wore as if somehow today the pain of wearing the constant reminder of her position at Maqbara was too much to bear.

Anger coiled within him, hot and dangerous.

What kind of monster bought a child, kept her inside Akram's most dangerous prison, and forced her to wear cuffs so that no one could possibly forget that, though many of the prisoners would eventually leave, Sajda never could?

The moment Javan was restored to his rightful place as heir to Akram's crown, he was going to punish the warden for everything she'd done. On the outside, it would certainly appear that the treasonous act of trying to murder Akram's prince was her greatest crime, but Javan knew better. He would punish her for Sajda first. It wouldn't give Sajda back her childhood, and it wouldn't take away the strange web of scars he'd glimpsed beneath her cuffs, but it would set her free of this despicable place. It was the least he could do for her as her friend.

Her friend.

If someone had bet Javan during his first few days in prison that he would come to enjoy spending hours with the girl who'd raised the hairs on the back of his neck at their first meeting, he'd have lost everything he owned. He'd been sure she was cold, uncaring, and dangerous.

He was still sure she was dangerous, and one day he planned to ask her who had trained her. It hadn't been Tarek, and she wasn't attached to any of the other prisoners. But someone with an excellent understanding of how to harness Sajda's speed, strength, and flexibility had shown her how to fight. Not just fight but win. Perhaps it was the woman Hashim's friends had mentioned when they'd followed Javan out of the infirmary. The woman who'd apparently been Sajda's friend and had died two years ago in the arena. He'd never asked her about it. The look on her face when Hashim's friends brought the woman up was enough to stop him. If she wanted to talk to him, she would. But someone had taken her under their wing and made sure she could defend herself.

It was more than a little humbling that he had to work so hard just to keep her from outscoring him in their sparring competitions. The thrill of trying to keep up with her, of pushing himself to move faster and fight smarter, kept something alive inside him, despite the shadow of despair he constantly fought to ignore.

He had no idea if it did the same for her, but he had other things to think about if he wanted to get out of Maqbara so he could punish the warden, save his father and his kingdom from the impostor who'd taken his place, and set things right. He had to survive the next round of combat and put significant points on the board. And he needed allies.

Quickly, he slipped to his knees, his lips already moving in a desperate prayer for help, though the longer he stayed in Maqbara, the farther away Yl' Haliq seemed to be. Eighth bell rang, sending a new wave of prisoners down to the arena to practice, and still Javan prayed, fragments of the sacred texts mixing with his own pleas for mercy as they fell from his lips.

By ninth bell, his knees ached, and his back was stiff, but still he prayed, his forehead pressed to the edge of his bed as he acknowledged the truth.

Beneath his anger at the warden, his budding friendship with Sajda, and the righteous belief that he would be restored to his destiny, fear curled tight around his heart.

What if this next round of competition was even more brutal than the last? What if he lost and remained trapped within the prison, at the mercy of the warden and the enemies he'd made?

What if he died? He'd be a prince stripped of honor, dignity, and the love of his family, turned into meat by the warden and forgotten by all.

His heart beat a frantic tempo against his chest, and he sucked in a slow, calming breath before the fear could paralyze him.

He wasn't forgotten. Yl' Haliq would hear him. He would see the great injustice done to Javan, and he would deliver him.

Javan climbed to his feet as tenth bell rang and Tarek appeared with a bowl of boiled vegetables and a wedge of flatbread.

"Have you seen her?" Javan asked as he accepted the food.

Tarek nodded. "She was at the stalls doing her job a few moments ago."

Javan moved toward the mouth of his cell, and Tarek stepped in front of him. "Where do you think you're going?"

"To see her."

Something soft entered Tarek's expression. "It does my heart good to see that you care about her, but I can't let you go down there now."

"Why not?"

"Because it's tenth bell. You're supposed to either be in your cell or in the kitchen. Combat is in four days. You can't afford to be beaten by the guards for breaking the rules."

Javan clenched his jaw. Tarek was right, but that didn't stop the prince from wanting to go see Sajda for himself, beating or no.

"Eat up and then go to rec hour," Tarek said. "Make those alliances and stay out of trouble."

Javan obeyed, eating quickly, though he saved his flatbread for rec hour, and then running through his approach over and over until eleventh bell rang. Tarek walked with him to level eight and the long rectangular room the prisoners used for their hour of rec time each night. Sajda stood outside the room with the guards as usual, though she wouldn't meet Javan's eyes.

An ache bloomed in Javan's chest as he moved past her and into the room, and he gave himself a mental shake. He couldn't think about Sajda or her reasons for ignoring him. It was time to focus on his strategy.

He needed allies.

Scanning the room, he found the four prisoners he and Sajda had decided would make the best allies. In the far corner, Hashim and seven others from level five were huddled by a fireplace whose flames hissed and popped. None of them looked up from their discussion. Dabir was missing from his usual place beside Hashim. One less threat to worry about.

Moving to the opposite end of the room, Javan approached his quarry. Grabbing a chair from a nearby table where soon a trio of women from level ten would play cards as they did every night, Javan spun it around, carried it a few steps, and plunked it down at the corner of a square table with two cups of dice and a fraying deck of cards with the symbols of Balavata's head families worked into their upper right corners.

"Mind if I join you?" he asked the four who were already seated, two of which were still finishing their dinners. Quickly he ran through their names as he sat. Intizara was on his right, a woman who looked to be about ten years older than Javan. Beside her sat Gadi, a man with smile creases at the corners of his eyes and nervous fingers. A woman named Kali sat beside him and then on Javan's left was a tall, narrow man named Nadim.

"It's a game for four," Intizara said, hauling her cards close to her chest as if he might announce to the others what was in her hand.

He shrugged. "Then I'll wait for the next round. It's been

a while since I've played thistles and thieves. Might help me to watch."

Intizara frowned, but Nadim said, "Fine, but we play for the pot, so you better have something to offer."

Javan watched silently as the four tossed out their bets—half of whatever they grabbed for lunch the next day, a short break from the morrow's chores while the others at the table did the jobs assigned to the winner, and even a small packet of dried apricots someone's family members had bribed a guard to bring in. As the game began in earnest, he leaned forward, propped his elbows on his knees, and ate his flatbread.

These four were his key to surviving Hashim's attempt to kill him in the next tournament round, and he was their key to having a better chance at staying alive. If he could get them to accept his offer and work as a team, all of their odds improved.

When the round ended, Javan said, "Time for me to place my bet."

Four pairs of eyes found his. The spit dried in his mouth, and he forced himself to swallow.

"What do you have to offer, boy?" Kali asked as she pinched a bit of her flatbread off and scattered the crumbs on the floor for Mal' Enish, the goddess of animals. When she noticed his gaze following her moves, she shook the rest of the crumbs free and glared. "Didn't see you giving an offering from your food."

"I . . . no, I didn't."

"That's no way to treat the goddess. There are mice in the prison. The kindness you show to the least of these reveals your true self to the world." The words from the sacred text flowed from her tongue with easy practice.

"I've always liked that passage." He smiled at her, but she

narrowed her eyes at him. Quickly, he said, "Here's what I have to offer, and no one has to beat me at thistles and thieves to get it. I want to fight with you four as a team in the next round of competition. I'll work with you to come up with a strategy that plays to our individual strengths, and I'll know where your preferred weapons will be hidden. In exchange, I expect you to stand and fight with me so that we can give ourselves the best possible chance of getting out of the arena alive." And the best chance of helping him gain enough points to qualify for the final round. It would be far easier to focus on killing whatever was going into the arena with them if he didn't have to worry so much about being ambushed by Hashim.

Silence descended across the small table, and the noise from the rest of the room pressed close. Cards slapping against table-tops. Swearing. Chairs scraping the stone floor while the sharp bark of mocking laughter rose from Hashim's corner.

"You've got some pretty nasty enemies," Nadim finally said.

Javan met his gaze. "I do. And having you four to help watch my back would help me stay alive. But I'll be helping you too. I'll know exactly where you can find your preferred weapons. And I've had combat training—"

"We know," Intizara said. "We've seen you spar with Sajda."

Gadi shuddered and muttered a quick prayer. "There's something strange about that one."

The others murmured in agreement, all of them watching him as if waiting to hear what he had to say on the matter. When he didn't reply, Nadim said, "I'm not agreeing to anything yet, but I'd like to hear your strategy for getting all five of us through the next round alive."

Relief unwound a bit of the tension that was strung through

him like a taut rope. Quickly he outlined his idea for a fight formation based on his strengths and theirs. He had no idea what they'd be facing—he didn't even think Sajda knew—but some strategy was better than none. When he was finished, they turned away from him, leaning across the table to whisper to one another while he sent a silent prayer to Yl' Haliq.

Finally, Intizara turned back to him and said, "You have a deal. We'll start working together tomorrow during sparring practice. But if Hashim comes at you outside the ring, you're on your own."

"Agreed." He stood as the guards shouted for prisoners to return to their cells before twelfth bell. "Thank you."

He had allies. He'd know where the weapons were courtesy of Sajda. And he would pray every chance he had that he could kill whatever he'd be facing in the arena before it killed him.

TWENTY-FIVE

TWO DAYS LATER, during the hour he was allowed out of his cell for chores, Javan crept out of the third level privy he was supposed to be scouring, took the stairs down to the arena, and found Sajda marking a sheet of parchment with the placement of the weapons for the combat round that was now two days away. Her back was to him as she stood in the center of the arena, black hair glowing almost midnight blue under the skylights as she gazed thoughtfully into the distance.

He hadn't talked to her since she'd left him behind to scrub the arena without her two days earlier. She hadn't brought his meals. She'd stayed near the stalls during sparring practice and chores. And though he was constantly aware that she was near, watching over him in case Hashim made a move, she refused to make eye contact and never came close enough for him to speak to her.

Tarek had brought Javan meals on both days, and had quietly deflected Javan's questions about Sajda until this morning, when he finally looked at the prince and said, "Stop asking me what's going on. Go find out for yourself."

Easier said than done. Javan didn't know what he'd said wrong in their last conversation, though he thought maybe it had to do with the cuffs she wore. The sight of them sent a spike of red-hot anger blazing through him as he slowly approached Sajda while hoping the guard who'd instructed him to clean the privy closets on the third level didn't catch sight of him and decide to beat him a day before he had to enter the next round of competition.

The faster he figured out what to say to Sajda, the faster he could get back to his chores and avoid compromising himself for combat. He opened his mouth to speak, but something warm and dangerously soft filled his chest as he watched her frown over the parchment.

He'd missed her.

He hadn't just missed their sparring sessions or her relentless pushing to build alliances for the competition. He hadn't just missed the way she gave him advice with cheerful pessimism or the way she questioned him closely about the outside world, guarded hope in her eyes.

He'd missed *her*. The eyebrow that rose when she thought he was wrong. The little smirk at the edge of her lips when she got the best of him. The light of fierce intelligence and challenge in her eyes when they talked.

Being her friend was like taking a ride on a half-wild stallion with nothing but your wits and your courage between you and a long, dangerous fall. It felt fascinating and dangerous—a test he still didn't know how to pass. Somehow, despite the fact that he was in danger from the beasts, the warden, the impostor, and his fellow prisoners, being around Sajda was like coming alive after years of sleeping like the dead.

He didn't want to go back to sleep. He didn't want to let go of the horse's mane and tumble to the safe, predictable ground. He'd known her for a month—less time than it usually took him to notice a girl at Milisatria—but here in the bleak confines of the prison where the few hours he spent with her each day were the ray of light in the darkness that was swallowing him, a month had been enough to know he wanted more of her friendship. More of her time. More of her.

And if he wanted that, then he had to find a way to fix whatever he'd broken.

"Do you have a minute?" he asked, staying at the edge of the arena to give her space if she still craved it.

She went still, and then deliberately took another minute to write a note on the parchment. When she finally looked at him, her eyes were distant, her expression cold.

His heart ached, a sudden shaft of pain that he didn't want to examine closely. Instead, he said, "I did what you asked."

She raised a brow.

He lifted his hand to tick the items off his fingers. "I made what I think is a solid alliance with Gadi, Intizara, Nadim, and Kali. We'll compete as a team for the next round. I memorized the weapon placement, and I've sparred enough to be as ready as I can be. You've fulfilled your end of our bargain, but I haven't. I still owe you a lesson before tomorrow. In case I die, remember?"

He lifted a brow of his own, a clear challenge he hoped she wouldn't be able to resist.

She held out for a long moment, and though he couldn't see the struggle on her face, he knew her now. The little finger she tapped rapidly against her thigh, the way her eyes narrowed when she looked at him—she was considering saying no.

The thought left him feeling anchorless, a boat tossed into the heart of a storm without a rudder.

Yl' Haliq, he was in trouble.

When did he start thinking of Sajda as his anchor? She'd tear him to pieces if she knew. It had been hard enough to get her to accept his friendship. Trying for more would be asking for her to cut ties completely.

Not that he wanted more.

Probably.

She rolled her eyes and stalked toward him, folding the parchment as she went. "Fine. We'll have a lesson. But only because I want to know the outside world, and you might die tomorrow."

Relief was a swift, shaky river of painful hope that surged through him like a monsoon.

He was definitely in trouble.

"Where should we go?" he asked. "I'm supposed to be washing the privy closets on the third level, so if we can find some place in that vicinity, it will help throw off the guards' suspicions if we get caught."

She scanned the honeycomb of cells above them, and then led him up the closest set of stairs to the third level. They exited behind a row of seats perched high above the arena floor. Several prisoners were sweeping and scrubbing the corridor to their right. Sajda turned left, and he followed her past a long row of seats, another stairwell, and finally to a door that led to a room twice the size of his cell. Faint beams of sunshine from the corridor's skylight gave the room a purple-gray twilight gloom. A large woven rug covered the floor and cherrywood lounging couches with pillows in deep jewel tones were scattered about.

"What is this place?" he asked.

"It's where the people with weak stomachs sit during the competition."

"If they have weak stomachs, why come at all?"

She gave him her people-are-generally-idiots, what-do-you-want-me-to-do-about-it? look.

"All right, let's sit." He sank into the cushions of a couch that rested against the far wall, out of sight of the doorway in case a guard walked by.

She eyed him warily and sat on the opposite end of the couch. She was tense, fists clenched, braced for him to approach subjects she didn't want to discuss.

"What do you want to learn?" he asked.

She watched him for a moment, and then said, "Where should I go when I get out of here?"

He eased back against a peacock blue pillow and considered her question. "That depends. If you want to stay in Akram—"

"I don't." The words rushed out, cracking her icy facade for an instant.

Her words hit him harder than they should have. He had to stay in Akram. There was no choice in the matter. He'd selfishly assumed she'd stay too.

Keeping his voice steady, he said, "Then let's talk about the surrounding kingdoms. There's Loch Talam to the north, Balavata to the south, and Ravenspire to the east."

"I want stars and wide-open spaces." The longing in her voice lingered in her eyes.

This was the real Sajda. The girl who'd been trapped underground for most of her life, forced to be with crowds of dangerous people. He wanted to tear open Maqbara's ceiling and let her breathe. Let her revel in the vast reaches of the sky above.

"There are small settlements along the road through the Samaal Desert, which is between here and Loch Talam. I know you said you don't want to stay in Akram, and that's fine, but you can't find any more wide-open spaces and star-filled skies than our desert. If you want the north, Loch Talam has a lot of lakes and rivers, and it's green and rocky. Mountains, hills, and friendly people. To the south, Balavata has the coastline, so you could have the sea with your stars."

She smiled, slow and wistful, and he caught himself before he moved closer to her. "I might like the sea."

"You might." He made himself smile at her, and she frowned. "That makes you sad."

"I'd miss you."

Her frown deepened. "Why?"

He laughed, though it hurt to do so. "Because we're friends. I care about you. I want to be around you."

A sound drifted in from the doorway, and Javan held his breath as the sharp clip of a guard's boots moved past. If he was caught in here, he'd have to talk fast to convince the guard he'd been cleaning. Maybe Sajda would have a convincing story ready. Something that would spare him a beating that could make surviving the next round impossible. He met her eyes, and they stared at each other in silence until the footsteps faded.

"Friendship is a lot of work." Her expression challenged him to deny it.

"Anything that matters takes effort sometimes, but friendships are also comfortable and easy. Like this."

"This is easy?" Her brow called him a liar.

He laughed again, and this time he meant it. "When do we ever run out of things to talk about? Or argue about? Or compete over?"

She smiled, but it was still haunted.

He could ask her what was bothering her and risk sending her running, or he could move on to the next subject she wanted to learn about. Before he could make up his mind, she said, "The only magical creatures I know about are those from Llorenyae. Are there others?"

"Yes. *Mardushkas* from Morcant are sorceresses. The queen of Ravenspire is a *mardushka* because her mother was from Morcant. There are rumors of a fae Wish Granter in the southern kingdom of Súndraille and of other fae living in Balavata. Loch Talam has a few who still know the old ways to work magic."

"What about dark elves?" This time the question didn't just crack her facade. It shattered it. Her eyes were full of misery, and her lips trembled.

He shivered and started to tell her they were disturbing wielders of nightmares who somehow swallowed the essence of things and used it as a weapon, but something in her expression stopped him. Feeling his way carefully, he said, "Most of them live in Ystaria, a kingdom far to the north of Loch Talam. A mountain range full of dwarves separates the kingdoms."

"Are they dangerous?" She traced her fingers over the runes on the cuffs she wore, and he had the sudden, sickening realization that iron held both fae and elven magic in check, especially when used with runes. Akram had won its freedom from slavery to the dark elves six generations ago using weapons, traps, and cages made of iron.

He swallowed hard, and studied her beautiful face with its

pale skin, midnight blue eyes, and long black hair that always covered her ears. She was shorter than most dark elves, even though she was nearly as tall as he was. But if she was part human and part elf, it would explain her incredible speed and strength. And it might explain why when she touched his bare skin with her hand, he felt as if he'd been hit by a tiny jolt of lightning.

The room felt as if it was spinning around him. He'd always believed the only good elf was a dead elf. He'd been given the honor of lighting an elven effigy on fire as a child. If you'd asked him a month ago what he would do if he were forced to be in close quarters with a dark elf, his answer would've involved his sword and little else.

Now he had to pick up his beliefs, one by one, and examine them for the flaws that surely ran through them. He couldn't imagine the world without Sajda in it, and he didn't want to.

"Javan, are they dangerous?" she asked, but it sounded as though she'd already decided on the answer.

He leaned toward her. "They can be. Just like the *mardushkas* in Morcant. Anyone with that much power can be dangerous, but the queen of Ravenspire is widely regarded as the most powerful *mardushka* to have ever lived, and she is kind, protective, and acts in the best interests of others instead of herself."

"So she's the exception?"

"There's always an exception. Magic isn't evil. It's what people *do* with magic that counts."

She looked away.

"Sajda, do you want to talk about what's bothering you?" he asked gently, and prayed that she knew she could trust him.

She shook her head.

He tried not to let it bother him. Instead, he said, "What else did you want to learn today?"

She met his gaze again. "I don't know how to meet people without threatening to hurt them."

He smiled. "That could be a complication in the outside world. When you don't need to intimidate people in social situations, you'll want to hold conversations about mutual interests, ask them questions about things they enjoy, eat with the appropriate dining ware, dance when asked—"

"Dance? Why would I want to dance with anybody?" She glared at him.

He laughed helplessly. "You might not. But if you're at a party or a fancy dinner or one day if you decide to get married, you'll be expected to dance."

"I'll just say no."

"You can certainly do so, but what if you want to say yes?"

"Why would I?" She shuddered. "Having a stranger's hands on me and having to move around together?"

There was a humming in his blood, a wild, reckless light burning in his chest, as he said quietly, "What if it isn't a stranger? What if it's someone you really want to be close to? And you don't want to be rude?"

"I always want to be rude." She grinned at him, and he looked away before she could see how badly he wanted her to agree to what he was about to propose.

"Think of dancing like sparring."

"Are you allowed to leave bruises?"

He laughed. "You're hopeless. No bruises, unless you're doing it wrong. But it's a give and take, an action and a reaction. You learn the moves, and it flows."

"I suppose you're a good dancer." She eyed him suspiciously, and he pretended to dust the wrinkles out of his prison-issued tunic.

"Best in my class four years in a row."

"So you competed."

"Kind of. It was for school, so it was for a grade. I wanted the best grade in the class." He gave her the same look he did when he was sure he could score against her in their sparring matches. "I'm still the best. You might want to quit before you discover that dancing is harder than it sounds."

Her brow rose, and the wild light inside him felt like it was consuming him a piece at a time.

"If you can dance, so can I. We both know I move better than you do." She rose from the couch, her expression defiant.

"You're going to take back those words in a minute." He stood and held out his arms, and then closed his eyes when she walked right into them. "Hold my hand . . . not that one, this one. My other hand goes on your waist."

"Move it any lower and you'll draw back a stump."

He leaned his cheek against her hair and laughed. "I wouldn't dare."

When he had her in position, he began softly counting a four-quarter beat while he moved her gently into the sweeping movements of the *pallestaya*.

"Why do you get to make me dip backward?" she demanded.

"Because I'm leading the dance."

She lifted her chin and gave him a long look. He grinned. "Memorize what I'm doing, and then if you want to lead, I'm happy to relinquish the honor."

"Fine. I'll learn it."

"Fine." He couldn't wipe the smile off his face as he spun her out and back in, swayed with his hand resting gently on her hip, and laughed as she hung on by the tips of her fingers and dipped twice as far as he would've taken her.

Her face was flushed pink with laughter as she came out of the dip, and she landed hard against him, her arms wrapped around his shoulders, her face against his chest.

He pressed his hands against the small of her back and swayed slowly while he prayed for this one perfect moment to stretch on forever.

She pulled back, with a shy, sweet smile he'd never seen from her before. In a flash it was gone, and she folded her arms across her chest. "I won, didn't I?"

"Won what?"

"The grade. The top prize. I dipped farther and spun faster and—"

"Yes, you won." He grinned, and she smiled back.

"This was nice," she said, and then before he could think of a reply, she snatched up the parchment she'd left on the couch and left him behind with the realization that somehow when he hadn't been paying attention, he'd started falling for Sajda.

TWENTY-SIX

"GET THOSE BEASTS under control immediately, or suffer the consequences," the warden barked as she swept out of her office, her hair scraped back into an unforgiving bun. "The doors open soon. We can't have our most important bettors feeling nervous."

Sajda hurried to comply, the skin beneath her wrists aching as her magic stormed through her. It was Exhibition Day, the day before the third round of the tournament when the betting heated up as the pool of crowd favorites narrowed to those who actually had a chance of winning the entire thing. The guards were escorting the surviving competitors into the arena where they'd be thoroughly examined by members of the aristocracy and merchant class who were interested in paying the warden's Exhibition Day entrance fee for the privilege of making a more informed bet on the upcoming round of combat.

A shape-shifter howled in its stall, and Sajda snatched a handful of sheep's guts to toss into its trough before the warden could decide to punish her slave for not feeding the creatures fast enough.

"I'll finish this row, little one," Tarek said as he limped toward her, a bag of sheep's guts dragging behind him. "You go on out to the arena to assist the warden. She's in a foul mood today."

"When is she in a good mood?" Sajda asked as she pulled off her leather gloves, hung them from their peg, and moved toward the arena.

The prisoners who were going to compete tomorrow were lined up across the middle of the arena facing the warden's platform. Their hands were shackled behind their backs, and a row of guards stood behind them holding the chains attached to the shackles.

Sajda glanced at the warden's platform, expecting to see the woman glaring down at the arena while her accountant readied herself for a flurry of bets on the upcoming tournament round. Instead, the accountant was sitting at her table shuffling parchment while the warden was nowhere to be seen.

The sharp crack of a whip cut through the air, and Sajda whirled to face the prisoners as Javan stumbled forward out of the line, his lips pressed tight against the pain while blood bloomed against the shoulder of his tunic. Behind him, the warden drew the whip into the air again, her dark eye lit with fury.

The guard who held Javan's shackles yanked the boy back into line, and the warden stalked past him to face the prisoners, the whip held ready.

"You will cooperate fully with everything the bettors ask you to do." The whip sliced through the air and bit into Javan's shoulder again.

He threw his head back as he grimaced, and blood dripped down his arm.

The other prisoners murmured, shifting their bodies away

from Javan as if worried whatever he'd done to anger the warden would somehow bring the whip down on them next.

What *had* he done to anger the warden? Sajda held herself still, her magic churning beneath her skin as her mind raced. It was unlike the warden to damage a competitor right before she expected to take bets on his chances of survival. Especially when that competitor had impressed the crowd.

The warden's voice rang out. "You will show respect and deference to everyone who examines you."

The whip snaked out, and Javan flinched as it dug into his already wounded shoulder.

Sajda frowned, magic itching in her blood. What could possibly be the point of injuring him before the bettors arrived unless the warden no longer wanted him to have a chance to be a crowd favorite? He was the underdog who'd wowed the audience with his unexpected display of both skill and compassion—the warden could make a killing on the bets people would be lining up to place on him.

"Finally, you will not speak." The warden raised her whip, and Javan's chin came up, his eyes meeting her gaze in challenge. "Not a single word. If you break this rule, I will personally cut out your tongue."

The back of Sajda's neck prickled with unease. In the five years since Prince Fariq and the warden had begun the tournaments, the warden had never instructed the prisoners to be silent on Exhibition Day.

But in five years, the warden had also never had an aristocrat who resembled the royal family shackled to the line of competitors. She couldn't do anything to change Javan's face, but she could make sure none of the bettors heard the refined, elegant polish in his voice. She could make sure no one speculated about the one aristocrat who'd landed himself in Maqbara.

For the first time since Javan had confessed to her that he was Akram's true prince, Sajda began wondering if he was telling the truth.

Magic hissed and scraped at her as Sajda met Javan's gaze and willed him to obey. The warden didn't bluff. His expression was stoic, but the defiance blazing in his eyes sent a cold wave of fear over her.

This is what came of having friends. Of letting herself get close to others. She couldn't afford to worry about him. He'd leave her, either by dying in the competition or by winning it. She needed to spend her time worrying about finishing her tunnel, deflecting the warden's suspicions, and making a decent plan for how to get the cuffs off her wrists once she was out of Maqbara.

Part of that plan meant paying close attention today so she could glean knowledge about the world outside the prison.

"Let them in," the warden called. The guards stationed at the far end of the arena opened the door that led up to the magistrate's office, and a small crowd of those who took betting on the tournament as seriously as the rest of Akram took betting on the horses filed in.

Sajda went to work. Meeting the visitors as they stepped into the combat arena while the warden climbed to her platform to oversee the bets, Sajda said, "Good morning and welcome to Maqbara."

A few of them nodded or murmured in response, though most didn't deign to speak to a slave girl. She continued, "As a reminder, the rules for Exhibition Day allow you to personally examine each competitor for a few moments. Once everyone has had a chance to make an examination, each of you may request a skills demonstration from three of the prisoners and may choose up to five skills for the prisoner to present. I will handle the weapons demonstrations, and the warden has chosen guards to run both the speed and strength tests."

The group nodded impatiently, their eyes already scanning the line of prisoners, looking for their favorites. Sajda glanced once at Javan, and found him watching the small crowd around her with desperate hope in his eyes. She cleared her throat and said quickly, "The warden has added one last rule. Today, none of the prisoners will be allowed to speak."

A woman closer to Sajda's shoulder frowned. "Why not? Questioning them about their background and experience is an important part of making an educated bet."

A short, round man who stood at the edge of the group said, "It adds to the risk, which adds to the fun. Scared your instincts won't be good enough, Lady Bah' Thrayn?"

The woman glared. "My instincts have already made me far richer than you."

Sajda took note of the woman's posture, the way her shoulders were thrown back, her hands hanging loosely at her sides. This was how a free woman stood. Not braced for attack. Not scurrying to do someone's bidding. This was how she took on the world and left her mark.

As the bettors made their way to the line of prisoners, Sajda threw her own shoulders back and strode toward the weapons table, arms swinging loosely as if she owned the prison and had nothing to fear. Unguarded. Unbowed by the weight of the warden's gaze.

It was like being naked in front of the entire prison, but she had to learn how to do it. When she escaped Maqbara, she needed to blend in.

The morning passed in a blur of activity. Sajda handed weapons to unshackled prisoners, watching closely to make sure they did a proper demonstration instead of turning the weapons against the guards or the guests. Some of the prisoners did a passable job at showing some expertise with the weapon they'd been handed. Some made it clear they'd survived to this point in the competition by sheer luck.

When Javan was hauled to the weapons area, a dozen or so bettors surrounding him, Sajda risked a quick glance at the furious set of his jaw before looking up toward the warden's platform. The warden was watching closely, her whip clutched tightly in one fist.

"Let's see what this boy's got," one man said. "This might be the one to bet everything on."

"Not everything, I hope," the woman who clung to the man's arm murmured. "We need something held back—"

"I have a major trade contract up for approval in Prince Fariq's office," the man snapped, silencing his wife. "You know he only approves contracts for those who attend the tournament, cheer loudly, and bet big. Without that contract, we'll lose a lot more than the amount I'm prepared to bet on this boy if he has enough skill."

Javan's brow furrowed, and he glanced at the man as if hoping to hear more about the way Prince Fariq awarded favor to those who supported the tournament.

Another man laughed. "Already saw his skills in the last round, didn't we? Bet this one had training from somewhere."

The rotund man who'd shut down Lady Bah' Thrayn's complaints spoke quickly. "Probably just another street rat who grew up fighting in the peasant quarter."

Sajda raised a brow and handed Javan a bow and a quiver of arrows, her hand brushing his for a split second before he turned toward the target mounted fifty paces away.

Blood from his shoulder wound caked his tunic, drying a rust-brown at the edges though the center of the stain was still a dark crimson. He hefted the bow, testing its weight and balance, and then reached for an arrow. His jaw tightened as he nocked the arrow and smoothly lifted the bow. Drawing back the string, he let the arrow fly. It buried itself in the center of the target. Two more arrows immediately followed, each hitting the center ring.

A few in the group surrounding him clapped lightly as he handed the bow and quiver back to Sajda. Blood flowed fresh from his shoulder, but he didn't seem aware of it. Instead, he turned to face the bettors and slowly looked each of them in the eye.

"Would you like to see Javan use another weapon?" Sajda asked.

"I think we've seen plenty—"

"The sword," a woman interrupted the fat little man, and he cast a quick frown up at the warden.

Sajda handed Javan a sword. Sending an icy smile toward the man who she now suspected was working with the warden, she said, "I think you'll find this prisoner is an experienced swordsman."

A murmur swept the group as Javan performed a complicated series of exercises, the sword moving through the air in smooth, competent strokes. Proof that he understood the mechanics of the weapon and was an expert.

Before anyone else could suggest another weapon, the warden's cohort swept Javan toward the strength test. As the others made to follow, the woman who'd requested the sword demonstration said, "That's no street rat."

"Did you see his face? Reminds me of the royal family."

"And he shares the same first name as the prince."

"He's had professional training. You don't get that unless your family has money."

The group moved too far away from Sajda for her to hear the rest of their conversation, but it didn't matter. The speculation would catch fire and spread. Every aristocrat who was attending the competition would be watching Javan tomorrow. He would be grist for the gossip mill for weeks.

If the warden thought she could contain the fact that she had an aristocrat in Maqbara, she was seriously mistaken.

Sajda glanced up at the warden's platform once more, her magic sizzling beneath her skin at the look of dark satisfaction on the warden's face. Surely she realized that even though she'd effectively kept Javan from telling his story to anyone with influence, she couldn't contain the curiosity. The rumors. And yet, she looked unperturbed. More than that, she looked pleased.

The skin beneath Sajda's cuffs stung as her magic hurled itself against the iron.

If the warden looked pleased, it meant she was already two moves ahead in the game, and that meant Javan was in trouble.

Sajda stared across the arena at the boy's back as he stood, proud and confident while the bettors prodded his muscles and discussed his merits as if he couldn't hear them. Something dark opened in her chest, pressing against her throat until she had to turn away or risk losing the last of the icy composure she was barely clinging to.

She didn't know how to save Javan from the warden. She had no idea what he'd be facing in the arena the following day. And even if she did save him, she would still be no closer to saving herself.

Throwing her shoulders back and relaxing her stance, she angled her chin to mimic the casual confidence of the aristocrats around her and mouthed their words, trying for the polished accent that marked someone as an educated, wealthy member of society.

The darkness within her ached, but she kept her expression cold and distant as she practiced looking like she was free.

TWENTY-SEVEN

THE MORNING OF his second round of competition Javan woke from a restless sleep with his stomach in knots.

The impostor was in the palace, sheltered by Uncle Fariq, a betrayal that still cut deep. Javan's father would surely be killed the moment he realized the impostor wasn't his son, or the moment he gave up the crown, whichever came first. Akram was in danger of being ruled by corrupt, dishonorable men. And the only way Javan could escape the prison and set it all right was to close the significant gap between himself and the competition's leaders today by destroying more innocent creatures without getting himself killed in the process.

He really didn't want to be killed. Was it selfish of him to want to live, not just for Akram or for his father, but for himself? To want the chance to dance with Sajda, to escape Maqbara, and to do all the things he'd turned down at Milisatria in the name of duty?

Climbing off his cot, he dropped to his knees and whispered

his morning prayers while the faint light of dawn filtered in through the prison's skylights. His chest felt too tight to breathe evenly, and his hands shook.

What would he be facing in the arena? He'd worked out a decent plan of defense and attack with Gadi, Nadim, Kali, and Intizara, and he was confident Sajda had hidden their preferred weapons where she'd said they'd be. But not knowing what he'd be fighting was a jagged blade that hacked at his composure until he wanted to scream.

How could he solve a puzzle when he didn't have all the pieces?

First bell sounded, harsh and clamorous, and the iron cell bars began their slow journey toward the ceiling. The corridors filled with the sound of prisoners making their way to the kitchen. Javan remained where he was.

Yl' Haliq knew how important today was. Surely he wouldn't let Javan fail.

He waited to feel the calming presence of Yl' Haliq, but there was nothing. The anxiety thrumming through Javan soured into fear, and he forced himself to exhale.

Fear out.

Courage in.

Yl' Haliq was with him whether Javan could feel him or not. The sacred texts were clear. Hanging on to that thread of reassurance, Javan climbed to his feet and turned to find Sajda standing in his doorway, Tarek just behind her. The early morning light gleamed against her black hair and lingered on her pale skin in a way that made Javan's heart beat a little faster.

"You look like you didn't sleep." Her voice was full of accusation.

"It's a little hard to sleep before something so important," he said as he stretched and then reached for a clean tunic.

"All the more reason to make sure you do." She turned away as he pulled on his gray tunic and sat down to lace up his boots. "You can't make any mistakes today."

"I know."

Tarek slipped past Sajda and handed Javan a banana and a bowl of lumpy porridge nearly the same color as the prince's shirt. "Eat. You'll want to give the food time to settle before the competition starts."

Javan nodded his thanks, and Tarek squeezed his shoulder and smiled while Sajda paced at the door of his cell, her mouth tight.

"Your allies can't make mistakes either," she said, shooting a glare at him before turning away again.

"I know." He ate the banana in four bites and then forced himself to swallow the lukewarm, congealing porridge.

"You have to watch out for Hashim and his gang. And for the warden. She isn't supposed to intervene, but don't trust her. If she already tried to kill you once, then she might still be working with whoever put you here." Sajda's voice sharpened. "And you can't turn your back on the middle of the arena. Not for a second. I don't know what's in there. The warden herself brought in a creature last night, and three of the guards who helped her were killed. I found their bodies at the edge of the arena this morning." Her voice shook at the edges, and she twisted her fingers together as if to stop her hands from trembling.

Javan's stomach clenched, and the food he'd just eaten turned to stone in his belly. Handing his empty bowl to Tarek, he walked to where Sajda still paced in front of his doorway, her graceful strides eating up the floor while her fingers drummed restlessly against her leg. It was such a change from her usual predatory stillness that it sent the anxiety inside him spiraling into fear again, though this time for a very different reason.

If the warden was still working with the impostor, what would she do to her slave if she realized Sajda cared what happened to the prince?

"Please don't worry," he said quietly while his pulse raced, and his stomach churned.

"I'm not worried," she shot back.

"Sajda." He reached for her, his hand brushing the bare skin of her arm. She spun toward him, and for a second, her dark blue eyes were haunted with misery and fear. Then she slapped a hand against the stone wall beside her, closed her eyes, and drew in a shuddering breath.

When she looked at him again, her cold, unflappable demeanor was back in place. Meeting his gaze steadily, she said, "You still have lessons to teach me, Prince."

"I know."

"So don't die."

He swallowed hard. "I won't."

Javan spent the entire walk down to the arena praying that he could keep that promise—for Sajda, his father, his kingdom, and himself.

The arena was full of reddish brown sand nearly as deep as Javan's waist. Patches of the sand glowed like blood beneath the skylights. Small black flags were planted above the location of the weapons Sajda had buried the day before. Aristocrats and some wealthy merchants in pale linen with brilliant sashes and wraps filed in through the door that led from the magistrate's office, checking to make sure the palace steward was recording their attendance as their voices filled the hollow space with the bright din of excited conversation and laughter.

Their laughter made Javan feel sick.

People were going into the arena to fight and possibly die for the entertainment of those who would never have to worry about entering Maqbara as anything other than a spectator. Javan prowled the space between the stalls and the arena's entrance, shaking out his arms and keeping his muscles loose, while he glared at the crowd.

"Don't waste your energy on them," Intizara said as she began pacing beside him, her expression fierce. "This is a game, and we're their pawns."

"We're people, not pawns."

She snorted. "What part of Akram do you come from?"

He hesitated, and then said carefully, "I was actually raised in Loch Talam. I only recently returned to Akram."

"That explains your fancy accent," she said. "I knew you couldn't be a real aristocrat like some of the prisoners think. Aristocrats don't end up in Maqbara. They're too busy accusing us of crimes—inventing the evidence if they have to—so they can take our businesses and enslave our children. This"—she swept an arm out to encompass the arena—"is just another way to show us that in Akram the rich now own us from our first breath to our last."

Javan met her gaze while anger burned hot and bright within him. "That goes against everything the sacred texts teach."

"The sacred texts don't seem to matter now that the king is in poor health and his cousin is helping with his duties until the prince returns."

She started to walk away, and Javan grabbed her arm. "Fariq is helping to rule Akram?"

"Not officially," she said. "But everyone knows he makes some of the decisions now. This competition was his idea. A way to entertain the aristocrats, keep the prison population down so that more can be sent here on nothing more than the word of those loyal to him, and line both his pockets and the warden's. The king only shows up at the end, and it's clear he's confused about where he is and what he's doing, but Fariq likes to check in on the competitors." She nodded toward the royal box, and Javan whirled to find his uncle and the impostor standing, their backs to the arena as they chatted with a few members of the aristocracy, a group of palace guards stationed by the door.

The muscles in his neck knotted, and something oily and slick coated his stomach as he glared at their backs.

He was in prison because of them. Risking his life because of their lies. Their corruption.

The truth burned on his tongue, and he longed to shout it for all the crowd to hear. His body trembled with the effort of keeping silent, but there was nothing to be gained by trying to expose the impostor now except a swift death sentence. Javan had no leverage. No advantage. And the one person with the power to reverse his situation wasn't here.

"Betting closes in a few moments," the warden's gravelly voice boomed out from her platform above the arena. "Competitors, line up."

Slowly, Javan turned his back on the royal box and joined

Intizara, Gadi, Nadim, and Kali at the edge of the arena, his hands curled over the wooden wall that separated him from the lake of sand on the other side and whatever horror the warden had hidden beneath it. He risked one quick glance toward the stalls where Sajda and Tarek stood. Tarek sent him a reassuring smile, but Sajda's expression was carved out of stone. He met her eyes for one brief moment, his chest tightening at the fierceness of her gaze, and then he turned back to the arena as the audience took their seats.

He couldn't think about Sajda or the impostor and his uncle. He needed all his focus to survive whatever waited for him in the arena.

"We have a special treat for your entertainment today," the warden said. "For the first time in the five-year history of this tournament, at great risk and expense, we've brought in a beast of myth and legend from the outer reaches of our own Samaal Desert. Buried beneath the sand is a *shy' tan amarryl*!"

The crowd gasped, and Javan's skin went cold. Sand demons were deadly and impossible to kill. How would setting an unbeatable beast loose against her competitors serve the warden? If everyone died, the competition was over, and her income stream would dry up until the winter tournament.

"A sand demon?" Gadi breathed the words beside him. "I thought those were just in bedtime stories to frighten children."

Javan had thought so too, but the warden wasn't interested in frightening children. He looked up at the platform and found her dark eye trained on him. She smiled and reached up to touch the bandage that covered the eye his arrow had taken. Understanding settled over him, heavy as a stone, and it was suddenly hard to breathe.

This was a death sentence.

He swallowed past the thickness in his throat and tried to force his frantic pulse to slow. The warden was working with Fariq and the impostor. Javan was supposed to have died in Loch Talam. When he'd shown up in Makan Almalik and confronted the impostor, he'd been sentenced to death at the *muqsila*. Instead, he'd ended up in Maqbara, competing for a boon from the one person who was sure to recognize Javan as the true prince: his father.

Of course, Fariq and the impostor couldn't let that happen. If the warden killed every competitor left in the tournament today, the takeover of Akram could continue without a hitch. The warden would probably receive a nice fee for her service to Akram's new ruler, and she could mount another tournament as soon as she'd replenished her supply of prisoners.

He was in deep trouble, and so were his fellow competitors.

The warden's voice echoed across the arena. "As you know, the *shy' tan amarryl* has the body of a lizard the size of a full-grown dragon with seven snake heads. It lives far beneath the ground and only surfaces to eat every ten years during a season of drought. Most have never seen one of these creatures in person, but you will get to see one in action today." Her voice lowered as if she was sharing a secret. "I can assure you the monster is most unhappy at being taken from its natural habitat. I doubt it will die willingly."

The crowd clapped its approval, and Javan clenched his fists to keep his hands from shaking.

The beast wasn't going to die at all. The storybooks all claimed it was invulnerable to the weapons of men. All Javan could do was hope to somehow survive.

The warden raised her voice again. "Competitors, fifty points will be awarded for every head you cut off, but be careful. For every head you remove, two grow in its place."

"Listen to me," Javan said quietly. His allies turned to look at him, their faces blanched with fear. "Grab your weapons and get into formation quickly. We'll fight off any head that comes our way without cutting it off, if possible."

"We won't get any points that way," Gadi said.

"We aren't going to need points if we're dead," Javan answered. "Killing one head makes the creature twice as powerful. Only take a head if you have no choice."

"Then how are we going to kill it?" Kali asked, her voice shaking as the crowd stamped their feet and yelled for the competition to start, many of them glancing fearfully at the royal box to make sure Fariq noticed their fervent participation. Behind her, a ripple shuddered over the sand as if something beneath it was moving.

"I'm working on that," Javan said, putting as much confidence as he could into his voice.

He looked past Kali to meet Sajda's eyes once more. They blazed with fury, and the runes on her cuffs were glowing.

"Competitors, take your places!" the warden yelled.

Javan turned away from Sajda, grabbed the edge of the arena wall, and leaped into the ring.

TWENTY-EIGHT

"A SAND DEMON? She's going to kill all the competitors, and the tournament will end before we've raked in the bets from the final two rounds," Fariq grumbled as he took a seat beside Rahim. Below them, the prisoners were crawling over the arena's wall and gingerly moving to the black flags that marked the location of the hidden weapons. Turning to the closest guard, he said, "Take note of which families are in attendance today and send someone to get an account of how much each family bet. There are several petitions lying on my desk. I'll need the information to make decisions in the morning. Especially since this will apparently be the final round of the event."

"We have bigger things to worry about than a silly tournament," Rahim said, his voice sharp. "There's plenty of wealth in the royal coffers."

The crown wasn't lacking an income. He'd seen the tax ledgers himself while quietly exploring the palace steward's office during a late night excursion just this past week. It could withstand not getting its cut of a sporting event.

"Fool!" Fariq hissed. "My cousin cut me off from all but a measly stipend seven years ago. This tournament is all that finances the FaSaa'il and our bid for the crown. You can't take over a kingdom and ensure the loyalty of your allies if you can't be generous with your coin."

"The crown is within reach," Rahim said. "You won't need coin to finance the FaSaa'il much longer."

Fariq opened his mouth to reply as Rahim leaned forward to get a good look at the competitors.

A boy about his age strode toward a cluster of black flags, four other prisoners in his wake. He held himself with a confidence and agility that were familiar. Bending to retrieve a pair of short swords, he slowly stood and locked eyes with Rahim.

The fury that radiated from the boy's body landed on Rahim like a physical blow, and the air left Rahim's lungs as if he'd been punched. Fariq was still talking as Rahim grabbed his arm, his fingers digging into the older man's skin.

"Unhand me this—"

"He's alive."

"Who?" Fariq yanked his arm free.

Rahim's voice was little more than a breath. "Javan."

Fariq's mouth snapped shut, and he whipped his head toward the arena.

As the warden shouted for the guards to wake the sand demon, Javan lifted his swords and gave Rahim a look that said the boy wanted to use the weapons on him instead of the monster waiting beneath the sand.

"That traitorous guard, I'll have his head." Fariq's voice rose. "I'll have his family's heads. I'll—"

"Calm yourself, Fariq." Rahim spoke through gritted teeth as the guards around them shifted uneasily. "The warden has clearly already assessed the situation and come up with a solution."

"If the warden had killed Javan in Loch Talam like she was supposed to, she wouldn't need a solution," Fariq said in a furious whisper.

Rahim frowned. "The warden was on the team of assassins?"

"She was my backup plan." Fariq glared at the arena, lines of tension bracketing his mouth. "She was supposed to kill him if the assassins failed. I told her to watch the academy in case he survived the attempt on his life after the commencement ceremony. It's not like her not to do her job."

"I don't see how one person, however formidable, could do a better job than a trio of assassins." Rahim clenched his fists in the folds of his robe. He was surrounded by incompetence. If he'd been in charge of killing Javan, if the FaSaa'il ever once bothered to listen to him, the prince would be long dead.

"The warden isn't just a person," Fariq said quietly. "She's a Draconi. She was supposed to shift into her dragon form and—"

"*She's* the Draconi who attacked the school the day before the commencement ceremony?" Rahim struggled to keep his voice down as the competitors near Javan sifted through the sand at their feet to remove the weapons buried there.

"What are you talking about?" Fariq turned his attention to Rahim.

"The headmaster increased security at Milisatria because of it. He got into the carriage with me to discuss Javan's safety since the Draconi had attacked the prince during some sort of exam." Rahim leaned closer to Fariq, his words falling like blows. "Javan wasn't supposed to die publicly, and certainly not before his commencement ceremony. It would be difficult to convince people that I'm the prince if they'd already seen the prince die. Your partnership with this woman nearly compromised our goals once, and now it seems she's had Javan under her roof all these weeks, and didn't see fit to either tell you or kill him herself."

The prison guards assigned to the competition hefted large rocks into the air and threw them into the center of the sand. They landed with muffled thuds, and the sand shuddered and then began sliding away from the thing that was slowly rising.

"It doesn't matter now," Fariq said. "No one in that arena is going to survive this."

A smile stretched across Rahim's face as a shiny black lizard with seven snake heads mounted on necks as long as two grown men lying end to end shook itself free of the sand and swung its heads toward the prisoners huddled at the edges of the arena.

Javan turned away from the royal box to focus on the threat, his mouth moving as he spoke to the prisoners who were working with him. Rahim clasped his hands together in a white-knuckled grip and leaned forward.

The crowd sucked in a collective breath as the heads all struck at once—seven glistening black streaks of lethal speed that left four prisoners bleeding on the sand. One competitor sliced off the head that came for him, and two more were rapidly growing in its place. The creature's golden eyes were bisected by a thick black bar of a pupil, and Rahim shuddered when one head rose to look around at the crowd.

He certainly hoped the warden knew how to control the creature.

The heads struck again, blurs of motion that were hard to

track, and the crowd screamed as more prisoners fell, more heads were hacked off, and still more grew in their place.

When the head closest to Javan struck, he lunged to the side, as did his allies. Again and again, they danced just out of range, and Rahim's palms began to sweat. Surely the boy wouldn't escape certain death again. No one could be that lucky.

Rahim sat, stomach churning, heart thundering in his ears, as the sand demon whipped its heads around, lashing out at anything that moved.

This time, Javan wasn't fast enough. He stumbled, and the demon's teeth sank into his back, tearing at the prince's flesh.

Fariq made a choked noise in the back of his throat as Javan hit the sand, blood flowing freely. The four who were allied with him grabbed him and helped him up, but he swayed on his feet.

Slowly, Rahim stood, triumph burning through him.

The monster struck again, this time latching onto one of the boy's allies. The man screamed as the snake's head tore into his neck.

Javan looked away from the creature, away from the injured man, and toward the side of the arena. Rahim stepped to the edge of the royal box to follow his gaze and found a tall girl with pale skin and black hair glaring at the prince as she mouthed one word over and over.

What was she saying?

He leaned further to get a direct look at her lips, and hands snatched his arms to hold him back, as down in the arena Javan yelled something to his allies.

"Step back, Your Highness," a guard said, her tone respectful but firm.

Javan's allies abandoned him and ran along the edges of the

arena toward the wall beneath the warden's platform.

"Let me go." Rahim tried to look at the girl again, but she'd stepped away from the arena's edge.

Had she helped Javan in some way? Surely she couldn't have much to offer. The prince was facing a sand demon. His weapons were useless.

"Your Highness, you are too close to the edge. Please, step back now."

The monster's heads swiveled toward the three prisoners running along the arena's edge, and then Javan was yelling. Jumping up and down, his face a mask of pain as he hefted a short sword.

Rahim's gaze swung from Javan to the running prisoners as the creature attacked Javan, its other heads still snapping toward the remaining competitors. Dread pooled in his stomach and clogged his throat.

Javan was buying them time. He knew something the others didn't.

"No!" Rahim yelled, his voice ripe with fury. "Get the ones who are running!"

"Your Highness!" Another guard joined the first to forcibly pull Rahim from the edge of the box.

"They know something. The girl must have told them." Rahim rounded on the guards and shoved them away. "Fariq!"

Fariq's lips were pressed tight as Javan sliced through the head that was tearing at his stomach and then fell back on the sand, a sword still held in his hand, though his grip looked weak.

"Sit, my prince," Fariq's tone was brusque. "It is unseemly to become so invested in the lives of mere prisoners."

Rahim glanced around to find all the palace guards watching him with narrowed eyes. His pulse spiked, his knees trembling with the effort to rein in the fury and find his royal composure before anyone could wonder why their prince wanted one particular contestant dead. Drawing in a shaky breath, he took a step away from the edge of the box and nodded once to show Fariq that he was under control.

Javan had been bitten twice. Blood was flowing. Even if the other competitors somehow found a way to defeat the sand demon, surely it was already too late for the prince.

The boy's allies reached the wall beneath the warden's box, shoveled sand out of the way, and revealed a gleaming copper faucet with a mouth as wide as two fists. Wrenching the handle, they cranked it all the way open. Water gushed into the arena.

At first, nothing changed. The creature attacked, its seven necks now carrying the weight of at least twenty-eight heads. Prisoners were screaming, fighting, or lying silent on the sand. The crowd was stomping its feet and cheering, many of them looking at the royal box to make sure their show of appreciation was being noted.

The water sank into the sand, and a large dark spot began expanding from the faucet's mouth as the water rushed toward the center of the arena. When it reached the sand demon, the creature hissed, all seven necks whirling to investigate the source of the water. In seconds, it was burrowing down below the surface of the sand, but the water was already there.

The monster thrashed, its heads breaking the surface.

"It can't breathe underwater!" one of the prisoners yelled.

Instantly, those who could still stand converged on the beast, wrestling with the heads, chopping them off and then plunging the necks into the watery sand before new heads could grow in their place.

In moments, it was over. The sand demon was drowned. The crowd was screaming its approval.

And the true prince of Akram was shakily climbing to his feet, someone's tunic pressed to the wound in his stomach, while he locked eyes with Rahim and glared.

Rahim glared back.

Sometimes when you wanted someone dead, you had to do the job yourself.

TWENTY-NINE

JAVAN WOKE IN the predawn darkness of the infirmary the morning after facing the sand demon, his body throbbing with pain. The monster had torn into his back and raked his stomach open. Every breath hurt, every movement was fire running through his veins.

But worse was the crushing knowledge that he'd failed.

His bargain with Sajda, his allies, and his strategy were worth nothing in the face of the warden's alliance with Fariq and the impostor. Yes, Javan had survived. But he'd gained no points; the warden was bent on killing him, even if it meant killing everyone else in the tournament; and the impostor now knew that Javan was still alive.

Still a threat.

How long before he came for Javan?

And how could Javan stop him? He couldn't defeat the warden, the crown, and his fellow prisoners combined. At the moment, he couldn't even get out of bed.

Darkness bloomed in his chest, heavy and absolute, and he closed his eyes.

Where was Yl' Haliq in all of this? Where was the steady presence that had comforted and guided Javan for so many years? Didn't he see the prince, abandoned and surrounded by enemies?

Tears pricked his eyelids, and he blinked rapidly.

Something rustled to his left, and he whipped his head in that direction, half expecting to see Hashim rising from his bed, but the man had been hurt worse than Javan, and he wasn't moving. Instead, Javan locked eyes with Sajda, who sat beside the doorway, her back against the cold stone wall.

She rose in one fluid motion and came to his side. For a long moment they stared at each other, and Javan couldn't think of a single thing to say. Finally, she reached past him to a shelf above his cot and grabbed a small bowl and a cup of water. Scooping up a spoonful of yellow-gold powder, she dumped it into the water, stirred briskly, and then sat beside him on the cot.

"Drink this," she said.

He stifled a groan as he struggled to get into an upright position. She placed the cup on the floor, wrapped her arms beneath his, and lifted. In seconds, his pillow was between his back and the wall, and she was handing him the cup again.

"Turmeric powder," she said. "It will help the pain."

He took an experimental sip, and then quickly downed the rest of the spicy drink. Maybe it would help dull the pain of his wounds. He wished there was something that would dull the rest of his pain as well.

She watched him carefully, and he scrambled for something to say. It wasn't her fault their plan wasn't going to work. She was caught up in all of it because she'd been loyal to Tarek. He prayed that loyalty didn't get her killed.

"You should leave," he said, keeping his voice low to avoid waking the other prisoners.

Her brow rose. "No 'thanks for giving me some medicine, Sajda'? Or 'thanks for spending the night in a doorway so that no one tried to kill me, Sajda'?"

"You spent the night here?" His voice rose. "Why would you do that?"

Hurt flashed across her face, so fast he almost missed it. "So that no one would try to kill you when you couldn't defend yourself."

He closed his eyes and tried to push the darkness inside him away. Tried to find the thread of hope he'd been holding on to for weeks. "I'm sorry," he whispered.

"It's okay."

"No, it isn't." He opened his eyes and met her gaze. "I'm sorry I got you involved in this at all. You shouldn't be here watching over me. You shouldn't try to help me with the next combat round. In fact, you need to stay as far away from me as possible."

Her eyes flashed. "You don't tell me what to do."

"I'm *not*." He drew in a deep breath, striving for calm. Maybe he couldn't protect himself, but he could protect her. "You're right. I don't tell you what to do. So I'm asking you. Please. Get away from me before my enemies decide to punish you for helping me."

She glared. "I don't know if you've noticed, but I'm pretty much all you've got. The warden just tried to kill everyone so she could get to you. Hashim might be too injured from the sand demon to hurt you at the moment, but that will change. And that boy in the royal box yesterday seemed very angry when the sand demon died. I don't think he wants you alive either."

"No, he doesn't. They all want me dead, and they're going to succeed, Sajda." He leaned forward, wincing at the pain that shot across his wounded stomach, his voice shaking. She had to listen. "They're going to succeed because they have all the power; and when they do, they're going to take down anyone close to me. I can't be responsible for your death. I *can't*. I might not be able to do anything else right, but let me at least do this."

She fell silent, and he stared at her for a long moment, his chest heaving with every breath, his composure fraying as he waited to see if she would do the one thing that would save her.

The one thing that would finish ruining him.

Then she straightened, throwing her shoulders back and raising her chin. There was fire in her eyes, and the runes on her cuffs glowed in the dim gray of the room. Leaning forward, she put a hand on his chest, and licks of heat spread from her skin to his. With one gentle push, he was back against the pillow, her face a few breaths from his.

"I'm not your slave," she said. "I don't take your orders."

The bottom dropped out of his stomach. "Sajda, no. I never said . . . That's not how I see you."

The heat from her palm raced along his chest, a thrill of lightning that sent his heart racing. "I know that. This isn't about how you see me. It's about how I see myself." She leaned closer, until he was drowning in the dark blue of her eyes. "I might wear the warden's cuffs, but I make my own choices. And I choose to help you."

He closed his eyes against the wave of pain and hope that threatened to undo him. "I've already lost everything, Sajda. I don't want to lose you too."

"Then you shouldn't have insisted on being my friend." Her voice was uncharacteristically gentle, and he opened his eyes to see fierce compassion on her face. "I don't turn my back on my friends."

"The warden will try to kill me again. So will the impostor and my uncle. Hashim—"

"When have you ever been afraid of a challenge?" She leaned back and pinned him with the look she usually gave him before they sparred.

"I'm afraid of this one," he said quietly.

"And that means you give up? You walk away and stop fighting? You give them what they want?"

His jaw tightened, and he looked away. "I'm not giving up. I'm acknowledging that the odds are stacked heavily against me. I was so sure I could fix this. So sure that my destiny was to rule Akram, and that Yl' Haliq would deliver me from this so that I could make things right. But he hasn't. Things just keep getting worse."

"So you fight harder. You fight smarter. And you don't tell your best ally to leave you alone."

"I don't know how to win," he admitted, forcing himself to look at her. "I don't know how to fight all three threats at the same time."

She smiled, and his pulse beat faster. "Hashim is badly injured. And sadly it looks like he is getting an infection from his wound. A shame so much dirt got in there after it was already bandaged."

He blinked. "Did you—"

"I doubt he'll be well enough to do anything to you for a

week or more. And the warden has a scandal on her hands, as does the crown."

"What do you mean?"

Her smile grew. "Oh, just a few well-placed observations and speculations with the right aristocrats during Exhibition Day. By now, the entire city should be on fire with rumors about the new competitor who looks so much like a Kadar. Many of the prominent families already hate what Fariq has done to the city and are just looking for an excuse to turn on him."

"And you made sure to give them what they needed."

"Like I said, I make my own choices. Now you choose to get better and keep fighting."

He leaned toward her, ignoring the burn of agony in his body, and wrapped his arms around her as the faint whisper of hope within him flickered into a flame. "Thank you for staying with me."

She stiffened at first, and then slowly melted into his embrace. Her body was warm, her breath tickled his neck, and the darkness that had opened up within him shrank a little before the unrelenting demands of her faith in him.

THIRTY

"OPEN THE DOOR," Rahim snapped as he entered the magistrate's office surrounded by his team of guards the day after the combat round against the sand demon. "I'm going to do an inspection of the prison."

"Inspection, Your Highness?" The magistrate hurried out from behind his large desk, his eyeglasses askew. "This is most unusual. Does the warden know you're coming?"

Rahim silenced him with a long, cold look.

"But of course, my prince. Whatever you'd like." The man hastened to lead Rahim and his guards to the tunnel that wound down to Maqbara's entrance.

Rahim didn't reply. Sweat beaded the man's brow as the silence extended throughout the length of the journey through the tunnel.

"My apologies, Your Highness." The magistrate's voice shook slightly. "The warden dislikes unexpected visitors, but that is no excuse for questioning my liege."

Rahim inclined his head in a slight acknowledgment of the apology and then swept inside the prison.

If the warden didn't want a surprise visit from the crown prince, then she should've made sure to kill Javan in Loch Talam like she'd been paid to do.

The tall girl with the pale skin and dark hair was sweeping sand from the arena floor so prisoners could shovel it into the open crates that lined the edges of the arena. She stilled as Rahim approached, and then slowly raised her gaze to his. Something cold skittered across Rahim's skin at the look on her face, and he gave her a predatory smile for the pleasure of watching her icy confidence dissolve into quivering obedience.

She raised her chin, something dangerous burning in her eyes.

His smile winked out.

Once he'd solved the problem of Javan, he was going to teach the warden's slave a lesson as well. He hadn't crawled his way out of the desert filth and into the palace just to have a slave refuse to give him his due.

"Where are the injured prisoners?" he asked.

"If you're looking for Javan, you should know—"

"*I'm* Javan," Rahim snapped. "Anyone claiming otherwise is a traitor who deserves death." His heart pounded, and rage licked at his veins.

Had the prince already turned the prisoners against him?

Something flickered in the girl's blue eyes, and she tugged at the iron bracelets she wore. "Of course you are," she said in a quiet, cold voice. "There is a prisoner here by the same name. You seemed interested in watching him fight yesterday. He was injured, so I thought you were referring to him."

It was a plausible explanation given how angry Rahim had been at the prince's survival, but it was unsettling that the slave had paid it any notice.

"You should know that he is one of the favorites among the aristocrats," the girl said. "They love to champion someone who has the strength to beat the odds." Her eyebrow rose. "Better return on their investment."

"What do I care about the aristocrats' betting?" he asked sharply.

"The crowd favorites are closely followed," she said, her eyes boring into his. "Rumors abound. Especially when one seems to resemble the royal family. It would be a shame for him to succumb to his injuries and fuel the speculation that he's a royal in prison by mistake."

Everything inside Rahim went cold and still. "Why would his death fuel speculation like that?"

"Because if he's in Maqbara by mistake, then there could be only one person who would benefit from placing him here. At least those were the rumors I overheard on the last Exhibition Day." She cocked her head. "I'm not sure what a group of suspicious aristocrats could do to a prince, of course. I'm sure I'm worried on your behalf for nothing."

He glared as his plan to simply slit Javan's throat and walk out of the prison disintegrated before the knowledge that doing so could jeopardize his upcoming coronation. One of the prison guards could talk. The magistrate could connect Rahim's visit with the death of the boy who looked like a Kadar. It was too risky to do the job himself, a fact that sent a flush of anger through his body.

Had the king heard the rumors yet? Rahim would have to

make sure every guard around the ruler was loyal to the FaSaa'il and then instruct them not to allow the old man any visitors. And he'd have to come up with a less personal way to make sure Javan died before the king attended the final round of combat. Quickly sorting through his options, he turned to the slave girl and said, "Tell the warden I want to speak to her and then take me to the infirmary."

She nodded, the barest inclination of her head that left him feeling like he was the one who'd been dismissed, and returned shortly with the warden.

Rahim kept it brief. "Announce to the prisoners that the aristocrat residing here and going by the name of Javan is an enemy of the crown. I will grant immediate release to any prisoner who kills him."

The slave girl remained silent and still. It was infuriating that Rahim couldn't tell if his words had made an impact.

"He's becoming a crowd favorite," the warden said. "If he dies suddenly, those betting on him will demand an investigation."

Rage curled through Rahim. Would every person he spoke to today question his judgment? Had they no care for the power he wielded over their pathetic lives? Leaning toward the warden, he snapped, "Then tell them to do it in the arena. I don't care. Just get it done."

Turning away from the warden, he motioned for the girl to take him to the infirmary and followed behind her as her long strides ate up the corridor. The infirmary was a long room filled with beds. Eight prisoners were currently in residence, including the prince. Torches illuminated the dim space, and a quick glance around the room showed Rahim that the prisoners were all badly wounded. Most were asleep or unconscious, and the two who were awake were lying on their backs groaning in pain.

No one even bothered looking at Rahim as he moved to Javan's bedside, leaving his guards and the slave girl behind in the hall.

Javan opened his eyes as Rahim approached, and anger swept his face. He struggled to sit up, and Rahim dug his hand into the bandaged wound on the boy's stomach and shoved him back onto the mattress. Blood seeped into the bandage, and pain bracketed the boy's mouth, though his furious expression remained unchanged.

Rahim leaned down and whispered, "Why don't you just die?"

"You first."

He bared his teeth. "Akram is mine now. The crown is mine. Your father is mine. You have nothing left to fight for."

"There's always something to fight for."

"Keep fighting then." Rahim shoved his fingers deeper into the wound, enjoying the hiss of pain that escaped the prince's lips. "It will only make my victory sweeter. You'll be dead by the end of the next combat round; but before you die, I want you to look in my eyes and know that I will personally kill your father once he gives me the crown. I was going to just let the poison he's been drinking twice a day do its work. We've become rather close these last few weeks, and I thought it the most merciful course of action."

"You know nothing of mercy. Or honor." The prince spat the words at him.

"Mercy and honor are for those who've never had to fight for a single thing they possess. I know everything about taking what is mine and destroying those who stand in my way." Blood soaked through the bandage and coated Rahim's fingertips. He bared his teeth in a vicious smile. "And the knowledge that I will kill your father, that he will suffer as he dies, is how I will finish destroying you."

Before the prince could reply, Rahim turned on his heel and left the room, and the prison, behind.

THIRTY-ONE

FIVE DAYS AFTER the false prince's visit to Maqbara, Sajda
paused at the door of the infirmary on her way from the weapons closet to the stalls. Javan was inside, still healing from his
wounds, but she didn't dare go talk to him. Not now that Hashim
and several of the other injured prisoners were awake and aware.

With the warden's plans to kill Javan failing, his popular-
ity with the bettors growing, and the false prince's bounty on
Javan's head in the next competition, Sajda didn't dare draw
attention to her friendship with Javan. For her sake, and for his.
It was one thing to spar with him during level fifteen's practice
sessions—she often joined the sparring sessions for the upper
levels, both to help the less capable prisoners with their skills and
to keep hers honed razor-sharp—or to use level fifteen for some
of the arena's less desirable chores under her direct supervision.
And keeping him from joining the others during mealtime could
easily be credited to Tarek's gratitude for Javan's defending him
against Hashim.

But something had shifted inside Sajda. A tiny crack in her defenses that she'd stopped trying to repair. When she was with Javan, she didn't have to pretend to be cold and indifferent. She didn't have to keep her distance. She felt free, but freedom wasn't what she'd thought it would be. It was a fire blazing in the heart of a rainstorm. It was the star-swept sky trapped inside her, and every time she stood near him, she could barely contain the power of it.

She couldn't risk being near him while their enemies were watching. Instead, she'd left Tarek in the infirmary to help the physician with strict instructions to shout her name if Hashim tried anything.

Turning away, Sajda brushed her palm against the stone wall outside the infirmary, drew on its icy strength, and then hurried toward the stalls as Batula shouted her name.

"They're here. Magistrate's door is already open. Don't like the looks of this shipment," Batula snapped as Sajda reached the stalls.

"You never like the looks of any of the shipments," she said as she pulled on her leather gloves and briefly envied Batula's iron vest.

Sajda had tried to wear a vest once five years ago when they received their first shipment of creatures from the fae isle of Lloren-yae, thinking that the discomfort of the iron was better than the risk of being disemboweled by the beasts she was handling. Instant waves of agony had driven her to her knees, and she'd lost her breakfast on the unforgiving floor of the arena. The warden had laughed and said monsters didn't get protection from other monsters. Sajda had spent the next few years mimicking every half-decent competitor in her spare hours, practicing until her raw strength and reflexes became a finely honed weapon she could use against the beasts; the prisoners; and maybe, if she was lucky, against the warden herself.

Turning, Sajda faced the entrance in time to see two dozen guards carefully maneuvering iron crates through the doorway and into the arena under the careful supervision of Hansel and Gretel, the twin bounty hunters who brought each order the warden requested from Llorenyae. Sajda had spent plenty of time with the twins in the five years since the tournament began. Hansel was a charming tease, but Gretel had become the closest thing to a friend Sajda had outside of Tarek and now Javan.

Quickly counting the crates, Sajda turned to eye the stalls, her stomach sinking.

She'd have to put something in the last stall—the one with her tunnel in it. Frustration set her on edge at the thought of going weeks without making any progress toward escape.

"Sajda, my mysterious rose, it's been too long," Hansel called out, flashing her a wide grin. The light that filtered in through the prison's skylights dusted bits of gold in his dark red hair and lingered on the runes inked into his arms.

Runes that matched the ones carved into Sajda's cuffs. If the twins had ever wondered about the similarity, they'd never mentioned it, though Sajda had caught Gretel eyeing the cuffs more than once.

"Stop calling her that. It's ridiculous." Gretel rolled her eyes at her brother and then whirled as one of the guards stumbled, nearly dropping his crate. She stalked toward him, the silver bells woven into the braided strip of shocking white that streaked through her dark red hair tinkling as she moved.

"Move with care, move with care," Hansel said to the guards.

"If you break it, you've bought it, and I do hate to clean up bloodstains."

Sajda moved through the line of stalls, opening doors and checking for weaknesses, even though she'd already double-checked them the day before.

It paid to be careful around the kind of beasts Hansel and Gretel delivered.

"You'll need netting around two of the stalls," Gretel spoke softly from the first stall as she eyed Sajda's progress. "One of the creatures has wings, and the other can climb."

Sajda nodded and moved to put netting in place. "Anything else?"

"Oh the usual," Hansel said as he joined his sister and winked at Sajda. "Teeth, vicious temperaments, and the occasional wee bit of magic easily contained by the iron in these stalls."

His gaze bounced off her cuffs and away, but heat burned in Sajda's cheeks.

Did they think she was a vicious beast who needed to be contained too?

"Three of the creatures are sealed in coffins," Hansel said, "and if I were you, I wouldn't break those open until the moment you truly need them. Once you let a reiligarda out of its grave, it's incredibly dangerous to try putting it back. Here." He handed her a leather pouch half the length of her arm. "We skimmed some grave dirt from each coffin for you. Put it on whomever is going to fight the reiligarda. The nasty things go straight for anyone who smells like they're the ones who disturbed the grave."

Sajda accepted the pouch gingerly. "I need to store three coffins?"

Hansel turned to answer a question from one of the guards, and Gretel said, "If you don't have an extra stall, you could—"

"I have a stall." Sajda placed the pouch on a shelf and moved toward the end of the row, her magic churning at the relief that flooded her.

She could keep the reiligarda in the stall with her tunnel, and she could still keep digging. Keep working toward the escape she so desperately craved.

"In here," she said, and then whirled toward Hansel as a crate crashed against the stone floor. The boy cursed, and Sajda moved quickly to assist him as a beast slashed at the crack in its crate with razor-sharp talons.

When the creature was once again contained, she instructed the guards to roll the reiligarda's coffins to the back stall where Gretel still stood.

"I'll do that," Gretel said firmly.

Hansel laughed. "One of these days I'm going to have to introduce you to the wonders of delegating menial tasks to others."

Gretel didn't reply. Instead, she waved the guards off and began maneuvering the coffins into the stall. "Sajda, you can help."

Sajda moved to the stall and grasped one side of the coffin, grateful to be wearing her leather gloves so that she wouldn't have to touch the iron directly. When they had the first coffin wedged against the far corner of the stall, Gretel said softly, "Are you in trouble?"

Sajda froze and whipped her gaze up to meet Gretel's piercing blue eyes. For a long moment, neither of them spoke, and then Gretel nodded toward the hay trough.

Turning, Sajda saw that the trough wasn't flush against the wall. The shadow of her tunnel peeked out from behind it.

Gretel stepped past her and shoved the trough back into place. "It's yours, isn't it?"

Sajda's heart pounded, magic screaming through her veins to hurl itself helplessly at the cuffs that bound her.

"That's what I thought," Gretel said, as if Sajda's silence had confirmed something for her. Glancing at the cuffs on Sajda's wrists, she said quietly, "Will you tell me what you are?"

What would the girl who hunted monsters do if she learned what kind of monster Sajda was beneath her cuffs? The world dropped out from under Sajda's feet, and her hands came up, fingers curled like claws ready to draw blood.

Gretel raised her hands, palms out. "I'm on your side, Sajda. I've spent a lifetime around those who are evil and those who are powerful. I know the difference."

Slowly, Sajda lowered her hands, her heart pounding painfully in her chest. "What are you going to do?"

Gretel smiled, and there was a shadow of sadness in her eyes. "I want to help you, if you'll let me."

"Why?"

"Because we're friends, and I don't have very many of those."

Letting her help meant trusting her completely, something Sajda struggled to do. Still, Gretel could have called for the warden the moment she saw the hole in the wall behind the trough. She could have just walked away without getting involved. Instead, she'd offered to help, and Sajda knew Gretel never said anything she didn't mean.

Gretel spoke quickly as Hansel shouted her name in the

background. "What if next time Hansel and I deliver some beasts, we smuggle you out in one of the crates?"

The crates. Made of iron. Sajda imagined the terrible waves of pain and sickness that would bring her to her knees, and swallowed back a lump in her throat. She could endure anything if it meant escape. Tarek could easily fit in a crate too. And if Javan was still trapped in Maqbara when winter hit and Hansel and Gretel returned with their next shipment, she'd smuggle him out in a crate as well.

Meeting Gretel's gaze, she said, "I'm listening."

Gretel glanced over her shoulder as if looking for eavesdroppers and then spoke quickly. "The order we're delivering now takes care of all the beasts the warden needs for the remaining rounds of the tournament. We won't be back until the winter order is placed. If you still need help then, I'll be ready."

Sajda looked at the iron crates and swallowed.

Gretel brushed her hand against Sajda's arm and said, "I'll bring wooden crates."

Sajda met her gaze and found fierce compassion on her friend's face. Would she still feel compassion if she knew what Sajda really was? "I can explain—"

"You don't need to. I shouldn't have asked," Gretel said. "I'll be here with a wooden crate this winter if you still need help."

"Three wooden crates," Sajda said. If Javan didn't win the tournament, he'd need a way out, and Sajda couldn't imagine leaving Tarek behind.

Gretel nodded. "Three crates. Be safe until winter."

"Until winter," Sajda said as Gretel left the stall.

Maybe Sajda would still be in Maqbara in five months when Hansel and Gretel brought the first shipment for the winter tournament. Or maybe Javan would win the competition, ask the king for his freedom, and return for her once he'd been restored as the prince. Her magic sizzled against her cuffs as she imagined what it would be like to be free.

THIRTY-TWO

RAHIM PULLED HIS royal purple sash across his chest and through the loop at the waist of his blue tunic. Checking his reflection in the gilt-edged mirror above his dresser, he practiced blinking the violent hunger from his eyes. Nearly two months of living at the palace and hiding how much he hated those who still treated him like a puppet was getting easier.

It was about to be easier still.

The coronation was scheduled in three weeks, just after the end of the tournament. He was sure the other prisoners would take the bait and kill Javan during the next round of combat, but he had another plan in place should that one fail. The FaSaa'il was in a fury over Javan's continued existence—rumors were growing into bold talk as people speculated about the prisoner who looked so much like their ruler.

Rahim wasn't worried. Rumors would never reach the king. The distrust Rahim had sown with the forged document from Fariq had blossomed into full-blown paranoia as the older man

272

refused to have any staff wait on him, to receive visitors, or to leave the palace unless accompanied by the one person he knew he could trust: his son.

On the day of the final tournament round, should Javan miraculously make it that far, a simple dose of saffeyena could be administered to make the king pliable and open to suggestion. If it seemed the king was fixating on Javan, a quiet word about rumors that one of Fariq's bastards had been sent to Maqbara would be enough to swing the king's favor against the true prince once and for all.

Turning away from the mirror, Rahim moved toward the door. He had a packed schedule of visits from the various aristocratic families who lived in or around Makan Almalik. Invitations to the coronation ceremony had finally been sent, and it seemed every wealthy aristocrat in the area wanted to greet him one-on-one and remind him of all they brought to the table as an ally.

Every wealthy aristocrat, of course, except those who'd had children at Milisatria with Javan. Those families were now exiled to distant political posts in Ichil and Eldr or had lost their lands, fortunes, and reputations to accusations of treason. All Rahim's idea, though he'd had to make it seem like Fariq had thought of it.

Soon, he wouldn't have to worry about playing the part of a good little puppet.

Soon, he'd be a god among men, and everyone who wanted to survive would do well to remember it.

The families who remained in the crown's good graces would either immediately accept Rahim as their king and repudiate the rumors about Javan, or they would find themselves in Maqbara.

The priests would continue their little charity work with the poor but would give a portion of all donations to the crown as a reminder of who truly ruled Akram.

And the FaSaa'il, who thought they'd found an uncouth little peasant who would obey their every whim, would go to their graves knowing they'd been outwitted at every turn.

Rahim's heart beat faster.

It had been a simple matter to mix a sleeping herb into the king's morning tonic so that he would remain in his bed for most of the day. And it was easy to arrange to have as Rahim's personal guard Abbas, the man who'd escorted Javan to the magistrate's office and then allowed him to go into Maqbara instead of executing him as ordered. The crowning achievement of Rahim's day was the ease with which he'd smuggled into the palace the three peasant assassins the FaSaa'il had tasked with killing Javan in Loch Talam. It had taken a bit of manipulation on his part to get the assassins' names from Lord Borak, but he'd done it. He couldn't pull off today's plan without them.

Leaving his bedroom, he moved through his opulent sitting room and then down the hall in the residential wing until he came to the dining room used only by the Kadars and their closest friends. Abbas followed at his heels, his eyes constantly studying Rahim as if searching for flaws in his claim to be the true prince.

It was infinitely satisfying that he would go to his grave still unsure which boy had been telling the truth.

Voices filled the dining room, and Rahim flagged a page who was standing at attention by the door.

"Yes, Your Highness?"

That title never got old. "Have all the invited families arrived?"

"Yes, Your Highness."

"Every member is present?"

"Yes, Your Highness. I checked the invitation list as you instructed."

"Excellent. You're dismissed," Rahim said as the kitchen staff began assembling the first course on a table beside the door.

"Very good, Your Highness." The page left, and Rahim nodded at the two maids who were checking that the orange florets that garnished each plate were in their proper places. "You may begin serving. I'll be along shortly. Abbas, please take a position in the dining room."

The maids curtsied, picked up the trays, and entered the dining room. Abbas frowned as if he wanted to argue that he should stay with Rahim, but a quick glare from the boy sent him into the room as instructed.

Rahim examined the tray of goblets the maids had left behind. Pale, golden apple wine shimmered in the sunlight that streamed in through the nearby windows.

His breath was a ragged gasp that sounded deafening in his ears, and his hands shook as he unstoppered a bottle Fariq had purchased from an apothecary weeks ago for the king's tonic.

Poison.

A soft white powder made from grinding cyallip seeds.

Rahim had ordered cyallip tarts for dessert even though there would be no one left alive to eat them. It had seemed fitting.

Tipping the bottle over each glass, he watched as the powder spilled into the goblets, spinning like a tiny sand devil until it disappeared into the golden liquid. A small amount, as was given daily to the king, would weaken the body, eat away at the immune system, and confuse the thinking as the body fought to heal the damage to itself.

The large amount he'd just mixed into each goblet would do far worse than that.

When the maids returned for the trays, Rahim had the bottle concealed in his pocket again. He waited until the maids were finished serving the drinks before excusing them.

"You can come out now," he said quietly. A rustling came from the drapes that flanked the windows along the hall and then the three peasants hired to assassinate Javan joined him outside the dining room. "You remember what to do?"

"Wait until you shout, and then enter and kill the guard," one of the men said.

"He's highly trained. I trust you brought poison-tipped blades as instructed," Rahim said.

"We're ready," the tall man said.

Turning away from them, Rahim entered the dining room and closed the door behind him.

The members of the FaSaa'il sat at the table glaring at him.

He met their eyes calmly.

"What is the meaning of this?" Borak demanded. "You don't call meetings with us. We call meetings with you."

Rahim raised a brow. "Then why didn't you refuse to come?"

"And have it be said that we disobeyed the prince?"

Moving to the head of the table, he inclined his head graciously and said, "I can see your dilemma."

"Where is Fariq?" Borak demanded.

Sweeping the assembled aristocrats with his gaze, Rahim said, "I apologize that Fariq is unable to join us as promptly as he wished. He'll be along as soon as he's able. In the meantime, we have excellent news. The coronation plans are proceeding without a problem. The king is fully in support. In a few weeks, all you wanted will be accomplished." He raised his glass as Abbas stiffened, his eyes widening as he stared at Rahim. "A toast! To the success of your plan and to many years of prosperous rule in Akram!"

They stood with him. Raised their glasses. Spilled a drop as an offering for Yl' Haliq before raising the liquid to their lips.

The shortest man went first—the poison working rapidly as it shut down his organs and dropped him to the floor. The others realized something was wrong, but they were already too far gone to do anything but fall to the ground, convulse briefly, and die as well.

Rahim set his goblet on the table with a click as Abbas scrambled for the closest aristocrat, calling for someone to send for the palace physician.

"Happy to oblige," he said. Raising his voice, he shouted, "Help! Bring the physician!"

The door burst open, and the three peasants rushed in, poison-tipped weapons drawn. By the time Abbas realized he was in danger, it was too late.

Rahim reached inside the pockets of his tunic for his throwing stars. The first star embedded itself in the tallest assassin's neck. The second burrowed into the shortest man's chest. The third man tried to run, but Rahim simply adjusted his aim and sent the final star deep into the man's back.

In moments, all three were dead, their blood spreading across the hand-painted tiles of the floor like a river. Rahim took an extra minute to arrange the bodies so that it would look like

Abbas had taken out the intruders and lost his own life in the process and then rehearsed the story he'd tell about being the last to raise his glass to his lips, seeing the others fall, and realizing that someone in the kitchen staff was a murderer. He'd call for a full investigation, and no one would doubt his word. After all, he was their prince.

His smile stretched wide and feral.

A god among men indeed.

THIRTY-THREE

THE NIGHT JAVAN was well enough to leave the infirmary, Sajda waited until twelfth bell rang, the bars dropped, and the prison fell silent before she quietly instructed Tarek to bring Javan to her. Tarek winked at her as he escorted Javan to the stairwell that led up to the old man's room on level eight and then left them alone.

The second Tarek was out of sight, Sajda froze.

What was she doing?

Sneaking a boy out of the infirmary when she knew what would happen if the warden discovered that Javan, of all people, wasn't where he was supposed to be. Worse, planning on taking him to the one place that had always been hers alone.

Her magic stung her veins, an anxious buzzing she couldn't ignore as she met his gaze beneath the moonlight that filled the skylights above.

He smiled, a slow journey of warmth that hammered away at her already shaky defenses.

"What are we doing?" he asked, his voice a low breath of air that brushed against her, sending a shiver over her skin.

She took a step back.

This could be a mistake. The kind of mistake that ripped out her heart and left it in ruins. She'd had enough of that in her sixteen years to last her a lifetime. If she was smart, she'd return him to the infirmary.

"Sajda?" He came closer, and she held her ground, her magic churning, her heart aching at the concern on his face.

Who knew if she'd ever truly escape Maqbara? Javan could lose the competition and his chance for an audience with his father. Gretel could change her mind about smuggling Sajda out. The warden could find the tunnel her slave was digging. Even if she did escape, would she ever find another friend who fit her jagged edges so effortlessly? If she backed down now, she might never know what he would do with her truth.

He faced his demons, both in the arena and without, and he was honest with her about every doubt, every fear.

It was absolutely terrifying that she wanted to do the same thing with him.

"Are you all right?" he asked, and she took his hand before she could talk herself out of it.

"Come with me," she whispered, magic dancing across her fingertips and on to his as she led him to the fifteenth level, past the mostly empty cells, and into the storage closet at the end. Leaping into the crack in the ceiling, she turned, braced herself, and offered her hand to help pull him up.

Once he was through the gap, she guided him around pillars and under support beams until they reached the corner of the ceiling where her skylight was waiting for them. The stars were just winking to life, and the moon was a thin slice of brilliant light high in the sky. She helped him duck past the last beam and then they crawled onto the blankets she kept there.

Javan stared at the blankets and pillows, at the skylight and the huge swath of sky above them, and slowly smiled.

"You like it?" she asked, and her cheeks warmed as she waited for his answer. This wasn't just a hideout. It was her dreams. Her secrets laid bare. It was the side of her she sheathed in stone every morning to keep it from the prison's taint.

"I love it. It suits you," he said, and the sincerity in his voice settled the churn of magic through her blood.

She sank back against a pillow and waited for her tiny blue star to appear. He lay beside her, his head on a second pillow, his arms crossed beneath the back of his neck. The silence between them was warm and welcoming, and she let it linger.

When finally her tiny blue star shimmered into focus, she said softly, "Sometimes I pretend I live there."

"Where?" He followed her finger as she pointed, and then said, "Seraphael."

"Seraphael? Is that the star's name?"

He turned to watch her face. "It's not a star. It's another planet like ours."

"I knew it." She smiled, wide and content, as she turned the word *Seraphael* over and over in her mind until it felt familiar.

"When did you discover this place?"

"I was nine. Exploring the entire prison at night trying to find a way out." She lifted her fingers to tangle them in the starlight, letting her magic drink in the cold purity and unbearable beauty until her blood seemed to sing with it. "I never did find a way out, but I found the next best thing."

"Will you tell me what this means to you?" he asked, his voice quiet.

She stretched her fingertips toward the starlight as far as they would go. It was never far enough. "It's freedom, or the closest thing to it that I can find."

Her heart thudded, and her breath caught as the words she'd never said to anyone gathered in her throat, surrounded by the icy distance of the stars that had always felt like home. And then he unfolded his arms and slid one under her shoulders, pulling her to his side where she could lean against him if she wanted.

She wanted. She wanted so many things that she could never have. But just for tonight, hidden from the eyes of the warden and the other prisoners, safe from the fear that Javan would be killed, she could pretend that the things she wanted were all within her reach.

Moving slowly, she tipped her head against his shoulder and wiggled until she fit against his side like the second half of a whole. When he squeezed her gently and rested his cheek against her hair, the words came pouring out.

"I would lie here and find the blue star . . . planet. And I would pretend that's where I belonged. If I lived there, I wouldn't be trapped underground, afraid every second of every day. I wouldn't be a slave." Her voice shook and tears slid down her face. "I have a mother who keeps me. A father who loves me. And I can go anywhere, do anything, without worrying that someone will see me for who I am and say the only good elf is a dead elf."

She pressed her lips closed and waited, every second an eternity, for his response. Did he hate dark elves? Was he afraid of them? Had she just lost something precious between them?

He pressed his lips to the crown of her head and said, "I'm glad you finally told me."

"I finally . . . Wait. You knew?"

His fingers traced lazy patterns across her back. "I figured it out."

"How?" She sat up and stared at him, her pulse racing, magic buzzing.

"It's all right," he said. "I only know because I pay extra attention to everything about you. When you asked me about dark elves, I could see it meant something to you. That my *answer* meant something to you, which made it personal. And then I remembered that runes carved in iron subdue fae magic, and that elvish magic is a close cousin, so it would dampen yours a bit. Plus you're so much stronger and faster than me, and I've never seen your ears."

"And you aren't scared to be around a monster?" It hurt to say the word aloud, but she had to be sure.

He sat up. "Why would you call yourself that?"

She shrugged.

"Sajda."

"It's what the warden always says." She couldn't look at him. "And the reason Dabir lost his mind is because he tried to attack me, and I hit him and drew blood, and then I don't know what happened. I just . . . The blood called to my magic, and I took some in my hands, and then I was seeing everything about him, and I knew how to tell a story—"

"You wielded a nightmare."

"You understand what I did?" She leaned toward him.

"Only what I learned in school. Dark elves can read the hearts and minds of the living things they touch, and they can borrow qualities, manipulate the physical being, or wield a nightmare that never leaves."

"That sounds pretty monstrous." She turned to stare at the stars so he wouldn't see the tears that were back in her eyes.

"It sounds like power. Power is neither good nor evil. It just is. It's what people do with power that matters. And I know you, Sajda. I know you better than I know anyone else. You are a girl full of courage, intelligence, strength, and beauty from the inside out. It isn't monstrous to defend yourself or others."

"Dabir might never get better."

"He'd better hope he doesn't because if I meet him again, he's going to have a whole different nightmare to contend with." His voice was flat.

She raised her face to the silvery starlight and felt its purity pour into her, a bolt of cold fire.

"What do you do with the starlight?" he asked.

She looked at him. "What do you mean?"

He smiled, his eyes lit with wonder. "I mean, you are literally swallowing starlight. Or your magic is. Have you seen yourself?"

She turned away from the skylight and held out her arms. Her skin shimmered, a brilliant silver-white that almost hurt to look at.

"Did you borrow something from the stars? Or is it something you plan to manipulate and use?" He sounded fascinated.

"I have no idea. I mean, I borrowed their essence—it's cold and pure—but I don't know if I could use it."

"Want to try?" He grinned at her, and she laughed, her tears drying on her cheeks.

He patted around the blanket nest until he found an old mug she used to keep filled with water until it cracked down the side.

"Here. See what starlight does to this."

She took it in her silver-white hands and let the magic that hummed and crawled beneath her skin seize the cracked porcelain of the mug. There was a flash of brilliant light and icy liquid silver poured out of her palms to coat the mug until it glowed like it had been dipped in real silver.

The cold bit deep, and she dropped it to the blanket. It struck and shattered into tiny fragments that melted into nothing.

"Whoa." Javan patted the blanket where seconds earlier the shards had been, and then met her eyes. "Just think what you could do with the sun."

Pain seared the skin beneath her cuffs and she pulled her hands to her chest.

"Do the cuffs make it painful to do magic?"

She nodded.

"That's why you have scars beneath them?"

Another nod.

"Maybe we can get them off of you."

She turned her left wrist and held it up until the cuff was illuminated by starlight. The runes were tiny shadows carved into its surface, and the lock was a slim crescent of darkness cut deep into the iron. "I've tried. I'd need a key, and only the warden and the magistrate's head guards have shackle keys. The magistrate's guards are only here during tournament rounds, and they don't keep their keys where I can see them. And the warden keeps the key hidden in her quarters."

His voice was still gentle, but there was a lethal edge to it. "The warden is the monster, Sajda. Not you."

She pushed him back down onto the blankets and curled up beside him. "You can sleep up here tonight. No one will find you. Once the bars raise tomorrow morning, we'll get you back in your cell. And then we have four days until the next combat round to get you back into fighting shape."

"Will you stay for a while?"

She leaned her head on his shoulder and watched the stars cross the sky until he fell asleep. And then she stayed a little bit longer just to pretend that the boy, who was going to leave to become the king of Akram, and the half-elven girl, who was going to escape to anywhere else, belonged together.

THIRTY-FOUR

IT WAS LESS than an hour before the next round of competition started. Javan followed Sajda out of his cell and into the stairwell that led to the arena. He was down to two allies in the arena. Nadim had been killed in the last combat round, and Gadi's leg had been injured so badly, he was unable to compete.

Every prisoner Javan passed fell silent, but this time instead of enmity, he saw anger in their faces. At first he thought they were angry with him, but when Kali and Intizara joined him on the staircase between levels nine and eight, Kali said, "Have you heard about the warden's treachery?"

Javan shook his head, nervous energy careening around inside him as if he'd swallowed lightning. What new threat was coming for him now?

"She announced to all of level five that any of them who killed you during combat today would immediately be released from Maqbara." Kali's voice was rough with anger. "We overheard several of them talking about it during breakfast."

"Just level five?" Sajda asked, her quiet voice giving nothing away, but Javan knew what she was thinking. She'd told him the false prince had made that offer for any prisoner, not just the ones who were the most experienced and had the most points in the arena. He'd already prepared a strategy that kept Kali and Intizara at his back at all times.

Maybe by only offering the bounty to level five, she thought it would cause less of an uproar among the prisoners and be less likely to reach the ears of the bettors.

Maybe she was superbly confident in Hashim and his friends.

It didn't matter. He had a strategy in place. He'd been praying all morning that it would work.

"Who's next?" Intizara demanded, her eyes darting toward the bottom of the stairs. "What's to stop the warden from using Hashim to kill anyone she pleases?"

"The whole prison is in an uproar," Kali said. "She's interfering with the rules of the tournament. None of us are safe."

"None of you were safe to begin with," Sajda grumbled. Kali and Intizara fell silent, giving each other uneasy looks.

"Don't mind her," Javan said. "She can't help being overly optimistic about those she likes."

"I don't like them," Sajda said as they reached the arena floor, where the small group of competitors was standing by the gate closest to the stalls.

Javan gave her the look he usually reserved for the moments when he wanted to goad her into sparring with him, and she sighed. "Fine. I like them a little. But only because they haven't tried to kill you."

They arrived at the arena to see Tarek put the final weapon in place and cover it with a black cloth. Once again, weapons were hidden so that each competitor had to gamble on where their favorites might lie.

Javan, Kali, and Intizara weren't gambling. He knew exactly where each weapon was located. Before Maqbara, he would have felt dishonorable for having an advantage over the other competitors. Now, as he faced the remaining twenty-three combatants, many who were allied with Hashim and favored by the warden, he was grateful for any competitive edge he could find.

Tarek left the arena, grabbed a small satchel that hung on a hook beside the first stall, and moved to Javan's group. Handing the satchel to Javan, he said, "Eat. You need your wits about you today, son."

Javan's stomach growled as he opened the bag and found an apple, a thick crust of bread with lentil spread, and three sugar dates. "Where did you find sugar dates?" he asked, his mouth watering. The last time he'd had these, he'd been walking through the outdoor market in Makan Almalik with his mother firmly holding his hand, her bright voice exclaiming over every pretty sash, jeweled headdress, and confectionery item she saw.

Grief slashed at him, a deep throb of pain that stole his breath for a moment. He kept his eyes on the food in front of him and waited for the ache to settle as Tarek said, "Did a favor for the cook. Figured you could use a treat after all you've been through."

"Thank you." He turned away from the others, took a bite of the apple, and sent a swift prayer to Yl' Haliq that the hurt would subside so he could concentrate. Missing his mother had been part of the fabric of his life for years. It seemed unfair that the loss could still sneak up on him without warning. Especially when thinking of her absence made the injustice of being thrown in prison instead of welcomed home by his father feel like the scab on a wound he just couldn't seem to leave alone.

"Are you all right?" Sajda was at his side, her voice quiet.

Was he all right? He was a prince trapped in a prison about to face terrifying creatures and lethal competitors for the amusement of the people he'd once belonged to; and if he survived, he was still going to be hunted by his enemies.

He picked up a sugar date, its sticky-sweet coating covering his fingertips.

"My mother used to give me these as treats when we'd go on outings together. I still miss her."

She was silent, and he was suddenly, excruciatingly aware that her mother hadn't taken her on outings for sugar dates and fancy sashes. Her mother had put her on an auction block and walked away.

He turned to her and offered the sugar date. "I'm sorry. My words were careless."

She had her stone-cold exterior firmly in place, but her voice was kind as she said, "You don't have to hesitate to share things with me. I'm glad your mother was good to you. Now hurry up and eat because your stomach needs to settle before you compete. I'm going to check on the beasts. You remember how to kill them? We've got everything you need with your weapons. You can't make a single mistake today."

"I remember."

"Don't die."

"I won't," he said and prayed he could keep his promise.

He finished his meal and joined Kali and Intizara to go over their strategy—form a loose triangle at the edge of the arena, one to kill a creature, two to fend off other prisoners. They'd take turns on kills unless they were inundated by the monsters Sajda was releasing.

The list of monsters and their point values went up on the wall opposite the stalls as the audience arrived in a cloud of bright sashes, jeweled hands, and the scent of cinnamon, peppermint, and fresh air.

Javan paced, swinging his arms, and forcing himself to breathe evenly as the nervous, precompetition energy tumbled through him.

Fear out.

Courage in.

He glanced at the list of monsters and his chest tightened. He was going to need every last bit of courage he possessed.

CLAWFOOT BEETLE—10 POINTS

TWO-HEADED SERPENT—15 POINTS

GARMR—25 POINTS

REILIGARDA—50 POINTS

ROC—100 POINTS

The beetles were a nuisance. A distraction, but they were no bigger than his foot, and though their claws could pierce leather and flesh, they could be crushed, kicked, or stabbed with minimal effort. The serpents had a head at each end, which meant you had to cut off both heads in order to kill them. They were more dangerous than the beetles, but they constricted their prey, which meant he could survive a bite if he was distracted fighting another monster when a serpent attacked.

He'd heard of a garmr before, but he'd never seen one until Sajda had sneaked him into the stalls two mornings before while the warden had been out on business. Huge black doglike creatures with shaggy hair, red eyes, and foam around their muzzles were a danger he couldn't ignore. There were five of them, and they attacked as a pack. It was crucial that he, Kali, and Intizara didn't get separated.

Which was going to be easier said than done because the reiligarda were a horror he'd only read about in his mythology class during seventh year. He still didn't know what the creatures looked like because they'd arrived in iron coffins filled with dirt taken from the graves they'd guarded on Llorenyae; and until they were disturbed, they would sleep. According to the stories, they looked like black skeletons with decaying strips of black grave clothes hanging off their bony frames.

The stories also said the reiligarda were relentless in their pursuit of those who wore the dirt of the grave that had been disturbed. The warden had of course ordered Sajda to smear grave dirt on each competitor in full view of the audience so that no one could claim someone else's favorite got special treatment.

That left the most threatening of the day's creatures: the roc. The enormous bird of prey was strong enough to carry an elephant in its talons. It would attack from above—there was already a huge net erected around the arena to keep the roc from going after the audience or from escaping. It was rolled up and tied off with ropes, but at the warden's signal, the guards would pull the ropes and trap the roc with the prisoners. Javan felt sick at the thought of destroying such a fierce and noble creature for the sake of this bloodthirsty game. There was no honor in it. No honor in killing anything that was joining him in the arena today, but he didn't have a choice. It was kill or be killed, and Javan desperately wanted to live long enough to save his father from the impostor. Long enough to save himself from Maqbara and take Sajda and Tarek with him.

"I'll take care of the roc first," Javan said to Kali and Intizara as the last of the crowd filed in, heading to either the betting table or their seats. "We can't risk being attacked from above while we're busy watching for Hashim's crew or the ground monsters."

And it would give him a badly needed one hundred points. It wouldn't quite be enough to put him in range of victory. He'd have to kill quite a few other beasts, both this round and the next, but it would help.

Quickly he whispered a prayer to Yl' Haliq to forgive him for the blood he was about to spill.

"I trust our weapons are in place?" Intizara asked softly as guards ordered the prisoners to move to the arena's wall and Tarek left to help Sajda, Batula, and the guards move the monsters into place, ready for release through the same gate the competitors were about to go through.

"In a triangle. Western edge of the arena. You're the fastest, Intizara. Get there first and claim all three if you have to. We'll be right behind you," Javan said.

The warden stepped to the edge of the platform and raised her arms. Heat boiled through Javan's veins as he glared at her.

She'd tried to kill him twice now. He was certain that if he hadn't made such an impression on the crowd during his first round of combat, if there hadn't been rumors and speculation that might damage Fariq's bid for power, she'd have killed Javan that very night. Instead, she'd had to look for ways to kill him that could be easily explained to the aristocrats who were desperately curious about the skilled fighter who looked like a royal. She'd aligned herself with the dishonorable impostor who was bent on stealing Akram for his own ends. And she'd hurt Sajda deeply.

She was going to die. Once he had the power of the throne behind him, he'd see to it personally.

Now she spoke, her gravelly voice filling the arena. "Welcome to the fourth round of this year's tournament. Betting is now closed. We are down to twenty-three worthy competitors."

She paused and the weight of her gaze landed on Javan and then slowly moved to Sajda. Javan's mouth went dry at the vicious malice in her eyes. She knew her slave was helping her prey, and Sajda was about to pay for her choice.

He started moving toward Sajda, looking frantically for a weapon that hadn't already been placed in the arena, as the warden said, "But today I have two surprises for you. A bonus treat, if you will. First of all, only the top three point earners in the competition will advance to the final round."

Murmurs swept the audience at this unexpected change in the tournament's rules, and a band of pressure wrapped around Javan's chest. The warden was hedging her bets in case Hashim and friends failed to kill Javan. He was nowhere near the top three point earners. To stay in the competition, he'd have to rack up significant kills this round, or all this would have been for nothing. He'd spend the next round locked in his cell like the rest of the prisoners who weren't competing, and his father would die as soon as he abdicated the throne to the impostor.

The warden continued, "Second, today we will have a new competitor for your enjoyment. Aren't surprises fun?"

She was going to put Sajda in the arena. Javan's heart slammed against his chest, and fear was a fire burning through his blood.

Sajda was powerful. Stronger and faster than anyone else entering the arena. The warden had to know that. Which meant she had a way to hurt Sajda and turn her into easy prey.

He reached Sajda's side as Tarek was saying, "Don't hold back, little one. Not this time. You fight with everything you've got. Let them see that you're a warrior to rival any of the prisoners."

Tarek didn't know the truth, then. Javan met Sajda's gaze and saw the tremors beneath the sheath of ice she was desperately trying to hide behind. If Sajda unleashed her true power in the arena, she might defeat the monsters, but she'd have revealed herself as something more than human to a crowd who believed, as he had once, that the only good elf was a dead elf.

She couldn't save herself from the warden, the guards, the prisoners, and the crowd who would be screaming for her blood. He couldn't save her from them either, which meant they had to work together to keep her alive without revealing who she really was.

"You can join Kali, Intizara, and me. Western edge, the triangle. Grab a weapon on your way to us. Don't be afraid to move fast enough to get your weapon of choice. No one will remember that once the monsters enter the arena." He grabbed her hand, her skin icy against the fire that seemed to be burning him from the inside out.

It was one thing to face his own mortality. It was another thing entirely to consider that the girl he loved might die for the crime of protecting him. The thought cut a vicious path through his mind, all teeth and talons and *fear*, and he had to work to keep the panic from showing on his face.

She opened her mouth to say something, and then the warden's voice filled the arena as she said, "Our new competitor may not seem like much, but I promise you he will bring a fascinating twist to today's combat."

He?

Javan met Sajda's suddenly panic-stricken gaze as the warden swept an arm toward the stalls and said, "I give you today's surprise competitor, Tarek B'halim!"

THIRTY-FIVE

"NO!" THE WORD was ripped from Sajda's lips before she could stop herself.

The warden smiled, and Sajda trembled. This was her punishment for saving Javan. She was going to lose Tarek, the closest thing to family she had since Maeli, the woman who'd shown her nothing but kindness and decency in the six years the woman had spent in Maqbara, had died in the arena two years before.

"I'm going in with you," she said to Tarek, as the older man lifted one trembling arthritic hand toward her.

"She'll kill you."

"She can try." Sajda shook, every ounce of the composure she'd borrowed from the stone that morning dissipating like it had never existed. "But you aren't entering the arena without me."

"He'll enter with me." Javan wrapped a hand around Tarek's shoulder as the guards shouted for him to return to the wall. "We'll put him in the center of the triangle."

"But something could still get to him." Magic screamed

through her blood, raking her skin from the inside, begging to be unleashed. Her cuffs glowed, her skin burning beneath the power of the runes.

"Nothing will get to him." Javan stepped close to her, close enough that she could see his pulse thrumming rapidly in his neck. See the quick rise and fall of his chest.

He was afraid.

So was she.

"Open the gate!" the warden called.

"I swear on my life, I will return him to you," Javan said quietly. "The only way you can defy the warden and enter the arena is by showing everyone who you really are. They'll turn on you in a heartbeat. Don't reveal anything to this crowd, Sajda. I'll protect him."

And then they were gone, Javan spinning Tarek toward the arena and rushing in behind the other competitors who were already grabbing the black cloths that covered the weapons and cursing if they hadn't found the one they'd hoped to use.

She watched, every muscle straining to run after them, stand in front of them, and destroy everything that came through the gate.

But Intizara reached the triangle of weapons first, followed quickly by Kali, and neither of them allowed another competitor to get to the weapons Sajda had hidden specifically for Javan.

The prince pulled Tarek across the arena to the deafening cheers of the audience, many who were on their feet, casting quick glances toward the warden in case she was the one in charge of recording who'd attended and how thoroughly they'd participated.

Sajda wanted to *hurt* them. Slice into their veins, let their blood pool in her palm, and whisper terrifying nightmares to them until they understood what it was to be afraid. To be certain that survival was impossible. Maybe she'd even take bets on how long they would last before their minds broke and they were lost.

"Is this the first crate?" a guard asked her, and she whipped her head around to glare at him.

He froze, and then glanced at her wrists. She followed his gaze to find that the runes were still glowing, her skin sizzling and scarring beneath them.

A quick look at the arena showed Tarek in the center of the triangle of Kali, Intizara, and Javan. Javan had the quiver strapped to his back, the short swords looped into his belt, and the bow in his hands. His expression was deadly calm as he faced the gate.

She knew him. He would protect Tarek or die trying. He'd give everything he had to keep his word, even if it meant he'd lose his chance at the final competition.

Her body shook until it felt like her bones were rattling beneath her skin, until the fraying thread that held her together inside felt seconds away from snapping.

She had to trust him.

She *did* trust him.

The realization did nothing to make her feel better.

The crowd was chanting now. "Release the beasts! Release the beasts!"

Sajda swept them with a glare. The beasts had already been released, and the crowd was sitting in comfortable chairs sipping dainty drinks and screaming for the blood of those who had no power to refuse their demands.

Still, she had a job to do if she didn't want the warden to decide to come after Tarek herself.

"Ready for the first crate?" the guard asked.

"Not yet," she snapped. Grabbing a dagger and the pouch of grave dirt Hansel had given her, she stepped into the arena, magic snapping, runes burning.

"We have some special monsters for you today as well," the warden boomed. "And to make the combat effective, our competitors have to be prepped."

Sajda moved quickly from prisoner to prisoner. A quick slash of the dagger across their arms. A handful of grave dirt smeared across their chests. She ignored the crowd. Ignored the muttered curses of the prisoners until Hashim whispered that Tarek was his. Then her hand lingered on his chest, full of grave dirt and magic, as she imagined sending her power into his veins to tear through his bones and boil his blood.

The buzzing swarm of magic in her palms bit into Hashim, and he stumbled back, cursing, his eyes widening as he stared at the burn on his chest in the shape of her palm. She bared her teeth at him and moved on.

She was fury and fear and magic held at bay by her cuffs. Every breath she took was tinged with desperation. Every step she took unraveled her a little faster.

"Some of our monsters are hunters." The warden sounded cheerful. "We have three reiligarda, and every prisoner now wears a bit of the grave dirt from the sites these creatures were supposed to guard. The scent of the dirt will bring the reiligarda straight to them."

Sajda's hands shook as she laid the tip of the dagger against Javan's arm while the crowd cheered.

"He'll be safe," Javan whispered.

She couldn't answer as she gave him a tiny cut and then smeared a small amount of grave dirt on his chest.

"As our grand predator today, we have a roc, captured high in the mountains that skirt the Samaal Desert." The warden's voice boomed. "Every competitor has been cut so that the scent of their blood will draw the bird."

Finished with everyone but Tarek, Sajda moved to his side.

"It's all right, little one. No matter what happens now," he said.

"Nothing about this is right." She laid the dagger on his arm and made a tiny scratch. Enough to satisfy the warden's eagle eye, but hopefully not enough to make him much of a target to the roc. "She's hurting you to punish me for helping Javan."

"You did the right thing," he said, his eyes clear and steady as they held hers. "I love you, little one. You remember that, no matter what. Promise me."

She swallowed hard against the swell of tears in her throat and pressed a tiny amount of grave dirt to his chest. And then before she turned away, she pulled him close, wrapping one arm around him while the other pushed the hilt of her dagger into his hand.

"Don't die. I can't—" Her voice broke, and she let him go. Walked away. Crossed the arena, a hollow shell full of furious magic trapped when she needed it most.

If she could get the cuffs off, she could destroy the warden. She was sure of it. She could bring the arena down on the heads of every person screaming for blood.

But she couldn't get them off. She couldn't do anything but follow the warden's instructions and put all her hope in the prince who'd sworn to protect Tarek.

"Release the first crate," she said to the guard as she walked through the gate. She met Javan's eyes across the arena.

He gave a small nod. He was ready.

She hoped the Yl' Haliq he always prayed to was truly on his side.

He was going to need the help.

The guard dumped the crate into the arena. Twenty large red beetles scattered, their legs scuttling over the floor while the claws on their raised front legs snapped viciously.

The competitors closest to the front of the arena began attacking the beetles as they came close, but Javan and his allies stayed still, holding their formation while they waited for the true threats to arrive.

"Release the serpents," she said.

A second guard helped the first wrestle a large barrel into the arena. They tipped it on its side, broke the seal, and ran for the gate, closing it behind them. Long brown and yellow snakes squirmed out of the barrel. Each serpent had a head at either end, each head raised to survey the arena while their bodies writhed, sending them across the floor in sinuous, muscular movements.

Intizara hefted her battle-axes and slashed at a snake that came close to the triangle. Kali was whipping a mace overhead as one of Hashim's crew closed in on them.

Javan stood still, his muscles tensed, his eyes slowly roving the arena, searching for a threat his allies couldn't dispose of.

Sajda was about to give him one.

Heart pounding, magic buzzing, she said, "It's time for the dogs."

The garmrs were housed in the stall closest to the arena's gate.

Yesterday, she'd laced their food with a sleeping herb so that she could enter their stall, snap an iron collar and chain around each of their necks, and loop the chains through a hook outside the door.

"Get the gate open, don't let anything out, and stay clear of their jaws," she said, moving to the stall as the guards did her bidding. Leaping to the top of a crate she'd moved beside the stall for this moment, she grabbed the chains and unlatched the stall door.

The pack of shaggy black dogs came out snarling. Their red eyes zeroed in on her, and their lips peeled back from their fangs as they began to circle her crate. She snapped the chains against their snouts, driving them toward the floor, and then she gathered her elven strength and leaped over their heads.

She landed just outside the row of stalls, and they instantly gave chase. She couldn't afford to put her strength or speed on display now that the crowd could see her, so she ran just fast enough to stay ahead of their foaming, snapping jaws. Skidding into the arena, the garmrs hot on her heels, she shouted, "Close the gate."

The guards slammed the gate shut behind the pack of dogs, and Sajda ran for the side, kicking a clawfoot beetle out of her way as she went. The dogs followed her, but they were slower now, distracted by the chaos as competitors fought snakes, beetles, and one another. She scrambled up onto the waist-high wall that edged the arena and let go of the chains.

A smart competitor could use the dangling lengths of chain to help defeat the dogs. A foolish or distracted competitor might trip on the chains and find himself fighting a losing battle against the pack.

She risked a quick look at Javan and found him standing directly in front of Tarek, his swords in his hands as two of the dogs charged. Her heart felt like it was tearing itself free of its moorings—thud, thud, thud—a reverberation she could feel in her spine.

Her wrists burned, as she balanced on the wall and considered leaping to join the fight.

She couldn't join the fight.

Not without the warden shifting into a dragon and destroying her, Tarek, and Javan. The warden knew what kind of monster she had for a slave, and she wouldn't risk allowing Sajda to turn the tables.

The best protection Sajda could offer Javan and Tarek was to stay out of their way and do her job. Keep the warden happy. Keep the aristocrats happy. And pray to a god she wasn't yet sure she believed in that the two people she cared about would get out alive.

Jumping off the wall, she strode toward the stalls and barked, "Bring out the reiligarda."

The guards looked terrified as they pulled the three coffins toward the gate. Lifting the first coffin, they balanced it on the edge of the wall until Sajda said, "Dump it."

Grave dirt and a vaguely humanlike body crashed onto the arena floor. Quickly the guards did the same with the next two coffins.

For a long moment, the pile of dirt and bodies lay still, but then it shuddered, a ripple that became more and more violent, sending grave dirt cascading across the arena floor in a swift-moving wave. Seconds later, three skeletons as black as the walls of Maqbara rose in swift, disjointed movements. Strips of rotting black grave clothes hung from their bones, and their eyes were burning black pits of rage.

"If you're there, please help Javan. Help Tarek." Sajda whispered the prayer and wondered if Javan's god would hear a girl the god's people thought would be better off dead.

The reiligarda jerked their heads toward the competitors and then moved—heads leaning forward, arms rising, hands outstretched, their legs jerking in quick strides that ate up the ground.

Sajda looked for Javan and found him bleeding profusely from a cut on the side of his head. The body of one dog lay at his feet, a chain wrapped around its throat, its tongue distended. Tarek was crouched behind Javan, dagger raised, his back against the arena wall.

Intizara was still in position, the ground around her littered with beetles and two snakes.

Kali was down, her throat torn open.

"And now for our grand predator—the roc!" The warden's voice boomed across the arena.

Sajda's hands were clammy as she and the guards wrestled with the roc's enormous cage. When they had it close to the gate, the guards backed away. Several of them grabbed the ropes that hung down from the length of netting that was rolled above them. A quick jerk of their wrists, and the netting tumbled down into place, surrounding the entire arena. Sajda climbed on top of the cage and leaned down to grab the latch.

A large hooked beak snapped at the bars of the cage closest to her hand. She was going to have seconds to let the roc free and get under the netting before it came for her. Drawing in a deep breath, she let her magic coil around her muscles and then she was moving. Flipping the latch, she jumped off the cage and slid under the netting as the roc exploded into the air.

The bird's body was the size of a large stallion, its velvet-brown feathers glowing in the afternoon sunlight. Its wingspan was easily the length of two cells end to end; and as it rose into the air, it gave a piercing cry that sent the remaining dogs whining onto their front paws, their red eyes gazing up at a predator who could eat them as a small snack.

The roc wasn't interested in the garmrs, though. It wasn't interested in the reiligarda, who were steadily crushing three competitors into a wall, their skeletal limbs moving with sickening speed and strength.

The roc wanted those who were bleeding.

And Javan was standing in a puddle of blood—his own, the dog's, and Kali's.

Sajda's skin went cold, her magic a rush of iced lightning that left her shaking with the effort it took to hold herself still.

"Get an arrow," she murmured even as he whipped an arrow to his bow.

The roc beat the air with its wings, rose to the top of the arena, and began circling.

"Now!" she said, not caring what the guards around her thought of the warden's slave shouting advice to a competitor.

Javan raised his bow just as two other competitors crashed into him, sending him into the ground.

"No!" Sajda lunged forward, her hands reaching for the net, but Javan was already up. Kicking, punching, swinging the bow like a weapon, and beating back the two who were doing their best to kill him. One of the attackers rushed for him again, and Javan sent an arrow into the man's chest.

The roc screamed as it dove, talons the size of Sajda's arms extended toward the melee. The crowd roared, and Javan looked up at the last second to see the impending threat.

Kicking the second attacker aside, he dropped.

Not toward safety, in front of Tarek.

A tiny sob escaped Sajda's lips as the prince stood in front of Tarek, bow raised though there was no time to loose the arrow before the bird reached him.

The roc slammed into Javan's chest, sending him stumbling back into Tarek and the wall. Its talons closed over his shoulders, and then Intizara was there, hacking at the bird's feet with her battle-axes.

The roc shrieked, a deafening cry of rage and pain, twisting away from Javan and back into the air, blood dripping from its talons. Javan lifted the bow and sent an arrow flying. It buried itself in the roc's side, but the bird continued circling.

Intizara whipped around to face an incoming reiligarda. The surviving prisoner who'd attacked Javan lunged forward again, running at Javan with a short spear. The prince pushed Tarek out of the way, and the spear grazed his chest, sending blood pouring.

The roc shrieked again and charged. The reiligarda sent Intizara flying into the wall and came toward Javan, skeletal arms reaching, its mouth gaping open in a soundless scream of fury.

"Remember, remember, remember," Sajda whispered, her hands locked in a white-knuckled clasp. "Come on. It's right behind you."

Javan backed toward the wall beside Tarek, his eyes on the approaching roc even as a reiligarda advanced from his left and the other prisoner came from his right.

The prince said something, and Tarek bent swiftly to grab a small bag tied to the black cloth that had covered the bow and arrow.

Another arrow from Javan buried itself in the roc's chest, and the bird reeled away as the reiligarda and the prisoner converged on Javan.

He went down, and Sajda was already tearing the netting out of the way when he kicked free just long enough to toss a few arrows toward Tarek before the prisoner grabbed his ankles and brought him back to the floor.

The reiligarda slammed its arms into the attacking prisoner, and as the man's grip slackened, Javan drove a sword through his arm. It wasn't a killing blow, but it was enough to make the man roll away and try to run. He didn't get far. The roc crashed into him, landing heavily on the ground and crushing the man beneath him.

Javan kicked and shoved at the reiligarda, but the skeletal creature was strong as iron and single-minded in its pursuit of the one who wore the dirt from the grave it had been meant to protect.

In the center of the arena, Hashim and two others fought the remaining reiligarda. All the dogs were dead. So were the serpents and at least nine prisoners. A few beetles cruised the floor, but no one was paying them any attention.

Terror was a blinding light trapped in Sajda's chest. Her magic swirled and scraped, begging for freedom, and she could barely breathe past the tears clogging her throat.

What would she do if she lost both Tarek and Javan?

She'd be trapped, alone in the bowels of Maqbara. As she

watched Javan struggle to keep from getting crushed by the reiligarda, a thread of anger blazed through her terror.

Why had he offered his friendship? Why had he made her laugh and think and trust? She'd been surviving just fine on her own for years. She hadn't known what she was missing. But now, she knew. She knew the depths of her loneliness if he died. She knew the void that would open within her. A void no amount of starlight would ever fill.

Tarek worked quickly with the materials he himself had left behind for the prince's use. Grabbing a small nest of rags wrapped in a ball of woven straw that had been smeared with pitch, he struck the tip of an arrow against a piece of flint held over the straw ball.

Sparks showered onto the ball, and it ignited.

Tarek yelled and jabbed an arrow deep into the ball. Javan gave another kick to gain an instant's reprieve from the reiligarda while he twisted at the waist, caught the arrow Tarek tossed his way, and plunged the flaming arrow deep into the chest cavity of the reiligarda. The creature stumbled, reached for him once more, and then collapsed to its knees as the fire ate through it.

Tarek already had another burning arrow ready. Javan sent it into the reiligarda who was fighting Hashim. Hashim was on his knees, his mace raised above his head in a futile effort to protect himself from the attack. He looked up as the skeleton dropped, and his mouth opened in surprise to see that Javan had been his salvation.

The third flaming arrow took down the remaining reiligarda, and then Javan turned toward the roc.

It was already dead. Crumpled into a heap of feathers and blood, Javan's arrows sticking out of its body.

It was over. Tarek was alive. Javan was alive.

And the warden was still bent on keeping Javan from the final round.

Sajda let go of the netting and ran toward the stairs that led to the betting table as the crowd thundered their favorite's name.

Did Javan have enough points to advance? He'd killed the roc, all three reiligarda, and a dog. That was two hundred seventy-five points. Plus, he'd killed another prisoner, a man who until that moment had been in second place. That meant that after the five-hundred-point deduction, Javan would get the rest of the man's points. It had to be enough to put him in the final round, to keep him a crowd favorite and the topic of conversation across Makan Almalik.

His safety depended on it.

Sajda flew up the stairs and stopped just outside the platform with the betting table. The warden's back was to her as she surveyed the carnage spread out across the arena floor. One of the judges was bringing up the results of the match. Sajda glared at the judge as if that would somehow influence whatever was written on the parchment the woman held in her hands.

"I'll take that," she said.

The woman hesitated.

"I'm the warden's right-hand girl. Do you really want to be on my bad side?" This time she didn't even need to borrow her composure from the stone. The sickening thought of losing Javan at the warden's hands was enough to make her feel like she'd swallowed ice.

The woman gave her the score sheet, and Sajda unfolded it with shaking fingers.

A prisoner named Iram was in first place.

Hashim was in second.

Javan was in third.

He'd made it. He was going to the final competition to fight for an audience with his father. And he'd given her a way to keep him alive.

Striding onto the platform, Sajda waved the score sheet in the air. The crowd fell silent.

The warden reached for it, and Sajda shouted, "Congratulations to three crowd favorites who will be advancing to the final competition."

"Give me that—"

"Iram, Hashim, and Javan are your finalists!" Sajda shouted. "Early betting opens now!"

The warden snatched the parchment from her hands and glanced at it. "You've overstepped your bounds, little monster."

"Have I?" Sajda met the warden's glare and for once didn't look away. "I simply announced the true winners and opened betting like we always do. Unless you were planning to announce results other than those on the parchment?"

The warden remained silent. Sajda turned on her heel and left the platform.

Tarek and Javan were alive. She'd ensured that Javan wouldn't be targeted before the next round of competition. The warden would never be able to explain it, plus she wouldn't want to lose the bets that were already pouring in for the newcomer who'd destroyed the ranks in his quest for victory.

Now Sajda just had to think of a way to protect Tarek as well.

THIRTY-SIX

TWO WEEKS AFTER gaining a spot in the final competition, Javan still had nightmares of the blood that was now on his hands. It didn't matter that the killings he'd done had been in self-defense. He couldn't stop hearing the awful wet sound of his arrow burying itself in a man's chest. Couldn't expunge the memory of the once-proud roc lying crumpled on the arena floor, slayed by his arrows.

He tried to tell himself that he'd done the only thing he could do. He'd survived. He'd get a chance to compete for an audience with his father in the final competition two weeks from now. And he'd kept his promise to bring Tarek out of the arena alive.

He was still protecting Tarek, though he was pretty sure the older man thought it was the other way around. Javan had spent a single night in the infirmary, but the guards who took roll at twelfth bell thought he was still sleeping there. Instead, at Sajda's request, he'd left the infirmary each night and slept on the floor of Tarek's room in case the warden decided to punish Sajda again by coming after the old man.

He didn't have a weapon, and he wasn't sure how he could defeat a Draconi without one, but at the very least, he could be a shield while Tarek ran for Sajda. Perhaps Yl' Haliq would accept his actions as penance for the blood he'd shed.

After another rough night full of violent dreams punctuated by the thunderous sound of Tarek's snoring, everything inside Javan felt coiled tight as he joined his fellow prisoners from level fifteen for the chore of polishing the arena's walls while Tarek helped the cook receive a food shipment. Sajda was by the stalls having just finished feeding the remaining beasts, none of whom Javan had been allowed to see. The warden was strict about her prisoners being surprised in their final round of combat. Sajda raised an eyebrow when she saw him.

"You look terrible."

"You could've warned me that Tarek snores like a lion. Like a pride of lions. Many, many lions." He rubbed his eyes and tried to shake off the exhaustion.

"Are you sure that's why you're so tired? He says you wake up screaming."

He swallowed hard and looked away. "The important thing is that Tarek is alive. I left him with the kitchen staff. He insisted. Said he had to do his job to keep the warden happy and that the warden wouldn't dare do anything to him in front of the merchants who are delivering food today. Intizara and several of her friends have kitchen duty right now, and she promised they'd yell for us if Tarek needs help." Javan yawned while Sajda took off her leather gloves and washed in the basin.

"Are you having nightmares?" she asked quietly as the other

prisoners hefted buckets and brushes and began polishing the walls.

"Yes." He lifted his own bucket of lye soap and reached for a brush. His body hurt, a bone-deep ache that throbbed with every move as his injuries healed. He wanted to curl up in a comfortable bed for a week, but closing his eyes meant seeing the terrible things he'd done.

"Do you want to talk about them?"

He shook his head. It was bad enough to keep replaying the memories in his head. Giving voice to them wasn't something he was ready to face.

She was silent for a moment, and then her expression sharpened. "You need to give me another lesson."

He blinked. "Now?"

"Unless you don't think you're up to it." There was a clear challenge in her voice, and even through the haze of exhaustion and guilt, something inside him sparked to life.

"I'll be fine." The thought of what she might want to learn, of the bright curiosity in her eyes and the smug smile on her lips when she was sure she'd excelled as a pupil was a welcome relief from the bloody thoughts that plagued him.

Sajda switched his bucket and brush for a broom and a mop in case any guards stopped them to ask why she was taking a prisoner on chore duty to the third level. When they reached the room the more sensitive aristocrats used to avoid seeing the tournament's violence, he lowered himself onto the softest couch in the room and leaned against the cushions. His eyes closed of their own volition. "What do you want to learn about today?"

"Jobs. I'm going to need a way to earn coin when I get out of here."

"There are all kinds of jobs. What kinds of things are you interested in doing?"

"I like stargazing. And fighting."

He opened one eye to look at her. "Is that the sum total of your interests?"

She thought for a moment. "I might like winning things."

He smiled as he closed his eye. "Nobody pays you to win things."

"Maybe I could teach other people how to win good grades at school." There was hope in her voice, and Javan's smile grew.

"You'd be a really good teacher if you didn't threaten to hurt your students, and if you kept the sparring to a three-bruise maximum."

"I don't want to teach fighting. I think I'll teach dancing instead."

His eyes flew open and locked on her face. She was serious.

He sat up. "Dancing?"

She smirked.

Yl' Haliq help him, despite the wreckage inside him, he couldn't resist that smirk.

"I've been practicing. All the moves you showed me, plus a few that I added to make it more interesting."

"I'm more than a little frightened now."

"Come on, I'll show you. It will be fun. Unless, of course, you can't keep up because you're too sore and too tired and too—"

"I can keep up with you." He was already on his feet, the exhaustion and guilt receding as warmth lit his chest.

The cold, suspicious Sajda he'd become accustomed to reading like a book with half the sentences missing had all but disappeared after their night beneath the stars. He wasn't yet sure what to do with the new, softer version she showed him when they were alone.

He knew what he wanted to do, but he'd yet to figure out what she wanted, and until he knew that, he was going to take things slowly.

She grabbed his hands and pulled him into position. One hand holding hers. One hand . . .

"Why is my hand on your shoulder and not your waist?"

"I'm leading." She gave him her I-dare-you-to-try-to-stop-me look, and the warmth in his chest spiraled into his stomach.

"Then I'm following," he said, and they began to dance, Javan humming the music he'd heard so often during his dance lessons at Milisatria.

She was right. She'd practiced. She spun him expertly and dipped him so low he thought for sure he was going to fall. But then instead of swaying for the sixth and seventh measure of the *pallestaya*, she let him go.

"New move," she said as she backed away. "Brace yourself."

"Brace for— Hey!"

She ran at him, leaped into the air, and landed in his half-raised arms. They tumbled backward, bounced off the couch, and hit the floor. Pain throbbed from his healing injuries, but he didn't care. She was unguarded, a flush tingeing her pale cheeks, her eyes bright with challenge; and for the first time since leaving the arena, he felt truly alive.

"I said brace!" She looked indignant, and he couldn't help the laughter that spilled out of him.

"Brace for what?" He gasped. "Did it ever occur to you to tell me what you were going to do so I could be ready? Thank Yl' Haliq there was a couch in the way."

She was sprawled on top of him, her hair mussed, the tip of one perfect elven ear visible. He reached up and gently smoothed her hair back in place. It was one thing for him to see her ears. It was quite another to risk another prisoner seeing them.

She leaned her face against his hand, and her eyes darkened.

The heat in his stomach spread through his veins, and his chest rose and fell rapidly as he ran a hand down her back.

Her eyes left his and wandered down to his mouth, and he was lost.

"I think I'm going to kiss you," he said before he could reconsider it. Doubt it. Stop the idea of kissing Sajda, the girl who wouldn't stay in Akram no matter how badly he wanted her to.

"Not if I kiss you first."

He laughed, a little wild, a little desperate. "Does everything between us have to be a competition?"

"Not if you just admit that I've already won." She grinned.

His stomach tingled, spinning in slow, delicious circles as he stared at her full lips. He couldn't seem to remember why this was a terrible idea.

"You can't win a game you haven't played," he said because, Yl' Haliq help him, he seemed determined to swallow fire while pretending he couldn't be burned.

This was a terrible idea.

He dragged his gaze from her mouth and found himself mesmerized by her dark blue eyes instead. The spinning in his stomach sent waves of heat surging through him.

"What are the rules?" she asked, smirking at him like she thought this was another combat maneuver she would excel at. Kissing him was a game she wanted to win.

Kissing her was going to ruin him.

This was a *terrible* idea.

He was going to do it anyway.

She leaned in first, and he tangled his fingers in her hair as her lips brushed his once. Twice. Tiny, delicate kisses that made the wanting worse.

She raised her head, and he pulled her back down. This time, the kiss lingered, and he took his time exploring the pressure of her lips on his, the taste of her mouth on his tongue. When they broke apart, there was a flash of grief in her eyes, and then she was on her feet.

"That's enough lesson for one day." Her voice was calm, but there was something beneath it.

He climbed to his feet. "Are you all right?"

Her eyes were too bright as she glanced at him and then away. "I'm fine. Just tired."

He didn't mention that he was the one who hadn't slept. He didn't say anything as she flashed him a little smile and then walked away.

She was always going to walk away. He knew that. Just like he knew that he couldn't ask her to stay.

Still, it felt wrong to have kissed her without telling her first that the reason he wanted her was because he loved her.

She might not listen, but that was a chance he had to take. He followed her into the corridor just in time to see her glance down at the center of the arena and begin to scream.

THIRTY-SEVEN

JAVAN RAN TO Sajda's side and peered down at the arena floor. His hands gripped the railing as his knees weakened. The air felt too thick to breathe, his blood too heavy to run through his veins.

Tarek lay in the center of the scarred wooden floor, his arms and legs staked to the ground with enormous iron pegs. A fifth stake had been driven through his heart.

Sajda wailed, a terrible, gut-wrenching sound that echoed throughout the arena, and then she turned and ran for the stairs. Javan followed, grief slicing into him with every step.

Tarek had been sure the warden wouldn't attack him while the merchants were present. Javan shouldn't have listened. Shouldn't have left the job of guarding Tarek up to Intizara. He should've insisted Tarek stay by his side. Maybe he couldn't have stopped the warden, but he could've tried.

Sajda reached the arena floor seconds before he did and stumbled into the arena, her arms wrapped around her stomach like she was trying to hold herself together at the seams.

He picked up the pace and intercepted her before she reached Tarek's side, his heart aching. "Let me take care of him for a minute, Sajda. You don't need to keep seeing him like this."

She shook, a leaf trembling in his arms, and didn't respond. Her eyes were glassy. Gently he pulled her against his body and held her. She didn't seem to notice.

Movement caught his eye, and he looked up to see the warden standing at the edge of the arena, close to the stalls. Her one eye bored down on him, and she gave him a vicious smile before heading toward her office. Perhaps she still had merchants to pay. Perhaps she'd done what she wanted and was content to leave Javan and Sajda with the aftermath.

Fury ignited in the hollow spaces of his grief, but he stayed where he was. Sajda needed him. And until he won the competition, the warden held all the power.

He couldn't wait to turn the tables.

"Tarek," Sajda whispered, her voice a ghost of its former self.

"Let me pull out the stakes," he said, desperate to help in some small way, though it wasn't nearly enough. "And then we'll take care of him."

"I'm stronger," she said, and stepped away from him. Bending, she grabbed the stake that held Tarek's left hand to the floor and yanked it out. A sob escaped her lips, and she went for the stake in his left foot. The iron left red burn marks on her palms, and the runes on her cuffs glowed like fire.

Javan stood, fists clenched, feeling useless. Every bloody nightmare he'd endured over the past two weeks, every shred of guilt he'd carried on his shoulders paled compared to this. Tarek had been his first friend in Maqbara. Without the older man's kindness and loyalty toward Javan, Sajda would've ignored him. There would never have been a bargain. Never any help. Javan would've been dead weeks ago.

He owed his life to Tarek, and the knowledge that he'd failed to protect him was a jagged stone cutting into him from the inside out.

When all the stakes but the one through Tarek's heart had been removed, Sajda fell to her knees beside the old man, curled over his chest, and cried. Her hands wrapped around the final stake, and she slowly pulled it out.

Javan got to his knees beside her, tears in his eyes, and said, "I'm so sorry, Sajda."

Her hands clutched Tarek's tunic, pressing on his chest, and the skin beneath her cuffs hissed as the runes glowed red.

She was trying to use her magic to reach him. Bring him back to life.

Dark elves couldn't bring the dead back to life, but Javan didn't tell her that. She had to try what she could. If he thought there was a chance of finding a shred of life left in Tarek, he'd be trying too.

When nothing happened, Sajda dropped her hands and slowly climbed to her feet. "I can't . . . I can't do this." She looked wildly around the arena. Javan followed her gaze, but the warden was gone. "She'll turn him into meat, and I can't be here."

Javan stood as well, his anger burning bright. There was nothing he could do to stop the warden. Nothing he could do to give Tarek a proper burial. All he could do was pay his respects in the best way he knew how, though it felt far too small in the face of this loss. "I'll say a lament over him. Yl' Haliq will welcome him and give him eternal rest. I wish I could do more."

She stood for another moment, trembling and grieving, and then she turned and ran.

Javan let her go. There was nothing he could do to stem the horror and loss she felt, but he could keep his word. He could give Tarek the dignity of a proper send-off before the warden desecrated his body.

Dropping to his knees again, he gently closed Tarek's eyes and straightened his clothing. He tried to pray, but the words caught in his throat, and he bent over Tarek as he struggled to swallow. To breathe. To do this one last thing for the man who'd saved him. Javan's voice was a shadow of itself as he finally choked out the lament, every word a dagger that pierced him. When the lament was finished, he stayed on his knees, tears burning his eyes.

"I'm sorry." Intizara's voice was quiet as she stepped onto the arena floor, a small satchel in her hands.

He raised his eyes to hers. She looked stricken. "What happened? You were supposed to yell if Tarek needed help."

He tried to keep the anger out of his voice, but it was there anyway, threading his words with grief and fury.

"I know." She looked at her feet.

"Then why didn't you? Did the warden stop you?"

"She set me free."

He went still, his hand resting on Tarek's chest. "Free?"

"She offered me freedom if I gave up Tarek without a fight. I'm sorry. I didn't want to leave without telling you the truth."

He was silent for a long moment as the anger ballooned inside him until he thought he'd burst from it. When she slowly looked up to meet his gaze, his voice was deadly quiet as he said, "You traded an innocent man's life for your own freedom."

"I held out as long as I could!" She took a step toward him, saw the expression on his face, and froze. "The others in the kitchen agreed quickly, and I was the only one left."

He rose to his feet. "So then you be the only one left. You stand in front of an innocent man, and you keep your promises. You behave with *honor*. You don't betray him so that you can get out of the sentence for your crime!"

"What crime?" Her voice shook with anger and misery. "I'm here because I slapped an aristocrat's son for grabbing my chest. He swore I assaulted him, and no one ever let me give my testimony. The others? Here because an aristocrat said they owed a debt they weren't paying. Only two of them actually owed wahda. The others were thrown in here to get them out of the way. To let someone more powerful take their business, their land, or their families to be sold into slavery."

He stared at her, his chest heaving, fury blazing, though he couldn't find it in himself to aim it at her anymore.

How many prisoners were in Maqbara because they hadn't been allowed to give any testimony or call any witnesses? How many were here on the word of an aristocrat who wanted to use the prison as a way to steal from those who already had less?

This was proof that the father he knew was no longer in charge of his kingdom. He would never have turned a blind eye to this. The aristocratic families Javan knew from Milisatria wouldn't either, and he was willing to bet the same could be said for most of Akram. This was the result of Fariq's treachery. His corruption had spread across the kingdom, a sickness paid for with the blood of his people.

Every person Javan had talked to within Maqbara said the same thing. The king was rarely seen now, and was known to be in poor health. Maybe he couldn't put a stop to the damage Fariq and the impostor were doing to the kingdom, but Javan could.

He just had to make sure he won the last round of combat.

"I really am sorry," Intizara said as the other prisoners who'd been meant to watch over Tarek joined her, carrying their meager belongings and refusing to meet his furious gaze.

"I am too." Javan stood in front of Tarek's body as the warden left the corridor that led to her office and walked toward the door that led to the magistrate's office, ignoring Javan completely.

Helpless anger filled him. He couldn't defeat the warden without weapons. He couldn't turn back time and save Tarek. All he could do was prepare for the upcoming round of combat and try to comfort the girl he loved.

Javan didn't wait to see the prisoners who'd sold Tarek gain their prize. He knew where Sajda would be. Turning away, he climbed the stairs to the fifteenth level and entered the storage closet.

Prayers gathered in his heart and poured from his lips in fractured whispers. As he closed the broken door behind him, he fell to his knees and cried beside the crate Sajda had used to escape into the rafters.

THIRTY-EIGHT

"THE KING IS no longer taking his tonic," Rahim said, bursting into Fariq's sitting room as his father was signing a pile of documents with a quill.

Fariq frowned, and waved his manservant from the room. When the door had closed behind him, Fariq said, "Watch your mouth in front of the staff. We don't need rumors. Especially since someone murdered the heads of the FaSaa'il right under our noses. If that isn't a clear sign that we have a traitor somewhere in our organization, I don't know what is. We don't know who we can trust."

Fariq had no idea just how true his words would turn out to be. Rahim turned from his father before he could see the rage that crawled through him at being given orders.

He was the future king.

He was through taking orders from anyone.

"Now, what is this about not taking his tonic? The palace physician refilled it just yesterday."

"Well, I don't know what he's doing with it, but he isn't swallowing it." Rahim turned back to Fariq, though the rage was still clawing at its cage. "His eyes are clear. He isn't shuffling around and running into things. He asked me several very pointed questions yesterday, and I think he knows the tonic was poison."

Fariq laid his quill down. "And did you answer those questions carefully?"

Rahim closed the distance between them. "I'm not a fool, *Uncle*. I deflected suspicion from me and agreed with him that he might be in danger and that he should double his personal guard."

"You *are* a fool." Fariq glared at his son. "You don't validate his fears and make him harder to reach!"

"If I hadn't agreed with him, I would have looked guilty. He was fishing for it. Asking me questions about my mother. About Milisatria. About the symptoms of his illness. About *you*."

Fariq froze. "He suspects me?"

Rahim nodded. Oh yes, the king suspected his cousin of trying to kill him and remove him from the throne. Rahim had made sure of it. It was unfortunate that the king's suspicion of Fariq had caused him to stop taking his tonic. Rahim couldn't afford to risk the king recognizing Javan and halting the coronation. Still, he could dose the king with saffeyena the morning of Maqbara's competition, and that would keep the king in a groggy state long enough to be seen with Rahim without acknowledging Javan, a certain way to stop the gossip about whether Javan was a royal. After the coronation, the king could have a well-timed accident, and Rahim's future would be secured.

"We must move quickly and carefully." Fariq turned to look out his window at the golden sunshine pooling on the mosaic tiles of his personal courtyard. "With extra guards, it will be tricky, but the key is to make it look like an accident."

"We can't kill him immediately after he hired extra guards and told them he thinks you're making a move against him and his son." Rahim's voice was cold as he slowly pulled his royal purple sash from around his waist. "The important thing is that I get the crown. I've promised him I'd reveal whatever it was Javan was supposed to show him at his mother's grave at the coronation. Made a big deal about wanting it to be a moment that honored her in front of the entire kingdom. He bought it. The coronation is proceeding on schedule."

"It's still more than a week away!" Fariq tapped his fingers on the table impatiently. "As the poison continues to leave his system, his thoughts will be sharper. His logic clearer. And if he suspects me, he'll come after me to protect you."

"It's what a loyal father would do for his son," Rahim said as he moved to stand directly behind Fariq's chair. "And, of course, it's what a loyal son would do for his father."

"What are you—"

Swiftly Rahim wrapped the sash around his father's neck, twisted it tight, and pulled. Fariq clawed at his son's hands, knocking the parchment and quill to the floor. Rahim dug his heels into the rug and held on. As his father's struggles lessened, Rahim leaned down and let every ounce of bitter rage he'd nursed for seventeen years out of its cage.

"The important thing is that *I* get the crown. Not you. Not the father who left his son to rot in poverty and filth for years." He twisted the sash tighter. "My new father believes me to be a loyal, honorable son worthy of being his successor. You've just helped me prove him right."

Fariq's body went limp, and Rahim slowly let go of the sash. And then he turned to find the king to report that someone loyal to the king had apparently uncovered Fariq's treachery and put an end to it.

THIRTY-NINE

JAVAN LOST TRACK of the hours as he bent over the crate in the supply room on the fifteenth level, his agony pouring out of him in broken prayers to Yl' Haliq, who had allowed all this.

The headmaster's death.

The impostor taking Javan's place.

Javan's imprisonment.

The corruption in Akram.

Meeting Sajda.

Losing Tarek.

Javan had been so sure of himself. So sure of the entire world when he stepped on the stage beside the headmaster to receive the sash he'd worked so hard for.

He was a prince, destined to rule. His father was a king full of honor and greatness, and Javan's task was to live up to his example. Akram was the jewel of the desert—her people thriving in a just society. He'd thought everything was carved in stone. A destiny ordained by Yl' Haliq himself.

But here he was.

On his knees in a dusty supply closet in Maqbara, surrounded by corruption and grief, praying though he no longer knew what to ask for.

He'd begged for deliverance, but he was still here.

He'd prayed that the injustice done to him would be made right, but instead he'd learned about the injustices that had been done to others. And here he knelt, broken by the truth that his father had failed. That pain was a way of life for so many of his people.

That pain was a way of life for Sajda.

He'd asked for mercy. For help.

He'd received silence.

Bending his head over his hands, he stopped praying. Stopped picking up every shard of grief, every splinter of anger to examine it anew. Instead, he went quiet, his heart aching as he let go of everything he wanted to demand. Ask. *Beg.*

For long moments, he stayed curved over the chest in the middle of the closet, silent and aching.

And then something shifted inside him.

A breath of peace. A soft whisper of comfort that didn't take away the pain but somehow made it easier to endure. The gentle touch of Yl' Haliq resting on Javan's battered heart.

And in the stillness of his mind, an idea formed, crystallizing before he realized what was happening. He clenched his folded hands as hope, soft and fragile, unfurled in his chest and took root.

He was right where he was supposed to be.

He was meant to hurt the way his people hurt. To see the truth of Akram from their eyes.

Their grief was his to bear. Their injustices his to make right.

He was destined to lose what he'd thought was his so that he could gain something far more important—wisdom.

He was destined to learn how to fight for his kingdom. For his people.

And he was destined to meet Sajda.

As if she'd read his mind, she dropped out of the crack in the ceiling and stared at him with weary grief on her face.

"What are you doing?" she asked, her voice husky from crying.

"Praying and waiting for you."

He got to his feet, moving stiffly, his knees protesting his hours on the hard stone floor.

"I was wrong," he said.

"About what?"

"Everything." He moved so that the crate was no longer lying between them. "I kept praying for deliverance. For escape. I was so consumed with the wrong done to me that I failed to stop and listen. To learn. But I've been listening, Sajda. And I know that I was always meant to be in Maqbara. I was meant to understand the corruption my uncle brought to Akram, the pain it causes my people, and the horrors that take place here in the name of sport."

He moved closer. "And I was destined to meet you. I wouldn't take back a second of my own pain if it meant that you and I would still be strangers. But my pain isn't the most important thing to me. Yours is. I would do anything to take back the heartbreak you feel. Even if it meant I'd never get to be your friend in the first place."

"Stop trying to make me love you." She stood across from him, her body trembling, her eyes haunted.

Love.

The word hung in the air between them, bittersweet with its wounds and its wild possibilities.

Gently he asked, "Is that what you think I'm doing?"

"Yes." She hurled the word at him, an accusation full of longing. "You protect me, you listen to me, you show me the stars, and make me *feel* things. Make me trust you. But I can't trust you. I can't want you. I can't . . ."

His heart ached with every beat, an unfamiliar, delicate pain that felt like walking into a strange house and realizing he was home.

"Why not?" He breathed the words and held himself still so that she wouldn't change the subject or brush him off. So that she wouldn't run.

Her hands curled into fists, held tight by her sides. Tears slowly welled in her beautiful eyes and slipped down her cheek. "Because you're going to leave."

The pain in his heart thrummed through his entire body at the dark grief that lay beneath her words. Of course she thought he was going to leave her. Her mother had left—pocketed the wahda from selling her strange, powerful daughter and disappeared. The female prisoner she'd been friends with had died two years ago in the arena. And Tarek, the closest thing to a father she'd ever known, was gone. Love must feel like a double-edged sword to her.

"Sajda—"

"Everyone goes away." Her voice shook, and the desperation on her face tore something inside him. "Everyone. You will too."

The tears glittered on her skin like starlight as he moved closer. Close enough to feel the tiny thrill of her magic reaching for him. To feel the heat from her skin lingering on his. With one gentle finger, he lifted her chin and looked deep into her eyes.

"I'm not the kind of girl people keep," she whispered.

"I'm not the kind of boy who leaves." He held her gaze as he raised his other hand to lay it against her cheek, her skin damp from tears.

"But that's what you want. It's what you've been working toward all this time."

"I find myself very conflicted about what I want," he said quietly. "I have a responsibility to my kingdom. To my father. But I want *you*, Sajda."

A tiny frown puckered her brow, and he smiled. "Don't start arguing with me."

"I'll argue if I want to. You can't just throw away everything—"

He kissed her, covering her mouth with his and swallowing the words he wasn't ready to hear.

He already knew what she'd say. He had to leave. Had to win the competition and be restored as the heir to Akram's crown of fire. And he couldn't take her with him. The warden would never part with her—not for any price, he knew that. New laws banned the selling of child slaves in Akram, but it hadn't freed those slaves who had already been purchased. And until he was established on the throne, he couldn't use the power of the crown to give the warden her death sentence and free Sajda. Couldn't change the laws to free the few slaves left in Akram and make sure others were spared the pain Sajda had faced.

She made a sound in the back of her throat and wrapped her arms around him, dragging him against her until nothing separated them. Her lips tingled, tiny bites of magic that pulled at him, seeking a way in.

He surrendered. Welcoming her magic into his mouth, into his blood where she could feel the heart of him. Where all that drove him—every fear, every doubt, every longing—would be hers for the taking.

It was like being scoured with lightning. He gasped and stumbled back, pressing one hand to his heart as it crashed against his chest.

"I'm sorry," she said, her hand hovering over his chest as though she wanted to take back the lightning thrill of her magic as it blazed through him.

"I'm not." He held himself steady as the blaze settled into a hum that prickled under his skin with a strange heat. "I wanted you to see for yourself. You don't need words and promises. You need truth. And your magic can give you that. Tell me." He swayed as her hand came to rest on the bare skin above his tunic, dragging the prickling heat through his blood and back into her.

She sucked in a little breath, her eyes gazing at something far away as she took what he'd offered and sifted through what her magic was showing her.

"Tell me," he repeated quietly.

Her voice was soft and full of hesitant wonder. "You don't want to leave Maqbara."

"Why not?"

"Because I'm here," she whispered.

"And?"

"And you blame yourself for Tarek, which you shouldn't. You're afraid you can't save your father. And you're afraid that if you fail in the tasks Yl' Haliq has given you, you'll lose yourself.

That you'll be broken." She flinched. "I'm sorry. I shouldn't have looked at that."

"I showed you willingly," he said, though meeting her eyes with all his secrets laid bare took more courage than going into the arena on combat day.

They locked eyes for a long moment, and then he said, "What else did you see?"

Pink blossomed on her cheeks. "Nothing."

He smiled. "Nothing?"

She shook her head, but she didn't move away as he leaned in. Framing her face with his hands, he said, "You didn't see that I want to sweep you out of this place and lay the world at your feet?"

The pulse in her temples sped up, and he pressed his lips to her forehead before saying, "You didn't see that I think of you every hour of the day? That when I catch myself staring at your mouth, I lose track of everything except how much I want to kiss you?"

He traced his lips down the bridge of her nose. "Or maybe you saw how winning a single smile from you makes me feel like I'm already a king. How you inspire me to be better, and how until I met you, I never knew I needed a girl who would constantly challenge me on every level."

"Javan—"

He moved to her mouth and hovered a breath away from kissing her. "You didn't need to hear my promises. You needed to see the truth for yourself. And you have to know now that I will come back for you. That I will take you away from here and give you the stars and the wide-open spaces you long for."

"I know." Her voice shook.

"And you have to know *why* I will come back for you."

Her lips trembled, but she didn't speak.

Closing his eyes and praying that she would accept the truth she'd seen in him, he whispered, "Why am I coming back for you, Sajda?"

She was silent for seconds, moments, *years*, and every breath he took was agony as he waited for her to accept it—to accept him—or to walk away from the risk that once again her heart would be shattered.

Finally, in a voice full of wonder and peace, she said, "Because you love me."

FORTY

IT HAD BEEN three weeks since Tarek's death, and Sajda still expected him to show up every morning with an orange for her breakfast.

She still noticed interesting things about the other prisoners that she wanted to share with him. Still thought of her workload in terms of what she would do on her own and what she would delegate to him.

And she would give anything to hear him call her little one again.

Her grief refused to subside, no matter how much calm she tried to borrow from the stone. It was a hollow space that remained black even when she swallowed the starlight.

The only comfort she'd found had been Javan's steady, solid presence—a bedrock she could stand on when everything else seemed to be shifting beneath her feet. He'd quietly begun to bring her something for breakfast every morning after she fed the beasts, even though it meant daring Hashim to attack him in the kitchen. During his chore hour, he'd taken on the tasks she would've usually given to Tarek. He'd sparred with her daily in preparation for the final round of the tournament, and he'd welcomed her strength and her speed, even when she left bruises because something inside her could no longer stomach the thought of holding back.

Every afternoon, she'd used the prisoners from levels fourteen and fifteen to help set up for the final round of competition, and she'd stolen a few moments between tasks with Javan to escape to the room on the third level.

Sajda hadn't wanted more lessons at first. It felt wrong to be planning to leave, to do more than just survive, when Tarek couldn't plan for his future too. But Javan had challenged her—bragging about the scores he received in mathematics, astronomy, and history—until she was irritated enough to show him she was just as good, if not better.

Now, she had a head full of facts she hadn't known before. She understood the history of the surrounding kingdoms; she could name the constellations as they spun past her place in the rafters; and she'd become so good at doing complicated math problems in her head that Javan had started getting grumpy when he needed to use a piece of parchment.

And now, grief had given birth to anger. She woke with her magic scraping at her skin, hunting for a target. She moved through her day with rage bubbling in the hollow space that had opened within her at the sight of Tarek's body. She lay down at night with a buzzing, humming power pressing against her cuffs in a futile effort to tear apart the things that held her back.

Soon she would be free.

Javan would come back for her. She knew he would. And the

warden would pay for everything she'd done. And then Sajda would have her stars and her wide-open spaces. Then she could leave the dust of Akram behind and never look back.

The thought sliced at her heart, a flash of pain she didn't want to examine closely.

But for any of that to happen, Javan had to win the next day's combat round, which meant he had to stop trying to talk her through what would happen if he lost and focus on the beasts he'd be fighting.

She faced him across the couch in the room on the third level as he said, "Just in case. It's the only thing I can think of to— Are you listening to me?"

"No. We aren't going to talk about you losing. We're going to—"

"We are absolutely going to talk about me losing." He leaned close, a feverish light in his eyes. "I plan to win, Sajda. You know I do. But we'd be fools not to have a contingency plan in place in case I lose. In case I die."

"Stop it!" She glared at him, and his expression softened.

"It's just in case. I need to know that I was able to do something to help you."

"Fine." She crossed her arms over her chest where the hollow space was now swirling with panic.

"If I go down, you take this." He held up a beautiful red sash wrapped around a square of folded parchment. "I'll wear it under my tunic, next to my heart. Get it to the king. You have the freedom to go up the stairs. You can reach him and give it to him. Tell him I'm his son, and I fulfilled my mother's *muqaddas tus'el.*"

"Why don't I just do that before the competition starts?" she asked. "Then you won't have to fight at all."

"Maybe you can. It depends on if the impostor is with him. If he is, I doubt he'll let anyone get near the king while I'm alive. He has too much to lose. But if I'm dead, or I've lost and can't have an audience with the king, then he might let down his guard."

"Or I could just smash through his guard, give this to the king, and throw the impostor into the arena." The rage within her blazed at the thought of hurting the person who'd taken so much from Javan.

"And be revealed as a dark elf? Be accused of killing the prince? The king would never look at what you have in your hands if you committed violence to get it to him."

"Fine. Now, are you ready to go over the creatures again?"

"We've gone over them for days, Sajda. I know them. I know how to kill them. I'm ready to fight. What I'm not ready for is leaving you behind, even for a minute." The misery on his face had her moving across the cushion that separated them until she could wrap her arms around him and lean her head against his chest.

She didn't want to be left either. Not for a minute.

But he'd come back.

She'd seen the truth in his heart.

He'd come back because he loved her.

She loved him too—a terrifying, exhilarating revelation she hadn't found the courage to put into words for him yet.

She had never said "I love you" to anyone. And even though it was true—she loved Javan fiercely and absolutely—saying it felt like dropping the last tiny defense she had. It was standing in front of a windstorm, arms wide open, with nothing to anchor her to the ground. It was jumping from a mountain believing that gravity couldn't touch her.

It was thrilling. Comforting. Terrifying.

And so she held him close, her magic humming along her skin and into his, and hoped he understood the things she didn't quite know how to say.

"I love you," he said softly.

She tipped her head up and brought his face to hers. Pressing her lips to his, she tried to memorize the way his chest rose and fell with every breath. The way his heart beat steadily beneath her hand while his mouth moved gently against hers. Warmth swirled through her, tangling with her magic until she wanted to send it into him and read his heart again. See his truth so she could hold it close after he was gone.

When she pulled away, he tried to follow, but she pressed him back into the couch. "I have to pull the weapons for tomorrow and make sure everything is sharpened and cleaned. You can't help with that. Prisoners aren't allowed to touch any of them outside the arena. The warden already checks up on me often when I'm working with the weapons to make sure I don't steal any for my own use. If you were with me, she'd have reason to punish you badly enough to make sure you'd lose the competition."

He stood when she did and wrapped his arms around her once more. "No matter what happens tomorrow, I don't regret being here, Sajda. I love you."

She leaned into him, and when the answering words lingered on her tongue, she opened her mouth; but the thread that held her together shivered and frayed, and the words dissolved. She left him there and hurried down to the weapons closet. She was focused on thinking through the weapons' layout she'd drawn up the day before—short swords in the center where Javan could easily find them. Bow and arrow for him on a hook to the west, far away from the gate to give him a chance to aim at the creatures she'd be sending into the arena. Spear on the opposite wall—

"Well, well, if it isn't the warden's little monster." Hashim smiled at her outside the door of the weapons closet, and she pulled up short. A quick glance around confirmed that they were alone in the corridor.

"What are you doing here?" she demanded, resting her hand on the wall beside her so she could pull the cold indifference of the stone into herself.

His smile turned vicious. "I finally figured it out. The way the warden calls you monster. The iron cuffs with runes carved in them." He gestured toward her wrists while everything inside her went still.

"Get out of my way. I have work to do." Her tone was as hard as the floor beneath her boots.

"I don't think so." He leaned against the closet door and tapped a thick, meaty finger against his lips. "It's so rare to catch you without your aristocratic guard dog that I think I'll stay and chat."

"Then I won't stick around to listen."

She turned to go but froze as he said, "Elf or fae?"

Magic screamed through her, a blazing heat in her veins, and her wrists ached as the runes glowed. Slowly she turned to face him. "Excuse me?"

"Are you a dark elf or a fae?"

"If I was either one, you'd be in trouble, wouldn't you?" She bared her teeth at him.

His eyes narrowed. "I felt your magic. Last competition, when you put grave dirt on me. You looked angry with me, and then there was this buzzing in my chest right where our skin touched. When you removed your hand, you'd left a handprint burned into my skin. See?" He pulled his tunic aside, and Sajda's mouth went dry as she saw the raised pink scar of her hand in the center of his chest.

When she said nothing, he sighed. "I guess it doesn't really matter which you are. My bet is elf because of how pale your skin is, but either way, I know."

Magic sliced at her, and she moved closer to him. He lifted his other hand, and she stopped as she saw the thick iron chain he held.

"Where did you get that?" she asked.

"Borrowed it from the last sparring session. No one noticed that I'd taken it from the arena. Guess you're still distracted by the old man's death."

She raised her hands, runes glowing, magic coiling in her palms. "I don't need these cuffs removed to hurt you, Hashim."

"I know. But I'm betting if I wrap you in this chain, it will be very difficult to use any of that magic against me. This is a lot of iron." He hefted the chain.

"And I'm betting I can hurt you before you do that."

He shrugged. "Maybe, but I'm not alone."

She turned and found three of his friends closing in slowly behind her, each of them carrying an iron chain.

"You didn't take four chains from the arena, Hashim."

"No, I didn't. I had a little help unlocking the weapons closet."

"The warden." Her breath came in quick bursts, and anger warred with panic.

The warden couldn't harm Javan directly without starting a fire of rumor and anger with her wealthiest bettors. But she could get to Javan by letting Hashim get to Sajda.

"The warden," he agreed. And then his chain whistled through the air, directly for her face. She dodged it, but then stumbled as a woman behind her snapped her chain across Sajda's back. Whirling, she snatched the chain, ignoring the burn of iron against her hands, and yanked the woman forward. A swift kick sent the toe of her boot into the woman's stomach. She fell, and Sajda turned on the others, but it was too late.

Two chains wrapped around her, pinning her arms to her sides. She hissed as the iron touched her skin. Magic tumbled and churned in her veins, but her hands were pinned, and the iron was slicing through her power, sending it spinning through her in fragments.

Hashim stepped in front of her, his chain swinging as if he might flick it toward her face at any moment. The air felt too thin, her blood too thick as panic roared within her.

She was trapped. No way to use her magic. No way to use her strength and speed. And no help was coming.

"What do you want?" she snapped, her voice shaky at the edges.

"What the warden wants. For me to win. She wants me to kill Javan during the competition." He smiled at her, and she nearly spit in his face. "But I think you and I can come to an understanding instead, which is why I asked her to let me use the chains. She didn't seem to think you'd be helpful, but you will."

"Why should I?"

"Because this is the best outcome for you. I leave, and no one in this hall breathes a word about what you are. You get to keep your favorite prisoner by your side. And the warden stays on the king's good side. My understanding is that the royal family doesn't want Javan to even be in the competition. I don't know what your aristocrat did to land himself in Maqbara, but he made enemies of the wrong people." He moved closer, the chain swinging. "As long as you help me, Javan will stay in Maqbara with you for the rest of his life."

She felt a flash of temptation followed instantly by guilt.

Javan would come back for her.

And even if he didn't, she could never be the reason he was forced to stay.

Hashim took her silence for agreement. "You're going to tell me where the bow and arrow and the short swords will be located tomorrow. Your boy can still fight, but he won't have his favorite weapons."

She laughed, cold and cruel. "Why would I do that? To force Javan to stay imprisoned here?"

"Because if you don't, I will reveal to the aristocracy that you are a dangerous creature of magic whose iron cuffs no longer restrain her. I'll show them your handprint on my chest as proof. It's almost the week of *Tu' Omwahl*. The memory of what your people did to ours is fresh. You're strong, but you can't take on an entire crowd of people who think the only way to protect themselves and their children from your kind is to kill you."

He was right. The crowd would devour her. She might take a few of them with her, but with restrained magic she wouldn't take enough.

Plus tomorrow couldn't be about her. Not even for a second. Javan needed to win so he could talk to his father and be restored to the throne. It would be harder for him to win without his preferred weapons, but it would also be hard for Hashim to win trying to use weapons that were better suited to someone else. And she could warn Javan. He was good at improvising.

"Do we have an agreement?"

She nodded, sickness moving through her as the iron chafed her skin.

Hashim leaned close and snapped the edge of his chain against her heart. "That's for burning me. And if you even think about betraying this agreement, I will expose you to the spectators and in the chaos that follows, I'll kill Javan."

The chains fell away, and Sajda reached one shaky hand into her pocket. Without another word, she handed over the weapons' layout and then brushed past him to enter the closet that the warden and Hashim had left unlocked while he was waiting to ambush her. Her hands shook with the need to carve into him, take his blood, and break his will into pieces.

FORTY-ONE

SAJDA CLOSED THE door behind her, her skin still burning from the iron chains, her heart beating a frantic tempo in her chest. Her hands shook as she began putting away the freshly cleaned weapons that had been used in combat practice that day. Tomorrow, she'd be up at dawn placing them in their assigned spots inside the arena while the warden watched.

For tonight, the swords went on the dusty black cloth. The mace hung on a hook beside the short spear and the chain. She picked up the bow and ran her fingers over the place where hours earlier Javan had stood in the center of the arena, and fired arrow after arrow in quick succession around the arena.

His strategy depended on getting the bow and arrow, and she'd just taken that from him. The warden would never agree to a last-minute change in weapons' placement. She gripped the bow with white knuckles, her heartbeat roaring in her ears, her magic blazing through her blood in desperation to protect Javan.

Oh, how she'd wanted to save him. To leap the wall and run

to his side, her magic clawing for the blood of his foes so she could whisper nightmares that would reduce them all to rubble.

Was it wrong to use her magic to hurt those who sought to hurt the boy she loved?

She wasn't sure she cared. If she had to be a monster, at least she could be a monster who kept the prince of Akram safe and helped restore him to his throne.

Something bumped the wall in the corridor outside the closet, and she froze, magic scraping at her skin. Had Hashim and his friends returned to torture her with their chains again?

"Did anyone see you enter?" The warden's deep voice filled the air.

Sajda shrank, huddling close to the floor, reaching for a pair of battle-axes as though that could save her if the warden turned her attention to the weapons' closet and discovered an eaves-dropper.

"I was careful."

She knew that voice—elegance and brute arrogance. It was the false prince. Her fists closed around the ax handle as she considered whether she could get past the warden long enough to kill the boy who'd taken everything from Javan.

"What is it? I have a prison to run."

"You have a boy to kill. I've run out of patience. Javan cannot be allowed to win tomorrow's competition."

"I'll make sure of it. If he doesn't die in the competition, then the points will add up to another winner." The warden sounded impatient.

"I don't have the same kind of faith in your abilities as Fariq. From the start, you have done nothing but create problems. You attacked Javan too early in Loch Talam, and didn't even manage to kill him then. You failed to report that he was in your prison, and by the time we found out about it, rumors about him were already spreading. And you failed to make sure he died in the last round of combat. You should've just killed him in between rounds and been done with it."

The warden's voice was a low, throaty snarl that sent a chill over Sajda's skin. "You'd better be careful how you speak to me. You need me as an ally, not an enemy."

"And you need me. Fariq is dead. The king will be dead shortly after my coronation. If you've made an enemy of me, you will lose this prison, your coin, and if you don't flee Akram fast enough, your life."

There was a long moment of silence, and Sajda hardly dared to breathe in case she gave herself away.

Finally, the warden said, "I can't just kill a competitor who is a crowd favorite. Not without raising a lot of questions with both my prisoners and the aristocrats. That's why I didn't kill him in the first place. The last thing we need are rumors about the boy with the resemblance to royalty who died mysteriously in Maqbara."

"Then you shouldn't have let him become a crowd favorite!"

"I was away when he arrived, and I didn't even know he was here until he was already in a competition and word was already spreading. *You* should've made sure he never made it to Maqbara."

"You bear plenty of blame for that as well. He must be killed. *Tonight*. The king's health has improved lately, and it's risky to let him see Javan. I'll dose him with saffeyena to confuse him, but I don't want to take chances. Kill Javan. We'll claim it was a jealous prisoner and punish one of them accordingly."

"If the prisoners think they aren't safe in their cells when they're following all of the rules, I could have a riot on my hands."

"Then you shift into a dragon and you kill anyone who riots. That will quell any dissent immediately. In fact, that's the best solution to all of this. Shift, burn Javan, and claim you'd discovered he was part of a plot against the crown. I'll support your claims. It will be simple."

"Easy for you to say when you get all the benefit and take none of the risk," she answered.

"Need I remind you that Fariq gave you an incredible amount of leeway in how you run your prison and how you gain your prisoners. I'm sure an investigation would uncover quite a number of inmates who aren't actually guilty of their crimes but whose room and board the city's taxes have been generously paying. And it would reveal that you're baking the corpses of the losers along with the destroyed beasts and using that to feed your prisoners so you can pocket the coin we send for their upkeep. As the new king, I can either continue to look the other way as Fariq did, or I can ruin you. Choose wisely."

In the silence that followed, Sajda quietly set the battle-axes down and pressed her hands to the stone floor. Her magic stung her palms as it drank in the heart of the stone, sheathing her in cold, immovable purpose.

"Consider it done," the warden said. "It's nearly twelfth bell. I'll burn him in his bed once the bars go down. There's no escaping from that."

The stone skin Sajda wore over her heart shuddered once at the thought of Javan dying in a stream of dragon fire, and then she rose to her feet, glaring at the door while she waited for the warden and the impostor to leave.

The moment the corridor was empty, she raced down its length and hurtled into the first stairway as the chain and pulley system shuddered into life.

If she didn't get there in time, Javan would be locked in his cell, and she wouldn't be able to get him out before the warden arrived.

She took the stairs three at once, bursting onto the next level and then sprinting up again. The iron bars rattled as they began descending from the ceiling.

Why had she put him on the fifteenth level?

Her breath sobbed in and out of her lungs, as she passed level three. Level four. Crashed into someone on level five's stairwell and never looked back.

Six.

The bars were a third of the way down now.

She reached for her magic. Let it coil around her muscles and give her power.

Seven.

Eight.

Nine.

The bars were halfway down. It didn't matter if anyone saw her run with inhuman speed. It didn't matter if she was revealed to be a dark elf.

All that mattered was that Javan, the boy who made her laugh and think and feel, survived.

Slamming her hands into the walls on either side of the stairs that led from level ten to eleven, she sent her magic shuddering into the wall and felt it give. Digging her hands into the stone, she created a new handhold on each side and flung herself to the top of the stairs in one leap.

Two thirds of the way up.

Twelve.

Thirteen.

Another handhold. Another leap.

She was almost there, but the bars were slowing. How much space would he need to get out? Was it already too late?

One more giant leap and she skidded onto level fifteen and bounced off the wall as she turned toward Javan's cell.

"Javan!" Her voice echoed throughout the upper levels of the prison, but she didn't care.

She ran, feet skimming the stone, as the door creaked toward its final stop.

He met her at the door as she flung herself between the bars and the floor, grabbed the iron railing, and locked her arms, refusing to let it fall.

The metal screeched, and she sobbed out a little prayer that she could hold it long enough. The iron bit into her skin, pain screaming up her arms.

"What are you doing?" There was a wild light of fear on his face. "You're going to be crushed. Move!"

He grabbed the bars and pulled, muscles straining as the door struggled to complete its journey.

"She's coming to kill you. Burn you alive. Slide under. *Hurry!*"

He kept his arms on the bars as he lay down on the floor beside her. "You slide out first. Then me."

"No. I can hold this."

"Sajda—"

She locked her eyes on his. "Trust me. I'm stronger than you can possibly imagine. Get out now before she arrives and takes your choice away."

There was a wealth of unsaid things in his expression, but he simply scooted down, keeping his hands on the bars to help with the weight, and then slid under. The second he was clear, she started to follow, and the door dropped a handspan.

"No!" he shouted, and lunged for the rail above her. Wrapping both arms around it, he pulled upward with all his might as she slowly wiggled free, trying to leverage as much pressure against the railing as she could while still getting clear of it.

"Clear," she said, and they let go.

The door slammed into the stone floor with a jarring thud, and from a distance, they heard the shush of leathery wings beating the air.

"She's coming," Sajda said, wrapping her hand around Javan's. "The closet. Quickly!"

They ran for the far end of the corridor. For the abandoned supply closet with its broken door. Sajda pulled the door open, practically shoved Javan inside, and then softly closed the door behind them. Seconds later, the dragon cleared the level, hovered in front of Javan's cell, and sent a steady stream of fire where moments ago, the prince of Akram had been standing.

"She might find us in here," Javan breathed.

Sajda's mind raced, skipping through her options and discarding them one by one until she found the only possible solution. "We aren't staying in here. It will take her some time to realize you weren't lying on your bed when she incinerated your cell. When she does, she'll track you by scent. Your scent might be all over the prison, but the strongest scent trail will be from where you've most recently been."

His face blanched, and she peeked out of the crack in the door to see the dragon still hovering just outside Javan's cell, watching the whole thing burn.

"If she tracks by scent, there's nowhere for me to run. You have to get away from me." Javan's voice was a desperate whisper. "Are you listening to me? Sajda!"

She pulled back from the door and met his gaze. "You already know I'm not leaving you. I'm going to take you down to the stalls. I have a hiding place there, and it will be very difficult for her to track your scent when it's mixed in with all the beasts we're housing. It's your best chance. Now let's go."

FORTY-TWO

THE CROWD WAS already chanting Javan's name when he slowly made his way out of the tunnel Sajda had spent years carving into the bedrock behind one of the stalls. She'd led him there the moment the warden was gone, creeping past the ruins of his cell by the light of the full moon. His bed was a charred, twisted lump. The rest of his cell's sparse contents were piles of ash on the stone floor, but it was the bed that held his attention.

He could have been lying on it, oblivious to the death that was heading his way. He already owed so much to Sajda, and now he owed her his life.

He'd stayed in the tunnel all night while Sajda smeared sheep's guts over the opening and the stall itself to throw the warden off his scent once the sun rose and she saw that the prince hadn't been caught in the inferno. He wasn't sure how long the warden searched for him, or what excuse, if any, she'd made to the other prisoners for trying to burn him alive. His world had narrowed down to the cool darkness of Sajda's little cave until she'd pushed the trough away from the opening and called for him to head to the arena.

The audience of aristocrats would make it nearly impossible for the warden to justify another attempt on Javan's life during the competition. At least that was his hope.

He left the stalls and walked to the arena, the parchment with a note to his father folded up inside his red sash and tied to his chest with a thin strip he'd torn from the edge of his sheet. He was thankful he'd decided to wear the sash at all times or it would've gone up in flames and, with it, the proof of who he was.

His stomach knotted, and his heart felt like it was hammering against his throat.

Today he'd finally see his father again.

Today he'd either become a prince again or die trying.

He reached the gate and stood a little ways from Hashim, who was already there, his fist raised in the air as his supporters screamed for him. Iram, the third competitor, joined Javan, and they surveyed the arena in silence.

The warden's platform was still empty. The weapons were secured beneath black cloths again, but it hardly mattered. Hashim knew where every weapon was located. So did Javan. And thanks to Sajda, he'd had enough warning about Hashim's treachery to form an alternate plan.

That plan included silencing Hashim.

Permanently.

The sacred texts were clear about the taking of an innocent life, but Hashim wasn't innocent. He'd tried to kill Javan, and he'd sent his minions to do the same in the last competition. There was every likelihood that he'd try again, especially because they each had over five hundred points now, so the deduction for killing another competitor would be more than balanced by receiving that prisoner's points. Javan could kill him in self-defense.

But he wouldn't.

Hashim had threatened Sajda with exposure. He'd whipped her with a chain. There was no possible way Javan was leaving Sajda behind in the prison if Hashim was still alive.

"We should fight back-to-back," he said quietly to Iram.

The young man looked at him in surprise.

"The beasts we'll be facing are lethal. If we don't have to watch our backs, we have a better chance of surviving," Javan said.

"Some of us aren't just trying to survive." Hashim turned to meet Javan's eyes. "Some of us are fighting to win."

Javan held Hashim's gaze and let every spark of righteous fury he felt show on his face. "I wasn't offering to fight with you." He stepped closer. "In fact, if I were you, I'd run from me. The monsters coming into the arena will kill indiscriminately. But me? I'm coming for you, Hashim. And I won't miss."

Hashim drew back, fear flashing in his eyes before anger washed it away. "Not if I kill you first."

Javan turned to Iram. "You like the spiked whip and the long sword, don't you?"

Iram nodded slowly, his eyes darting between Hashim and Javan.

Javan smiled grimly. "He isn't your ally, Iram. You're just another body standing between him and victory. Now listen. The whip is on the floor in the northeast corner. The sword is hanging on the wall directly beneath the warden's platform."

Iram's gaze widened as he peered around Hashim to check the position of the black cloths that hid his weapons of choice. "Why would you tell me that?"

"Because you and I aren't enemies. We can fight back-to-back. It gives us one less foe to worry about."

"And if I refuse?"

Javan shrugged. "Then you'll at least know where your weapons are and hopefully you'll get out of this alive."

He glanced at the stalls, where Sajda was calling orders to the guards as they positioned the competition's monsters for entry into the arena. The pale skin of her arms was burned red where the chains had held her, and a deep welt rose over her heart, courtesy of Hashim. She'd assured Javan that it would fade. That it was nothing. She was used to the pain of her cuffs, but he didn't care.

Hashim had imprisoned her. Threatened her. Hurt her.

He was going to pay dearly for that.

A ripple of excitement ran through the crowd, briefly silencing the cheering. Javan looked up as a trio of royal guards stepped through the door on the far wall. The air suddenly felt thick, time moving in slow motion as the guards walked forward and Javan caught his first glimpse of the royal family.

Of his father.

He was different from the man in Javan's memory. His shoulders stooped a bit, his black hair had gray at the temples and throughout his beard, and there was a shakiness to his movements. His piercing gaze had dimmed into something faraway and confused, but though he was different, he was achingly familiar. The same quiet kindness in his eyes when he looked at the boy he thought was his son. The same raised chin and calm expression that demanded perfection from those around him even as he strove to deliver it himself.

He hadn't delivered it.

He was walking into a pit of corruption, violence, and injustice, and by sitting in the royal box, he was sanctioning it all. Did he know that? Or was the confusion on his face a symptom of a once-great mind that no longer understood his present circumstances?

Javan's heart ached as he watched the king. He wanted to run to his father. To speak to him and hear him call Javan by his name. Whatever his father had become, he was still the gravity that had held Javan to his duty for ten long years. His respect, his regard, was what Javan had been working so hard to earn.

Javan clenched his fists and held himself still as the impostor took the king's arm, purple sash flowing, face alight with fierce pride.

Hashim wasn't the only person Javan needed to silence today.

Another trio of royal guards followed the pair as they slowly made their way to the closest staircase and up to the first level. Javan frowned. Uncle Fariq hadn't come. Javan didn't know whether to be relieved or disappointed. Without his uncle's influence, it might be easier to convince his father that he was the true prince. But he'd also wanted to confront his uncle's betrayal in front of all of Akram.

The warden stepped to her platform as the king and the impostor took their seats above Javan's head. He craned his neck, but he wouldn't be able to see into the box until he was in the arena, and at that point, he couldn't afford his focus to be split between his father and the monsters who were coming to kill him.

The crowd fell silent as the warden raised her arms. For a split second, she locked eyes with Javan, and he shivered at the fury on her face. Turning away, he met Sajda's gaze, his heart thudding in strange, jarring beats.

He might die.

He might win.

Either way, he might not see her again for a very long time.

He tried to put everything she meant to him in his expression. Her eyes darkened, and she pressed one pale hand to her heart, and then she lifted her chin, jerked it toward the arena, and gave him a look that was pure challenge.

She wanted him to win. To gain an audience with the king, be restored to the throne, and leave Maqbara. Even though it meant leaving her behind.

"Competitors, enter the arena!" the warden called.

Hashim was first through the gate, and he went immediately for the short swords lying in the center of the arena. Javan sprinted past him as Iram went for the whip and then the long sword. The prince had just put his hands on the bow and arrow when the warden yelled, "Bring in the beasts!"

Slinging the quiver onto his back, he hooked the bowstring over one arm and raced for the battle-axes. With only one sharp edge, they weren't as good as the swords, and they were certainly heavier, but they were better than fighting with his hands.

The crowd was seething with anticipation. The monsters for the final round were a mystery. The scoreboard was shrouded with a black cloth, and the crowd would get the excitement of seeing each creature as the warden announced it.

Javan whirled toward the gate in time to see a guard yank on the rope that held the netting above the arena. The crowd clapped wildly as the netting fell. The prince risked a quick glance at the royal platform and found the impostor glaring at him with naked hatred.

The king was sitting quietly, a frown on his face. He wasn't looking at the arena.

The crowd erupted into cheers as Sajda and another guard ducked under the netting with a cage the size of a barrel of mead balanced between them.

"Our first creatures are vampire bats that can smell blood from three leagues away. They attack in swarms and drink the blood of their prey until the prey is dry." The warden sounded cheerful at the prospect. "Each kill is worth ten points."

Sajda lifted the latch on the cage door, and the bats flooded the arena, leathery wings beating the air, fangs gleaming as they circled, searching for blood.

Javan was going to give them what they wanted. Whipping an arrow into his bow, he sent it straight for Hashim.

It buried itself in Hashim's shoulder, and he went down on one knee. The crowd surged to their feet in a frenzy as Hashim pulled the arrow free and threw it to the ground, but Javan couldn't hear them. His world was the thunder of his heart, the weight of his weapons, and the horrifying beasts being led to the gate by Sajda.

The bats shrieked and dove, a spiraling swarm of black bodies and white teeth. Hashim screamed as they landed on him, tearing at his bleeding wound with their fangs. Javan focused on the gate as Iram moved to stand beside him.

"Sa' Loham, what is that?" Iram breathed, his hands clutching his weapons with desperate strength.

The warden's voice echoed over the sound of bats. "Our next pair of beasts are the legendary rencapal! Each kill will be worth fifty points."

The two enormous horselike creatures Sajda was leading into the arena were nearly twice as broad as an Akramian racing stallion. Their coats looked to be made of shadows that shifted and twisted independently of the creatures' movements; their eyes glowed black; and their hooves and teeth were iron.

"Demon steeds from the mountains north of Loch Talam," Javan said quietly, another arrow already at his bow. "Don't let either of them get close. They can trample us in seconds."

He sent an arrow into the chest of the rencapal on the left. It screamed in furious pain and charged.

Whipping another arrow into the bow, he shot again.

The beast kept coming.

Yl' Haliq be merciful, what did it take to kill this thing?

The second rencapal took its cue from the first and charged as well.

"The whip!" Javan yelled as he nocked another arrow.

Iram slashed at the incoming beasts, his iron-studded whip cracking through the air. One rencapal shied. The one with the arrows sticking out of its chest kept coming.

It was twenty paces away.

Javan sent another arrow, this time into its neck, and its nostrils flared as it bore down on him, black eyes glowing with rage.

All he'd managed to do was anger it.

Tossing the bow to the ground, he grabbed the battle-axes and readied himself. When the steed was five paces out, he dove to the side, slashing at the tendons on the creature's massive forelegs as he went.

The rencapal crashed to its knees. Leaping on its back, Javan quickly sliced the artery in its neck. Blood gushed, and the beast slowly toppled.

Javan leaped clear, and it was only after he heard the rush of leathery wings that he realized his hands were covered with the creature's blood. Iram's long sword swooped past Javan's head, and the bodies of five bats went skimming across the arena floor.

Javan whirled, looking for the other rencapal, and saw Hashim on his feet, bleeding profusely from his shoulder, the ground around him littered with the bodies of the rest of the vampire bats. The other steed was slowly backing away from the snap of Iram's whip as the warden yelled, "Turn loose the were-jaguars! Fifty points a kill."

Javan ran for his bow, scooped it off the ground, and sent an arrow flying into the chest of the first were-jaguar that cleared the arena gate. The other two were right behind it, unnaturally long limbs and sleek bodies gleaming in the afternoon sunlight. Hashim abandoned the short swords and grabbed a spear instead. The rencapal screamed and charged the closest jaguar as Hashim threw the spear into the third shape-shifter.

That made one hundred points for Javan. At least one hundred points for Hashim, depending on how many bats he'd killed. Iram had only killed five bats, but even with Iram's low opening score, Javan was still in third place.

Javan needed to take both of the top predators being sent into the arena. As the rencapal stomped the were-jaguar into oblivion, Iram drove his sword into the side of the beast. The creature twisted, lashing out. Its hind legs, with its sharp iron hooves, crushed Iram into the wall. The man slid to the ground and lay still.

Javan tore his eyes from Iram and faced the gate as Hashim moved toward the center of the arena, keeping a safe distance between himself and the injured rencapal.

The worst was yet to come. A chill slid over Javan's skin as an earsplitting roar shattered the air, briefly silencing the crowd. The faint skittering of bony legs and claws followed the roar, and Javan swallowed hard as Sajda and the guards led a pair of muzzled, shackled monsters toward the arena.

They were sending in both at the same time.

He drew in a shaky breath as the warden clapped her hands for attention.

Fear out.

Courage in.

"As our grand finale, we have two vicious monsters! The first is the legendary triceleon from Llorenyae." She waved her hand in a grand gesture, and as if on cue the three-headed lion roared, the chain netting around its mouths trembling with the force of the beast's anger. "The second monster is the rare jorogumo—a spider devil from the country of Ichil! One hundred points each."

The jorogumo was a female spider several handspans taller than Javan. Her bulbous body was supported by eight bony claw-tipped legs, but her upper body looked vaguely human, as though a woman's frame had been embedded in the center of a spider's body. Her face looked somewhat human too, though her mouth opened and closed in a perfect circle with an equally perfect circle of fangs inside.

Sajda and the guards whipped the muzzles and chains from the creatures and slammed the gate shut behind them. Briefly Sajda met his gaze, her eyes fierce. He felt his heartbeat steady, his thoughts slow.

This was it. His last chance to free her from the warden. To free Akram from the impostor. He glanced up at the royal box and found his father leaning forward, watching intently while the impostor sat beside him, fists clenched.

The lion padded toward the bodies of the slain were-jaguars, one face looking at Javan, one looking at Hashim, while the other gazed at the injured rencapal that was stomping its hooves as it sized up this new threat.

The spider skittered to the side, claws clicking, and huddled against the wall beneath the warden's platform.

Javan nocked an arrow and sent it flying toward the lion. It struck the head that was gazing at him. The beast roared, shaking its heads. Hashim raced forward and grabbed the spear he'd sent into a were-jaguar as Javan sent another arrow into the lion's second head.

Hashim yanked the spear free as the lion snarled and came for him. Javan sent another arrow, but it missed as the lion sprang for the threat in front of it.

The prince started moving as the lion crashed into Hashim, bringing them both to the floor. The beast roared in pain as the spear went through his chest and out its back. It slashed with its claws, its uninjured jaws yawning wide as it snapped at Hashim.

Javan skidded on the blood of a fallen were-jaguar and caught movement out of the corner of his eye. Pivoting, he barely had time to brace before the injured rencapal slammed into him, one iron hoof connecting with Javan's hip and sending him sprawling.

He rolled out of the way as iron hooves drove into the floor where seconds ago he'd been lying. The beast reared again, blood pouring from its sides, and Javan sent a battle-ax into its chest.

Its hooves crashed into the floor, shaking Javan as he

scrambled back. The ax hadn't nicked the artery, and until he did that, the creature was just going to keep coming until it killed him. Rolling quickly to the left, Javan readied the other ax and gauged his move. The rencapal reared, screaming in fury, and when its hooves hit the floor again, Javan was already running.

Grabbing the mane, he swung himself onto the creature's back, its shadowy skin as slippery as the wind. Tangling his fingers in its mane, he leaned down and slashed the artery in the creature's neck. Then, leaping clear, he turned to find Hashim, bleeding and breathing heavily, crawling out from under the lion's corpse.

That left the spider.

Javan whirled to face the wall where the spider had been, but she was gone. In her place was the thick, glistening edge of a web anchored to the wall before spreading up into the empty space overhead.

A rapid clicking sound reverberated through the arena, directly above Javan's head. He looked up just as the spider dropped, wrapped her bony legs around him, and pulled him high into the air.

FORTY-THREE

The crowd screamed as Javan hurtled into the air. The spider's legs pulled him tight against the bulbous circle of her lower body. Fear was a razor slicing his thoughts to ribbons.

His arms were pinned. His legs were pinned. He couldn't get to the battle-ax he held in his hand. Couldn't struggle or he might fall to his death below.

Prayers formed in his mind, wisps of panicked words and desperate thoughts as the spider slowed and came to a stop in the web she'd spun above the arena. He was so close to seeing his father—to setting everything right. He couldn't die now. Not like this.

Over the yelling from the aristocrats who either wanted him to plunge to his death or to get out of the spider's grasp so they could collect on their bets, a girl's fierce voice shouted, "Turn the ax to the left!"

He twisted his wrist, following Sajda's instructions, and felt the blade in his hand connect with something. Immediately he started sawing, jerking the ax back and forth while he prayed for something to give.

Something had to give.

He hadn't come this far to fail.

A sticky rope wrapped around his feet, and he realized that some of the spider's legs were moving, rapidly coiling a rope of web around his ankles. He sawed faster with the ax blade, though he wasn't sure what good it would do if his feet were trapped.

"Push!" Sajda yelled.

He obeyed, shoving the ax blade forward as hard as he could. Something snapped, a sickening crunch that briefly loosened the spider's grip. He leaned back and looked down. He'd sawed through the bend in one of the beast's middle legs. It dangled useless, a thin yellow fluid leaking out. Web wrapped around his ankles at least four times, and the other legs were tightening again.

It was now or never.

The spider was no longer pinning the wrist that held his weapon. He pulled his arm up as far as it would go and then plunged the ax blade into the hard shell of the spider's lower body.

The creature wailed, a guttural, raspy sound that sent shivers over Javan's skin. Spinning in midair, she held Javan with her front two legs as she swung her wounded body away from him and shoved her head close to his, her mouth gaping.

He flinched at the humanlike face with its vicious, round, teeth-filled hole and swiped at her again with the ax. This time, she saw him coming, and she dropped him.

He plunged headfirst toward the arena floor. Screams rose, but then the web around his ankles jerked him to a stop several lengths from the relative safety of the ground.

The web shook, and he looked up in time to see her scuttling toward him, teeth snapping.

He swung his body, jackknifed at the waist, and drove the ax into her head as she reached him. She shuddered, and the entire web shook. And then, she slowly rolled off the web and dropped toward the arena floor.

Javan sliced through the web around his ankles, twisted as he fell, and landed on top of her. He raised the ax again, but she shuddered once and lay still.

The crowd erupted, but Javan wasn't finished.

He hadn't killed all of the monsters who deserved to die.

And he had a promise to keep.

He slid from the spider's back, landed on shaky legs, and looked up. Sajda clung to the netting at the edge of the arena, her face paler than usual, her eyes full of furious relief when they met his. The runes on her cuffs were glowing, and he quickly looked away before anyone followed his line of sight and wondered about the slave girl with the fiery runes carved into her iron bracelets.

The crowd were on their feet, shouting and cheering.

All except the king.

Javan froze as he locked eyes with his father. He was standing at the edge of his platform, his hands clasped as if in prayer while he stared at Javan, a frown digging into his forehead. Behind him, the impostor slowly got to his feet, his eyes on the king.

Javan looked at the closest judge. Had he won? He'd killed both rencapals and the spider, which gave him two hundred points. Was Hashim still alive, or had he succumbed to his wounds?

He turned to look for the older man just in time to see Hashim charge, Iram's discarded whip in his hand.

The leather cracked the air with a vicious snap. Javan moved to the side, but he was too slow. The tip struck Javan's chest and bit deep.

Blood poured from the wound as Javan faced Hashim. He ignored his shaking muscles. The pain that throbbed from his injuries.

Hashim was done terrorizing Sajda. Done using people to further his own violent ends.

And he was all that stood between Javan and an audience with his father.

Whispering the lament for the dying, even though he wasn't sure Hashim deserved it, Javan hefted the battle-ax and waited.

Hashim circled, with Javan turning to keep the man in sight. And then Hashim raised his arm to flick the whip again. Javan waited until the whip jerked forward, slicing through the air toward the prince, and then he ran straight for Hashim.

The whip fell as Javan slammed into Hashim, grabbed the man's tunic, and brought them both crashing to the ground. Hashim dropped the whip and fought viciously with his uninjured arm, punching Javan's face and fighting to get control of the ax. Javan grabbed Hashim's shoulder and dug his fingers into the arrow wound he'd given the man at the start of the competition. Hashim cried out, but then he brought his knees up, planted his feet on Javan's stomach, and sent the prince sliding.

The ax spun out of Javan's hand and skidded across the arena.

"Get up! Now!" Sajda's voice cut through the crowd's screams, cold and furious.

Javan's body protested as he rolled away from Hashim, who

was stumbling toward him with the whip again. His chest was pouring blood. His ears were ringing. And it felt like his jaw was going numb.

He was going to pass out if he didn't put an end to this soon.

The whip glanced off his back as Javan moved toward the far western edge of the arena, climbing over a dead rencapal while Hashim pursued him.

His legs refused to hold him when he slid over the beast's back, and he fell to his knees. The whip slapped the rencapal's hide, barely missing Javan. Behind him, Hashim was laughing.

"Nothing can save you now. Not that little dark elf *ehira*. Not your aristocratic manners. I win. I'm getting out of here, and you're going to die in this hole."

Javan crawled forward, hissing as the whip connected with his leg, and then laid his hands on the weapon he'd left behind at the start of the competition.

Hashim was still laughing, the whip raised over his head, as Javan whirled, raised the bow, and sent an arrow into the man's chest.

The whip fell with a clatter, and then Hashim sank to the floor and lay still.

Javan dropped the bow and slowly got to his feet. The floor vibrated with the thunderous cheering of the crowd, but he didn't care about them.

He'd done it.

He'd won his chance to show his father the truth.

Weary relief shook him, and he had to work just to stay on his feet. The wound on his chest sent a shaft of pain straight through him as he pulled his tunic over his head and untied the red sash that was folded up beside his heart. A tiny piece of it was frayed now, caught by the lash of the whip.

A few months ago, this sash had represented ten years of duty and sacrifice, but those words meant something different now. When Javan had first worn the sash, he'd been proud of his accomplishments and certain of his ordained destiny. Now as he unfurled its silken length, he knew that his duty went far beyond the expectations of his parents, and sacrifice was more than the willingness to give up one thing to get another.

Sacrifice was an old man refusing to let a naïve boy be crushed by his enemies, even though it cost that man his own life.

Sacrifice was a wounded, abused girl finding the courage to make her own choices without backing down.

And sacrifice was what had been demanded from the people of Akram for five long years under Fariq's corruption. From the inmates imprisoned on false charges and forced to compete in this barbaric tournament to the aristocrats trapped into cheering for the bloodbath or risk losing their lands and livelihood to Fariq's greed. Javan was going to put an end to all of it.

Sajda tore the netting out of the way and ran across the arena as he stood swaying, his eyes on his father. When she reached him, she wrapped her arm around his back, and he leaned on her.

"Come on," she said softly, a wealth of pride and grief in her voice. "Let's get you home."

She helped him move to the center of the arena while the crowd cheered, the warden stood still as a statue on her platform, and the king clasped and unclasped his hands, his eyes on Javan.

Carefully, Javan lifted the sash. The crimson silk glowed softly in the afternoon sunlight, and the king sucked in a breath.

"I did it, Father," Javan said loudly. Ignoring the pain in his chest, he raised his arms higher, the sash held firmly between them. "I honored my mother's *muqaddas tus'el*. I made her proud."

The king met his son's eyes and smiled, confusion and wonder on his face. Javan trembled with relief and bittersweet happiness. No matter what had happened, no matter what his uncle had done in the name of the crown, Javan could come home. He could make it right. And he could use the power of the throne to free Sajda.

Then everything seemed to happen in slow motion. The impostor lunged forward as if to join the king at the edge of the platform. His father said, "Javan!" in a voice that caused an ever-widening ripple of silence to spread through the crowd. And the impostor seemed to trip and crash into the king.

The king tumbled from the platform and into the arena.

"Father!" Javan cried as the king landed in a sickening sprawl of limbs and blood.

The prince stumbled to his father's side, Sajda right behind him, and dropped to his knees beside the king's head.

"Javan," the king whispered, his breath whistling in the back of his throat.

"I'm here." The prince looked up at the royal platform where the impostor stood surrounded by guards, an unconvincing look of horror on his face. "Get a physician!"

"My son." The king's hand fluttered away from his chest, and Javan wrapped his father's cold fingers in his.

"Don't go." Javan's voice broke. "I just got you back. Please, Father."

For a moment, Javan thought he would hang on. He would keep breathing, the physician would treat him, and everything could be as it should be. But then the king exhaled, and his chest went still.

Javan pulled his father's head into his lap and curled over him while grief and rage bled through him in equal measure.

He'd lost everything now. His father. His chance to return home and make things right. His ability to force the warden to let Sajda go free.

"Get on your feet, prisoner!" The impostor's voice filled the arena as guards hurried from the platform toward the king.

Slowly, Javan placed his father's hand back on his chest, folding the crimson sash beneath the king's fingers, and then climbed to his feet. Grief was a long, slow slide into utter despair, but fury was the rope that tethered him to this moment.

This boy was the cause. The root of everything that had gone wrong.

And now this boy would be acknowledged as the new king. He would win. There was no one left to believe Javan if he challenged him. No one left to see the injustice and make it right.

"I am the king now in the wake of my father's unfortunate accident," the impostor said. "Do you deny it?"

The crowd murmured at the strange question, and Javan met the impostor's eyes.

"Don't challenge him," Sajda whispered. "It's an excuse to kill you for treason."

She was right. Javan could practically see the execution order forming on the impostor's lips.

But he was still owed a boon from the king. The impostor couldn't deny it without raising questions from the aristocracy— something he could ill afford to do in light of his part in the king's death.

There was still one promise Javan could keep.

"I do not deny it," he said, his voice steady though everything inside him shook. "I believe I am to be granted a boon, Your Highness?"

The title tasted like ashes in Javan's mouth, but he didn't hesitate.

The impostor frowned, glaring down at Javan as if hunting for the trick he was sure the prince was playing on him. Javan waited, his body still, his heart bleeding at the sight of his father lying at his feet. At the hope that had shriveled within him until only the bitter dregs were left.

Finally, the impostor glanced at the crowd who waited expectantly on the edge of their chairs and then said, "I suppose you want your freedom."

Sajda drew in a sharp breath and whispered. "You can still be free. You'll find another way back into the palace. Someone else will recognize you and then you can—"

"Not my freedom," Javan said in a loud, clear voice. "Hers."

The crowd gasped, and the impostor's eyes widened as Javan turned to Sajda. "For my victory boon, I ask for the cuffs to be removed from the warden's slave and for her to be set free."

FORTY-FOUR

SAJDA STARED AT Javan while his words rang in her ears and the crowd whistled and cheered their appreciation for the unexpected twist to the end of the tournament.

He could have asked for his freedom.

He'd asked for hers instead.

And now he stood before her, broken and bleeding, with steady resolve in his eyes, but grief written in every line of his body.

"Javan," she said quietly, "you can't. It's more important that you get out. You can go to the other aristocrats. Convince them. You can—"

"If he agreed to give me my freedom, he'd either exile me or send assassins after me the moment I left Maqbara."

"But you're good at improvising. You could find a way to eventually take back your throne." Her voice shook as the resolve in his eyes hardened.

"I'm not leaving you here, Sajda. I made you a promise. Now I'm keeping it."

Tears gathered in the back of her throat, and she pulled him against her, his blood staining her shirt as he wrapped his arms around her and leaned his face against her hair.

"I love you," he whispered, and her magic churned, scraping at her skin.

He'd just traded his life for hers. There were no words she could give him, no pretty promises that would ever match the depths of his sacrifice. Still, she had to try.

Pulling back just enough to look into his eyes, she said, "I don't think I deserve this."

His smile was gentle and full of pain. "You deserve the stars, Sajda."

She shook her head and the tears spilled onto her cheeks. He leaned down and kissed her as the crowd cheered and screamed. The impostor called for the magistrate's guards to unlock Sajda's cuffs and remove her from the arena. The warden shouted a protest that was nearly drowned out by the wild applause of the aristocrats as one of the guards removed a cuff key from his pocket. And still Javan kissed her, his lips lingering on hers like he needed to memorize the way she felt in his arms.

She wanted to memorize it too. Capture the roughness of his lips and the heat of his skin and the beat of the heart he'd given so completely to her. She wanted to fight the guards and stay with Javan. Tear the impostor to pieces and the warden too and give Javan the life he deserved.

How could she accept his sacrifice when she'd made none of her own?

The guards pulled her away from him, and he raised an arm toward her, his expression carved out of unspeakable loss as she was taken to the center of the arena where the audience could fully appreciate the boon that had been granted.

"Think of me when you watch the stars, Sajda," he said as the guard slid the key into her cuffs. Her magic buzzed, a swarm of hornets trapped in her veins.

She couldn't accept this sacrifice without making one of her own.

Without showing Javan the words she'd been unable to say.

A hard, brilliant light sparked to life in her chest as her cuffs clattered to the arena floor.

"You don't know what you're doing!" the warden yelled, her voice furious.

Furious and fearful.

Slowly Sajda turned to look up at the warden's platform. At the woman who'd bought her, abused her, and trapped the magic that was now blazing through her with wild abandon. The warden's eyes met hers, and the woman took a small step back.

Sajda flexed her hands, marveling at the way her magic gathered in her palms without pain. Without scarring the flesh of her wrists.

"Sajda, no. Don't reveal anything," Javan said, as Sajda turned from the warden to pierce the false prince with her gaze. His eyes widened, and she smiled, fierce and vicious.

She was a star.

She was a galaxy.

She was the power of the universe barely contained, and this impostor had destroyed the boy she loved.

Letting every bit of strength she possessed coil around her

limbs, she plowed her fists into the guards who surrounded her, sending them flying across the arena floor and crashing into the wall.

The crowd gasped and murmured uneasily, but she wasn't listening.

Let them see her for who she really was. Let them tremble. And let them come for her. They wouldn't reach her in time to save the one who'd hurt Javan.

"Sajda!" Javan reached for her, but she only had eyes for the traitor prince.

Power was an intoxicating light that scoured her from the inside—an impossible stream of energy that begged for release.

She was done holding back.

Sprinting across the arena floor, she crouched and then leaped for the royal box.

The jump was at least the length of six men lying end to end. She cleared the height easily. The false prince stumbled back, his hands up as if he could ward her off. As if he could stop what was coming.

No one could stop her.

She was a creature of strength and magic and nightmares, and he was her prey.

The guards who still remained on the platform lunged for her. She batted them away like they were nothing and snatched the false prince's tunic.

"Please," he said, his voice high and shaky. "I'll give you anything you want. Coin. Land. The deaths of your enemies."

"You'll give me the truth," she said, and smiled as he trembled.

Hauling him to the edge of the platform, she eyed the jump back into the arena. Javan stood below her, his fists clenched, his eyes wild as the crowd screamed that she was cursed. A dark elf. A nightmare.

Additional guards stationed at the magistrate's office were pouring in through the door that led out of Maqbara.

Let them come. She would destroy them all.

"Please," the impostor beside her begged, and she jumped, dragging him with her.

The ground rushed toward her feet, and she landed in a crouch. The boy landed hard beside her, his tunic still clutched in her hand, and something in his leg snapped.

He screamed. The crowd pushed and shoved toward the stairs, but every stairway, every opening was blocked with the incoming guards.

Above Sajda, the warden shifted into her dragon form and roared.

"Sajda, run. *Run!*" Javan said as the dragon left the platform, beating the air with her wings, smoke pouring from her nostrils.

"Watch him," she said to Javan, gesturing toward the false prince, who was sprawled beside her moaning about his broken leg, and then she was moving.

Away from the impostor. Away from Javan, who would be safe from the dragon if he stayed beside the boy the warden had helped put on the throne. Toward the center of the arena where the midafternoon sunlight blazed through the skylights like golden fire.

The dragon circled, every beat of her wings sending a gust of wind to batter Sajda's body as she stood in the haze of sunlight and raised her arms.

Her magic hummed, tangling with the rays of light and swallowing them whole.

It was blinding power churning through her veins to pool in her chest.

It was unbearable heat scouring her from within.

It was *fire*.

And she was its vessel.

The dragon dove for her, mouth gaping wide as flames gathered in the back of her throat.

"You wanted a monster?" Sajda yelled, her skin blazing with the need to release the sun-filled magic that churned within her. "Let me show you how monstrous I can be."

Sajda took three running steps and jumped.

She collided with the dragon in midair, slammed her hands into the scales, and sent every drop of sunlight into the warden.

Fire exploded from her fingertips, wrapped around the dragon's body in brilliant bands of red-gold light, and then sank beneath the scales and into the warden herself.

The dragon roared, a terrible cry of agony that echoed through the arena, and smoke began rising from her scales. Sajda let go, twisting as she fell so that she landed once more in a crouch on the arena floor.

The crowd shrieked in panic as the dragon spiraled, smoke pouring out of her, scales drifting into ash as she dropped toward the first level of seats. She struck a platform full of aristocrats in fancy clothing, and flames erupted from her body, dancing over her muscle and bone like rays of pure sunlight. The people pushed and shoved to get away from her as the fire brightened, a white-gold light impossible to look at, and then the dragon's body collapsed into ash and drifted slowly off the platform to rain down onto the arena floor.

The magistrate's guards hesitated at the gate that led into the arena, swords drawn. Sajda turned to face them as Javan said in his polished, aristocratic voice, "Stand down."

The guards flicked him a quick glance, confusion and scorn on their faces, and he repeated, "I am Prince Javan Samad Najafai of the house of Kadar, esteemed prince of the Kingdom of the Sun and heir to Akram's crown of fire, and I order you to stand down. No one who tries to harm this girl will live to see tomorrow."

"I am the prince," the impostor called, his voice full of pain and fury.

Sajda bared her teeth and stalked toward him. He dug his elbows into the floor and tried to scoot away from her. He didn't get far before Javan planted a boot on his stomach and held him still.

"You're going to give me the truth," Sajda said in a loud, clear voice. "You're going to give all of us the truth." She turned to face the crowd who were huddled in groups, their terror-stricken eyes glued to her. "Would you like to hear a story?"

A few aristocrats had forced their way past the contingent of guards at the mouth of the arena and were trying to reach the door. Sajda raised her voice, "Anyone who leaves this room without Prince Javan's permission will deal with me."

The fleeing aristocrats froze, and Sajda swept the crowd with her gaze. No one moved.

"Once upon a time," she said, "there was a prince born of a good king and queen. He was taught to be faithful to Yl' Haliq, to his parents, and to his people. His mother died when he was young, and she made him promise to excel in school, to become the best at everything so that he could become the best ruler for his kingdom. For Akram."

She glanced at Javan, and found warmth in his eyes as he watched her. Giving him a tiny smile, she turned back to the crowd.

"This prince was taken to the academy in Loch Talam for his education. He spent ten long years there, never returning home because he was committed to studying longer and working harder than anyone else so that he could honor his mother's dying wish and meet his father's expectations. So that he could return to Akram ready to rule you with justice and fairness when it came time for him to sit on the throne."

She turned her gaze on the traitor prince, and he shivered beneath the fury in her glare. "But there was another boy. A boy who didn't belong in the palace, though he wished he did. And he conspired against the prince. He knew the prince's father hadn't seen his son in ten years. He knew he looked enough like a Kadar to pass for Prince Javan if he could keep his facts straight. He sent a dragon and a team of assassins to kill the prince so he could take his place. But the prince didn't die because, as you've all seen during this tournament, he is very skilled at surviving."

A murmur swept the crowd.

"When the impostor realized the prince hadn't died in Loch Talam, he ordered him to be executed. An old guard recognized the true prince and put him in Maqbara instead. And here he's been, all this time. Competing and winning so that he could gain an audience with the king. With his *father*. So that he could claim his rightful place as your prince and help restore order and justice to Akram. And so when the impostor realized that Javan had won, and that all was about to be revealed, he killed the king so that he could order Prince Javan's death and steal the throne once and for all."

She crouched beside the false prince, magic stinging her palms. "Didn't you?"

She dared the boy to lie. To give her a single excuse to swallow the sunlight and turn him into ash.

He gave her a defiant look. "You can't prove any of that."

He was right. Turning him to ash wouldn't prove his words. It wouldn't give Javan back what was rightfully his.

But swallowing the sunlight wasn't the worst that she could do. She reached out and scraped a nail down the side of his arm. Blood welled, and she let it drip into her palm. Her magic sizzled against it, and she could already see his fears, laid out before her like a succulent meal of terror and darkness.

"Do you know what I am?" she asked quietly.

He stared at his blood in her palm and then slowly raised his eyes to hers.

"I'm a dark elf." For once the words didn't sink into her with the heavy weight of shame and fear. "I can take your blood and read your fears." She leaned closer. "I can give you unspeakable nightmares. Nightmares that never end. Your mind will shatter. You will break. And yet your heart will keep beating. Your lungs will keep breathing. You'll be trapped in an unending loop of your worst fears until you grow old and die."

He trembled and looked beyond her toward Javan. "Please," he whispered.

Sajda grabbed his chin with her free hand and wrenched his face toward hers. Her voice was loud and clear, echoing across the silent arena. "You don't speak to him. You don't even *look* at him, do you understand me? You took his father and his freedom, and now you are dealing with me. And you have three seconds to admit what you did before I give you exactly what you deserve. Did you impersonate Prince Javan and kill the king?"

Slowly, he nodded.

The crowd gasped.

Sajda wiped his blood on his tunic and stood to face Javan. "People of Akram, I give you the real Prince Javan."

Javan held her gaze for a long moment and then turned to the crowd, his brown eyes glowing with steady calm. "There is much to do in the coming days. I will call an emergency meeting of the heads of every aristocratic family in Akram so that we can get to the bottom of who was involved in this deception and begin to put things right. And of course, we will move through the proper, lawful channels for my coronation. But not before we hold a royal funeral for the king."

He drew in a shaky breath and glanced once at his father's body, lying peaceful and still several lengths away. "As acting king, I declare that Sajda is under the crown's protection. Any harm that comes to her will be considered an act of treason and will be punished accordingly."

Warmth that had nothing to do with the sunlight flooded her, and her lips quirked in a tiny smile as he continued.

"I further declare that this boy is a traitor to the crown and will be held in Maqbara until his trial. The magistrate will appoint a temporary warden until a permanent replacement can be found. I will remove the stain of dishonor on Akram's crown and make our fair kingdom a place of justice and peace for all people." He glanced above the platforms to the cells that lined the stone honeycomb above them. "For *all* people."

The applause began in scattered fits and starts, but then the crowd came to its feet and clapped, cheering for this unexpected ending. For the prince they'd never known was missing.

Javan pulled Sajda into his arms, and she was surprised to realize that he was trembling.

"Thank you," he said softly. "You scared me half to death."

"You scared me more."

"I can't believe you revealed yourself to them. You sacrificed yourself for me." His hands tightened, fisting in the back of her shirt.

"You sacrificed yourself for me first."

He pulled back to give her a look, and she raised a brow.

He smiled. "This isn't a competition."

"Of course not." She grinned, and then he was kissing her, and it was warmer than the sun's fire and purer than the starlight.

It was air in her lungs and fire in her heart.

It was magic.

FORTY-FIVE

IT HAD BEEN two weeks since Sajda had killed the warden, extracted a confession from the boy who'd taken Javan's place, and entered the palace with the true prince. Two weeks of fragrant baths and delicious food. Of silk dresses and maids anxious to comb her hair or fetch her anything she might want.

Two weeks, and she felt like she was coming apart at the seams.

Every eye that watched her, every hand that served her, every whisper that died when she walked into a room were a thousand tiny knives scraping at her until even the calm she borrowed from the palace's stone floors couldn't help.

Magic prickled and hummed in her blood, a painful itch that grew worse as she huddled in her soft bed at night, eyes wide open as she stared at the walls.

The air inside the palace didn't stink of beasts and burned porridge, but the tang of Makan Almalik's dust still rested bitterly on the back of her tongue. The people who served her smiled and thanked her for saving their prince, but she wondered how many had lit an effigy of a dark elf and cursed her kind with the same mouth that praised her now.

Tossing her bedcover aside, Sajda dressed quickly and then moved to the balcony outside her bedroom that overlooked a tiled courtyard and a grove of lemon trees. Pushing the door open, she leaned against the carved wood railing and looked up at the vast expanse of the night sky.

The stars were shards of burning glass bathing the ground in silver and white. Reaching one hand toward them, she let her fingers tangle in the starlight. Let her magic curl around it, cold and pure, and welcome it inside her.

There was freedom in the starlight. In the distant beauty that couldn't be captured or contained. There was peace where no eyes could watch her and no voices could whisper. Where there were no cages, be they gilt-painted or carved from stone.

"I am a star," she whispered, and silvery light drifted off her fingertips like frozen lace. "I am a galaxy."

The frenetic buzzing of her magic settled, and she tilted her face toward the sky.

It was lonely in the starlight, but loneliness was better than being surrounded by another kind of prison. There was just one thing missing in the starlight.

Javan.

Tears burned her eyes and slid down her cheeks to drip like silver-white diamonds to the balcony below. She couldn't stay here where the walls closed in and the air still smelled faintly of Maqbara. She couldn't stay, but leaving was going to carve out a piece of her heart.

A sound cut through the stillness, and she opened her eyes

to see Javan standing on his own balcony a short distance to the west. He was watching her, and the pain on his face made part of her want to go to him.

The rest of her longed for the wide-open spaces of the desert where she could be alone with nothing but the stars and her freedom for company.

She held his gaze for a long moment, and then judged the distance between the balconies, gathered her elven strength, and leaped. He raised his arms as if to catch her, but didn't touch her as she landed in a crouch and then stood in front of him.

For a long moment, they watched each other. Tears gathered in the back of her throat, and she let the starlight slide off her fingertips. Let her magic coil and churn as she reached for his hands.

His skin was warm against hers, and he caught his breath as she stepped closer and laid her head against his chest.

"I'm sorry," she whispered.

His shoulders bowed, and for a moment he was still. And then he let go of her hands so that he could wrap his arms around her. She pulled him close, memorizing the heat of his skin and the imprint of his body sheltering hers.

"When are you leaving?" he asked, and the pain in his voice sent her magic thrumming through her blood.

She wanted to take the hurt away. Promise to stay and somehow be the girl who could survive inside a palace like she'd survived inside a prison.

But she swallowed the words and simply held him instead. She wanted more than to just survive. She wanted to heal. To stop being afraid. She wanted to carve the word *monster* out of her and replace it with something better. Something that fit.

"Javan," she breathed as she tipped her head back to look at him.

He smiled, though there were tears in his eyes.

"I'm sorry," she said again.

"I'm not." His voice was steady. "You owe no one an apology, Sajda. Including me."

"But I'm hurting you."

He gently touched her cheek with his lips. "Sometimes it hurts to love someone. I wouldn't change it, though. I wouldn't change a single thing. I love you." He met her eyes. "Please remember that no matter how far you go, I'll always be here if you decide to return."

His voice shook a little, and she leaned up to kiss him. His lips were rough and a little desperate, his hands fisted in the back of her dress. She tilted his head so she could get a better angle, and her magic surged through her, a thrill of pain and pleasure.

When she stepped back, she held his gaze one last time, and tried to find words for the way he was the one place she knew she was safe. For the way his smile made her cheeks glow or the way his faith in her settled the rough edges of a wound she still hadn't truly examined.

The words wouldn't come. Instead, she whispered, "Thank you for freeing me and for letting me go."

And then before more tears could spill over, before the magic that was hurling itself toward him instead of toward the open sky could tempt her to make a promise she wasn't sure she could keep, she leaped back to her own balcony, grabbed the pack of supplies she'd assembled earlier in the evening, and left the palace behind.

FORTY-SIX

THE DAY AFTER Sajda left, Javan was crowned the new king of Akram. No one had warned him how heavy the crown would be. He stood in the tiled entrance of the palace and tried to ignore the dull ache in his temples as he greeted the royalty who were visiting Akram to pay their respects to Akram's new king while also visiting the grave of Javan's father.

It had been two weeks since he'd won the tournament in Maqbara, lost his father, and then gained his freedom and his throne thanks to Sajda. He hadn't had a single peaceful night of sleep since. His dreams were filled with the blood he'd shed, and his ears echoed with the screams of those who'd died in the arena. His days hadn't been much better. He'd spent his time working through the royal council, the palace staff, and the aristocratic families who lived in Makan Almalik, hunting for corruption, assessing his kingdom's needs, and searching for the right people to take over both Maqbara and the magistrate's office so that every prisoner's case could be reviewed.

Javan wasn't going to allow anyone who'd been sent to Maqbara without evidence to stay in that place of darkness and pain.

The impostor, however, was going to live in Maqbara until a trial could be held. Part of Javan hoped the boy would receive a death sentence for his actions. Part of him couldn't stomach the thought of more bloodshed, even for someone who deserved it.

He adjusted the heavy crown on his head and wished that Sajda was standing next to him.

Her name sent a bone-deep ache of misery through him, and he resolutely stretched his smile wider as he reached a hand toward the next pair of royals who attended his coronation. Above him, moonlight flooded the glass dome of the palace entry, gilding the enormous diamond chandelier a dazzling white.

Somewhere, Sajda was staring at the same sky. The starlight would turn to liquid silver beneath her skin, and she would be glowing in a way that almost hurt to see.

"Are you well?" The boy whose hand Javan just realized he'd been clasping for too long stared at him intently, his dark eyes narrowed as he pulled his hand free and took a step back.

"My apologies," Javan said, wincing as the ache in his head redoubled.

"No apology necessary." A beautiful girl with golden skin and a wide smile elbowed the boy and then leaned toward Javan as if she wanted to tell him a secret. "The key to surviving these interminable meet-and-greet ceremonies is a healthy supply of snacks."

Javan's eyebrow rose. "Snacks?"

She grinned. "Works every time. Chocolate is especially good if you've got a headache. Of course you don't have a handbag to smuggle food in, but you're the king! People have to obey you. You can send a page to the kitchen at any time."

"Chocolate." Javan smiled what felt like his first real smile since he'd watched Sajda leave as the girl tapped a finger against the beaded exterior of her handbag. "You're carrying snacks right now, aren't you?"

"You never know when you're going to need one." She extended her hand for him to lift to his lips. "I'm Ari."

The boy sighed, though he seemed just as bemused by Ari as Javan was. "She means she's the Honorable Princess Arianna Glavan of Súndraille."

The girl looked pained. "I'd prefer just Ari."

Javan nodded solemnly. "I'll think of you as Ari, the girl with the snacks."

She beamed, and then they moved on, beckoned by a page to a hall set with refreshments. Javan greeted several others, and then ducked out a side door to the courtyard, its fountains frozen solid.

His breath fogged the air as he removed his crown, nearly groaning in relief as its weight lifted.

If only it was that easy to lift the other weight he carried.

The nightmares. The corruption in his government. The wounds that needed to be healed across his kingdom.

And the way he missed Sajda with every breath he took.

"Your Highness, all the visitors have arrived." A page spoke from the doorway behind him. "Are you ready to give your welcome speech?"

Javan let the ache of missing Sajda settle into his bones, and then squared his shoulders. Placing the crown back on his head, he took one last breath of the peaceful night air and then prepared himself to fulfill his duty.

To make his parents proud. To lead his people with honor and compassion. And to be the kind of king who understood what sacrifice and love truly meant.

"Your Highness?"

He rose to his feet, turned to face the page, and said, "I'm ready."

EPILOGUE

JAVAN STOOD ON the balcony that overlooked his courtyard at the palace and watched the stars flicker to life in the velvet sky above. The chill of night was quickly chasing away the thick, lazy heat of another summer day in Akram, and nightingales sang in the lemon grove that rose on the hill behind his courtyard. Malik sat at his feet, his golden leopard eyes blinking sleepily.

Tonight, nearly eight months after leaving Maqbara behind, he would host Akram's first kingdom-wide ball. Everyone was invited, from peasant to aristocrat. When a member of Javan's royal council had protested the inclusion of peasants, Javan had removed him from his post and appointed someone else in his place.

Ballrooms across the city were open tonight. Every aristocrat was hosting an event. Every kitchen was busy assembling buffets fit for the finest tables in the land. And the palace itself had three halls converted into small ballrooms, five rooms hosting buffets, and of course the main ballroom.

It was a small step toward unifying his people, but it was an important one. He'd personally addressed invitations to the former Maqbara prisoners he'd released when an audit of the magistrate's office revealed that nearly half the prison's inmates had no evidence to support their convictions. He wouldn't blame them if they refused to set foot in Makan Almalik again, but he hoped they would. He'd given them justice. Now he wanted to give them a sense of community. Of belonging.

He would dance tonight with the daughters of aristocrats, butchers, goat farmers, and guards. Many of the aristocratic young ladies had already been paraded in front of him while their fathers offered a list of ways their family would make a good alliance with the crown and their mothers mentioned that of course he would need a queen, and her daughter was very accomplished.

He'd brushed them off with as much dignity as he could, giving the girls themselves a quick, sympathetic look. He understood all too well the pressure of living up to your parents' expectations, sometimes at the expense of what you really wanted.

The person he really wanted was wandering the wide-open spaces of the world, far away from Akram.

It had been eight months, and his heart still wandered with her.

He'd have given anything she asked for, anything she needed to keep her by his side, but in the end, he hadn't made the offer. She'd told him from the beginning that she could never stay in Akram. He'd loved her too much to beg her to change her mind.

She hadn't promised she'd come back, and as he'd watched her leave, he'd known there was a good chance she wouldn't.

She'd find freedom somewhere far from him, and she'd stay. She'd think of returning, but no matter how many open skies she slept under, no matter how many stars she counted, Akram would still be the shackle she couldn't bear to touch again.

Now, as he stood on his balcony adjusting a purple sash against his silk tunic, he breathed in the night air, full of citrus and jasmine, and promised himself that one day he'd search for her.

One day, when his kingdom was settled. When no one was questioning his rule. When there were no more pockets of corruption to root out and destroy. He'd put a regent in charge, and he'd search the world until he found her.

And if she was happy—if she was truly free—he wouldn't approach. He'd watch from afar, satisfied that the girl he loved was thriving, and he'd return to Akram, leaving his heart behind with her.

A gong sounded from the palace's main courtyard. A call to enter the ballrooms and begin the festivities.

It was time.

He whispered a prayer that wherever Sajda was, she was safe and happy and at peace. Then he took one last breath of the citrus-tinged air and nodded respectfully in the direction of his parents' graves.

Fear out.

Courage in.

It was time to bring his kingdom together.

"Do you have a dance partner yet?"

The eerily quiet voice came from behind him, and his breath caught in his chest. For one awful second, he thought he was dreaming. That he'd conjured her out of need and want, and when he turned, his room would be empty. Slowly, heart pounding, he turned, and there she was. Standing in his doorway, her skin glowing like starlight against the brilliant blue of her silk gown, her black hair hanging loose and free down her back.

He crossed the distance between them in five steps, scooped her into his arms, and held on tight.

"You came back." His voice shook as he buried his face against her hair.

"I did." She sounded shy.

He closed his eyes as his hands lay against the bare skin of her back. "I thought you might not want to see Akram ever again."

"I didn't come back for Akram."

He pulled away, and she smiled. The shadows that had haunted her eyes in Maqbara still lingered, but stronger than her ghosts was the light of tender hope that glowed on her face.

"I want to show you something," she said as she pulled one of his hands from her back and placed it on her heart instead. "Can you feel that?"

He waited, and then nearly jumped away from her as the strange, prickling heat of her magic gathered beneath his palm, stinging and buzzing.

"You don't need words and promises," she said.

He smiled. "I said that to you once."

"And you were right. But I haven't said nearly enough to you. Will you let me show you?" she asked.

He nodded, and then her magic pierced him, moving through his blood like a thunderstorm. He staggered, and she caught him. Steadied him as her truth was revealed.

"Tell me," she said softly.

He met her eyes. "You're hurting still, and you aren't sure you'll ever be whole."

Her eyes darkened. "What else?"

"You found the stars and the wide-open spaces you crave, but . . ." He frowned and then his heart began pounding, his stomach tingling.

"But?" she asked, and he started smiling.

"But something was missing."

She raised a brow, and his smile felt too big for his face.

"What was missing?" she asked.

"Me." Wonder filled him at the truth that glowed like a jewel in the midst of her magic.

She leaned close, her lips a breath away from his. "Why did I come back, Javan?"

Everything inside him fell into place—the grief of what he'd lost, the burden of ruling his people, the longing he felt for the girl who'd sacrificed herself to give him his kingdom—as he said, "Because you love me."

She kissed him, wild and pure and sweet as her magic swirled between them.

"I love you," he breathed.

She grinned. "I said it first this time. You're getting slow living in all this luxury."

He laughed. "Do you still remember how to dance?"

She gave him a look that sent his pulse thundering. "I remember that I'm already better at it than you are."

"Want to prove it?" he asked as faint strands of music from the orchestra floated in through his open window.

"Fine. But it's not my fault if your people take one look at my skills and decide to give me the crown instead."

He laughed as he led her through the tiled hallways of the palace, her hand tucked in his arm, her eyes lit with the joy of challenging him.

For the first time since he'd entered the palace as its ruler, he felt at peace.

ACKNOWLEDGMENTS

Thank you to Jesus, who gives me strength and is my hope.

Writing books is a mostly solitary endeavor, but none of my stories would ever hit the shelves if it wasn't for the incredible support I have from family, friends, and my publishing team. A big thank-you to my husband, Clint, for being my biggest fan, for taking on extra duties when deadlines approach, and for always being invested in me. Another thank-you to my kids—Tyler, Jordan, Zach, Johanna, and Isabella—for helping me get my work done and for being proud of me. Also a huge thanks to my parents for jumping in to assist in household projects, grand-kid wrangling, or assisting me with my job, and to my sister, Heather, who is always one of my first readers, and my brother-in-law, Dave, whose support makes it possible for me to step out of my busy life to do book travel or to hide away in my office and hit my deadlines. Nobody cooks noodles like you, Dave.

I'm also grateful to Melinda Doolittle for being my beta reader and biggest cheerleader; to Jodi Meadows, KB Wagers, and Shannon Messenger for writing sprints, great advice, and even greater friendship; and to Kayla King and Beth Edwards, who shoulder extra weight to keep YABooksCentral.com running for me when I'm traveling or on deadline.

I'd also like to express my undying appreciation for the incredible publishing team at Balzer + Bray. Seven published works in, and I am still constantly impressed by your talent, dedication, and skill. From my rock star editor, Kristin Rens, who always pushes me to create the best version of the story that I possibly can, to Kelsey Murphy, Kristin's always awesome assistant, to the amazingly gifted Sarah Kaufman and Alison Donalty, who design my covers, to my publicist, Caroline Sun, and the rest of the publicity and sales team, you are simply stellar, and I owe you at least nine hundred cookies delivered by Tom Hiddleston himself. I'm also grateful to Martha Schwartz for doing such a thorough copy edit on a book that needed a lot of double- and triple-checking, and to my sensitivity reader for loving Javan and Sajda and for helping me finesse the culture of Akram so I could tell the story as it needed to be told.

More gratitude goes out to Holly Root for being the agent in my corner. You remain one of the best life choices I've ever made.

And finally, a huge thank-you to YOU, my readers. May you lose yourself in my stories, laugh, cry, swoon, and stay up way too late turning pages. Meeting you and talking books and fictional worlds is the best.

TURN THE PAGE FOR A SNEAK PEEK
AT THE COMPANION NOVEL

THE BLOOD SPELL

ONCE UPON A TIME . . .

THE WRAITH CREPT through the darkness of its forest prison, hunger gnawing at its bones. It was skeletal now, brushing against the thorn ferns and moss-covered tree bark with bony fingers that rattled in the breeze.

Once, its strength had been unrivaled. Its magic unmatched.

Until its sister had joined forces with others against it.

Now the wraith haunted the vast, damp darkness of its cage, a shadow bound by a spell it couldn't break no matter how hard it tried. The thought of vengeance was the meat and marrow of its dreams. It was the strength that bound its bones together and the breath that filled its lungs. Some days, memories of the ones who had trapped it blazed to life, leaving behind the scorched bitterness of shackled rage. But most days, it could feel only *hunger*.

As the gray-black light within the forest sank into the total darkness of yet another night, the wraith stalked the edges of the vast prison, hurling itself against the invisible spell that bound it here, feeling the magic spark, blister, and burn.

One day, it would break free. It would rush over the hills and move through the long stretches of farmland that stood between it and the city. It would find its sister and those who had helped her hunt it down, and it would destroy them all.

And then it would feed and feed and feed, and there would be no one left to stop it.

Hunger stabbed. The wraith dug its fingers into the closest tree trunk, gathered its magic, and shrieked, a long, razor-tipped wail that shivered through the air, sending birds screaming for the skies as the sound winged its way across the distance between the wraith and the city that sheltered its enemies.

The iron bells that hung along the road to warn people when a fae monster was near clanged wildly. The wraith lifted its face as their discordant, chaotic melody reached its ears, and smiled.

ONE

Mornings were a curse.

Bernadina "Blue" de la Cour yawned and blinked at the golden sunlight that bathed the streets of Falaise de la Mer, the capital city of Balavata. People bustled along the wide main roads that cut through the large city like swaths of ribbon, hurrying toward the open-air market that was held once a week in the heart of town. Others moved along the warren of side streets that curled away from the main roads and burrowed through each of the city's nine quarters.

Everyone seemed cheerful. Or if not cheerful, at least fully awake.

Blue didn't know what it took to wake at dawn and be cheerful about it, but whatever it was, she didn't have it.

"Isn't this a beautiful morning?" Papa asked as they moved through the iron arches that marked the entrance to the Gaillard quarter and headed for their alchemy shop. The arches were meant to weaken anyone with fae magic in their blood, but they'd never affected Blue. Maybe it was because the magic in her blood was harmless. Or maybe it was because the royal council was wrong about iron arches doing a single thing to protect the people from the kind of fae magic that *wasn't* harmless.

Blue shrugged away her thoughts and took a sip of the hot spiced chicory Papa had made for her before they'd left their farmhouse on the outskirts of the city. The drink tasted of bitter chicory root, sweet cream, and nutmeg, and it almost made up for the fact that the sea fog was still clinging to the edges of the city.

Nothing good came from getting out of bed before the sun had chased the fog away. Actually, nothing good came from getting out of bed before the noonday meal, but in seventeen years of trying, Blue had yet to convince Papa of that.

Papa slung an arm around her shoulder and laid his cheek against the pink headscarf Blue had hastily wrapped around her short black curls. "Almost awake?" he asked, laughter sparkling in his voice.

She grunted and took another sip as they reached the corner where he would turn left to open up the shop and she would turn right to join those moving toward the large square where the market was held.

"It's only one day a week that you have to get up at dawn," Papa said, his smile a wide slash of white against his light brown skin. "Need any help at the market today?"

Blue yawned again. "I'll be fine. Ana is meeting me there to help carry my purchases to the shop." She hefted the burlap sacks she'd tossed over her shoulder before leaving the farmhouse, though she knew as well as Papa that she'd carry most of them herself. Hiring little ten-year-old Ana, one of Falaise de la

Mer's many homeless, as a delivery girl had been more a decision of the heart than of practicality.

Papa nodded and reached for her nearly empty cup, the smile disappearing from his face. "Be careful. Don't let anyone catch you using your magic to check the goods before you buy them. Remember—"

"No one will believe I'm harmless, no matter what I say. I know." She finished his oft-repeated warning for him and leaned up to plant a kiss on his cheek. His skin was thinner now, sagging at the edges as strands of silvery gray worked their way into his close-cut black hair. There were laugh lines fanning out from his brown eyes, and sometimes when he thought she wasn't watching, he leaned heavily against the shop's counter at the end of the day as if being on his feet for hours on end was wearing on him.

He returned her kiss and then studied her face with a smile. "You remind me of your mother. She was always the most intriguing woman in any room. And she didn't like to take my warnings about her magic seriously either."

"I'll be careful. I promise."

She couldn't find herself in his face—she had her mother's dark brown skin and eyes, Grand-mère's pointed chin and sharp cheekbones, and the tiny stature of her mother's side of the family. In fact, the only proof Blue could find that she shared blood with her father, who was the son of a tall, dark-skinned man and a woman with the pale skin and smooth hair of her Morcantian ancestors, were the curls that lifted from Blue's scalp and framed her face.

But she didn't need to see herself in his face to feel every inch his daughter. They shared the same affection for the alchemy shop. The same passion for helping others. And the same love

5

for a simple, uncomplicated life at their farmhouse, their garden, and the sea that bordered the cliff at the edge of their property.

Turning, Blue made her way toward the market. Falaise de la Mer was a busy port city that attracted people from Balavata and several of the surrounding kingdoms. But no matter how many moved into the city, the heart of Balavatan culture remained a celebration of food, artistry, and a fierce will to survive. Along the broad sides of buildings and homes, colorful pictures made from paint mixed with sand told the stories of Balavata—from the festivals to honor their folk heroes to the rise of the head families to the sea with its changing moods and constant bounty. The history of her kingdom surrounded Blue as she ducked through crowds, grumpily eyeing those who seemed wide awake and thrilled about it.

When she neared the eastern edge of the quarter, she cast a quick glance at the Gaillards' pale blue mansion. As one of the kingdom's nine head families, the Gaillards had coin to spare. Blue supposed they spent a fair amount of it on managing their quarter and the southern villages assigned to them—they answered to the queen for the safety, economy, and upkeep of their portion of the kingdom—but anyone who owned five carriages for a family of three could certainly afford to use some of their wealth to help the destitute who huddled in the city's back alleys, begging for food and taking jobs no one else wanted just to survive.

Blue had long since stopped hoping the head families would do right by those who needed them most. Instead, she'd taken matters into her own hands.

And today would be a test to see how close she was to succeeding.

Thrusting her hands into the inner pocket of her light summer cloak, she brushed her fingers against the cold chunks of pale yellow metal she'd created after staying late at the shop the night before. It had taken Blue far too long to realize that help for the children who slept in alleyways and foraged through trash in her quarter wasn't coming from the magistrate, the Gaillards, or even the queen. Once she'd accepted that if she wanted to solve the problem, she was going to have to do it herself, the answer had seemed obvious: she'd use her talent for alchemy to turn ordinary metal into gold.

Ten months later, after more failed experiments than Blue cared to count, she was close. Maybe even close enough to count it a success. She'd know soon enough, and once she could produce gold, she would buy a big home, hire tutors and provide fresh food, and gather up every child she could find so that they could finally do more than just survive.

She reached the northern edge of the quarter and followed a crowd through the gate that led to the market. The square was divided into twenty rows of stalls with small seating areas at the end of each for those who'd just purchased crisp gelleire fish or a platter of fried apple cakes, a Balavatan staple. The center of the square was dominated by a large raised stage, surrounded by benches. Some days traveling theatrical troupes put on shows or brokers auctioned off exotic creatures procured from far-off kingdoms. Other days, magistrates from each quarter brought a prisoner or two up on stage for public punishment, depending on their crime.

Blue looked toward the stage and winced as she entered the field. Nine flags—each with the crest of one of Balavata's head families—hung from the scaffolding. It was a magistrate day. Last time, she'd accidentally seen a woman get whipped for the crime of stealing silver dishes from her employer. She'd rather not see anything like that again.

Turning away, Blue hurried down the ninth row of stalls toward one of her regular vendors, passing brightly patterned dresses with seashells embroidered along their hems, glittering beaded jewelry, freshly baked bread, and a stall featuring boots from the best cobbler in the city. There was another woman already talking with Maurice when Blue got to his stall, her voice rising as she debated something with the old merchant.

Ignoring them, Blue moved to the back of the stall to examine the crates of seeds, bark, roots, and dried berries that Maurice regularly procured from the fae isle of Llorenyae.

Casting a quick look over her shoulder to be sure no one was watching, Blue let her hands rest on a crate of yaeringlei seeds, feeling the gentle rush of the small magic she'd inherited from her mother tingle across her palms, seeking a connection with any natural thing—plant, animal, or mineral.

If they'd been harvested correctly, the large, pebble-size seeds would leap toward her magic, eager to be used. If the fruit that encased them had been forced from their bushes before they were ripe, the seeds would lie dormant, refusing her advances.

The crate's wood was rough, and bits of it curled toward Blue's hands as if eager to be used in her potions. She shot another look at Maurice and his customer, but they were engrossed in their discussion.

The seeds within the crate leaped for her hands, tapping against their wooden home like bits of hail against a window. Maurice's gaze jerked toward her, a frown digging into the sagging skin between his eyes. Blue stepped away from the crate and shoved her hands into her cloak pockets, a chill racing over her skin as the woman turned to face her, pale skin flushed with anger at Maurice.

She'd seen this woman a few times at the market or when Blue and Papa spent time at the castle, and Blue had no interest in catching her attention now. Dinah Chauveau, head of the Chauveau family, had a reputation for ruthlessly running her quarter and for making life miserable for anyone who tried to cheat her.

She also had a reputation for zealously punishing anyone caught violating the law against magic.

Swallowing hard, Blue gave Maurice and Dinah a wobbly smile and hurried toward a selection of jewels resting inside a locked glass case. Her breath felt too thin, her blood too thick as she turned her back to them and prayed they hadn't seen anything that could get her in trouble.

"We can resume our discussion of your failure to meet the terms of our contract once you get her out of here." Dinah's voice was cold and precise.

"What can I get for you today, Blue?" Maurice asked from beside her elbow. His brown face was folded in on itself, like a grape shriveling beneath the harsh summer sun, and his hands shook a bit with age, but his eyes were as shrewd as ever.

"Pink sapphire!" Blue's words were too loud, too rushed, and she folded her arms over her chest to give her hands something to do as magic tingled across her palms, reaching for the jewels that Maurice was pulling out of the case.

"I don't have pink today, but here's a blue and a white, and both are just as lovely," he said.

Blue shook her head. "I need pink for the potion I'm working on."

"I can get my hands on one soon enough and have it delivered, no extra fee."

"That's fine." Blue turned toward the crates and began rattling off the list of other items she needed, an itch between her shoulder blades where Dinah's gaze rested. Blue hadn't had a chance to check the rest of the ingredients she wanted to buy, but there was no way she could risk it now.

Maurice quickly wrapped up her purchases and loaded them into her burlap sacks. "Where's that young girl you use for deliveries and such?"

Blue frowned as she reached inside her cloak for the metal she hoped would pass as gold. "I'm not sure." Ana should've been here by now. She was usually very prompt, and she knew Blue needed help on market day.

"If you can't carry all these yourself, I'll deliver the rest later for a small fee." Maurice's eyes brightened, and Blue laughed.

"I've experienced your small fees before, Maurice. I can carry it all or find a child to help me."

Schooling her face into a mask of composure, Blue pulled out the chunks of pale yellow metal she'd created the night before. It was almost gold. And maybe almost would be good enough. She didn't want to cheat Maurice. She just wanted to test her experiment. And if anyone in the market could instantly spot a fake, it would be Maurice.

His eyes narrowed as she handed him the chunks of almost-gold. "Pretty pale for gold." He held it up to a bar of sunlight slanting in through the roof and turned it this way and that.

Blue flinched as Dinah took a step closer, her gaze on the metal as well.

Maurice brought the metal up to his mouth and bit gently.

His brow folded into a frown. "Soft like gold, but the color's a little off. Where did you get this?"

Her face heated. "The shop."

It was as much of the truth as she was willing to give them. If anyone realized what she was doing, she and Papa would no longer be safe. Blue would bet everything they owned that one of the less scrupulous brokers who managed the illegal gambling dens throughout the city would be at their door within an hour with a plan to force Blue into working for him. And if a broker didn't get to her first, somebody else would.

Everyone in the kingdom would want a piece of the girl who'd figured out how to use alchemy to turn ordinary metal into gold.

Maurice's voice was rough. "Somebody cheated you, Miss Blue. This is a good imitation, but it isn't gold. Do you remember who paid with it?"

She shook her head and hurriedly grabbed a handful of coin out of her other pocket. Laying the coin out on Maurice's table, she took the almost gold out of his hand and pocketed it again.

"That's useless, Miss Blue," he said. "Unless you want to turn it over to the magistrate so they can hunt for the person who gave it to you."

"Oh, no. That's fine! I mean, obviously it's not fine, but I'm sure I can use it in one of my potions or something." Her voice was too bright, but she couldn't seem to change it. Gathering her bags from Maurice, she slung them over her shoulder, staggering a bit under their weight, and then bid a hasty farewell to Maurice, nodding respectfully to Dinah on her way out.

Scanning the crowd around her once more, Blue hurried to the end of the row. Where was Ana? Had she forgotten it was market day? Or had another, more lucrative job come up?

A tiny whisper of fear poisoned Blue's thoughts as she stopped to examine the crowd again.

Children went missing in Falaise de la Mer. Everyone knew it, though no one could really explain it. It was always the children whose parents were in prison or who'd died working dangerous jobs for one of Balavata's brokers. Children no one would really miss.

But Ana wasn't a girl no one would miss. She had a regular job with Blue at the Mortar & Pestle. She had friends. And to the best of Blue's knowledge, no one had gone missing from the Gaillard quarter for years. Besides, Ana had failed to show up twice before, and both times she'd returned after a few days, apologizing for leaving Blue on her own and explaining that she'd been hired for a cleaning job by one of the wealthier families of the city, who paid Ana twice what Blue could.

A shout broke through Blue's thoughts, and the crowd around her surged toward the stage, carrying her with it.

"The laws of our land have been broken. The queen wishes you to bear witness!" a man's voice boomed from the center of the stage. Blue dug her heels into the soft ground to avoid being pushed past the first row of benches as guards from each quarter brought prisoners onto the stage to have their crimes read aloud and their punishments delivered.

"Up first, we have Selina Bisset, who has been accused of breaking the law against using magic."

People around Blue murmured and shot fearful looks at the stage, where a woman stood facing the crowd, her hands tied behind her back. Blue was too far away to see the expression on the woman's face, and she didn't want to.

"According to the law, no person shall use fae magic in any

form." The man held a scroll in his hands, his eyes scraping over it as he read. "No magic may be used for healing, for spells, for altering the physical appearance of objects or people, for divining the future, or for affecting anything that lives on the land, the sea, or the air. It was the use of fae magic that turned the witch Marielle into a blood wraith who drank the blood of our children and terrorized the streets of Falaise de la Mer."

Actually, it was the misuse of fae magic that had created the blood wraith, but Blue knew no one was interested in the nuances. Not when most of them remembered the wraith haunting their streets, destroying lives in its unending quest for power. She took a few steps backward before running into a solid wall of bodies standing close behind her.

The crowd murmured louder, and Blue caught many of them saying the name *Marielle* like a curse.

The man onstage turned toward the woman. "You were seen using fae magic to transform rotten fruit into fresh in an attempt to deceive your customers. Do you deny the charge?"

Blue closed her eyes. There was no point in denying the charge. The magistrate wouldn't have brought the woman here if he didn't have at least three sworn witnesses. Blue's hands burned as if her own magic was reaching for the woman on the stage, and she clenched her fists and tried to take another step back.

Whatever the woman said in reply was lost as the crowd began chanting, "Death to witches!"

Not everyone who had fae magic was a witch, either, but that was another nuance no one who remembered the blood wraith wanted to discuss.

"According to the law of Balavata, under the blessing of

our gracious queen, I hereby sentence you to death," the man shouted.

Blue's stomach lurched, and she turned and fought her way through the crowd as the guard next to the accused woman drew his sword from its sheath with a metallic hiss and plunged it through her chest.

From *New York Times* bestselling author
C. J. REDWINE

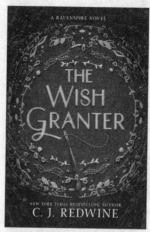

Don't miss more dark and dazzling tales in the
New York Times bestselling Ravenspire series!

Don't miss a book in this daring series

DEFIANCE

C. J. REDWINE

BOOK 1

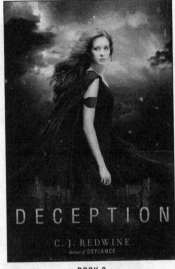

DECEPTION

C. J. REDWINE
Author of DEFIANCE

BOOK 2

HARPER**TEEN**IMPULSE

OUTCAST

A DEFIANCE NOVELLA

C. J. REDWINE
Author of DEFIANCE

DIGITAL NOVELLA

DELIVERANCE

C. J. REDWINE
Author of DEFIANCE and DECEPTION

BOOK 3